GOOD
SCAMMER

GUY KENNAWAY

MENSCH PUBLISHING

Mensch Publishing
51 Northchurch Road,
London N1 4EE, United Kingdom

First published in Great Britain 2023

A catalogue record for this book is
available from the British Library

ISBN:
978-1-912914-62-3 (paperback)
978-1-912914-63-0 (ebook)

Typeset by Van-garde Imagery, Inc., • van-garde.com

1

An eleven-year-old boy called Clive 'Bangaz' Thompson leapt from the prow of a fishing boat onto the talcum sand of Negril. Maas Henry, a man agile in thought, word and deed, jumped out behind and waded through the shallows holding a weathered wooden sign nailed to a post. He passed it to Bangaz, who tried to stand it up in the dry dirt.

'Mek it lie flat pon the ground.' Maas Henry shoved it onto some roots that roped across the sand. 'Let dem find it. You haffi lay the bait so dem cyan see no hook.'

They found a comfortable spot under the heart shaped leaves of a sea-mahoe and waited, watching the boat full of tourists leave the hotel and chug towards them.

As it arrived, Henry walked down the beach shouting, 'Welcome one and all. Welcome ladies. Welcome Tom, Harry and Dick! I give you your official welcome to mi island paradise!'

All the tourists were white back then. Henry eyed up the women wobbling out of the boat and held up his hand to an admirably large woman in a billowing floral dress.

'Milady. Let me help you ashore.'

Once up to her knees in the warm, clear water she tried to free her hand but Henry had it firmly gripped. He smiled at her.

'Nice 'at. Bangaz, hurry up carry the lady bag.'

Bangaz did as he was told. The tourists were on a $10.00 morning Island Adventure tour arranged by the hotel, which included a boat ride to a little island 500 yards from the shore, drinks and snack on the beach, and boat ride back looking for turtles. Maas Henry was nothing to do with the official tour, but was an enthusiastic joiner of any activity which looked profitable. Little Bangaz had been dragged onto a building site many times and told to start moving blocks while Maas Henry gave orders to the workers, both for the fun of it and so that, when the owner turned up at the end of the day, Maas Henry could point to what Bangaz had done and say, 'Ya haffi make fair payment, slavery days done,' enough times that he finally wore the man down and the two of them walked off with a few dollars, which Maas Henry kept.

Maas Henry made a play of brushing some imaginary dust from a bamboo bench and invited the bosomy floral woman to sit.

'I am Robinson Crusoe and this my likkle man Friday,' he said. 'You come to rescue we? Or stay with me on my magical island?'

The bench looked like it might have nails sticking out of it so she held back, and anyway she didn't want to get cornered by him.

'I must say, this is really is idyllic. I mean, wow.' She slowly turned away from Maas Henry and tried to get back to the group.

'Lady,' said Henry, who was having none of that, 'what is your name?'

'Barbara.'

'Welcome. Sit down, Barbara. You want coconut? Banana?'

'No, er, well I think the guys from the boat have refreshments for us.'

'You want ganja? You want a likkle smoke?'

'Gee, no, no, it's a little early in the day for that.'

'Never too early. This a Jamaica, milady!' Maas Henry said.

She tried again to get back towards the group, who were standing round a cooler holding Red Stripes and scrunching up their eyes.

Seeing the For Sale sign on the ground, Barbara said, 'Is that for real?'

'You like honey? Bees' honey?' Maas Henry said, pretending not to have heard. 'I can get you the bestest honey inna de world. Mi can bring it to you at your hotel, my fine lady. Or you can come to my community and I can cook pork and chicken for you.'

'Is this island actually for sale?'

'That just one old sign mi grand-daddy put up when he wanted to sell the island.'

'Oh. I guess I better go back now.'

'Mi just chill out here,' said Maas Henry.

Bangaz settled down near Maas Henry and watched the Jamaicans from the boat chat with the whiteys using their loud, simple tourist personas, which involved a lot of Ya mons and high fives and always laughter whatever the situation. Some of the crew performed the limbo and sword dances in the hotel lobby. It was all a fun part of the fooling of the whitey, which was the bedrock of the tourist experience; a tradition started in 1642 when a rich white man sprawling on a ball and clawfoot chair in a big house in Bristol, England, was sent the first fraudulent accounts by his plantation manager in west Jamaica.

'Do you know about this place?'

Bangaz looked up to see a wiry white guy craning over him. Maas Henry stopped pretending he had dropped asleep and said, 'Dis a fi mi grand-daddy piece.'

'What?'

'This is my grand-daddy land,' he translated.

'That lady there, she said she saw a For Sale sign. He selling up?'

'He don't want it cos him have to pay land tax. Government tief.'

'Are the taxes big? May I ask what they are?'

'Four tousan every year.'

'Four grand? US bucks?'

'No man. Jamaican.'

Maas Henry looked as blank and as foolish as he could, which was very when he wanted to, while he watched the whitey work out how much four thousand J was in US dollars. Henry knew the answer: thirty. 'Mi grand-daddy kiant afford that money so him moss sell out it.'

'It's quite a spot he's got here.'

It wasn't to Bangaz. It lacked the basic requirements of a decent place: tarmac, cars, current, music, food and school.

'Bot noboday want fi buy it. Not anybady. Grand-daddy would give it away but it give him a likkle income.'

'How's that?'

'Every boat that come have to have him permission to land and have to pay fee.'

'How much?'

'Ten dollar a boat. So him tell me.'

The white man looked around, walking a couple of paces to his left to see further down the beach. 'It's all of the island, right?'

'That's the bad bit,' said Maas Henry. 'Cos people want neighbour dem. The island too lonelyish and quiet for people with no-one elkse pon de place. Island too private, you know?' He shook his head sadly.

'How much was your grand-daddy looking for?'

'Ole 'eap. Him want too much. I tell him, I say please grand-daddy don't be so greedy. Lower the price. But him never go below fourteen tou-san' US dollars. Maybe twelve.'

A petite woman with short dark hair came over. 'Chris, we're going I think, if they're not too stoned to steer the boat.'

'Marie, look. This island's for sale. This man's grand-father owns it. They want twelve grand for it.'

'Sorry, he always does this on holiday, finds some ruin and falls in love with it. Come on you.'

'No, seriously Marie, it's the whole island. Look I'm interested to meet the old man, if just to hear the story. Can I meet him?'

'Him hard fi catch,' said Maas Henry, 'as him live deep inna de bush, but mi can't go look for him cos mi car brok. Can you give me a help a fix mi car and mi will carry him back down to the hotel?'

'What's wrong with the car?'

'Gearbox want fix.'

'What's wrong with it?' Chris asked.

'Mi drive home Sunday and hear de engine mek one rasping noise, but mi nuh take it personal. Monday afternoon mi a go up a Blenheim and it bruk dung in Dias and the car nuh move back or forwards.'

Chris rubbed his forehead.

'Mi cya fix it,' Maas said.

'When? Only I'm leaving in, er...' Chris said.

'If me have fifty US it cya fix easy. But me don't.'

'Is that all it is here?' Chris said. He caught his wife's eye. She silently told him to pay it in a way only a couple who had been together for twenty years could communicate.

'Come on, Chris,' she said. 'They're leaving.'

'Hang on Marie. Look. I'll pay for that, here,' he gave Maas Henry fifty, 'and bring your grand-father to the Coconut Grove Hotel. I'm room...'

'Mi will find you!' shouted Maas Henry, 'wid ease. Don't worry yourself bout dat.' 'I'm called Chris. And you are?'

This question momentarily wrongfooted Maas Henry, but after hesitating he said, 'Mi call Henry.'

'Okay, but we leave in a week. You will bring him, yes?'

'Of course,' and Maas Henry used the phrase that Bangaz knew to be a sign that things were about to get messy: 'Nuttin can g'wrong. Trust me.'

When the two of them had pushed the tourist boat off the sand and waved goodbye, Maas Henry looked at the bank notes.

'Memba,' he said to Bangaz. 'Everyting we tek from dem, dem tek from we first. Never forget that.'

2

Unless you saw the sun set in Negril every day, it was impossible to believe that you weren't watching a unique event. Chris felt Marie squeeze his hand as they looked across the sea at the pinkish sky shot through with a golden glow. The huge orange disc of sun was slowly dousing itself in the water, igniting the ocean. Every night, give or take the odd storm, this spectacular light show entranced the people. It was an appropriately exotic end to a sensual day, like God himself was a little bit high and just having fun.

Over the boat's wake the little wooded island receded. Marie squeezed Chris's hand again.

'We're buying the island!' Marie exclaimed to the two boatmen. They smiled and nodded enthusiastically.

'Ya man! Irie vibes. No problem!' they shouted over the engine.

Back in the hotel room, Chris came through from the bathroom rubbing cream on his mosquito bites, radiating sunburn and excitement. Marie lay on the bed applying aloe vera to her scorched neck.

'Can you believe how stupid they are?' Chris said. 'A whole island? Twelve grand?'

'He said fourteen.'

'But immediately dropped to twelve. Totally declared his hand. What a dipshit! They'll probably take ten, you know? They clearly know sweet

F A about business negotiation. If the grandson is like that, what is the old man gonna be like? This is the steal of the century.'

'Did you hear him say that boats need permission to land on the island?'

'Yeah,' said Chris going back into the bathroom.

'That means we can just ban them. Have total privacy. A private island. Ours.'

Chris said 'Uh huh,' from the bathroom.

'It has got to be one of the most beautiful in the world and only 500 yards from shore,' said Marie, sitting up. 'Come on, hurry up. Let's go down to the sea grape terrace. You know how I love a bit of limbo and a sword dance with my cocktails,' she laughed.

3

Almost the only truthful words Maas Henry spoke that day were the ones about his car, an eight year old Toyota Corolla, being bruk. But Maas Henry had a plan to fix it. He had seen an identical Corolla behind the mesh fence of the Thrifty Rental car lot in Montego Bay, and it was to Thrifty that Maas Henry and Bangaz were travelling, bungled up in a taxi.

Bangaz had the day off school because his class was on a field trip to Donald Sangster International Airport to learn about transportation, and to inspire the pupils to become air traffic controllers, pilots or check in staff or, if they wanted to make big money, baggage handlers. The pupils were conducted around the cabin of an aircraft. For most of the class it would be the only time they ever boarded a plane. Marva, his aunt, wouldn't pay for the trip, so Bangaz was hanging around his yard when Maas Henry called him.

At the car rental company, Maas Henry pushed open the door to the air-conditioned kiosk and looked the girl, bulging out of her striped uniform, up and down.

'My young nephew visit me from mi sista in town,' he said, indicating Bangaz. 'And I want to take him round some of the beauty spots of St James and Westmorland, so need a car for couple days.'

She came round the counter, dragging her feet, and took Maas Henry out onto the car lot. He let her take him to a Suzuki.

'No, uncle! This one!' Bangaz said, standing in front of the Corolla.

'Okay,' said the girl, who sucked her teeth and slouched back to the kiosk for the key.

Maas Henry sped the rental back to his yard and was soon underneath it, despite it being supported on a lump of semi rotten timber, a stone, and an old wheel rim. After a quick look he went off in search of a beer and a tool. Any tool, because like so many ingenious Cove mechanics he could replace a gear box with a wrench, kitchen knife and broken claw hammer. His bungalow had a plastic Georgian style front door and windows in only two rooms. The rest was raw concrete with steel rods sprouting into the air. People driving by saw a ruin, but it was a palace rising from the dirt.

Block by block, Maas Henry was stepping towards the finished project which, at the current rate of progress, would be in 2098. Around his house, he had arranged a collection of rotting cars and broken furniture. His sitting-room was three plastic chairs around a rusty chest freezer under an almond tree. An electricity pole at the entrance was a maypole of cables. It was perfection itself to Maas Henry.

Maas Henry lay on his back under the rental, where he cuss and use bad word on the nut dem. In an hour the gear box dropped with a thud and a stream of black oil glistened on the dirt. He dragged it out, stood up, popped a beer and poured out the first sip of Dragon Stout. He looked at Bangaz and said, 'Like Anancy Spider we have to be tricky to survive. You know?'

'Yes sah,' said Bangaz.

'Your mumma tell you bout dem Anancy ting?' Maas Henry disappeared under the other car.

'Mi mumma dead, mi a tell you.'

The principal folk character all Jamaicans were taught about as children was a cunning spider called Anancy, who tricked his way through life. There was not a folk tale about Anancy renting a car for twenty-four-hours to steal its gearbox, but Bangaz took the point.

A white man drew up in a rental car. It looked to Bangaz like it could be the boss of Thrifty Motors, come to check on his rental. Holding on to a big spanner, Bangaz glanced at the gearbox sitting in a pool of sump oil, smiled weakly, and swallowed.

'Hello little chap,' said the man. 'I am looking for Henry.'

Bangaz looked down to see Mass Henry's feet drawing out of sight under the car.

'I never see him from morning,' Bangaz said, and pretended to loosen a nut with the wrench. A small green parrot made its syrupy call from the breadfruit tree. Bangaz saw the man staring at Maas Henry's Dragon stout on the car radiator, so he picked it up and had a drink of it.

'What are you up to here?

'Me fix mi car,' said Bangaz lightly.

Chris pointed at the gearbox. 'Is that the gearbox I gave your uncle fifty dollars to fix?' He tutted. 'Do you know where he is? Only I'm leaving tomorrow.'

There was a clink and clatter and a shout of 'Yes! Chris! Whuppen?' And Maas Henry stood up wiping his hands, his smile totally convincing. 'Blessings and guidance! This good news!'

4

The next day, Bangaz sat where cars slowed down selling ackee or pear or banana depending on the season. Lacking uniform, lunch money and even shoes because Marva considered them an unnecessary luxury, he missed out on a school, and never learnt to read or write with confidence.

It was by the bridge that Maas Henry found Bangaz, as arranged after the white man had left his yard, and told him to get in the car.

Maas Henry pushed Bangaz in the seat next to the shrivelled and bent figure of an old, deaf man from the other side of the community called Moxton. Maas Henry drove them to a low, ill-built office block not far from the seedy centre of Negril where a slow crowd of hustlers, hookers, higglers and stoned tourists wandered about looking for the next event in their lives. Maas Henry jumped out and walked toward the building which had a sign that Bangaz couldn't read which said Howard Reynolds Attorney-At-Law.

'You stand here, you don't move,' Maas Henry told Bangaz. 'A man soon gonna come outa the door.'

Sure enough, a man in black trousers and short sleeved white shirt with a button down collar came out of the office, got into an SUV and drove off.

'Dat Liar Reynolds. When you see him come back, if we are still inside, you run in and give me a warning shout.'

In their taxi, Chris and Marie were slung from side to side as the driver took the curves of the West End road, swerving at dogs and children to avoid potholes. They had been staying in a clammy hotel room getting high and making plans. Marie wanted the island to be a spiritual retreat.

'First thing,' she said. 'We ban all boats from the hotel.'

'We can't do that, hon,' Chris said.

'Okay. We make it 200 bucks to land. Sort the wheat from the chaff. Top end only.'

'I think there are traditions we have to honour.'

'It's our island, duh ... so we make the rules, right? We are the chiefs. That's one of the main reasons you get a private island, eh? To make your own rules. Along with the spiritual retreat, we can make it a tax haven.'

'I doubt we can do that. Look, we have to act like responsible chieftains. The island is in Jamaica. We have to respect the culture. Irie?'

Marie chuckled to herself. 'Just wait till Terry and Di find out. Can you picture their faces? We got a private island. Yeah. It's ours. ALL ours. Yeah, in the Caribbean. Yeah it's got a beach. Yeah, we are putting a house on it. Yeah. Oh, can we come on your yacht this summer? Now you want to ask us? That poxy little thing with the stuffy bedrooms and nowhere to put a drink down? No, no we can't come cruising with you in the Keys because WE'VE GOT OUR OWN PRIVATE FUCKING ISLAND you patronising ass holes.'

Through occasional breaks in the fence Chris glimpsed a flash of sea, the back of a villa, and a woman with a big hat and bikini looking at her phone. On the other side of the road was a succession of broken bars, empty lots, rotten houses and dissolving cars behind rusting zinc.

'You ever think,' Chris said, 'what would have happened if the Israelis had been given this island instead of the mid-east? Can you imagine what they would have made of it? With this rainfall and sunshine? These people let so much go to waste. Sometimes I despair at the way the Jamaicans don't appreciate it. They are so lazy, and stupid.'

'Honey,' Marie said, her eyes flicking at their driver.

'What?'

'It sounds kinda racist.'

'It's just fact. You know? I mean look at the situation we are in. A whole island for eleven grand. How stupid can you be?'

When the taxi drew up, Marie recognised Bangaz hanging around the dry and dusty forecourt of the lawyer's office.

'That's the little boy who was there on our first visit. Cute!' Marie said, and then shouted to Bangaz, 'Wha gwaan! No problem, ya man.'

Bangaz smiled obligingly and shook hands with the pair, essaying a courtly bow he had seen pon teevee round at his friend Adi's.

Maas Henry leapt forward. 'Chris, mi brudder! Welcome. Everyting ready. Mi have grand-daddy and liar here. Grand-daddy!' Maas Henry poked Moxton, 'him deaf mi sorry to say.' He then shouted at Moxton: 'Dis de white man gonna buy fi we island, okay? Come inna de liar office.'

Old Moxton was dimly aware that he was involved with one of Maas Henry's schemes, although he couldn't have told you what it was. But Maas Henry had promised him a help, so he went along quite happily, a simple smile on his leathery face as he was ushered into the building .

Inside, already in reception, was a large slow man with a spherical head and thick beard called Branda who had briefly been in prison with Maas Henry for pig theft and now stood waiting before them in his four-piece funeral suit. It was not ideal casting, but Maas Henry worked with what was to hand.

'Here is the esteemed man himself,' said Maas Henry, introducing Branda as 'Liar Reynolds, Gentleman of the Bar Association of Jamaica, Attorney-at-Law and QC.'

Chris said, 'Pleased to meet you. Oh by the way, I hope you don't mind I actually checked you out. You know, I looked you up on the internet.'

Maas Henry's smile sagged.

'You do hear all kinds of things about Jamaica,' Chris continued. 'But don't worry, you vetted clean. We're all good.'

Maas Henry opened the door onto an apparently ransacked room, which was where Reynold's partner had practised before his arrest and subsequent appointment as MP. He then found the correct door, and pushed Branda towards the leather seat behind the desk, which Branda settled into with a smile of such joy and achievement you'd have thought he had just passed the Bar exam.

Old Moxton sat there looking convincing as Chris and Marie, on the edge of their seats, looked over the survey map (stolen from the Minister of Land's Office) and the sale contract (run up by a lawyer in Mo Bay who owed Maas Henry a favour to do with a woman) and took out their pens to sign. To avoid taxes, which turned out to be exorbitant, they had agreed to pay cash. Chris took out a thick envelope and proceeded to count the American bills on the desk.

Branda found a pen in the drawer and handed it to Moxton.

'Sign it, Grand-daddy,' Maas Henry said.

When Moxton saw the wad of American currency, he thought: That a ole eap o money. Maas Henry jinall me. All me ago get is a flask of JB and chaser.

He croaked, 'Mi change mi mind. Mi nuh sign. Mi nuh sell mi island.'

'What?' said Chris.

'Bludclaat,' said Mas Henry. 'Sign it here,' he pointed to the document.

Maas Henry placed the pen in his top pocket.

'Mi never go sell it out. Mi love it too much.'

'You've already agreed. You can't go back on it,' said Marie. 'Can he?' she asked Branda.

'Mi want mo' money,' Moxton croaked.

'Hey old timer, we've completed the negotiation, right?' Said Chris.

Moxton got himself up on his legs and, with bent back and shuffling steps, tried to make for the door. Maas Henry blocked him, and with a tight grip of his arm said, 'Stop dat. Wha' you want?'

'Mi wan five ondered,' said Moxton, pointing at the money.

'More?' said Chris. 'Jesus.'

Maas Henry stared at Moxton.

'Five hundred more, you sign?' Chris asked.

Moxton nodded.

Chris took out another envelope and counted 500 onto the desk. Maas Henry reached across but Moxton grabbed it and jammed the notes in his trouser pocket.

As soon as Moxton signed and everyone had shaken hands, Maas Henry said, 'Right, ladies and gentleman, mi Liar here is late on his way to court to defend an innocent man. I am afraid we must leave forthwith and forthright.'

Emerging from gloom into searing sunshine, Chris blinked and said, 'Honey, how about we take a boat and go sit on our own island, eh? How good does that sound? What a feeling! I actually own a private island in the Caribbean.'

Mr Reynolds' car drew up, and the big man got out and strode towards the group. Having had a few highly unsavoury dealings with Maas Henry in the past, Liar Reynolds nodded curtly and carried on his way into his office. Once, Maas Henry had turned up to court intoxicated when Reynolds was defending him. When the judge brought down his hammer and said 'Order!' Maas Henry had called out 'Gimme one rum and orange juice, bar tender!'

Maas Henry said to the couple, 'Hold on. We muss have a drink to celebrate the sale.' He indicated Bangaz to follow, but pushed Moxton away. With his arm around Chris and Marie's shoulders he led them into the Corner Bar, saying 'what are you gonna buy me? I think this call for champagne.'

Bangaz sat in the corner savouring the Pepsi Marie passed him. It was the first drink he had ever been bought and he planned to stretch it out for the whole day, and possibly into the next. He watched Chris and Maas

Henry chat at the bar. Both men could not have looked happier, though Maas Henry's happiness was to last longer than Chris's.

Later that day, after landing on their island, Chris and Marie were just settling their towel on the sand to watch their first sunset from their new paradise, feeling very at home, when the security detail from Plantation, the hotel closest to the island, arrived and told them to leave.

'Island close at six.' said the uniformed man.

'Huh? I don't think so,' said Chris. 'We just bought the place. I ask you to leave.'

The guards exchanged glances.

'Please?' said Chris. 'We are having a private time here. As owners.'

'You must leave the island,' said the guard. 'Six o'clock it close to tourist.'

'I got information for you,' said Marie, jabbing her finger at him. 'It's closed to assholes. You wanna get fired? Get off our property.'

'Come on,' the guard put his hand on Chris's elbow and tried to lead him off. Chris shook his arm and stood his ground. That turned out to be a mistake as he was picked up and tipped into the boat while screaming, 'I own this place!' Marie followed him soon after shouting, 'Assault! Battery! I am gonna sue your asses off!'

The manager of the hotel opened a drawer and took out an identical document to the one Chris was waving about. Then he looked back in the drawer and took out another one.

'You is not the first I am afraid, sir,' he explained to Chris. 'It is very regrettable. These bad people operate a fraud and I am afraid you get catch up in it.'

'But your boat guys heard me talking with that louse,' Marie said. 'I told them he was selling it to us! Why didn't they say anything?'

'They are just ignorant, never understand nothing,' he waved in the direction of the water sports hut on the beach, where the boatmen were counting the 500 US that Maas Henry had tipped them.

'This is not over,' said Chris.

'You want me to throw that away for you?' the manager said, pointing at the sale document.

'No,' said Chris.

He was clutching the papers when, the next morning, he and Marie emerged from a taxi and stormed towards Attorney Reynolds' office. Unfortunately, Bangaz happened to be in the car park, having identified Negril as a place of opportunity.

'Hey, hey, you...' Chris snapped, as he turned from the taxi.

Before Bangaz had time to think, Marie grabbed his arm. 'You are coming with us,' she said and marched him into the office.

Bangaz smiled. 'Milady!' he said brightly. 'Whuppen?'

'That's what we are gonna find out,' said Marie.

Chris pushed open the door to Mr Reynolds' office.

'Who are you?' he said to the fit, handsome young man behind the desk.

'Brian Reynolds, Attorney-at-law,' the man said in a soothing baritone. 'And how may I help you?'

'But I've met Mr Reynolds. Yesterday. You're not him.'

Reynolds chuckled. 'I am Mr Reynolds.'

'I signed this document right here,' said Chris clutching the deed of sale, 'and I counted out eleven grand of our cash on that desk. For this worthless piece of shit.'

'We don't know it's worthless,' said Marie. 'It's evidence of fraud. We can sue with it.'

'What did you buy?' said Reynolds, leaning back in his chair.

'An island,' said Marie.

'The one off Plantation Hotel?' Reynolds inquired.

'Yes,' said Chris.

'I am sorry to say that you have been the victim of a confidence trickster. That property belongs to the Jamaican Government,' Mr Reynolds said softly.

'This boy,' said Marie holding up Bangaz limp arm, 'was with the man who conned us. He's an accomplice. An accessory before, during and after the fact. We want to get our money back and get him and his uncle charged. What's his name, your uncle?' shouted Marie at Bangaz.

'Him name Maas Henry,' said Bangaz. He knew Chris knew Maas Henry's yard so it was pointless denying he knew him. 'But he gone a foreign. He tell we now he make a money he fly to Miami this morning. He leave out for airport early. He pack him bag and go.'

'We've got to report this to the Police,' said Marie. 'He's stolen our money.'

Mr Reynolds held up his hand.

'You paid eleven grand for that island?'

'Yeah,' said Chris bitterly.

Reynolds let out a low whistle, raised his eyebrows and said, 'What you think it's really worth?'

Chris looked confused.

'A million?' asked Reynolds. 'Two million?' He let a silence fill the room. Then asked, 'So, who really is the thief here?'

'Are you kidding?' Marie said. 'Did you just say that?'

'Have you ever heard of reparations?' Mr Reynolds coolly inquired.

'What's that, another con?' said Chris.

'Oh no. It's quite straightforward. It's the payment of money owed to the people of Jamaica.'

'What? For slavery? That stopped nearly two hundred years ago. That's, like, eight generations.'

'Yes,' said Liar Reynolds, 'and while you have been passing your money down from father to son, we have been passing your bill down from generation to generation. Adding interest too. Because you refuse to pay what is owed, and we have grown a little tired after 190 years of waiting for our compensation. You must accept it is reasonable for us to seek redress?'

'But this has nothing to do with us,' said Chris.

'Right,' said Marie. Bangaz felt her grip on his wrist loosen.

'You have always stolen from us,' Reynolds said.

Bangaz jaw drop open. He had never heard a black man chat to a white so. And Mr Reynolds was so gentle and polite. Marie let go of him arm.

'You two,' Reynolds said calmly, 'prove you are still trying to steal from us. May I suggest you respectfully stop stealing? Now, please leave, I have work to do.'

At Maas Henry's car-strewn yard the next morning, an SUV drew up and Mr Reynolds climbed out.

'Maas Henry,' he called.

After a precautionary pause, Maas Henry appeared round the side of the house.

'Ah, Mister Reynolds, sir,' said Maas Henry. 'Always good to see you.'

There followed an expletive laden rant from the lawyer, with a few yelps of pain from Maas Henry, who eventually went back to the house and returned with some bank notes in his hand. He handed over 500 bucks and the atmosphere improved.

'Next time you tell me first, you understand?' Reynolds said. 'I will draw up the paperwork for a thousand and get out of my office for another thousand. Deal?'

Maas Henry's lupine features lit up with a wide smile. 'Deal sah!' he said.

So although Bangaz never really went to school, it wasn't really true he didn't get an education.

5

Willy Loxley-Gordon read those first four chapters to a fifty-year-old Bangaz, who sat on the porch of the house in Campbell Cove where Willy had lived for more or less thirty years. He had a round face with a little nose and bright blue eyes, but the neat features which had once been cheeky and handsome were beginning to show signs of fear and even defeat.

Willy said, 'What do you think? You like it?' He ran his hand through tufts of his white hair while he waited for the answer.

Bangaz bent his head to one side and sparked a lighter, his hand studded with big rings, one with a ganja leaf picked out in diamonds. His knee was jiggling fast.

'It don't start at the beginning,' Bangaz said. 'What about when me born?'

'That's not how you write books,' Willy said. 'Tings nuh go so. You haffi begin with a story to catch the reader.' Thirty years in Jamaica had taught him basic Patwa, and as an ex-pat in France would speak French, so Willy spoke the local language, out of consideration, respect and the wish to better communicate with his friends.

Bangaz nodded. 'But this my story, not yours,' his bulging eyes sparkled.

'I meant to ask you about that,' Willy said, breathing heavily as he moved his bulk in the lopsided chair, 'as it relates to my payment situation. How much money were you thinking of paying me to write it, roughly?'

Willy knew well that Bangaz was a millionaire with an extravagant villa on the hill and a fleet of blacked out cars.

'Money?' Bangaz pulled deep on his spliff and tipped some of a flask of JB white rum into a thin plastic cup.

'Well,' said Willy, 'I wrote that on spec to show you what I was capable of. If you want to proceed with this biography, well, I have already incurred quite a few out of pocket expenses and I was hoping in addition you could maybe, if you liked how it's going, er, possibly pay me some kind of advance against sales? If you like it? You see I am a professional author of over forty years standing...'

'Pay you?' Bangaz stood up in mock fury. 'Cho! Mi a scammer, Willy! You lucky mi nuh charge you. This a book gonna make you rich. It the story of Clive Bangaz Thompson life. The biggest scammer in the whole of Jamaica. Top operator. King pin. From him rags to him riches.'

'I am aware of the potential, but the thing is I am a little short at the moment. You might say, financially embarrassed.'

That was an understatement. Poor Willy was, at sixty-five years of age, bankrupt and a long, long way from home. Not that he could ever go back to blighty. He might be able to sell this house in Campbell Cove but it wouldn't buy him a box in England. He had once lived in Belgravia, where he had contributed to the cultural life of the beau monde. He had not, however, contributed any National Insurance and had no private pension, so a dignified retirement in the UK was out of the question. His outlook was dire. That's why he was reduced to importuning the gangsta in front of him who was now dancing to some music that floated through the trees and onto the water.

Willy had spent a year on a book about Ian Fleming, Noel Coward and the smart expatriate set they ruled over in Jamaica in the 50s and 60s. The outline and a sample chapter, which he had emailed with hope in his heart to his old publisher, had been returned by an automated reply saying his editor no longer worked there, and the Orientalist and Travel Writing department had been renamed the Black Voices imprint. Willy had written a lively pitch to the new chief editor, Zuri Bennet-Henriques. Zuri had not replied.

Willy's agent, a genial and decent man called Claude, had retired a few years ago. New representation had not been forthcoming. Claude had taken a look at his proposal as a friend, and said, 'Willy, I worry you're out of touch out there. This proposal is far too colonial, too backward looking. Nobody's interested. Or rather nobody in publishing is interested. Don't you, dare I say it, have a black subject? You have lived there thirty years. While Ian Fleming and Noel Coward were living their charmed lives amongst their servants in the 50s and 60s, black writers in Kingston were struggling to be heard. That's what people want to hear about. Although, having said that, even if you tried, er, I'm afraid you are not what they want ... as a writer. It's not your fault. Your options are very limited I'm afraid, and as you know I am no longer in the business.'

Willy had panicked, then remembered a conversation he had in a bar. 'There is this man in my community here. He's a gangsta of sorts. A top scammer. He's the Pablo Escobar of scammers, you could say. He wants to tell me his story.'

Claude listened and said, 'That has potential. If you were under thirty, black and female I'd probably get you a commission for it. Yes, that's the reality we all face. Us old white men have had our day.'

With those alarming words gnawing at his confidence, Willy had agreed with Bangaz to write his story, which had brought them to this moment on his porch.

'Nu worry bout nuttin, Willy!' Bangaz shouted waving his spliff around. 'You gonna bingo with this book. Trust me,' he flashed a smile. 'But tell me the honest truth, why you start it when mi already age eleven? It will start ...' He pointed at the keyboard, '...Clive Thompson was born in the Parish of St John on 23rd Feb 1978. That is the first words of my book.'

22

'Look,' said Willy, 'I'm not taking dictation, okay? We are doing it my way or not at all.'

'Very good,' said Bangaz. 'Very good. But memba mi idea dem wicked and powerful. Chuss me.'

'We will have to see how it's received,' grumbled Willy.

'Anedda ting. Why you write in Patwa?' Bangaz shouted.

'Because people chat in Patwa.'

'Yes,' said Bangaz. 'When dem talk, but not you when you is describing things. You say people dem. This is not proper English. In English it never says dem. That is not English. And English don't say pon. Dem say on the television. Not pon teevee.' He suck teeth.

'I wrote that to give a flavour of Jamaica.'

'Don't!' snapped Bangaz, waving his finger as he held the lighter. 'I want mi book to be in the Queen's English. It must write properly. No Patwa. You write Bangaz jaw drop open. English don't say that. Dem say Bangaz jaw dropped open. Seen?'

'But Patwa doesn't have any tenses. It don't got no tenses. It's all in the present tense. You never say dropped.'

'But is you writing it Willy, and you speak English. That is why I choose you.'

'Well I'm keeping it as drop. For the vibe,' Willy said.

'That just a ignorance. And I want proper spelling all fully correct. You want fi make me look like a idiot? Enuh!'

Willy sighed. 'Look Bangaz, I know you're clever, I'm sure you're cleverer than me. So you will understand that I am trying to render reality here. There is no wrong or right way. English is no more the right way than Mandarin Chinese. But you do all speak Patwa. And lots of you hardly speak English. Patwa is the national language though the big people dem try to pretend differently. You can't depict Jamaica without adding some language into the recipe. To do it in a formal English style would be preposterous...'

'....A dat mi a want. Formal English style. Words like preposterous, and hitherto and aforementioned and regarding and sincerely. Proper words.'

'In that case you should get someone else to do this. Serious ting,' Willy said.

'There is nobody elkse. You is my writer. A dat mi decide.'

'Well I can't do it your way. And we shouldn't be doing it your way. Just trust me, okay?' Willy said. 'I've been writing a long time.'

Bangaz stood up and patted his pockets for the lighter which was in his hand. When he saw it he smiled. 'Okay. We do it your way Willy. But no fuckery, understand?'

'Agreed,' said Willy. 'A sprinkling of Patwa but no fuckery.'

'Good. Very good.'

'I hope this doesn't turn out to be a waste of time,' Willy muttered.

'Dem ago love this book,' Bangaz said bringing the lighter to his spliff. 'A great white man write bout a great man. Dem haffi love it man. You famous!'

Willy smiled ruefully and shook his head. 'I'm not. If I ever was, I'm not a name any longer. I once wrote, back in the 90s this was, a book which sold a respectable number of copies, about Ian Fleming.'

'A who name Ian Fleming?'

'Wrote the James Bond books.'

Bangaz thought about this for a moment and said, 'You write the James Bond books?'

Willy smiled, slowly shook his fluffy white head and chuckled, 'I'm afraid not. Things would be rather different had I done that.'

'You haffi keep belief,' said Bangaz. 'That's all. Truss me. Nutting can g'wrong. Rain a com.'

And with that, the man was on his way, loping across Willy's yard towards his SUV, which started before he reached it. 'Later!' he shouted.

It was August, high summer, hot, still and sultry. Olympic rings of moisture left by successive tumblers of Appleton Estate rum glistened on the desk. Heavy drops of rain began to tap on the zinc roof, accelerating from tack tack tack to a clattering thrum as the cloud belched water over the house. Through a silver bead curtain that dropped from the eaves, Willy watched the water of the cove turn smoky with bouncing droplets. It rained so hard that outside, in the open air bathroom, Willy's shampoo bottle filled to the brim through the hole at the top.

Sitting at the table, untidy with dirty plates and stained liquor glasses, Willy was about the only thing in that whole house that was washed up. He sighed, pulled his laptop towards him and began to write.

6

On the night of the 23rd Feb 1975, the tail of a storm which had brought the East coast of the US to a frozen standstill whipped across Jamaica and brought a choppy, argumentative sea to Cove with a moaning wind which rattled the windows and boards.

The cold air sent Marva Thompson to the blue barrel of clothes in the corner of the room. The barrel had been sent down by cousins in Michigan in response to Marva begging daily for a help, and she had cleared it at the wharf with high hopes which were mainly dashed when she prised off its lid; she cuss and use bad word when she see that half of it was filled with American winter clothing, for which there was no use. But this cold front now changed that. Bent double over the barrel, Marva dug around and found a bobble hat, scarf, puffer jacket and fur lined boots. She was just pulling on her gloves ready to brandish the outfit around Cove when her step sister, fifteen-year-old Tanisha, raised herself on the bed and said, 'Mi think the baby a com. Help me. You haffi carry me a hospital.'

Marva said, 'Now?'

'Yes,' said Tanisha. 'Yes. Hurry.'

Marva suck teeth.

'Please,' said Tanisha pushing her foot into a slipper.

'Why you haffi pick now?' Marva said. 'You a selfish gal, you know dat?'

'Please, help me.'

Marva shoved Tanisha in the back of a taxi and ordered the driver to take her to the hospital in Lucea. Then she adjusted her ski hat and headed off to Dahlia, a woman she knew had no barrel clothes.

She stepped off the bus at Dahlia's yard.

'It cold?' Marva asked Dahlia. 'Boy, mi never notice it in mi jacket. You don't got no jacket? Careful you nuh catch cold...'

Marva then headed to Green Island where she knew of a few sufferers who could be relied on to have no jacket or hat, who she could gloat at.

Tanisha arrived at the hospital with a fever, and was made to sit on a chair in a corridor in a whistling draught while in labour. She had a seizure around midnight, and never regained consciousness. At four in the morning, Bangaz came into the world and Tanisha left it. Bangaz often wondered if she saw him before she died, and had a recurring dream of passing her like a ghost in a hospital corridor, reaching out his hand to touch her.

Tanisha's mum was dead from a car accident and her father long gone. And there was no sign of the baby father. So the hospital sent a message to Marva to come for Bangaz.

Marva turned up at the hospital the next day in a black polo neck apres-ski sweater and goggles even though the weather had turned hot again. She looked down at the infant that had been placed in her arms, adjusting the lanyard for her ski lift pass. He had a cute round face, bowed lips and bright eyes, searching her face for love.

Marva wanted to go down to the morgue and shake her sister's corpse until it burped out the name of the baby father. She had an idea he was rich and married. Even if he wouldn't take the baby he could give Marva a help with a money.

Back in her room she gave him his first bottle.

She kissed his face and said 'You name Clive.'

7

After turning in, moderately happy at meeting his 500 word target, Bangaz turned up at one in the morning and shouted outside Willy's door.

'Yo, Willy! Mi want mi writer!'

The house creaked as Willy shuffled to the door. 'I'm not your writer,' he muttered.

'Come on, Bossy. Tek up your laptop. Mi wan fi chat.'

Willy opened the door in his nightshirt. 'I am not your writer. You are my subject,' he said. 'And this kind of thing ... I am prepared to work unsociable hours, but in consideration of a payment. This is over and above. A fair payment is due if this happens again.'

'A joke you a-make,' laughed Bangaz. 'Also, this book. It gonna have my name on the cover too.'

'Well, I'm not sure about that. Let me think about it,' Willy said wandering outside for a pee.

The rain had passed and it was a hot summer night, the moon throwing deep shadow on the porch, the cove silver, the sky sewn with stars. Back in the house, Willy flicked the switch on and off until the bulb on the wall lit up. Bangaz was in his white merino, baggy white shorts and slippers. He pointed at the laptop. 'Sit dung,' and then clicked his lighter at his spliff. He spoke without pausing while Willy tried to keep up on the keyboard.

8

For years, Bangaz's distant relatives fought over how much money they had to give Marva to keep him. She was a tall strong woman with an unconventional parenting style, which included shouting at little Bangaz: 'Ya madda go dead and leave you fi mash up mi life. Ya mash mi life, ya crawsis pickney.'

Bangaz got the blame for Marva's woes, which were many and varied. Her lack of a big house, the absence of boasty furniture: the pickney fault. Him mash up everyting.

At sixteen, Bangaz had a pregnant girlfriend called Pauline. She was a short, pretty girl with a kind smile on a heart shaped face. Born and raised in Kingston, she had come west after she had been run from her yard by her madda, because her step-father rape her.

Marva let Pauline com to stay cos Marva said she could do house-work and cook for her and Wayne, who was Marva's boyfriend. One day Pauline fell in a culvert and broke her foot. She begged not to work, and Bangaz tell Marva she could not do no work, but Marva say she don't have nutn wrong and she can do house-work and washing.

'Nuh bodda start limp!' Marva shouted at Pauline. 'Cause it nuh gonna work. Yuh tink yuh smart. Limp all yuh want yuh still affi do work.'

The next day Pauline collapsed and go to hospital where dem say her bone bruk in two place. Pauline have her foot in cast but Marva say she can wash dishes and spread bed.

9

'When Marva discover Pauline get belly,' Bangaz said, his throat strangling any emotion, 'that day she trow we outa de yard. She say, "lard god Clive, mi know Pauline bad, and now she gonna run way and leave mi with the baby because she know mi good with pickney and everyone want mi fi raise dem baby."'

Bangaz halted for a moment as the memory crossed his mind. 'Blud-claat woman.' he sighed. 'Couple of bredren tell me I can disown the baby,' he added.

Willy nodded while his fingers flew over the keys, stopping only to turn off autocorrect.

'Mi friend say that I can run Pauline outa de yard, and stay at Marva yard, and forget bout her. Even Marva tell me to run Pauline. She said it probably not my baby and that Pauline try fi trick me in to wear a jacket. Just let the girl go on with it alone, she told me.

'But so I had no father, I am not doing the same to my pickney,' Bangaz said. He waited for Willy to write that down before continuing. 'So I tek up mi woman and I tek up my ting and I leave Marva yard. I move into a room in a bruk dung house whey roof leak, but rat nuh run over us inna the night. Things bad but Pauline take my hands and say she believe in mi, and she know I will find a way to look after my family.'

10

Bangaz got a job in an all-inclusive. It was the only work around. The sugar cane industry had crashed, and the manufacturing sector in the form of an underwear factory in Sandy Bay had failed to take off. The American executive who closed it down after three unprofitable years said it was the only time during a life in the garment trade he had seen a pair of underpants with three leg holes.

Bangaz took the test for Plantation, which was one of the big new hotels in Negril. He failed. The results of the exam were always the same: the people who passed and were best suited to being a staff member always turned out to be the prettiest girls with the palest skin who looked likely to at least flirt with Mr Hawkin, the well-padded hotel manager. In the end, Bangaz was recalled because he could swim and the hotel was expanding so fast they were short of life guards.

Bangaz had been at Plantation for a good few months when he met the Williams family from Manchester, England. There was Daddy called Aiden, Mummy called Mandy, Caddy the daughter who wore a pickney wrist band but looked 19 or 21, and the two kids Cliff, 10 and Bruce, 6.

It was Bangaz job to sit up a ladder and watch the beach so he see plenty pretty gal dem, but Caddy hot. On her first day, Bangaz's best friend Ample, who was a waiter in the restaurant, see Caddy and Caddy see Ample. She turn to look at Ample as he carry a tray of cups to the tourists and she trip over Bruce.

Ample was tall and loose limbed with soft eyes, big ears and an easy smile. All the tourist women love him, but he wasn't a gallis—a man who go up and down and trick and fuck every girl he meet. He was soft and kind.

Ample had noticed Caddy but paid it no mind. It was dangerous to have sex with a guest. Yes – that was one of Mr Hawkin's rules. That kind of thing could get you disappeared. In the time Ample and Bangaz had been at the hotel, two good bredren lose their job with immediate effect after being found in a guest bedroom. The guests, however, were never given an explanation. They were left to wander around the hotel looking for their lovers. One woman ended up having sex with a sacked waiter through the links of the fence.

Caddy was thrilled when she sat down for dinner on the second night and realised that Ample was their waiter. He said, 'Water, milady?' pouring from a steel jug with one arm behind his back.

'Can't I have a drink?' Caddy said. 'I am meant to be on holiday.'

'No,' said Aiden. 'You're not 18. Have an alcohol free cocktail.'

'Okay.' She looked into Ample's big soft eyes and said, 'May I have a virgin sex on the beach, please?'

Ample looked straight back trying not to smile. 'Very good, milady. Straight up? Or on the rocks?'

'Straight up,' said Caddy.

'Can I have a Red Stripe,' said Aiden, 'and Mandy? A pina colada, and two apple juices. Thank you.'

'Very good, sir,' said Ample, swivelling on his feet, adjusting his tray and shimmering off across the dining table.

'Caddy!' said Aiden.

'What?' his daughter said.

'He was a bit fresh,' said Mandy.

Caddy spent the days curating her suntan on a sun-bed, angled away from the rest of her family, and making unnecessary trips around the hotel to scope out Ample.

As he had the job of life guard, Bangaz never liked to point out to anyone exactly how safe the beach was. The soft sand shelved away so reassuringly and the Caribbean sea unfurled like a roll of silk. The only danger was lightning, so he made the most of shepherding the guests out of the water when a summer storm blew over.

He picked up plenty of English, happily calling out, 'Top of the morning milady,' or, 'Yes buddy. How you doing today? Give me a high five,' and saying, instead of no problem, man, 'not a problem, my good man.' He had just said 'Have a nice day,' to Caddy when he ran into her father, who he enjoyed having conversations with. Aiden wore a tie-dye singlet, cargo shorts and an old green forage cap with a ganja leaf insignia.

'Hey, Clive! Ya man,' said Aiden to Bangaz. 'Good to see you. Would you teach me a couple of Patwa phrases? I think I should stretch my linguistic horizons.'

'For sure!' said Bangaz, who was doing the same thing. 'Give me a quick second,' he said, dropping a cup into a garbage bin.

'How do I say: Hello, how are you?' Aiden asked.

'Easy! Whuppen? You good? Or Y pree?'

'Whuppen!'

'Yes mi brudder!' Bangaz shouted back, suddenly seeing Mr Hawkin glaring at him from under an umbrella.

'Blessings and guidance,' said Aiden, putting a five dollar bill into Bangaz's hand who passed it back, forcing out the hardest words he had ever to say: 'I can't accept that.'

Aiden waved him away, picked up his Steel Pulse tote bag and headed off the beach. 'Caddy,' he called. 'I'm going to the bar. Do you want a juice?'

'Fruit punch, please,' she said in a monotone.

Mr Hawkin walked up to Bangaz and said 'Give me that. It hotel property.'

'I never ask for it,' Bangaz said, passing the bank note over.

Aiden returned with a tray of cups. He handed Caddy hers. She idly wondered if Ample had poured it, enjoying embroidering her day with thoughts of him. She gave it a sip, tasted rum, and smiled. She put her arm up in the air and clicked her fingers. She knew he was watching her from the deep shade behind her.

11

'Wheel up! Pull up,' said Bangaz, stopping Willy mid-sentence. 'How you know what Caddy thinking? Or what she say to her daddy? How you know what happen when you cyan see it and nobody tell you?'

'I'm imagining it,' Willy said. 'You can do that in books.'

'This fockry,' stated Bangaz.

They had been sitting reading on the porch from early, and the sun was now directly overhead, blasting heat and light onto the yard, scattering every person and every animal into the shade. Willy screwed up his eyes at the glare.

'It's a bit unconventional,' Willy said.

Bangaz ruminated on it.

'Did you like "embroidering her day" as a phrase?' Willy said.

Bangaz grunted.

'Sometimes you have to break the rules,' Willy said.

'For sure,' said Bangaz, nodding. 'Because sometimes the rules only serve certain people.'

'You can say that,' said Willy.

'So dem muss break.' Said Bangaz, adding, 'Jamaica style.'

'Jamaica style,' agreed Willy.

12

'I do find these name badges barbaric,' Aiden said to Mandy as he settled onto his sun bed. 'Clive tried to refuse to take a tip. They're fired if they accept them. Their badges literally say: No tips, please! It's the please that's so offensive. It's our money, we can spend it as we want. This place is beginning to remind me more and more of a real plantation.'

'Please Aiden. We're on holiday.'

'Clive told me yesterday he had to pay five US dollars for his badge. And it is against the rules to take it off. I was having a very interesting conversation with him about pay and conditions...'

'How did he handle the excitement, Dad?' Caddy called over her shoulder.

'You know what he said to me about the hotel industry?'

'I have a feeling you're gonna tell us whatever we say,' said Mandy.

'You two are such tourists,' said Aiden.

'Yeah, trying to be,' said Mandy, lying back and closing her eyes.

'He said Windmill grind slow, but grinding still. Quite astute, don't you think? The hotel has fake tourists called shappers, who shap them out. They give tips and take their badge number and report the staff who accept them. They are called secret shapper.'

'Shopper,' said Mandy. 'Secret shopper.'

'Oh yeah,' said Aiden, 'of course. 'Don't you think that's like almost slavery?'

Answer came there none.

'Aren't you two at all interested in any of the social and economic conditions of places you visit?'

There was silence broken by Caddy saying, 'No. Next question.'

'For god's sake just lie back and relax Aiden,' murmured Mandy. 'It's called a holiday. We're trying to get suntans, not A levels.'

'You remember that time Dad wanted us to go on a tour of German concentration camps?' Caddy said, her eyes closed.

Mandy laughed.

'Another great family holiday,' said Caddy, 'from the man who brought us a long weekend visiting extinct coal mines in Yorkshire. With two toddlers.'

'No – I admit it, the beach is great,' said Aiden. 'Astounding! Look at that turquoise. But it does get boring after a week. For an inquiring mind. I want to see and learn about the real Jamaica.'

Aiden left them on the beach and went to reception.

'Hi – I'd like to look into taking a trip somewhere.'

The slender, almond eyed woman at the desk – one of Mr Hawkin's protégés – suck teeth and said, 'Tour bus leave Wednesday, 170 US Dollars per guest. Minimum eight passengers.'

'Uh, ok,' said Aiden. 'Where does it go exactly?'

'Native village, craft market, river view. One moment.' She answered her phone and listened for a while, staring at Aiden. Then she murmured 'Carry me one chicken and rice and vegetables, no fry.'

Mr Hawkin hovered into view. 'Sir! A very good day to you. May I be of assistance?'

'I was just asking how I go about leaving the hotel to take a look around the countryside. Do a bit of exploring, you know?'

'Our advice is not to perambulate beyond the perimeter of the hotel. What were you particularly hoping to see?'

'I'm not sure, I suppose some village life.'

'But this is a village here! Leaving is not necessary, or recommended. Are the staff not friendly?'

'Very. It's just that I'd like to meet some Jamaicans who are not in the hotel industry.'

'Why?'

'I want to see life up in the hills, away from the tourist honey pots. See how the citizens are.'

'They are dirty. Wifey would not be partial to them, I assure you. And your daughter, she would not be safe. We cannot guarantee her safety outside the perimeter of the hotel.'

'It can't be that bad. I am an experienced traveller. I'm just after some local culture...'

'.... We have limbo and sword dancing in the lobby on Thursday and Saturdays....'

'.... just to spend a bit of time with some ordinary folk, I suppose. Just go into a local bar and talk some Patwa.'

Aiden touched a nerve there. It was another of Hawkin's rules that tourists should never have to hear Patwa. At staff meetings, Mr Hawkin often emphasised that tourists 'have not journeyed to our nation to hear a dutty, ignorant language on their vacation. Speak properly! Speak English,' he commanded. Anyone heard speaking Patwa was risking their job.

Another of Mr Hawkin's rules was that no tourist be allowed to leave the compound – though the tourists were not allowed to know about this rule.

'Bearing in mind productivity ratios going forwards,' Mr Hawkin had said at the staff meeting, 'and insofar as under which certain principles shall be adhered to willy-nilly, the guest individual shall, whomsoever they be, prefer to enjoy a sub optimal visitor experience when beyond the curtilage of the hotel. Now, is that clear?'

'Yes sir, Mr Hawkin,' everybody said about the words that none in the room, including Mr Hawkin, understood.

Bangaz stood in his white shorts and short-sleeved shirt with LIFE GUARD on the back, listening and learning.

As they filed out, a security man said 'Mr Hawkin sir, I is not sure what I muss do, I did not hear you clearly.'

'Mm,' and 'yes,' a few others mumbled, gathering around the oracle.

'Frighten the tourist dem,' Mr Hawkin said quietly and smiled. 'Mek dem scared to leave the hotel. Understand now?'

The more tourists believed it was too dangerous to visit Jamaica unless you stayed inside a fenced compound, the more business the hotel got. Bad mouthing the country and its people was good for the all-inclusive business.

To free up Ample and Caddy, Bangaz got mummy and daddy fully intoxicated. Every time they asked for a drink he made their rum very stronger. This allowed Ample to spend more time hovering around Caddy with his tray, and finally he took her for a walk in the manicured grounds with nobody noticing.

'Where's Caddy?' Aiden asked, steadying himself on the umbrella.

'Probably talking to Ample.' Mandy slurred.

Aiden lowered his voice. 'I'm pretty sure that guy's gay. They have to keep it covered up here.'

'He's doing a good job of that,' Mandy said.

Bangaz was rubbing sun tan oil on a thick German divorcee as he watched Caddy touching and laughing with Ample up on the pool deck above her parents. Ample was admiring the rosey blush on Caddy's pale skin and enjoying staring into her green eyes.

At the end of the shift each day, Bangaz and Ample left the rarefied atmosphere of Plantation through the security gate. They had to let the guard dig about them a bit, and then they were pon de street again, amongst the noise and litter and grime of Jamaica. The minibus pulled over to pick them up and rattle them down the road, passing through Orange Bay and

Green Island to Campbell Cove where Pauline sat waiting with baby Jenna in their bare wooden room. Bangaz never stopped off at a bar or idled on the road on his way back to her.

Ample said, 'You have to remove mummy and daddy for me. Enfree we out of the tangle. I can't get nowhere when her father look pon Caddy so hard. And I like the girl. She cool and she friendly; we talk.'

'No problem,' said Bangaz. 'Lang time Aiden want fi tour outside the hotel. Him chat nuff bout it. So mi happy to help,' said Bangaz. 'I will carry mummy and daddy and the kid dem to Cove for a cook out on the beach. That will give you plenty time to do your ting.'

13

After grooving the sand with the sunbeds and planting the umbrella in the ground, Bangaz said to Aiden, 'How about one day I will take you out on a tour? I can take you to my community. It call Campbell Cove.'

'That sounds lush,' said Caddy, a little over enthusiastically, but she was in on the plan, and had to get rid of them for the day.

'I bet it's great,' said Aiden, trying to rouse enthusiasm from Mandy. 'What do you think?'

'Will you be there, Clive?' Mandy asked. A journey in a cramped mini-bus to an unknown destination didn't really appeal when compared to a day on the beach drinking cocktails and reading Veronica Henry romances.

'At your very service, milady.'

'It could be fun,' said Caddy, giving it plenty.

Aiden said 'You are finally getting the culture bug, Caddy.'

And the outing was arranged for Bangaz's day off.

The evening before they were due to go, when they were all in the kids' hotel room, Caddy moved smoothly into phase two of operation Virgin-Sex-On-The-Beach: she announced she wanted to stay behind.

'I forgot about the PADI course,' she lied. Caddy had been doing a diving course in the hotel swimming-pool. ' It's our first open water dive,' she said. 'I really don't want to miss it.'

'So you're not coming?' said Mandy. 'Thank you very much for joining in on the family holiday. Not.'

'If diving is her passion, I think it's a good idea she gets her certificate so she can continue with it. And if we're still out when you get back from the dive, you can spend some time with that Shakespeare. Remember, young woman, you've got exams to sit in five months.'

Little Cliff took advantage of this conversation to go into the parents' room, find Aiden's wallet and steal three 20 dollar bills from it. He scrunched them up in his hot hand and dug them in his shorts' pocket with the wrappers from the chocolates he found on his pillow.

The next morning, with a rucksack stuffed with water bottles, diving masks, suntan oils, swimming costumes and towels, the family set off on their adventure without Caddy, though first they were stopped at the gate by security and sent back to reception to get the paperwork in order.

Aiden approached the desk. 'What is this about us having to sign something to leave the hotel?'

The woman with the almond eyes and high heels looked at Aiden, said 'Waiver,' and slid a piece of paper across the desk at him. Aiden started to read it.

The hotel accepts no responsibility nor liability for any instances of kidnap, rape, theft, knifing, shooting — whether with pistol, rifle or shot gun, not excluding assault weapons — which occur outside the hotel's perimeter fence. Nor will the hotel accept any responsibility in the event of a guest contracting denghi fever, red fever, scarlet fever, cholera, AIDS or small-pox....

'This is fear-mongering,' said Aiden.

'You may not exit the hotel without it being sign,' the woman said looking at her nails.

'Just sign it, what does it matter?' said Mandy.

Aiden signed furiously, and passed the paper back. The woman looked at it, pushed it back without saying anything.

'What's wrong now?'

'Name, address, date of birth, mother's maiden name and date of birth of father.'

'For...?' Aiden said under his breath.

Mr Hawkin appeared in the doorway. 'Mr Williams, why are you putting your family in the path of danger?' he asked.

'We just want to meet some local people.'

'Take the Calico Jack island tour and turtle watch. Only 40 dollars per person. US. You can meet and talk to the boatmen while you consume one snack and one beverage on the beach of our deserted island. Or let me sign you on a jungle canopy zipwire and 4 by 4 adventure trip at a cost of 100 US each.'

'Look, if it's all right with you, we are going to leave the hotel for a day, and trust in the kindness of the Jamaican people. Mandy, kids, come on.'

The family emerged onto the street.

'Aiden!' Bangaz hissed from under a tree. 'Milady! Cliff! Bruce!' He beckoned to the family, who crossed the road and started climbing into the old minibus. Setter welcomed them from the driver's seat raising a plastic cup of rum and smoking a spliff.

'Bungle up!' he said.

'Clive, there are no seat belts,' Aiden said.

'No need! Nutn can go wrong, trust me,' Bangaz said.

'Hold on, I've left my wallet in the room,' Aiden said patting his pockets.

'Don't worry,' said Mandy. 'I've got plenty.'

'Setter is the best driver in the village,' Bangaz said from the front.

That was true, but the word 'best' meant something different when describing a driver in Jamaica. It meant fastest. With a fierce rev of the engine and a gentle departure they set off east, slowly gathering speed, leaving the hotels of Negril behind them until they hit maximum velocity on the long straight through the mangrove marsh, a speed which Setter maintained no matter what occurred on the road ahead of him. Over-taking on blind corners, swerving potholes, scattering a crowd of school children, the minibus hammered towards Campbell Cove.

'How far is it?' asked Aiden.

'Soon reach,' shouted Bangaz.

They drew up in the heavy shade of an almond tree by the fisherman beach at Cove, where Bangaz's bredren were keenly waiting. The people of Campbell Cove loved tourists and longed for them to stop, but as the foreigners were held in captivity in the new all-inclusive hotels, they hardly ever got the chance to give them a good welcome. As Aiden and Mandy alighted from the minibus, a bottle of beer was placed in their hands.

Maas Henry was primed, and sprang off the bench to greet the arriving party. 'Welcome to fi we likkle community, milady,' he said trying to grasp Mandy's hand. Mandy was too busy dealing with the anxiety of watching Bangaz lift the two boys straight onto Champion Buoy shouting 'Mek we go and catch couple lobster for breakfast,' to notice Maas Henry, though she did momentarily notice Troy, the slim rasta owner of the beach bar,

'Where are the life-jackets?' she called.

'We don't got none,' Bangaz replied. 'Soon come.'

'I'll go,' said Aiden, wading after the boat and clambering in. 'Sit down boys,' he said as Bangaz's friend Omar started the outboard. Omar was one of Bangaz school friends, or rather truancy friends, because as a half albino he had been picked on by the school bullies, and had preferred to spend his time selling fruit by the road and playing in the bush with Bangaz.

Champion Buoy cut a V through across the calm water, skating over the coral reef like a plane over cloud. The boys faced forwards, their hair spread by the wind, gripping on to the boat, serious, scared and thrilled. They turned and smiled at their father. They, along with all the Jamaicans, shared none of Mandy and Aiden's fears.

With the shore far away across a field of deep blue, Omar throttled back the engine and drew up alongside a bunch of white bleach bottles, leant over and pulled on the weedy rope until a cage appeared through the clear water. He hauled it dripping onto the rim of the boat and tipped it onto the floor. The boys backed away, shrieking with delight but both clutching onto Aiden's arms. A dozen lobsters thrashed about in the cage. Omar reached in and took out four, holding them by their backs while their claws worked the air. He threw them into a bucket and tipped the cage back into the water. The closest Cliff and Bruce had ever been to live seafood was a battered cod finger; they stared open-mouthed at the animals, jumping when they snapped their claws.

Aiden held onto the boys' waistbands as they raced over the water back towards the thickly forested hills. A single strand of blue smoke rose from the beach into the uninterrupted blue of the sky. Underneath this smoke was a driftwood fire lit by Troy, which Mandy was staring into as she took another pull on the burning spliff which she had found in her hand.

'That was just, wow! Wow! Amazing!' Aiden called as he waded from the boat.

Mandy tore her stare from Troy's torso, which she had been studying closely, particularly the total absence of even a pinch of fat on the skin that ran over the ridges of his stomach. 'So is this!' she said, holding up the spliff. For some reason she had stopped hiding her spliff from the kids. It was probably something to do with the Campbell Cove beach vibe. But in all honesty Cliff and Bruce had much more interesting things to think about than what their mum was doing. 'It's something called Eye Grade,' Mandy said. 'You've got to try it.'

While the boys helped Omar and Clive draw the boat onto the sand, Aiden stood next to his wife and took in the beauty of the Cove.

'This is the kind of place I've been talking about,' he said to all in earshot. 'Proper Jamaica.'

This elicited a generous sprinkling of Yeah mons from Maas Henry and the other men who had gathered to enjoy a rare encounter with a tourist.

'What an experience for the boys to see the lobsters coming up alive from the deep. And now we're going to eat them.'

With a stroke of his machete, Bangaz opened the lobsters and laid them on the rusty grill over the driftwood fire, which Troy was gently rearranging with a stick, his dreadlocks falling in front of his face. Mandy had wondered what the locks would feel like at the back of his slender neck if she held them in her fist.

Aiden perched on a log. 'It's a certainty that pirates would have sailed into this harbour. Don't you think so, Clive?'

'English pirates?' asked Bangaz.

'Not necessarily, though the English controlled these waters for hundreds of years. It would have been privateers, most likely.'

'What is privateers?' asked Omar, keen to learn now school was in the past.

'A very English invention. They were criminals, but encouraged and protected by the English. As long as they didn't steal from us they could do what they wanted. The privateers did our dirty work, basically. Attacking ships, robbing settlements, murdering Spaniards and the Dutch. If they got caught, the English pretended they didn't know them. If they didn't get caught we rewarded them and made them lords and knights. In 1563 there was an interesting case in the High Court in London about the technical definition of a privateer—'

'For god's sake Aiden, lighten up,' Mandy said.

'They were criminal who the king protect?' Bangaz asked.

'Yes,' said Aiden.

'Big man ting,' said Maas Henry.

'Ya man,' said Aiden, 'a dat,' pleased to use some Patwa. He took a couple of pulls on Mandy's spliff, and was now back in 1563, on the prow of his privateer, his booted foot on the rail, a gleaming cutlass in his belt, prowling into Campbell Cove after water, rum, women and song.

Troy reached up and plucked some fresh leaves from the tree. As much as Mandy wanted to watch the boys being shown how to catch crabs in the shallows by a dreadlocked child, she found it hard to move her stare from where Troy's shorts had slipped down to his muscly loins, both at the front and the back.

14

Back at Plantation, Caddy was standing on the decking by the water sport office holding her mask and fins, pretending to be lining up to get on the boat with her fellow PADI trainees.

'May I get you something to drink?' A low voice said behind her.

'There you are,' said Caddy. She put her hand out to touch Ample, but he pulled away.

'Juice? Water?'

'I just wish we could have some privacy, so we can talk properly. Can you sneak into my room?' Thus phase three of Operation Virgin-Sex-On-The Beach proceeded.

'If the camera sees me the Supervisor get rude on me. She ago suspend me.'

She said, 'come to below my balcony.'

Caddy took the curving concrete path through the palms and glossy shrubs to her building. She waved her magic card and entered her room. She took off her flip flops, put down her mask and fins, slid back the window, and went out to look for him. He was walking on his long legs down the path holding at his shoulder a tray and two cups. He smiled, put the tray beside a bush of little white flowers and gazed up.

Caddy pointed and said 'Use this drain pipe...' but she need not have.

In a few athletic moves he was on the balcony beside her.

'You look like you've done that before,' said Caddy.

'No. You make me quick and strong. Next time I shall do it with a tray and a cocktail for milady.'

'No, it's nice you not serving me for once. It's my turn. What do you want me to bring you?' They had left the balcony and she was by the bed. Ample stood in front of her. Six foot three.

'Bring me some love,' he said, holding out his hand.

'Double or single?' Caddy asked.

'Make it a double.'

She came to his arms and stood on her toes to kiss his mouth.

'I accept tips,' she said. 'Ow. What's that?'

'Mi pin, hold on.' Ample started taking his badge off.

'No,' Caddy said, 'You are not meant to take that off. Take off your shirt. That's allowed.'

He took off his Plantation shirt. Caddy had seen eighteen-year old boys with their shirts off in England. They didn't look like Ample. He hadn't worked at the hotel long enough to fatten an inch of his body.

'Now I feel left out. Take off my shirt.'

'Yes, my lady, it will be my pleasure to, but first let's have a little smoke.' He took a 50 dollar bag of weed and wizla out of his sock, and sat on the bed. He flattened the paper, cupped it in his hand and start to bill a spliff, with Caddy leaning on his shoulder watching him.

'You have a piece of card or paper?'

'Use this,' Caddy offered him a business card her mum had left on the desk. Ample folded it, placed it in the groove, and with a roll and a lick completed the job.

'You have lighter?'

'Hold on.' Caddy nipped through the door to her parent's room and found Aiden's lighter in the ashtray next to his wallet.

'We better go on the balcony,' Ample said.

They spread a couple of towels, sat on the floor and talked about their lives, Caddy transfixing Ample with descriptions of travel and shopping and school. Ample offered music and movies in return. When they were high enough and comfortable enough with each other, they went to the bed.

'I better put this back so your parents don't know we've been here,' said Ample holding up the lighter. 'Where was it?'

'In the ashtray by the TV,' Caddy said.

15

In Campbell Cove, the standard fisherman beach breakfast cookout was well under way. From the shore, Mandy watched a fisherman steer his boat through the lane in the coral and onto the sand. When he turned off the engine it made a clicking sound as it wound down. Troy and Maas Henry walked into the water to help slide the boat up onto the beach and look to see how much catch was in the buckets. Troy could see some fish, so turned away and put another bit of wood on the fire. The fisherman sorted his catch. Some to take home, some to sell and some to cook on the beach for his friends. Maas Henry sat on a root with the bucket between his knees and start to scale the parrot and snapper. Troy pulled tin foil off the roll and laid each fish with okra, peppers, onion and thyme before folding them and placing them on the fire.

To Mandy it was all such a beautiful blur. It seemed she had set up a line of credit with Troy, who was pouring JB rum and popping Red Stripes for Bangaz, Omar, Sitter, Maas Henry and Bunna who appeared from nowhere, and who were all really friendly. Bunna was the only person in Campbell Cove to own a crash helmet, which he wore that morning on the beach. Motorcyclists didn't wear helmets. After a particularly gruesome accident a helmet was found with a decapitated head strapped in it, so people said they didn't work. Bunna's helmet was particularly noteworthy because Bunna didn't possess a motorbike or even a bicycle.

Cliff was looking for shrimps with a five-year old boy called Gutta who didn't seem to be under any parental supervision. They used the mask to catapult pebbles into the sea until the strap broke. Aiden was sitting with the men having an earnest conversation about the iniquities of slavery. Mandy had told him to stop it, but he wouldn't, so she had followed Troy into his dark shed to look for ice. The bar was no more than a plywood box with a wild mosaic floor made from the off cuts the tilers stole from the hotel construction sites. Inside, Troy seemed more naked than dressed. A cloud of vapour puffed out of the chest freezer he leant over to retrieve a tin bowl with a big lump of ice in it. He stabbed at it with a pick, sending splinters and shards that tingled when they touched her skin. He picked a bit the size of a lump of coal and stuffed it into her soft plastic cup. Unscrewing the rum bottle, he looked serious as he poured the liquor over the ice.

He reached under the counter for cigarettes and offered Mandy a Craven A which were upside down in the pack. Her hand went out, then back, then out again, then hesitated in the air, then back. Then she picked a cigarette out. Troy palmed her the lighter. She lit the cigarette, inhaled, closed her eyes and said 'Fuck that's good.'

Under the tree Aiden was enjoying the attention of the gathered men, who leant forward to listen. It was unknowable how much they understood as he was talking English, and they were mainly speakers of Patwa. They were aware he was talking about the past, which was not a subject they were particularly interested in, but he was apparently saying things they didn't know about. Only Bangaz with his better English grasped it. But they all saw how intense and serious Aiden was, and that counted for a lot. He was angry, but at who it was hard to tell.

'You haven't heard of the Zoah massacre?'

They looked confused. Maas Henry, sensing advantage said, 'Ya man. Zoo massacre,' and nodded enthusiastically.

'What is it?' said Omar. 'You nuh know 'bout it.'

'Tell we,' said Bangaz.

'This should have been taught to all of you in primary school,' Aiden said. 'It's basic Jamaican history.'

'Dem nuh teach wi nuttin,' Omar said.

'Right,' said Aiden, nodding grimly. 'The Zoah was a boat, a ship, that transported slaves from Africa to Jamaica...'

With those words he felt the attention slacken. Maas Henry did not want to hear about slavery days. Would the white people want to talk about slavery days if they had been the slaves?

Bangaz leant forward. 'What happened to this ship?' Information from the outside world was so rare. He was hungry for it. He was assembling a huge jigsaw which he had never seen the picture of. The people inna foreign had seen the box.

'There was a rule,' Aiden told Bangaz, 'that if you were in danger of losing the whole cargo, it was permissible to jettison a portion of it to save the rest. The insurance would pay out for it. This was established with a cargo of coal which caught fire. They threw half of it overboard to save the rest and save the ship. And the insurance covered the loss. The captain of the Zoah decided that to save half the slaves he had to cut down how much water was being drunk. So he threw overboard 142 men and women to drown, and claimed the insurance on them.'

Bangaz understood just enough of this to make his throat sting. He could hear the catch in Aiden's voice.

'For Christ sake Aiden,' Mandy said, appearing from the shed, flushed with the thrill of her brief flirtation with Troy. They had not touched, and they had barely exchanged a few innocent words, but both had enjoyed a little Jamaican moment, which would give Mandy an inner tingle for hours, and Troy a what-might-have-been memory to treasure for years.

'We should all know the real history, not the one the hotel or their school presents.' Aiden continued.

'Pur-lease put a sock in it for a minute. We are trying to chillax here, not start an armed uprising,' Mandy said.

Aiden took a crack at a bit of Patwa: 'Me am holding a reasoning, a meditation.'

Bangaz said 'Mi wole a reason, mi wole a meds. Not hold.'

'Mi wole a reason,' repeated Aiden. To Bangaz he said, 'and to make it worse, when they arrived in Black River, there was still plenty of drinking water in the ship's barrels.'

Aiden essayed a suck teeth, without a huge amount of success, but hoped that Bangaz and Omar appreciated the gesture.

Later Aiden said, to no-one in particular, 'an apology is in order, man....'

16

The sunlight moved through the trees, the shadows crossed the beach, and the sea turned from pale blue to cobalt with white caps in the distance. When the fish came off the grill, Troy slid each one onto an almond leaf and passed them around. They were small and bony. The villagers were expert at separating the flesh from the bones with their fingers and mouths. After food, Omar lifted the engine off the boat and stored it in the concrete bunker where it would be safe for the night amongst the other outboards.

Another spliff was built and lit. A box played music. Aiden, in his UB40 1982 European Tour T-shirt and a tam he'd bought from a vendor the hotel had allowed in for a few hours, got Mandy to take a photo of him with Maas Henry and Bangaz.

'Troy!' she called. 'Come in the photo too. Get closer, that's it.' Suddenly it all made sense to Mandy: her anxieties about child safety and flirting and not knowing what was going to happen, faded into a lovely warm exciting buzz. It was like the song which was playing in the background said: every little thing was going to be all right. She felt her shoulder touch Troy's. It was fine. It was fun. It was innocent and glorious at the same time.

Aiden was holding a big spliff when the shutter clicked. He felt so happy. He chill with him posse, with him crew. He was a fully resolved traveller in Jamaica.

Later in the day he bumped fists with Bangaz and said with tears of joy in his eyes: 'We are all the same race, man. It's called the human race.'

'You cut we, we have the same blood,' shouted Maas Henry.

Ample and Caddy were dozing in each other's arms when they heard the door open in her parents' room.

Their bodies froze, locking onto one another, and they watched with wide, silent eyes as Aiden raced into the master bedroom, grabbed his wallet off the bedside table and hurried out of the room.

'Shit that was close, you better go....' They pulled their clothes on and kissed goodbye as Ample dropped over the balcony and disappeared into the garden with the tray at his shoulder.

Aiden passed through reception and back out onto the road where Mandy was lingering with Banga, Troy and Setter the driver.

'Here,' Aiden said, looking in his wallet. 'What?' he murmured, rifling through the compartments.

'Don't worry, I've sorted it,' said Mandy. 'What an amazing day,' she sighed. 'Truly awe inspiring.'

'Ya man,' said Aiden. 'Every time.'

'Blessings,' said Bangaz.

Meanwhile, Ample was climbing down the front of the building. In the garden he picked up his tray and the cups and threaded his way back to the restaurant, buttoning up his tunic. Caddy, leaning blissfully against the rail, watched him go with a lingering smile.

'There you are, Cads,' said Mandy, appearing behind her. 'Let's get dinner. The boys are starving. I want to hear all bout your day.'

Caddy raised a secret eyebrow thinking to herself, I bet you really don't.

Five minutes later they were settling down at their table in the restaurant. After a fuss with menus and seating arrangements, Aiden turned to Caddy, 'So how was your afternoon?'

Ample arrived at that moment, making her blush and ignore the question. He leant over Caddy's shoulder and poured, with clinks, icy water into the glass.

'Do the family all have a great time on a village tour?' Ample asked.

'It was amazing,' said Mandy.

'Just incredible. Ya man. So beautiful and so interesting. Amazing people. We went to a place called Campbell Cove,' Aiden continued.

'That is my community!' said Ample. 'My yard is there.'

'Well we all loved it. But Caddy stayed here,' said Mandy, turning to her, 'You really missed out.'

'How was your day today milady?' Ample asked Caddy.

'Fine. Great actually,' she said, looking into her water as she sipped it.

'Oh right,' said Mandy, 'How did the open water dive go?'

'It was great,' said Caddy.

'Frightening?' asked Aiden.

Caddy thought about it for a second. 'At the beginning, but then I settled into it and it was fun.'

Ample nodded as he filled Cliff's glass.

Mandy said 'Did you go very deep?'

Caddy snorted a laugh, but covered it with a cough. 'Yes, very.'

'Did you touch the bottom?' Asked Cliff.

Caddy and Ample exchanged glances trying not to smile. 'Nearly,' Caddy said. 'Maybe next time.'

Ample stopped pouring and stared at Caddy, widening his eyes.

'Hey there's your dive master!' said Aiden, waving towards the beach. 'What's his name?'

'Him call Glenroy' said Ample, turning to go back to the bar.

'Glenroy! Yo!' called Aiden, emboldened by the day's many successes, and believing the gap between the Jamaican people and him rapidly narrowing.

The watersports' manager approached on his short legs, a little non plussed, and then smiled when he saw Caddy. Caddy turned pale.

'What gwaan? Glenroy, is it? How did my girl do today?' Aiden said.

'She was just great sir. One or two technical aspects to improve on, but she's a natural.' His little eyes sparkled at Caddy.

Caddy gently breathed out, feeling how beautiful it was. She was being looked after by all of the staff in the hotel, all of them backing Ample.

After food, Mandy went to the shop with the mask that Bruce had broken.

Standing in front of the cigarettes and sun tan oil, Mandy felt a sweet urge to buy a pack of Craven A and take them home to Manchester to relive every now and then – not often – the brief Jamaican moment with Troy in the shed, with the shards of ice and the twists of smoke from the spliff.

The woman looked up from her phone and glanced at the mask. 'Dat brok?'

'Yes, it just seemed to snap. Sorry.'

'You have receipt?'

'No, but I bought it three days ago – from you! Don't you remember?'

She stared impassively at Mandy.

'No receipt, no refund.'

'You must remember,' said Mandy. 'You had run out of till-roll and wrote the receipt on a business card.' Mandy remembered clearly enough. Even though she was the only customer in the shop the listless security man at the door wouldn't let her out without a receipt, so Mandy had to go back to the counter and wait while the woman found a biro and wrote one.

'You must have receipt for refund,' the woman said.

Ange said 'Okay, okay,' and headed back to the rooms to look for it.

Caddy was out on the balcony leaning against the rail remembering the delights and glories of the afternoon. The lights were going on along the paths, the festoons added gaiety to the beach, and the moon was laying a trail of fire across the bay. She breathed it all in. Oh god it was amazing to be alive, and even more intense to be alive in Jamaica.

Mandy had searched her room and stood in the door scanning the kids' bedroom. Bruce had a habit of squirrelling away little things that he found.

She looked in the drawer of the desk, then behind it, then around the bedside table. Her hand went down the side of the bed and her fingers felt something. She pulled it up. It was a badge. It said, Hi, my name is Trevor. No tips please! Ample's badge. How did that get there? She was about to call Caddy, but hesitated and slipped the badge in the pocket of her cut-offs as she stood up. She would show Aiden first; she didn't want to jump to conclusions. She restarted her search for the receipt which took her through the sheets, the pillows, onto the single bed, and in and around the cupboard before the bathroom. There, she flicked on the light. Kids' carnage. Towels, flannels, underwear, toothpaste, toothbrushes, and a small dalek shaped bin. She took the lid off the bin and looked in to see the white liner ballooning from the sides. She put her hand in and felt for paper. She found some and pulled it out. But what was this?

She pulled out a used condom, no knot in it. She tilted her head, blew out her cheeks, and dropped it back into the bin.

Aiden was in their room also looking for something.

'Honey.'

'Yeah? Sorry. I just do not understand where—' But he stopped dead when he saw her expression. 'What? What is it?'

'Turns out Ample's not gay.'

'Whaa? What?'

'I found this,' she said with an arched brow, holding the name card up between her index and middle finger, 'And I found a used condom in the bin next door.'

Aiden closed his eyes in a grimace.

'While we were at the village?' he said.

'I suppose so,' said Mandy.

He tapped his foot and scrunched up a fist as his brain synapses made connections. 'Clive must have been in on it.' He said, hurt. 'And the dive-master,' His anger was rising. 'She's seventeen!' He stood up to explode.

'Don't ruin it. Don't ruin it.' Mandy pleaded, her hands grasping his and her eyes searching for his. 'It's been such a special day for us, can we try to let it go? Please?' She pulled him close to her.

Aiden twitched.

'No. We've been fooled,' he stepped back. 'I'm going to tell the manager.'

'Aiden, she's a minor here,' said Mandy. 'Can you imagine what might happen? We can't...'

'They were all in on it,' he said. 'How could they have done that to me? She's a child for God's sake.'

'We better ask her what happened,' said Mandy.

They called Caddy through and closed the interconnecting door saying 'Cliff – look after Bruce for a minute.'

Caddy looked at her parents, not quite able to meet either gaze.

'Darling,' Mandy said. 'What happened this afternoon?'

'What do you mean?' She scratched the back of her neck where she could feel the heat creeping up.

'Did you have a man in your hotel room?' Aiden asked. He sat hunched on the dressing table stool.

Caddy said nothing.

'Well yes or no?' Aiden barked.

'Yes,' Caddy said.

'All we want to know is was he here by your invitation?' Mandy said.

Caddy folded her arms. 'You mean was I raped? The answer is no, I wasn't. Definitely not. So you can forget all about it as it is none of your business.'

'How did he get in? Asked Aiden. 'Did he have people covering for him, from the hotel...?'

'No he climbed over the balcony, OK. Like Romeo, if you think about it. I guess that's what happens if you let a girl read too much Shakespeare.'

'Look, I'm just..' said Aiden.

'I'm not a child, Dad. Okay? Stop interfering. I'm fine. I had a nice time. I like him and he likes me. We're going to meet again after Christmas.'

'Well that's not happening,' said Aiden.

'I won't need your permission,' said Caddy, and left the room.

Aiden swore under his breath. Then he stood up, felt for his wallet and looked in it.

'Of course. Of course,' he said.

'What?' said Mandy.

'The sixty bucks,' he said. 'That's where it went. Ample took it. No one else has been in our room.'

Aiden pulled open the door. 'Caddy. Did you take money from my wallet?'

'Oh shut up,' she said. 'Of course not.'

'Right. Thank you.'

Back in his room Aiden seethed. 'I'm reporting him. I'm sorry, I'm willing not to report rape, for the sake of Caddy, but I will not tolerate theft. Stealing from us! When we have been so kind and friendly to them!'

'He'll lose his job,' Mandy said.

'He should have thought of that. She's our little girl.'

'She's not a little girl.'

'No. Well I'm going to see that manager right now.'

'Aiden. Aiden, please. Don't ruin this.'

17

Caddy woke before dawn and was out in her bikini roaming the gardens in the lavender light, counting off the minutes until Ample came on shift. But 10 a.m., when he told her his shift began, came and went, and Ample never appeared. She went to the bar and asked where he was.

'Look like maybe he sick out, or not feeling too good,' the kindly old barman called Hudson said to her. He had once said to her 'It's nice to be nice.'

She went to look for Bangaz, but the chair on the ladder was empty, and the sand looked unraked.

Mr Hawkin had enjoyed having Ample and Bangaz directed to his office when they came on shift. In the windowless room under the air conditioning slits, Mr Hawkin stood behind a desk with a brass sign with his name on it. Ample spotted his a name badge that said 'Trevor' strewn on the desk and sighed. With exaggerated satisfaction, Mr Hawkin sat heavily in his executive chair.

'The toleration level,' Mr Hawkin said, 'in this hotel, of over-fraternisation with the guests, is zero. And the toleration of theft is also zero. Do you understand?'

'No, sah,' said Bangaz honestly. 'Mi nu unnerstan.'

'You have sex with the girl, you tief her farder money from him room. And you,' he turned to Bangaz, 'were part of the conspiracy.'

'I never take no money. Mi nu tief.' Ample protested.

'I took them for a cook out.' Bangaz said evenly. 'On my day off. They have a good time. They tell me that.'

The door opened, 'Mr Hawkin, can I have a word with you going forward?' the receptionist said, shooting a withering look at the men.

'Is it important?'

'Yes.'

Mr Hawkin went out into the corridor.

'What is it?'

'They don't have any lobster for your lunch, would your preference be for snapper or steak?'

When the weighty matter of what Mr Hawkin was eating for lunch was settled he came back to his office. 'You are henceforth terminated from current employment status,' he said. 'And going forward based on this will pertain to the status of ex-employee.'

The two young men looked confused.

'Blaadclaat, you fire!' Mr Hawkin shouted. 'Come out. Now!'

They trooped back down the corridor, out to the security kiosk and were spat back onto the street.

Mr Hawkin reported Clive Thompson and Trevor Johnson to the tourism industry regulator, to ensure neither of them got a job in another big hotel in Jamaica ever again.

And they couldn't even get a job at a little bar. Only hot gal dem get bartender work.

Caddy never heard from Ample again, so she started to think that Aiden was right: Ample had got into the room that afternoon to steal money. Otherwise he would have sent her a message, if for no other reason than to explain his disappearance. She cried on the beach behind her sunglasses. Maybe it was true what they said about Jamaica, and Jamaicans.

At the end of the week the Williams family took the airport transfer coach which sped through Campbell Cove, close to where Ample and

Bangaz sat on the bamboo bench by Troy bar, waiting for the fishermen to come in with a food.

A week after the Williams returned home Aiden was on his haunches in front of the washing-machine, pushing in the dirty laundry, when he found some crumpled up bank notes in the tiny pocket on Bruce's cargo pants. He took them out, checked they were three 20s and stared at them.

A few minutes later, still sitting on the lino, he heard the kitchen door open and slam.

'Caddy?'

'Yuh?'

'I'm in here,' Aiden said, standing up.

She put her head round the door.

'I owe you an apology. A big one.'

18

Bangaz tried to get any job but couldn't find anything. He lived with Pauline on the hill in Cove in a single room home, made of rough unpainted boards raised on knobbly rocks. Their furniture was a bed, a little dresser and a plastic laundry basket for clothes. On the dresser stood a mirror and a couple of ornaments on plastic doilies. All of this was lit, in the usual way, by a single bulb on the wall.

Jenna was born and he couldn't afford enough food for Pauline to get breast milk. He felt wretched and vex bad with the world. But he never felt like leaving Pauline. When Pauline come back from hospital she drop asleep on the mattress and leave Bangaz with the pickney. Her diaper was heavy but he don't have any more to change it. She bawl, but Pauline too tired to wake up so Bangaz cradle the baby in him arms and go and beg a money for a pampas and a food for Pauline. He walk through the bush and look at Jenna's moonlit face wrapped in a towel. He said, 'Don't worry. Daddy gonna provide for you. Daddy gonna look after you.' And he looked up said, 'I swear by the moon and by the stars I will do this for you.'

Bangaz walked down to the beach side where the Campbell Cove fishing fleet was drawn up on the sand. The old dug-out canoes were falling apart and different craft, representing the community's resourceful and imaginative post-colonial era were lined up at the water's edge. There was a yellow windsurfer with Sandals written on it in faded letters which was propelled by a pole with plastic plates nailed to each end. Beyond that was an old chest-freezer with its lid torn off, and beyond that was Champion Buoy, the first boat to be powered by an outboard engine.

Bangaz was down there to look for a food from Troy, who went inside him shed and give Bangaz a fish in foil to take back to Pauline. A white BMW, clean and criss, drew up by the bamboo bench. When the glass run down Bangaz recognised his bredren Adi who lived in Mo Bay. Adi look well fed, prosperous and happy.

'Adi,' croaked Bangaz, pulling up his pants cos them loose he get so thin. 'Can mi talk wid you?' he approached the car. 'Me have a hungry pickney and baby mudder and I don't got no job and I beg you a little help, please.'

Adi gave Bangaz a couple of bank notes from his top pocket.

'Blessed are you,' said Bangaz. 'Respect and guidance, always.'

'Come and work with me,' Adi said from the pine scented interior. 'I am in Freeport, Montego Bay. Can you do that?'

'Bangaz bent forward, clutching Jenna tight, his hands together in supplication. 'Mi will do anyting to make a money. Anyting.'

'You gonna work in a call centre.'

'If I can do it I will. Chuss me and tank you, Adi. Respect.'

19

Call-Sure was on the first two floors of a new concrete building near Montego Bay's Freeport. Male employees were made to dress like business executives in a two or three piece suit, and the women wore stockings and heels, even though they were only ever on the phone. Pauline pressed a shirt and pants and Bangaz borrowed good shoes and got the bus to Freeport to report for work. To support the computers and servers the place was kept so cold that at lunch break Bangaz, who didn't own a wind-breaker, ran out to warm up.

Adi was a supervisor and made Bangaz sit by a woman called Tammi who tell him 'how ting run'. She wore medical glasses and white stockings. The work involved booking service appointments for engineers for white goods in Chicago, and chasing up some debts for a car loan company in Canada.

Bangaz felt his dread and hatred of school surface like a harbour shark when a script was put on the desk for him to read. He stared at the English words, unable to open them.

'Start at the top,' said Tammi. 'Good day sir or madam, depending if it man or woman, and say How can I help you today?' Her finger rested on the script.

'How do I say this next bit in English good like you?' he said.

Tammi happily showed off her reading, and Bangaz managed to memorise enough to pass the day without being exposed, but he wasn't going to be able to keep it up for long.

When he got back to Cove he sat in the doorway looking out at the yard scratched by fowl Pauline raise.

'You good?' she asked.

He never replied.

'What's happened? You lose the job?'

'No,' he said to Pauline. 'This rough, I tell you. I don't know mi cya do it. I don't read good enough. My cya read. Mi ago look for different work, like construction: cast concrete can be.'

'No,' said Pauline. 'You can do this.'

But Bangaz could not ask Pauline to help him. He was through with asking for help, or receiving it. He saw help as violence against him, and wanted to strike out at it. He wanted to tear the script into little pieces. He could not swallow, he vex so bad. Tears prick him eyes. Even when he worked out what a word on the script was, it was a bludclaat English word, a word in a foreign language he barely speak. The English language was a trip wire the whities left across every interesting doorway, to stop the little people entering into national life. The trip wire, if you looked closely, was marked English spelling, syntax and grammar. It was certain to send everyone sprawling, for only the English and their lackeys could lift their dainty feet to step over it.

'Hush now,' said Pauline. She looked at the script, and took his hand tenderly.

With the baby on the bed crawling over them, Pauline read the script with her finger moving from word to word. All Bangaz's repressed fury melted when she explained what it meant to him in Patwa. Every night he memorised new words and learnt to read the responses. At the end of each session, Pauline role-played being a customer, to help Bangaz perfect it.

'Hello! Is that the service centre?' she started, when dishes washed and the baby drop asleep.

'Good day madam, how can I help you today?' Bangaz said.

'Mi pum pum bruk dung,' smiled Pauline.

Bangaz laughed. Pum pum was the Campbell Cove word for vagina.

'Just to be clear,' he said, glancing up from the script, 'you are calling because your pum-pum has stopped working?' It was a requirement that they repeat back to the customer their request.

'Ya man. It want service.'

'I can help you with that. Is it under warranty?' asked Bangaz.

'It ungle eighteen year old but it seize up.'

'Just to be clear, you are calling because your pum pum seize up?'

'Ya man, so mi a tell you.'

'That may not be covered by the warranty. But I can send round an engineer to assess and diagnose the problem.'

'It want a rodding.'

Bangaz snorted with laughter, then cleared his throat.

'We 'ave engineer dem...'

'Engineers, with an S', Pauline said.

'We 'ave...'

'H H H have,' Pauline corrected.

'We have engineers in your area next Wednesday,' Bangaz said. Pauline nodded and smiled. 'Do an afternoon or morning appointment suit you, madam?'

'Does.'

'Does an afternoon or morning appointment suit you, madam?'

'Come ya,' said Pauline pulling Bangaz to her. 'Well done. You clever. You learn fast, man.'

After sex, because neither of them could wait until next Wednesday, Bangaz stood up, remembered the script and said, 'Is there anything else I can help you with today, madam?'

20

Call-Sure was run by two flamboyant and camp men, one called Gucci and the other Gabbana, and they were not in a hurry to tell people their real names. Some said they were from Nigeria, others said they were American. No one knew. Gucci, short tubby and with a neckerchief always tied, was the eyes and the fists of the partnership; and tall, willowy cashmere clad Gabbana was the brains. Gucci liked to get things done. He had killed more than three people, one by slamming his head in a car door in front of a large crowd outside a nightclub after a dispute about parking. He was never charged as the forensic evidence got lost and there weren't any witnesses.

A year or two before Bangaz joined the company, Call-Sure was simply a business that collected bad debt. It bought junk debt off American corporations, money that was going to be written off, and tried to get paid on it. If you bought a couch or TV and moved house three times to avoid making the payments, the loan company eventually gave up on you and sold your debt to Gucci and Gabbana. They trained their staff to track down the debtors and persuade or threaten them with various bogus sanctions to pay a percentage of the outstanding figure to close the account. The hundred dollar debt you owed was sold to Gabbana for six dollars and they aimed to collect forty on it. It was a moderately successful business.

One day, someone in the call centre accidentally dialled the wrong number and spoke first softly and then threateningly to a random old woman who owed nothing. Whatever protestations the woman made, the caller insisted the fridge she had bought had not been fully paid for. For one reason or another the old lady went for her bag, got out her bank card and paid $40 US. It was only when Gucci went through the day's business that the mistake came to light.

Gucci told Gabbana, and a lightbulb went off over their heads. They were late in the office and the cleaner thought the place was empty. But when they found the switch and sat back down again they smiled.

'You realise what this means? It means, in the right circumstances, we don't need a debt to collect a payment,' Gabbana said.

'We just need a good story,' said Gucci.

'A very good one,' agreed Gabbana. 'And a sucker.'

The two of them wrote the first script, in which they told the client that they had had a big win on the lottery but, to access the prize, they had to pay a handling fee, up front, which varied from $US100 to $US5,000. This type of telephone scam had been in existence in one form or another for many years, but it was the twist that Gabbana gave to it which made the difference. He realised that although the script was important, more important was the selection of the clients. He created the first, and historic, lead list. It was the lead list that changed the history of Campbell Cove and far, far beyond it.

Compiled, owned and protected by Gucci and Gabbana, the Call-Sure lead list was their unique contribution to the global scamming industry, and one of the principal reasons western Jamaica was to turn into an international centre of excellence for the trade. Using contacts in the call-centre industry, Gabbana mined the data to extract the details of vulnerable people who made very bad decisions around finances. Gambling addicts, wealthy bi-polar sufferers, customers who were defaulting on a large mortgage, people with unsustainable credit card debt, people who missed payments on

that expensive couch or fridge – all of the above were on Gucci and Gabbana's lead list.

Although Adi was an old friend of Bangaz, Bangaz did wonder why he
had been so keen to give him a help. Then he found out: Adi had brought
Bangaz in to steal the scripts from Gucci and Gabbana's office. It was a
dangerous mission, and Adi wasn't going to do it himself. The bosses went
across the mall at lunchtime to get a box food of mutton or oxtail and rice.
In the hour they were out they left a woman called Terry-Ann on the door.
Stout and thick and no-nonsense, Terry-Ann was not known for amorous
follies. However, it was generally agreed that nobody could resist Adi's
considerable charms, which included being able to promote or fire anyone
on the floor. When he turned his bulk toward a woman she went weak at
the knees, or lost her job.

Bangaz gave the word to Adi, who took Terry-Ann out onto the stairs
and worked his sweet charms. Bangaz then walked through the office door,
head up, shoulders back, went to the table and took from a pile of papers two
different scripts. He then left the office, ran down the stairs, hurried across
the mall car park to Productive Business Solutions where a thin woman with
protruding eyes called Shawna Kay took the scripts and put them into the
photocopier.

'Give me two copies,' Bangaz said. He decided he had earnt his own
scripts. While he waited, Bangaz looked across the car park at the cook
shop where the bosses were sitting at a plywood table.

She handed him the copies, he paid and tipped her and walked back
to the office. You weren't searched going back into Call-Sure, so Bangaz
loped up the stairs three at a time, passing Adi who gave him a pained
expression over Terry-Ann's shoulder, slipped into the room, placed the
scripts on the table, and was just about to leave when he saw a CD case on
Gabbana's desk.

He had, twice, coming in early on an 8am shift, seen Gucci carry this
CD from the safe along with some scripts and note pads, so he knew it
was something important. Bangaz glanced through the glass into the hall

where the arriving staff were settling into their cubicles and the afternoon's work.

'So I take a risk and aim higher,' he yelped at Willy. 'I did it for Jenna, I did it for Pauline and I did it for mi self, cos I was not going to live like sheep. I am a lion. From when me born I know it, but they try to oppress me, take my mumma away from me, I get Marva and no help. But this felt like my moment.'

He picked the CD up, slipped it in the back of his waist band, returned to his cubicle and pulled on his head set. Within seconds he was organising a drying-machine service call in Ottawa.

21

Back in Campbell Cove, Bangaz walked in the fast-fading dusk towards the ball ground, past the madman who lived in the cemetery who stood by a smouldering fire, ankle deep in rubbish.

There were five houses in Travis's yard. Travis was the only friend Bangaz had who owned a computer and laptop. All of all his siblings had houses in the yard, each representing how well they had done; from Hyacinth's two room bungalow, to Patsy's two-storey home with eight big rooms and porches all grill up, which Patsy visited once or twice a year because she was a business executive in the US.

Travis's house was more modest. Bangaz stood in front of the bungalow, and called 'Bra!' which drew out a handsome young man with chiselled features and a sharp roof top trim. He grunted, and Bangaz went onto the porch, stepped out of his shoes and followed Travis into a cluttered room crammed with dark furniture, lace table cloths, paper flower arrangements, and, crucially, a computer and printer in the corner.

Bangaz took out the CD and said, 'Can you tell me what's on this?'

Travis dropped the CD into the tray, moved the mouse and dragged the chair up as he looked at the screen.

'Documents. Five,' he said.

'Can you print them?'

There was a pause. 'I don't got enough paper,' Travis said. 'The first one is 27 pages. Shall I carry it tomorrow?'

'No.'

'I can find some scrap paper.'

He printed on the back of old Computer Studies coursework. Bangaz gazed at each page as it chattered out of the machine. There were hundreds of names, addresses and phone numbers. Hundreds. Even thousands. Some had bank details beside them. Column after column. He turned the pages over in his hand, wondering what they meant and what they would bring. They felt like his lottery ticket.

While Bangaz walked back to his yard, the moon rose through the trees on the hill and cast a white glow over the pasture. Inside his home, he tied the pages of paper in a scandal bag and knotted the handles.

Before he left the house the next morning, Bangaz hid the package under the mattress but, a quarter of the way down the track, he turned round, retraced his steps, took it out from the bed and hid it in the fowl coop, under a thick layer of do-do. But even then he worried about it being found if Gucci and Gabbana send people to him yard.

When he returned from the day's work at Call-Sure, he changed out of his work clothes and went to the fowl coup. Reaching under the sawdust he pulled out the package. Sitting in the door of the house with his slippers dangling off his feet, he carefully untied the knot.

'Did nobody say nutn today?' Pauline asked.

'Nutn. Everyting cool.'

'Nutn unusual?' she said.

'No,' replied Bangaz, pulling out the top page, picking up his cell phone, and dialling a number off the first column. 'Hello, is that Mr Willis, Mr Kenneth Willis?' he said, launching himself off his seat into the yard.

'Speaking.'

'Good evening, sir,' said Bangaz. 'I am calling from Global Sweepstakes and Lotteries International of 1165 Hyatt Way, Chicago, Illinois,

7692. I am pleased to inform you that you have come up as a winner on this month's draw....'

There was a pause, an intake of breath, then: 'I goddam knew it! I knew I was gonna win that!' Kenneth shouted back. 'I have been on this streak of bad luck as long and lousy as a decomposing python ... I knew it was about to change. I felt it this morning. Goddam it. At last, a break! How much have I won, son? Tell me it's not twenty bucks.'

'No sir, it is not twenty,' Bangaz was walking round under the mango tree. He squeezed up his eyes. 'It is four hundred and seventy-eight thousand, six hundred and fifty-three US dollars.'

There was a pause. 'Say that again.'

That was a problem, because Bangaz had forgotten what he had said. He was going to have to settle on one figure and stick to it.

'That is a sum in excess of four hundred thousand dollars, sir.'

Kenneth was a small man with a horseshoe of mousy hair above his ears and blinking eyes behind horn rimmed glasses. He called himself a computer geek, a numbers man, a data obsessive and a dotcom investment specialist. He had perfect judgment about stocks and bonds, but his timing had been beset by bad luck. He had been using a system he had developed for roulette. You could not fail. You just had to have time. When he had lost their vacation cash he had said to his ex, 'Baby, don't you see this is a good thing? It's great news! It just means the payout when it comes is even bigger. It's just probability. Sheer math. Ha!' He had laughed. 'Just watch.' His investment business tanked and he was currently doing odd jobs. That very morning he'd fixed a hole punched in a bedroom door by some rich folk's kid in Greenvale.

'So when do I get it?' Kenneth asked Bangaz. 'Goddam it. After the run I've had, Lady Luck smiles again!'

'You receive the payment in full by bank certified cheque as soon as you have paid the clearing fee.'

'How much is that?'

'Three hundred dollars, sir,' said Bangaz

'And to think I almost quit gambling! How do I pay?' he shouted.

22

After Bangaz had another night of sex with Pauline, he couldn't stop thinking about the lead list, so rich was its promise. Leaving Pauline asleep with Jenna snuggled into her, he stole out to the fowl coup, removed the package, picked another number, and dialled it.

She was an elderly lady called Marjory Bell. She took the call in her neat bungalow in Kentucky on the edge of the grounds of the big house where her daughter and son-in-law, the Congressman, lived, largely ignoring her. She turned down the television and went to the phone on the wall by the kitchen. She was not fast and it often rang out before she reached it. She glanced at her watch: 10.00pm. It must be important.

'Hello?' her voice quavered.

An early part of Bangaz's script was 'are you between the age of 40 to 50, 50 to 55, 55 to 60, 65 to 70, 70 to 75, or over 75?'

'I am 82, young man,' Marjory said. 'And my memory ain't so good,' she said. 'That's why I can't remember buying that ticket. But I guess I bought it, okay. I do buy them occasionally. I like to think I'll win some day and I'll give it to my grandkids.'

From the tone of the Marjorie's voice, her age and accent, Bangaz instinctively reduced her winnings. What was right for Kenneth would overwhelm Marjorie.

For the old lady it was a $128,000 win, with a release fee of a 100.

He told Marjory Bell to pay by Western Union.

'We are based in Jamaica, and you must send it to me direct, so I can input it to the data to Payment division, head office in Ohio.' He knew the script pretty well, and kept the powerful words like data and input coming fast.

A small and dim warning light was flashing in the back of Marjorie's mind.

'But why Jamaica?' she asked without conviction, because she didn't want it to go wrong. Marjorie imagined the swimming-pool she was going to buy with the prize. How the water sparkled as her grandchildren leapt in and splashed about. They never had enough to do when they came to see her. That was one of the reasons they didn't walk over so often.

'That is because it is an offshore bank,' said Bangaz. 'This is a large kiash, this is a large sum of money, and you are in the United States and you are over 65. It exclaim you from being a higher tax brucket wid the IRS....'

Marjorie couldn't make head or tail what the young man was saying.

'Because the lawyer under offer already taken care of that process,' Bangaz was going a bit off piste here, grabbing the sentences from the script and stitching them together as best he could, feeling what she needed to hear. 'When you live in the country you have to try to get the most of the money you can get because you know government is going to tax you so if you feel you can give your grandkids five thousand, then you are going to leave with a reduced winning sum and cheque.'

He could feel he was taking the old lady with him. He was going to buy block and cement to build a flush toilet and tile bathroom for Pauline and Jenna.

23

Waiting on the roadside for the minibus the next day, Bangaz snapped the CD into four pieces. He dash away each bit out the window a mile apart on the coast road.

There was a crowd at the door of Call-Sure.

'Wha gwaan?' Bangaz asked.

'Dem search de building and search everybody who go in.'

'Dem lose one CD,' Tammi said.

'It wipe,' said someone else.

The atmosphere was dark on the floor. Through the glass, Bangaz saw Gabbana shouting at Terry-Ann while Gucci sat in a chair watching them horribly closely.

Bangaz kept calm.

When he saw Adi he said, 'What's all this about?

'Sambady tief a CD. The boss vex bad.'

'Oh,' said Bangaz.

Adi said, 'is this something to do with you?'

'Me?' said Bangaz. 'No. Nat me.'

'It was on the table by the scripts.'

'No. I never touch no CD. I get the scripts, like you tell me to, but put them back. I give the scripts to you,' he said pointedly. Adi scowled.

Bangaz had not told Adi he had taken copies for himself. 'Don't he got no back up?'

'Yes. Dem have back up on hard drive. But he want to know who take it. You never take it?'

'No,' said Bangaz.

'Who take it gonna meet whole heap of trouble.'

Later, as Bangaz sat in his cubicle and gave a washing machine engineer instructions about finding a house in Long Island, New York, he saw in the corner of his eye Gucci coming up behind him.

'Is there anything else I can help you with at this time?' Bangaz said, finishing the call.

'Hold on a moment,' said the voice behind him.

He turned round as if he were shocked to see the boss standing there, short and thick, humming with fury. Bangaz was icy inside but let himself look a bit flustered.

'Boss,' he said, 'you good?'

'Was it you?' Gucci said.

'What?' asked Bangaz.

'Who tamper with my possessions? Who stole what don't belong to you? Who takes my livelihood from under my nose?'

'I was searched when I left. They searched me,' said Bangaz. 'I don't know nutn about that. I wish I could help you, Mr Gucci.' Bangaz pulled a pleasant, quizzical face.

Gucci said, 'I am watching you. You get that?'

On his lunch break, Bangaz walked out of Freeport, weaved and skipped his way through the tight traffic and teeming pavements of downtown Montego Bay, to arrive under the yellow awning of the pharmacy and novelty store next door to Western Union. He waited in the short queue, a large proportion of which was sexy women, and showed his ID to the girl at the counter. She looked at her screen, nodded, opened her cash drawer and counted out $300 US in ten dollar bills. Then she said, 'Wait.'

Bangaz hesitated, about to run.

'You have a second,' she said. 'One hundred. Marjorie Bell.'

'Yes,' said Bangaz.

Bangaz did not take even an icy mint sweetie or a bottle of water out of that 400. He went to the Chinaman supermarket and bought Pampers, milk, baby food, Babygro and a slippers for Pauline, and took them back home and laid them on the bed for his woman. She hug him up and thank him.

'You is my hero and you is Jenna hero. You are a good man. We was hungry and now you find a food for us. Mi love you. You make me proud.'

Her words warm his heart and softened the fist that was clenched in his belly. In his whole life no woman had ever told him he made them proud.

'Come ya,' she murmured.

He held her close and spoke into her hair. 'This a hustler world, Pauline,' he said. 'Ya cya trust nobody and nutn, but mi wan you fi know there is one ting that is not a scam: and that is my love for you and Jenna.'

'Like our love for you. It nuh scam. Nevva,' Pauline said, hugging him tight and kissing his neck, until he felt small tears prick his eyes. 'Till the end of time. Foreva n eva.'

Gucci and Gabbana's lead list turned out to be a lottery ticket, and a winning one at that, so Bangaz bingo. Big time.

Although mobile phones had been around for a few years, many folks in the States were still carrying on as if they were in the safe and protected era of the landline, when a ringing phone meant contact from familiar, reliable and usually respectable friends and acquaintants. People didn't cold call on the landline in those days. On a landline, calls were easily traceable to an address and probably a person. The cell phone and the cheap sim card fire-bombed all that.

In the early cell phone era the caller was admitted without any checks right into the trusted space of the receiver. Marjorie Bell metaphorically opened her front door wide to Bangaz, took his coat and hat, and conducted him through to the lounge as guest of honour allowing him to admire her collection of valuables on the mantlepiece and side tables.

The first months were so rich in rewards, Bangaz said to Pauline, 'I muss leave Call-Sure. A muss. Dat place a waste of time for me now. I can make hole heap more money inna the yard.'

'It too dangerous to leave, with Gucci's eye pon your back,' she said.

24

'Hold on,' said Willy. 'Hold on a minute, just stop right there. Yes. Pull the bloody hell up.' he raised his hand, stopped Bangaz talking and leant back from the keyboard with a creak of wicker. As usual Bangaz was standing at the end of the porch jiggling up and down, barking words at Willy. It was late afternoon. The cliffs on the other side of the cove were glowing in the sunset. The water was dark. Out to sea a couple of booze cruise catamarans were hurrying to port under motor after depositing their drunk tourists in Negril who would travel by coach back to their hotels.

'You want 'tap?' Bangaz said.

'Do I want to stop? No. I'm cool. But we have a problem, my friend,' Willy said. 'Marjorie Bell. How am I going to write a book, or a book that people want to read, about someone who steals money from an old, unsuspecting lady in America?

'I neva put no gun to her head. She send it down from her own free will,' Bangaz said.

'I just cannot seem to be condoning scamming,' Willy said. 'This creates a major obstacle.' He looked around and lowered his voice. 'What you must realise, you must know, is that out there in the rest of the world scammers are not held in such high regard as they are around here. In fact, they are hated.'

Bangaz adopted an expression of hurt outrage.

'Yes. Out there in the rest of the world,' said Willy. 'I know people here don't think so. Look, I don't want to be personal or disrespect you Bangaz, but some people, well, quite a lot of people, think scammers are just human rats. You know? We have to start from that point. I've written long enough to know you cannot expect the reader to go along with an unlikeable protagonist.'

Bangaz took a suck on him spliff and bore his gaze deep into Willy. The old man vex Bangaz bad.

'You white people,' Bangaz said. 'You come to us black people with your bible, right? With your bible,' Bangaz flashed a vicious smile. 'And you show it to us, and you tell us is the word of God. And you say God say we must be the slaves, and you must be the masters.'

He paused. Willy glanced at him sheepishly, nodding lightly.

'And you,' Bangaz said, 'you call we scammers. You is the scammers!'

'Keep your voice down,' Willy said. People from the village often wandered through Willy's yard to go fishing or look for bait on the rocks.

'That's another thing.' Said Willy, looking around. 'I'm getting nervous about how many people know we are doing this together. I don't want to be called an informer. It could get nasty.' Willy's old face showed the anxiety. He bit his lip. 'Christ I could do with a drink.'

Bangaz shouted, 'Gatta!' and a voice called back from the car. 'Go a Barry for chicken. You want chicken, Willy?'

'Yes please.'

'And go a Sharon and carry back a flask of Appleton, couple beers, hot, and couple chasers.' He sat down, and then stood up. 'You ever rent a car?' He asked Willy.

'In the past, sometimes,' Willy replied.

'It a scam. They tell you a cost and then it's excess fee, pick up charge, cleaning charge, compulse insurance. And if you meet in a accident you still haffi pay for damage.'

'I know what you mean, but—' Willy said.

'I hear tourists say air ticket a scam them mek them pay extra for seat and food and every little ting. Even Pot Noodle a scam. The regular and large pot are different size but have same portion of noodle. You know? And car parts. Pure scam. My cya buy a door hangle for mi BMW. Mi haffi buy the hangle and the inset and the lock all in one piece even though I ungle need hangle. Dem scam me.'

'Yes, but—' Willy said.

'You is scammers, you British and American, you just you call it fine print or regulation or protocol. You never need no visa, Willy, but visa pure scam. Chuss me. Dem tek your money and never gonna issue no visa. No Jamaican hardly ever get tru wid British Home Office. It another scam. But it fully legal under your law.'

A lanky youth with a headscarf tied in a knot at his chin marched into the yard and passed three bags with a clink of bottles up to Bangaz.

Bangaz flipped off a bottle top with his lighter and tipped the first sip of his beer out onto the ground. That was for dead friends. Willy focused on his rum, lifted it to his lips and felt the sweetness and warmth send help down his throat.

The chicken came in tin foil which Willy opened beside his laptop. He reached for the hot pepper sauce removing its tiny red cap and blotting his food. They ate in the Jamaican manner: in silence, their chairs turned half away from the table, as if alone, spitting bones out over the porch rail to be pounced on by slinking dogs.

The time for more talk was when food done.

'Bangaz, my friend,' said Willy, 'You've never really said why you're doing this?' Willy wiped his mouth and pointed at the laptop. 'I mean why are you telling me all this? You realise there's no guarantee of money in it?'

'I want mi story tell, you know?'

'Before you die, is that it?'

'No man live forever, Willy.' Bangaz looked down at the spliff he build. 'Mi wan fi go out wid a bang. Seen? Mi want people fi know mi story, an me wah people fi know the choppa story.' Choppa was the new local word for scammer.

Willy had worked out why he was involved. It was because Bangaz could only tell this story to a white man. It was too dangerous to tell to a Jamaican. The survival mechanism that got them through slavery days was still in place: never ever snitch. Never be an informer.

'Only I'm beginning to think I might be in danger, here,' Willy said.

'No,' said Bangaz. 'You nuh in no danger. I can protect you.'

'But what if you die?'

'You in no danger from no scammers.'

'Why?'

'Because you is gonna glorify we. You ever hear of Mario Puzo?'

'Sure. How do you know about Mario Puzo?'

'I see one TV documentary about him. He write about the mafia, seen?'

'He wrote The Godfather.'

'And the mafia love him. You know why?'

'I guess because he glamourised them,' said Willy.

'Good. Very good,' said Bangaz. 'You is gonna glamourise we. People gonna read your book and love us. Seen?'

'I shall sanctify you, if it saves my ass,' Willy laughed.

'Very good!' cried Bangaz. 'Sanctify. Good. Good. Very good.'

25

Bangaz ignored Pauline's advice. After the next payday he just stopped going in to Call-Sure. People were always quitting. They just couldn't deal with that shit any more. Everybody knew that.

Sitting on an old plank nailed between the mango and an almond tree, Bangaz made his calls while around him kids picked fruit off the ground to sell on the roadside. In the mornings he went to Western Union to pick up his money. He was there so much he made friends with Siddi, the fat woman with a squint who work there. Every time he bingo he give her a few hundred J tip. Her chubby hand took it off the counter and placed it in her bra.

One morning, Pauline came back from the market in Lucea with a copy of the Gleaner. She put the week old newspaper on the bed where Bangaz was lying with Jenna.

'Look,' she said.

On the front page was a photograph of Gucci and Gabbana with their hands cuffed behind their backs, being led away by two police. The headline read: Pair arrested in $350 million mail fraud.

Pauline read the story:

'Police arrest Jamaican businessmen Brian 'Gucci' Suarez and Danny 'Gabbana' Kuanu for mail fraud in dawn raid at their private addresses. The pair appeared in Montego Bay Circuit Court where they were refused bail and kept on remand while the United States Federal Government applies for their extradition.'

She put down the paper and smiled.

'I guess you are safe,' she said.

'We are safe,' he said. 'A dat! Blessings! Yes!' he shouted. 'Jah give we guidance!'

He looked at the newspaper and read on: 'Police entered the properties at Freeport and a villa in Montpelier, Montego Bay, and seized computers, phones and hard drives, which Inspector Morris said would be combed through to establish the nature of the crim ... crim-in-al ... criminality of the accused.'

'You read good,' Pauline said.

It was a bright morning. The heat of the summer had passed and the air wasn't so heavy with humidity. A sweet breeze blew through Campbell Cove, and Bangaz felt it on his smiling face as he walked with a bounce down to the fisherman beach. He hummed like the buzz of the clippers he could hear where a man sitting on a chair trim. The twisting column of smoke that came through the leathery leaves of the sea grape meant that Troy was cooking. When Bangaz reach he saw Troy, Ample, Maas Henry, Toffee and Bunna smoking weed by the bruk fish cages.

Bangaz mounted the three uneven steps into Troy's bar and bought everyone a drink. It was time for another smoke, and Troy took three 50J bag o' weed out of the cardboard box and put them on the bar. When the drinks were done, Bangaz bought some more.

Buying two round of drink was unprecedented. An hour later he bought everyone a third, creating that morning a myth which was many times retold in the community. Word was spreading of Bangaz's elevation in life.

On the porches and in the bars dem say 'Bangaz rise up fast. Him live in a old bruk dung house, but him always carry kiash pon him, and Pauline start change hairstyle and nails regular. Something a gwaan, for sure.'

When his bredren around him, Bangaz said, 'gather round, mi have sump to tell you. Sump important. You want to know where mi get mi money?'

He took a script out of his pocket, unfolded it, and said 'this how you can make some too.'

He briefly explained the lottery scam, and passed the script around.

Maas Henry handed it back. 'Mi kiant read dat,' he said.

'I can get Pauline to help you. She help me,' said Bangaz.

But Maas Henry had no intention of submitting himself to that indignity.

Troy looked at it and glanced at the back. 'Mi nuh business wid dat,' he said, handing it back. 'Mi cool wid dat,' and he placed his spliff back in his mouth.

'Why do they send down the money?' Ample asked, staring at the words.

'If from five tousan the only thing you gonna give is just a hundred dollars anyone would take that risk,' said Bangaz.

Ample looked again at the script. He could pronounce the English words, and had experience of white folk: he knew how rich, entitled and simple many of them were, and he believed the words might work. He also had something else which was to come in useful from his time at the hotel. He had seen the wastefulness of the white kids, and witnessed how much freedom and money they squandered. And of course the memory of the incident with Caddy and her family still burnt hot in Ample's heart. He had been hurt and he had been betrayed and he had been accused of something he hadn't done. That was not stuff you forgot. Here was an opportunity to get even. That anger helped him memorise the script.

Toffee listened from the edge of the group. He was a youth with a fat belly and bandy legs. He had always been withdrawn and quiet at school, maybe because he was so small. It was true he never felt like he fitted in. No girl ever wanted to friend with him. He put his hand out for a script.

Maas Henry shouted 'This a big man ting!' at him, making Toffee flinch and withdraw.

'No,' said Bangaz, 'everybody can do this who want.'

''Xcep Bunna,' said Maas Henry, 'Bunna eh idiot.'

'Bunna can try,' said Bangaz, looking at Bunna's daft, lopsided smile.

26

'Why did you tell everyone in the community? Why didn't you keep it secret?' asked Willy, taking the lighter from Bangaz's outstretched hand. 'Wasn't that just dangerous?'

'I have to share it with mi people. Mi muss.'

'But wouldn't they talk?'

'Let them chat, let them make them funny noise,' said Bangaz. 'I want people to know. Mi turn big man. And dem haffi know mi rich. And I want to help the sufferer dem. Give the people a hand. You know me, Willy. I want to share. If you give a man a fish, you feed him for a day. If you teach him to scam you feed him for a lifetime.' And he took back the lighter, lit him spliff and tug on it deep.

27

Bangaz gave Ample and Toffee the money to buy a little phone and sim card at Digicel. And he gave them each a page of the lead list. Toffee liked using the phone. On the phone he was not small with crooked foot. On the phone he had smooth brown skin, long legs, big brown eyes and dreadlocks which the white girls loved. He could be someone better on the phone. He could escape himself, as a scammer.

Ample sat on a bench by the fisherman beach, talking into his phone.

His phrases would waft across the sand. 'I am calling from the offices of the Publishers' Clearing House in Columbus Ohio.'

Nobody cared, and nobody noticed. Nobody noticed, that is, until a month later Toffee passed by on a brand new motorbike. And a month after that he had a girl on the back, her arms tight around him. He dropped her at Troy bar and wheelied for two miles from Campbell Cove to Green Island and then turned smoky donuts in the middle of the crowd of kids outside the school where he had been bullied. He passed through Campbell Cove three or four times a day, sometimes with a uniformed schoolgirl clinging to him.

More people joined in: Bunna had a go, but Bunna lacked something to make it work. He was happy with little, always smiling and always positive. He didn't feel compelled to get more. Then Omar took it up. Travis too.

Bangaz supplied three scripts. The first was the original lottery scam, the second an IRS story about unpaid taxes. Unless the client paid up in double quick time, the IRS were going to seize his house, car, TV, wife, basically anything they could think of in Cove to scare them. The third script was a bogus accident insurance pay-out, in which the scammers pretended that an out of the blue payment was being made for either an ancient car accident, or workplace pollutant. Naturally, it just needed the handling fee paid up front.

In the bars and on the porches, in the deep shade of the midday sun or in the smoky dusk, you could always hear a Cove yout saying, 'Good evening, sir. I am calling from Global Sweepstakes and Lotteries International of 1165 Hyatt Way, Chicago, Illinois, 7692. I am pleased to inform you that you have come up as a winner on last month's draw...'

Bangaz was busy leading his own new clients to their first payment and old ones to the second third and even fourth, because when the promised winnings didn't appear in their accounts, he easily came up with a simple obstacle that could be removed with another, then another, payment. Handling fee, security deposit, bank charge, extra legal fees, cost of drawing a certified cheque, photocopying, legal advice, miscellaneous expenses. All of these were presented, and all had to be paid. And nearly all were paid by the madly optimistic and trusting people on Gucci and Gabbana's lead lists.

Some days Bangaz was walking out under the brown and yellow awning of the pharmacy next to Western Union with a $US 500.00 in his pocket. Some days, much, much more.

Omar, whose freckly face and ginger hair were for many years a fairly permanent feature on the bamboo bench outside Troy's bar, and who was not known for pursuing a professional career with fierce determination, went into Courts in Lucea and bought a bed, sideboard, TV, component set, fridge, freezer and cooker. For his madda. With cash. And then returned four days later and put more cash down for the same stuff for himself.

In the same month, Toffee gave his motorbike to his brother and turned up in a newish Honda to Troy Bar, and out of the passenger door stepped Lady Gizzada, a 300 pound thirty-year-old go-go dancer of national repute whose principal area of operation was on the beach and in the clubs of Negril. She had eye lash like awning, bumpa batty and a much admired body squeezed into gold hot pants and brassiere. Toffee tossed the car keys up in the air and caught them, leading Lady G into the shed and buying her a pink pussy: Campari and rum cream. He took a wad of notes an inch thick from his pocket and tump it pon bar top.

'Mi bingo,' he said.

People group up to look at his brick of cash and Lady Gizzada herself, until he led her back to the car and took her to TT Guest House on the hill above Green Island for the night for his own, if not her, pleasure.

28

Adi, Bangaz's old supervisor at the call centre, par with big people. That meant his friends were prosperous and important, and that he didn't have time for Campbell Cove no more. But when Maas Porter died of sugar, as diabetes was called in Campbell Cove, Adi came to the candle-light and parked his white BMW facing out, near the tufted ball ground. The candle-light was the first in a touching series of ceremonies when someone died in Cove. A few days after his death, friends and relatives lined the road and path to Maas Porter's yard with candles in brown paper bags of sand. There was a bar open but most people stood around without drinks, talking in subdued murmurs.

Under a blue canvas tied between trees, Troy cooked pots on open fires: chicken soup, conch soup, pork, fish, and a vat of rice. He ladled portions into styrofoam boxes and handed them to the people who stood around, avoiding the porch where Maas Porter's daughter Sonia and son Cremo sat, each with one bandaged leg. Amputation was the only treatment of diabetes for people who couldn't afford insulin.

As the dusk gave way to night, the lines of candles brightened into a path to heaven. Adi stared at the lights; he was Maas Porter's nephew and feared the disease.

Bangaz was picking up a generous round of drinks as the big man came through the door of the bar.

'Keep the change!' Bangaz called to the bartender. Those words were so precious to him. To be able to say them, at last. 'Adi!' he called. 'Bredda! Y pree? Everyting up?'

They touched knuckles, and exchanged pleasantries. Toffee sat on a stool, leaning against the raw wood and shouting at every girl who walked by, 'Com ya!' grabbing those who slowed down, tussling with them until they hit him and walked away, laughing and jeering over their shoulders.

As Bangaz and Adi walked into the dark, Adi noticed Bangaz's new diamond socks and new check shirt buttoned at the top with the rest left undone. His criss trainers had not come second hand from no blue barrel, that was for sure.

Adi said, 'Gucci want him lists back.'

'I don't know about his lists,' Bangaz said, adding, 'You tell him we tief him script?'

Adi suck teeth. 'Mi never tell you a tief the CD, Bangaz. The lists serious, man. He will find out you have him lists. Look...' Adi waved his hand at the bar where Ample, Omar and Toffee were buying drinks for their bredren. 'He is going to come after you all,' Adi said.

'Him a prison,' Bangaz said. 'Dem ago extradite him go a 'Merka. Dem nat even sentance him yet.'

Adi looked at Bangaz, quietly astonished at his confidence. Adi himself was terrified about the CD going missing.

'Nuhbadi nah trouble me,' Bangaz said walking away. 'Dem cyah touch mi. Mi nuh fear dem bwoi. Mek him know dat wen yuh chat to him.'

That night, as Bangaz took off his necklace and laid it by his new cologne on the lace mat on the dresser, Pauline said, 'Yuh nuh feel say dem ago trace back all a yuh bingo dem to the CD?'

Bangaz stretched out beside Pauline and brought his hands behind his head. 'Nutn like dat, Pauline,' he assured. 'If dem com mi ready'.

'Mi a fret you know, Clive,' Pauline only called him Clive when things serious. 'I scared for Jenna, and this one.' She looked at her belly. 'Mek we move house, maybe go down the other side, far away or mek we try fi file to go to USA.'

'You cyah file. Smaddy haffii file fi you. Smaddy affi married to you, who is a citizen, or your family member. Like that you gonna get a green card easy. So we never gonna get through with green card,' Bangaz said.

'I don't think we is safe here,' said Pauline.

'This a good yard. We are in our community near our friends. That is the best protection. Dicky and Waller always pass by and they know we. They will tell us if any stranger come look.'

His neighbour, Sparrow, had gone to America on the farm program in the 80s as a strapping young man, had run off, and was living twenty years later as a janitor in a block of apartments in Miami. Every few months Sparrow sent money down to his brother Dicky and uncle Waller who, over thirty years, had built a house on a plot of land on the hill above Bangaz's yard. They were just fixing the windows so it was nearly finished, but nobody knew if Sparrow himself was going to leave the States and reach back down to Cove. Sparrow had never seen his house except on his phone. Because he was an illegal immigrant, and would never be allowed back into the States if he travelled to Jamaica, the journey home would be his last, and he would once again be swapping one life for another.

29

Bangaz chop ten pon him new couch, dozing the afternoon away with a cell phone on his belly, occasionally opening his eyes to admire the pyramids of marl, builders' sand, and new monument of fresh blocks framed in his doorway. These were for the house he was constructing.

A thousand miles north of Bangaz's reclining body, Danielle Tinknell was sitting under a ceiling fan in a 1950s themed cocktail bar in the town of Naples, Florida, USA. She figured the fan was just for show as the AC was doing its job, blasting cool air at the customers, despite the doors being thrown open to the views of towering condos on a humid summer evening.

Her boyfriend, Andy, slumped into the chair beside her: curly blond hair, good jawline and blue eyes a little too close together.

'What's going on?' Danielle asked.

'You and I could be celebrating something, like, really big,' Andy said, looking around for a waitress.

'What's happened?'

The waitress appeared between the palms and took their order for a couple of daquiris. As soon as she was out of earshot, Andy leant forward.

'This afternoon, when I was in the apartment...'

'I thought you were going to a job interview.'

'Lucky I didn't. Listen to what happened. The landline rang, and it was this guy. He asked for Andy, and I asked what it was about. I was thinking it might be a debt collector because of that business loan. I said, "Is this about money?" He said, "well yes sir, it is," and he told me that his name is Pablo, and he works in a mail room at Fed Ex HQ in Ohio. He said next door was the accounts department.'

'Andy, what are you talking about? Where is this going?'

'Just listen, okay? He told me has a friend in the accounts department and she has told him about a bank account where the money is put for all the parcels that are never claimed or delivered. Loads of little payments, five, ten dollars, but it really adds up, Pablo said.'

'Why was he telling you this?'

'He said he had what he called a money making proposal.'

Danielle looked unimpressed.

'He and his friend have worked out that they can access the account and make transfers from it, because it's never actually checked. You see, the money doesn't really belong to anyone.'

'Does it really work like that?' said Danielle. 'I somehow doubt it.'

'It's money waiting to be claimed by customers. But they never do!' said Andy. 'And Pablo said they just need someone outside the company to send the money to.'

'Why ask you?' said Danielle. 'I mean, do you know him?'

'No. I told you.'

Danielle stared at Andy.

'But that's the whole point, Dani. He needs someone he doesn't have any connection with. I'm random to him.'

'Not just him,' said Danielle under her breath.

'He wires the money to me, and I wire it on to him, after taking a cut. And I mean a good cut, babe,' Andy started laughing with the joyous thought.

'That sounds dangerous and totally illegal,' Danielle said. 'Also, have you ever heard the phrase If something sounds too good to be true, it probably is?'

Andy looked dismayed. 'But you are,' he said.

'What?'

'Too good to be true.' He flashed her a smile.

'Oh Andy, you say the cutest things. Do you really think I am?'

'Of course you are honey. You are too good to be true, but it's true.'

Danielle blushed as she sipped from her straw.

'I won't be doing anything wrong,' Andy whispered urgently. 'They're the ones who are doing the transfer. They can't prove he spoke to me.'

'The FBI can track it to your bank. Then you're implicated...'

'Not necessarily. Do you remember Arty?' Andy said.

'Oh god, him. What happened to him? Arty? Why Arty?'

'He lives at his parents' place over the winter. He's really getting on top of his drink issues. Remember when I ran that jazz venue with him? The Oxford Jazz Joint?'

'That tin hut the other side of Alligator alley? That place was a dump.'

'You said you loved it.'

'What about it?'

'We formed a corporation, the two of us. Arty and me. This is back in 2005, right? It's all dissolved and over, it fell apart, it had to, because it was part of our personal growth journey. Lessons learnt, right? But it still has a bank account. I know, because I still get statements and bank cards. They are totally useless, because the account is empty. It always was. And my name was never on the account. Arty's was. But like I said, I still have the card and the passwords.'

'Andy! Are you insane?'

'I can get the money, put in there and then either take it out in cash or transfer it off-shore. I have actually been looking at this and it's not as difficult as you think. You just have to pay.'

Danielle put her hand on his arm. 'Why would you ever risk being put in jail?'

Andy leant towards Danielle. 'It's fourteen million dollars.'

Danielle slowly leant back in her chair. She felt herself blushing again. Andy looked as though he was about to burst apart with excitement. He held his mouth shut trying not to smile too much. He nodded and mouthed 'fourteen.'

'Fourteen?' Danielle whispered.

'And we get five. Five.' He held up four fingers, then realised and put his thumb out to make five.

'We can leave Naples, baby. We can quit this fucking dump. And you can quit being a realtor. I know how much you hate it. Think of where we could go.'

'Would you take me?' Danielle asked.

'Babe! You're my partner. You're my compadre. You've stuck with me through thick and thin. You're my bestie and my lover. I ain't going unless you're coming.'

'So, you get fourteen into the account?' Danielle asked.

'I get fourteen transferred in,' said Andy, 'Million. And I have to transfer nine straight to an account Pablo has set up in The Cayman Islands. That's where he says we can have our accounts if we want. Five million for him, and four million for the woman in accounts. Basically all she has to do is leave her desk for five minutes. And five million for me.'

'How come he's giving her so much?'

'She's critical. Plus he likes her and she needs the cash. She's disabled. Actually he called her crippled. Shows how recently he migrated to the States. He's from the Cayman Islands, and has a wife and five kids to look after. He says it's been a real struggle as one of the children has a breathing problem and the medical bills are, like, terrifying.'

'But he's giving you nearly a third.'

'He said – he's such a nice man, humble and quiet. He's in a wheelchair too. They put all the disabled staff out of sight down in the basement.

His biggest fear is not being paid the money from me, so wants to make sure I feel happy, and that he is cool with giving me five. He used the word cool. He says five million meets all his needs and any more is greedy. You have to like a dude who says that.'

Danielle stirred the foam with her straw. 'You haven't told anyone, have you?'

'Just you.'

'Good,' said Danielle. 'Don't. Arrange a time to speak to him next when I can be there. I want to hear what this guy sounds like.'

'Sure, we're talking as soon as he's got Ange fully on board.'

'Who's Ange?'

'The woman in accounts.'

'Oh. OK.' Danielle shrugged and drained her glass. 'Come on, let's go home.'

Danielle paid. They weaved through the tables of snowbirds – the generic term for the white, middle-class, mainly elderly mid-westerners who wintered in Florida – and a bell-hop in an ill-fitting uniform opened the louvred doors and let them out onto the upscale streets of downtown Naples.

30

Danielle was perched on the edge of a floral couch in the 29th floor apartment she and Andy were house-sitting. The place belonged to some clients. Andy had fitted the motorised fly screen which had jammed shut, so they couldn't get onto the balcony. He motorised blinds and drapes for the folks of Naples, so they didn't have to go to the trouble of standing up and closing them by hand, but that meant Danielle had to look at the view through the mesh. It wasn't much of a loss: a couple of condo tower blocks and miles of swamp. The ocean was in the other direction.

Danielle's head almost touched Andy's as they stared at the laptop on the coffee table.

'Read it out,' Danielle said.

Andy concentrated on a piece of paper in his hand: 'Tequilashot all one word. Arty made the passwords,' he said as Danielle typed.

'Boom,' said Danielle as the account appeared on the screen. Balance: $1.56.

'Well that's about to change, big time,' murmured Andy.

The phone vibrated on a coffee table book called Caribbean Style Interiors.

'That's Pablo,' Andy said. 'Right on time.'

'Good evening. Am I speaking to Andy?' Bangaz said from the bamboo bench in his yard, admiring the bunches of mangoes weighing down the branches of his tree.

'Hello, yes, it is. Is that Pablo? Is everything okay?'

'It is. We are making the transfer on Sunday night, 2am, quiet time here between security shifts. First, give me your bank account and Swift Code for the transfer. Go ahead.'

Andy read the account numbers off the screen; Danielle nodded.

'The money will appear in your account on Monday by 9am Eastern Daylight Time,' said Bangaz. 'It will be fourteen million, six hundred fifty-four thousand, eight hundred and eleven dollars exactly. When it arrives, please ring this number to confirm and make an immediate transfer to the account I will give you now. You have a pen and paper?'

He waited while Andy picked up the pen. He heard Andy's breath shortening with excitement. It was now a familiar sound.

Bangaz read off a piece of paper covered with random bank account numbers and Swift Codes which Travis had supplied. Travis had not taken to scamming, he didn't have the edge. But Travis ran a profitable business in the service industry to the scamming trade, coming up with technical advice and IT support with banking and telecommunication.

'Repeat that account number,' Bangaz said. 'Pay close attention please....'

Andy read the number back.

'Correct. Very good,' said Bangaz.

Danielle creased her face and mimed something.

'Hold on, I have a pan on the cooker,' Andy clamped his hand over the phone.

'I think I can hear crickets in the background,' Danielle whispered. 'Where did you say he was?'

'Pablo, where are you?'

'I am in the workers canteen at Fed Ex in Ohio.'

'But I can hear crickets in the background, isn't that crickets?' Andy asked.

'What? Oh! I wish! That's our broken AC unit here. Down here in the basement we have no windows, just lousy AC units.' He lowered his voice, 'but all that is about to change, right?'

With the call finished, Andy folded the bit of paper, hid it in Danielle's book of poems about Empowerment, and went to pour two glasses of Chardonnay. As he watched the wine swilling into the stemware he thought about the cash making its way towards him. He had been planning to share it with Danielle 50 – 50, but he hadn't mentioned the exact split and, as he picked up the drinks and walked through to the lounge, he began to feel less inclined to hand over too much.

He was going to say, 'I'm giving you two mill, okay? How does that sound?' But he actually said 'I'm giving you a million,' and handed Danielle her wine.

'What! Oh wow! Thank you hon!' She kissed him, tears in her eyes.

'It's been a hell of a journey, you and me,' said Andy, seeing her crying and feeling his throat tighten. 'You took me on at a low ebb. A very low ebb, babe.'

Andy's career as a minor porn star had come abruptly to an end, and he had found himself unqualified for life outside the sex trade. But Danielle had literally picked him off skid row and helped him back on his feet.

'I owe you everything,' Andy said, 'it's great to be able to show you some gratitude and pay you back.'

Danielle had fallen in love with Andy, invited him to live with her and supported him in every way there was, even on the nights he got wasted. With her savings, she bought him the motorisation business, though it turned out it didn't suit Andy's skill set.

'You know you don't have to.'

'I want to. Cheers.' It was true, he felt great being generous.

The glasses clinked. They looked into each other's eyes, brimming with excitement. Andy's body hummed like a tuning fork. There was a new drug in his blood. The money drug. Everyone in Naples was quietly on pharmaceutical doses of it. Andy had only known it in homeopathic doses. But this was straight from the dealer.

Danielle said 'I am super-stoked, Andy.' For three years she had stood by and watched the snowbirds buy condos for 800 grand without thinking about it. She wondered where they got all that money, and why she would never know sums like that. In Naples you were the unusual one if you were poor.

She didn't even have her own apartment, not even a little concrete box with a view of a wall and an AC unit. Every day she got up and forced her thoughts down: I don't want to be a realtor. I want to be an artist. I want to live in a studio by the sea with a lot of glass and make work inspired by the ocean and the sunset.

Andy went back to the place where he lived since Danielle caught him using sex lines. He lay awake in Pablo's world: the hour of 2am approached. He closed his eyes, thinking of the money flying down the wires and landing with a thump in his lap.

31

Danielle woke from her dream; she had been at her easel, where the work flowed effortlessly from her brush. She picked up her cell phone.

'We rich?'

'There's been a hitch, but it's not a problem,' Andy said.

'The money's not in the account?'

'No, but it's not the problem. It's just a hitch, a delay.'

'What kind of hitch?'

'Pablo rang me just after I left for work. Last night the management unexpectedly put a second person on Ange's shift, so she was never alone in the room. So he couldn't make the transfer without being observed.'

'Is he going to try again?'

'Of course, but he has to be dealt with, this new person. He's a Polish guy called Marcin.'

'What do you mean dealt with?'

'They have to get him out of the room tonight. Pablo's already spoken to him. He's told him that he needs the room empty.'

'What reason did he give?' asked Danielle.

'He told him he needed the place empty to have sex with one the cleaners. You know, a quickie. The problem was the Polish guy asked which cleaner. Pablo told me all this. He only knew one cleaner so said her name: Ann. This was a mistake because Ann is married to Marcin.'

'Shit...'

'Yeah. So Pablo had to give a watered down version of what we are actually doing. Like we are getting thousands, not millions. Marcin said he's happy to see and say nothing, but he wants a share.'

'How much,' Danielle said.

'A thousand bucks,' Andy said.

'Oh. Okay. Well that's not a problem. So we're back on,' said Danielle.

'But he wants it up front. Before we make the transfer.'

Something irritating nipped in Danielle's mind. She brushed it aside.

'I guess that's reasonable,' she said.

'So you told Pablo to pay him.'

'Kind of. He hasn't got the grand. He's only on 480 a week and he has the family to think of. You know, the medical bills. He said he had a friend he could ask but it meant cutting us out, as he would have to do the whole thing with this other guy.'

'Cutting us out?' Danielle said.

'He said he only had two hours to raise the thousand, so I said I'd give Marcin the money and deduct it from the cash I transfer to Pablo.'

'Andy, you sent him a grand?'

'Not quite. I wanted to ask you about that.'

'Right. You haven't got a grand.'

'I borrowed ten grand from the bank.'

'You borrowed ten grand?'

'It was so easy. What does it matter, Danielle? It's nothing now! But I don't get it till tomorrow. I swear it's coming so can you make the transfer and I will pay you back as soon as the loan comes in?'

'Andy.'

'Please, Dani. Millions of dollars depend on it.'

'Okay, but, you know — I don't want to be totally negative, but it sounds fishy.'

'You got to Western Union it to him. Not him, actually, to his brother, in Jamaica.'

'Why?'

'Pablo's lost his ID card. Get a pen. His brother's called Clive Thompson. He teaches in Jamaica. He's going to send it direct to Marcin.'

'That's funny, that's my uncle's name, Clive Thompson; my mum's sister's husband.'

'It's quite a common name, I guess,' said Andy.

'Okay, I'll do it,' she said.

32

Willy had a tricky relationship with alcohol, but not as tricky as the one he had with his daughter. At least with the rum he had fine moments of clarity and joy, even brilliance, before the descent into confusion, regret and bitterness. With Holly, he had never got it right, and had never been able to make her or himself happy.

Holly lived in Kingston where she worked in the media, which meant everything from styling an advert to driving a foreign director around to scout locations. She was driving from Negril back to the capital with a car full of clothes from a music video when she realised she had some time to spare and decided to call in on Willy.

The house in Campbell Cove was a perfect place for a child to grow up: right by the seaside and surrounded by kind neighbours and their kids. This was why it was particularly annoying that she had never felt welcome there. Willy said he couldn't cope with her on his own and the only women in the house were too flaky for her mum, Kayenne, to entrust her to. Kayenne and Willy had never lived together. For Holly, the idyllic place held only a few painful memories.

She turned her SUV through the drunken gateway and parked in the shade. Dressed in a long, tight African print skirt and a white lace top, she slipped into her shoes which she'd taken off to drive. She walked towards the house, patting the thick dreads coiled on her head, and radiating a city sophistication not often seen in Campbell Cove.

She called 'Yo,' ironically as she approached his house.

Willy appeared at the end of the porch. 'Oh, it's you,' he called weakly. He kissed her on the cheek. 'So good to see you. I was just having a little, er, think.'

Holly moved past him, put her sunglasses and clutch on his kitchen table, and started collecting up empty flasks of Appleton and old Gleaners off the floor.

'Don't, don't, please,' Willy muttered. 'Bunna will do it when he comes in.' Bunna used to work in the yard and around the house for a wage but now hung around, unpaid, trying to be useful in the hope that Willy would find a few bills for him. 'I've let things rather go to rack and ruin I've been working so hard.'

Holly plucked the cushions from the day bed and pounded them till gusts of dust jumped out, then rearranged them symmetrically. To Willy, there was something a little alarming about the violence of her thumps.

'Leave that, they're fine,' he said. 'You've done enough.'

She knew he lied about having a house keeper. The cockroaches were apparently so in control they didn't seem frightened of Holly, in fact one ran directly at her in a clear territorial challenge, but being a Jamaican woman she soon lick it dead with her fancy designer sandal (made in Jamaica). She later found, with a spasm of sadness and frustration, the self-help book she had given Willy swollen and stuck together on a broken chair in the garden.

'Come and sit down and tell me about you,' his crumpled old face smiled. 'Shall I go and make a drink, or an iced coffee?'

She bent down to pick up a sheet of paper, stared at it and passed it to Willy.

'JPS,' he said. JPS was the national electricity company.

'21 grand,' Holly said.

'Yes,' said Willy miserably. 'I'm hoping for some royalties...'

'I'll pay it,' she dipped into her hand bag and took out five bank notes. 'Dis a for the current bill, yuh understan?'

'Yes yes yes,' he said. 'Thank you. You have saved me from the darkness once again, my love.'

Holly carried on clearing up, emptying ashtrays.

'What's this?' she said, looking at another piece of paper. She passed it to him.

He read, in his own writing: Notes on a book about a righteous Jamaican scammer. Willy smiled weakly.

'You're not writing about scammers are you?' Holly asked.

'One has approached me. He asked me to write his story.'

'Mi hope yuh hope yuh tell him fi go suck out him mumma dutty pussy hole.'

'I didn't, actually.'

'You're not writing it, are you?'

Willy said nothing.

'You're not writing it?' she said again.

'It's the story of this community, of this country...'

'It is not,' she snapped. 'It is not our story. Plus it could get you killed. You know what they're like. Ruthless. Ruthless. What the fucking hell is wrong with Tea parties with Noel Coward and Princess Margaret?'

'No-one wants to read about them anymore,' Willy said. 'No one's interested. And I kind of understand why.'

Holly sat down and looked at her phone. While scrolling she said 'Who is this guy, anyway?'

'He knows I write books.'

'He's trying to scam you, you know that don't you?'

'I have considered it, yes. But I don't actually think he is. He's from this community.'

'That means nothing.'

'I know. But I've always liked him. He's very bright, and he has a story which I think is interesting. The British taught the Jamaicans to scam by modelling it. Slavery was only survived by scamming the enslavers. When the politicians ignore the people on subjects like reparations, scamming is a political duty.'

'How's he gonna do it? Get close to you for your banking information? Good luck if that's his plan,' she laughed.

'He wants the story of his bredren told.'

'About how they jinall old ladies and then buy guns and shoot innocent Jamaicans for fun? Nice story.'

'You see, that's what you all think.'

'Because we all live here, and we all know. Just because you like them and are nice to them does not mean they won't rob and kill you without a second thought. Dem are bludclaat crawsis and destruction. And you? Yah mek dem turn you in a informer.'

'No. He's decent, and I'm not snitching, I am singing praises. We've agreed on that.'

She ran her hand around a garbage sack to open it up. 'You are seriously going to write another book about the violence and deception of Jamaicans to add to all the others and bun bad lamp fi we? Is like yah throw salt ina we cut. Why yah dweet? Because there isn't quite enough negative shit said about us?'

'I'm am artist...' Willy started, but Holly cut him.

'This is my country, my life,' her voice tight. 'We're trying to go forwards, become civilised safe and reliable, and you are taking us back.'

Willy scratched his head and looked at the floor.

'Can you, for once in my life, not undermine me?' Holly said. 'Can't you write something about how bright our future is? Our movies, our music, our nature, our eco-tourism, our innovation. Be positive about Jamaica. Please, Dad. It's my future you're trashing. I live here. I don't want to have to migrate to America. I can't go to the UK because you never married Mum and you never file for me and they are so fucking racist they won't let me even go on holiday there. Thanks for that. But even if I could I hope

I'd stay here. Everyone has to leave here because of this shit. Even Tashy is going, and she loves Jamaica. You know? I want to prosper in a positive Jamaica. Yuh undastan? Is it that hard for you to help make a place where kids are educated, the streets are safe, garbage is collected, and the taxi driver or police don't come on to me? Where the electricity bill doesn't have a service charge on it for the Minister of Energy's wife's shoes? Can you fucking do that for me?'

Willy moved out of her way and stood in the corner while she swept around his chair. 'I am sixty years old and nobody is interested in my work,' he said.

'You're sixty-four,' she said without looking up.

'Okay. And I am sinking here. I am struggling. No-one wants my books. I am running out of money, this place is falling down. And my health isn't so strong. My hearing's shot and my eye-sight's not so sharp. I wore a mismatching pair of slippers for two days until someone pointed them out. You think I like my daughter to pay my current bill and see me like this? I want to stand up. I want to be a man. I want to be a success.'

Holly suck teeth.

Willy said. 'I want to make you proud of me. To make you respect me.'

'Spare me, please,' said Holly.

'This project is going to sell.'

'Pickney nuh care if daddy successful, Pickney want daddy to be there when a bed time.' She swept the dust off the porch into the yard. 'And you didn't manage either,' she said under her breath.

'That is rather ancient history,' Willy said. 'It was a long time ago, and you know your mother wasn't easy.'

Calmly, Holly said, 'Yes, I know that. I was the one who had to live with her for my entire childhood.'

Willy nodded. 'I'm sorry,' he said. 'Leave the mess, please, but thank you for helping. I let things slip. I'm not going to do that again.' He sighed heavily and said, 'Tell me what you've been up to.'

'I've been on a video shoot in Negril,' she said, leaning the brush against the boards and picking up her phone. 'With Shaggy and Sean Paul.'

'And what's the song about? Cake recipes?'

Holly didn't look up from her scrolling.

Willy said, 'Murder and scamming, no doubt. But it's fine for them to say it.'

'Hmm?' she said, pretending not to have heard. 'They don't actually. They don't do that.'

'But you know what I mean. Vybz can't stop going on about it. So I hear in the bars.'

'Yes, well I wish he wouldn't. From a Kartel everybadi head start swell.'

A rumble of distant thunder made her glance at the sky.

'Rain a fall,' she said.

A squally breeze kicked up some leaves, and some brooding clouds brimmed over the hill and hurried towards the house over a grey mesh of rain.

She picked up her keys and said, 'I'm off.'

'Thank you for dropping by, my love,' said Willy. 'I'm sorry—'

'Stop apologising. Do something positive instead, will you?'

'Of course, of course. What?'

'Do not write about any scammer or scamming. Can you do that one thing for me? Mi a touch road. I want to catch Dub Club tonight and have a prep day on a chicken commercial Monday. The glamor of show biz.'

With those words the rain hit the zinc roof with a crash. The bead curtain of water hung from the eaves as the deluge dropped from the sky. Holly sat back down. Everything was suspended when rain fall. There was little wind and no change in temperature. The shiny sea turned matt, its surface smoky with bouncing droplets.

Holly dug around her Vuitton bag for a some kush and wizla. The rain was too loud for inessential conversation. She built a spliff, lit it and smoked.

Willy found a flask and a glass and poured himself a rum.

'You want one of these?'

'I'm good.'

They sat in silence and watched the rain sheeting down over the Cove. Then from the river came a brown line moving out to sea. This was the sludge that came down the hill and into the water, pushing its way out. The rain intensified to a percussive clatter and then yielded a little.

'How is err, err, that nice bamboo farmer?' Willy said.

'Kevin,' said Holly.

'Yes,' said Willy.

'I split up with him four years ago,' Holly said.

The rain intensified, hammering the metal, pouring off the gutter in a silver tongue. A crack of lightning rent the air and sent a shiver through the house.

The rain ceased as fast as it started, leaving dripping trees and gurgling rivulets. A car revved its engine, a box started playing music.

Holly collected her things, stood up and pointed at Willy's laptop. 'Get writing about The Magic of Mustique, or Princess Margaret's hats on her jubilee visit to Jamaica in 1906 or whenever the bladclaat woman come.'

Holly stared at her father.

'A joke me a make,' she said.

He nodded. 'I know.'

She picked her car keys up. 'I must go.' Orange dashes of sunlight appeared high in the trees as she crossed the wet yard under the glossy leaves.

Willy checked she had gone, cleared a space on the table, dried some residual liquid with his shirt sleeve and placed his laptop down. He sat, fired it up, took out his notebook, opened it, and started reading. Then he took a breath, leant forward and typed.

Writing for Willy was usually like hacking a tunnel through granite with a toothbrush. But today the rock opened up. The toothbrush had touched a magic button. A door in the rock swung open to reveal Bangaz in his white shorts, thigh length socks, Liverpool shirt and huge gold necklace with KING suspended on it. Bangaz conducted Willy into the mountain down well-cut, lit tunnels. As fast as Willy typed the next sentence formed in his mind. He went to the kitchen and came back with some cold coffee. The sea darkened and the line of the horizon sharpened as the sun dropped. The water chatted and gulped at the rocks, urging him on. The night opened like a curtain, ushering in the crickets and chirruping frogs. With the storm clouds gone, the moon was rising. The sea slithered and slopped at the rocks. The roll and catch of a distant bass line and the traffic both fell away. Silence. And the tapping of his keyboard.

33

Waller, in baggy trousers with a high belt and turn ups, his shirt rolled up his muscled forearms, stopped by the house and put down his old bag of carpentry tools.

'Pauline,' he said softly.

'Ya man,' she said from inside.

'A bredda dung de road a check fi Bangaz.'

The house creaked, and Bangaz opened the door wearing only his shorts.

'You nuh know him?' he asked.

'Me never seen him. Him aks wish part you live.'

'Tank you.' Bangaz softly closed the door.

He put his finger to his lips and his ear to the wooden wall.

A woman down the path was shouting 'Dis a fi Bangaz Thompson yard? Wishart Bangaz Thompson yard? Tell mi, pickney! Get outa mi way! Mi look for Clive Thompson.'

Bangaz sighed, opened the door, put his head out, and watched Marva and Wayne, both of who fat up, labouring up the path.

'Lord! Oh my lord. Kiss mi neck!' Marva called out when she glimpsed Bangaz. 'There he is! Mi blessed child. I have been sick with worry since you gone. Sick, oh Lord! Tank god mi find you.'

She grabbed Bangaz and engulfed him in a tight embrace, tears coursing down her face.

Pauline and the two girls, now five and three, came to the door.

'Pauline! Mi daughter! God be praised! And two pickney! Look how dem favour dem Aunti Marva!'

Wayne staggered to a halt behind her, out of breath and wiping the sweat from his neck with a cloth. He at least had the decency to look a little sheepish, nodding at Pauline and Bangaz, saying, 'Yes.'

'Yes, Wayne,' they said.

Pauline and Bangaz stood watching Marva say hello to the children, then she turned to them.

'Pauline! My number one daughter-in-law. Look how beautiful you grow! Bwoy mi miss you. Mi heart bruk when you lef!'

Wayne said, 'Mi hear tingz a gwaan good for you.'

'We good, man' said Bangaz. 'Give tanks and praise. We have life and that is the main thing.'

'That is the best thing,' said Wayne, though he wasn't certain of that. A good meal and a flask of JB Rum was possibly better than his current life. He stood with his hands in his pockets, gazing out towards the tree-tops and the distant view of the cove, particularly admiring the concrete blocks, sand and marl piled in front of him.

'Clive,' said Wayne, 'Mi a beg you a shoes money so mi can go look for likkle work.'

'Wayne!' said Marva. 'Don't bother the man with talk like that! A family dat! Yuh nuh pressure family for money. Cho!'

'Wayne,' said Bangaz. 'True you is family, you know? So mi will help you, wid pleasure.'

He went into the house, which now had three rooms, padded over the new tiles through to his bedroom and opened the drawer of the dresser. It was scattered with bank notes. Some of it was the cash Andy had Western Unioned. He grabbed a handful and went back out, allowing Marva to see the wad. Her desperate, pained and pitiful expression softened Bangaz's heart.

'Forgive me, please,' she croaked. 'Mi done wrong but I repent of me sin dem. Trust me....' She put out her hand, begging for money.

Bangaz peeled off a good few bills and laid them pon her palm.

Marva gasped, then howled, and crushed Bangaz in another embrace, picking his feet off the floor. 'Oh mi prodigal son. For as the psalm say, none is so blessed than the madda who receive back the prodigal son. Give tanks and praise. Amen.'

When Marva had had a good look around, ooh and ahhing at all she saw, they walked the curved path through the yards down to the main. At Troy's bar, Bangaz peeled off more notes to buy Marva and Pauline a Magnum and the kids a champagne soft drink.

'Praise him!' whispered Marva. 'Praise him to the highest!'

'Bartender,' said Bangaz, 'Mi a buy everybody a drink.'

The place had been so busy Troy had employed a bouncy, pretty girl called Deliesha. When Bangaz walked in she reached behind her without looking and grabbed the JB bottle to pour him a flask.

'Chip chop,' she said. Campbell Cove for What's up.

Clever and charismatic, Deliesha could have got any job in a hotel or even a bank, but her sights were set on one single ambition: to leave Jamaica and reach a foreign. She was as impatient and restless as someone sitting with their bags in a hotel reception waiting for check in time. From when she was sixteen she had been trying to get a passport. She was now twenty-one.

Applying for a passport was more an art than a science when parents had drifted off and family records were torn or lost, and Deliesha never mastered it. She had never tracked down her father, let alone his date of birth and birth surfiticket. Her mother had lost her papers in Hurricane Gilbert. Deliesha's plan when she got her passport was to file in America, using her aunty Denise to invite her. If she didn't get through with that she had the option of marrying a US citizen to get a green card, but that was a long process and she would either have to pay a man a lot of money or risk marrying a stranger who might get ideas about keeping her in his home.

So, while in Jamaica, she didn't bother with a career or a relationship. She acted like she was just passing through, though with her work at Troy bar she showed everybody what they would be missing when she leave out and reach up.

The space behind the bar, and sometimes the bar top, was Deliesha's stage, and she moved around it smartly to get everybody a drink, then she opened the book. All bars had a book. Deliesha's was a lined school exercise book, its pages filled with curving columns of numbers, many scratched out. Only Deliesha could interpret the book, but the book was never wrong. She found Bangaz's page and started writing in biro.

Bangaz took his drink out and said to Marva, 'What I have, I share wid my bredren and sistrine.'

'Be careful dem nuh take you for no fool,' Marva said. 'Memba family always come first. Regular.'

A small, fast assembling crowd took their beers and murmured thanks.

'He is my son, yuh know,' Marva told the people, basking in the glory. 'Mi raise him from him born, cos him own madda dead in childs birth. True I save him life.'

Bangaz let Wayne take a spin on his new motorbike, and gave him a bills to fill it up with gas, to give the man something useful to do. Wayne was next seen an hour later, during which time he had circled Green Island and spread the legend of his stepson's ascent in the world and his own close connection to him.

Standing against the rail of Troy's new porch, Bangaz realised how happy he was to see Marva again. Whether her tears were fraud or real they were wet enough, and stirred in Bangaz a deep wish to be loved even if it was by someone as dodgy as Marva. She had fat up and life had worn her down, but she was still Marva, gazing fondly at him and indulging Jenna.

A van drew up and a middle-aged man in a short-sleeved shirt, dark trousers and leather shoes got out and wandered towards the bar looking confused. He held a piece of paper.

'Troy Bar, Campbell Cove?' he said.

Bangaz nodded towards the bar. The man called 'drinks delivery.'

Troy appeared from the gloom in a singlet, shorts and slippers, spliff hanging from his lip.

'Four Hennessy and six Krug Champagne?' the man queried.

'That's correct,' said Troy. 'How much?'

'It must be nice to drink champagne,' cooed Marva. 'Boy, mi never do that. Mi life too miserable. Well I suppose some people can't live that life-style through no fault of them own.'

'Bring us a bottle on ice,' Bangaz called out to Deliesha.

The driver walked back to his van shaking his head.

Deliesha brought out a bottle of Krug nestled in the ice bucket and passed a plastic flute stolen from a hotel to Marva. Bangaz felt his cell phone buzz and walked away from the shed across the tarmac and onto the sand to take it.

'Andy. Perfect,' he said. 'I can't talk for long, the boss is in the building. Thank you for calling back ... I know, I know, I know. We had to postpone again. Marcin felt sick and didn't come in, so we have to wait till he turns up again. But he has two week annual leave start Monday so I don't think we are going to be able to do the operation until next month November time. Or maybe even next year now ... Yes. I do know his replacement; Micky, a white guy from Boston, and I have asked him but he wants two grand up front, so I said no way!'

When Bangaz walked back to the shed, Marva was saying to a crowd of little boys, 'You hold champagne flute just so,' as she pointed her little finger in the air.

Later, tipsy on Krug, Marva approached Pauline. 'If yuh feel like yuh need a break or smaddy fi watch dem pickney, yuh can always say Marva! I am here! Yuh know mi love dem pickney, yuh can drop dem off fi couple day, although mi affi go put on back de current. Mi owe tiefing JPS six grand so di nastiness dem cum cut off mi light. Lard I don't know where mi cya find dat. But if you don't mind pickney sit in dark, dem cya turn wid me any time.'

34

As the unofficial chairman and CEO of Campbell Cove Choppers Inc, Bangaz needed an office which reflected the breadth and success of the operation. His friend Bunna, too easy-going for scamming, had got a job as a caretaker for a white man's holiday villa in Campbell Cove. It boasted a swimming-pool, wide porches on the front and back of the house, an outside shower and sunbeds under umbrellas to lounge on. The white man often disappeared for months in Europe or America, so the place was perfect. Bangaz asked Bunna, while he stood in the white man's yard leaning on a rake, if it would be cool for a couple of bredren to chill by the pool as they did their work.

'I cannot let you do that,' said little Bunna. 'I know you are my bredren and everything but Archie give me orders that nobody can use him pool or him yard or go pon his porch while him inna foreign.'

Bangaz listen carefully, suck teeth and say 'Nuh worry bout nutn, Bunna. Nutn can go wrong. Everyting ago alright man. Nuh worry yuself. Everyting cool, chuss me.'

Bunna said 'Well if you say so Bangaz mi cool with it, but respect the place, and nobody use no furniture or go in the house. And when Archie reach dung you haffi go, understand?'

Every morning Bunna would greet Bangaz, saying anxiously 'You nuh done yet?' and as Bangaz marched into the villa Bunna would stand in the yard saying 'No! Nuh chubble none a the good chair dem.... Okay, one chair and one cushion... No! No No! Not the couch, man. Be cool. Mi beg you. The white man gonna vex bad wid me if you bruk him ting. No! No clothes! Ok. Take and wear and put it back this one time. Not again.'

With the help of the guys who ran the pools at the all-inclusives, Bunna had finally mastered the swimming pool, which was now crystal clear with polished water. Ample served cocktails. The vibe was perfect. Bangaz felt rich before he even started making his calls.

35

'It get we in the right frame of mind,' Bangaz explained to Willy.

'I bet,' said Willy.

'For sure,' said Bangaz, tilting his head to light his spliff.

'Thank god for what was his name? Archie? The white man.'

'Ya man, Archie,' said Bangaz.

'Except,' said Willy, looking up from his laptop and scratching his head, 'he was not called Archie. Was he?'

Bangaz gave Willy a non plussed shrug.

'He was called Willy, and it was this house, wasn't it? The bathrobe,' Willy said, 'Red satin, yes, with black lapels and a gold belt? You ruined it. I bought that in Jermyn Street. You know how much I yelled at Bunna about that? I thought it was him using all my stuff.'

'No man, Bunna cool. And him never snitch. Him cool,' mused Bangaz.

'I used to vex with him bad,' said Willy, 'poor man. Plus you broke that chair. I loved it. And what about my towels?'

'But everyting cool now, eh?' said Bangaz. 'Forgive and forget, my friend. It coulda worse for you.'

'How?'

'I coulda sold this house whole eap o time,' Bangaz chuckled. 'Every white tourist who come onto the yard think me own the place. I could sell it out to them so easy. Hey buddy, nice place you got here. You own this place? Sure do. I struck it rich in import export. I was thinking of maybe it's time to sell and move on.... One time, Willy, I was on the phone to a client getting ten grand and a tourist offer me a hundred grand for this house at the same time. Bludclaat, true mi haffi laugh.'

'You want me to thank you for not selling my house behind my back? Jesus. Who am I working with?'

'Me. Bangaz Thompson. Kingpin. Top of the line chopper. You cya work with nobody elkse but the king.'

Willy sipped his rum and stared out through the thicket of overgrown foliage obscuring his pool.

'You reminded me of the old days,' Willy said. 'Oh, the parties I used to have in this house. Patrick Lichfield often dropped in. For a laugh. If he was on the island. Chris loved him. Everyone did. Sir Patrick. He was a baronet...'

Bangaz stared blankly at Willy, deeply unimpressed.

'... Johnny Gold too, he ran a nightclub in London called Tramp. Wonderful place. Michael White, the famous impresario. Happy days. And the women...' Willy fell silent, ruminating. 'Those were the days. God how we laughed. The 70s and 80s were actually wonderful decades. This place was always full of great characters. Real mates, you know? Gianni Campini, Count Gianni Campini. His party trick was stopping ceiling fans with his head. Played a marvellous game when he poured a bucket of ice down your trousers and then looked to see who had the smallest prick. It was called Piccolo diccolo. Top company, Gianni. Well, they all were.'

He used the past tense because two of his old muckers had died in car accidents and, even more tragically, others had got married. Those had been Willy's glory years. But one day he discovered that he couldn't afford the chemicals for the pool. Or for himself, for that matter, because he had run out of money. He had been used to flying from Kingston to London in March to enjoy the summer in London, but was forced to stay in Campbell Cove alone and tough out the sweltering season. The pool went green and started to stink, so he emptied it. Some noxious liquid nevertheless remained in a leafy puddle in the deep end. Rats fell in and expired, exhausted from trying to climb the sides.

Willy patted the newspapers, books and magazines for his Craven A. When he had one in his mouth Bangaz palmed him a lighter, then pointed at the laptop, but Willy ignored him.

'Do you remember my Chevrolet Impala?' he said as a distant smile formed on his crumpled face. 'Powder blue. Now that was a classic car. With the girls on the back seat.'

Bangaz remembered that car. It used to speed past him sitting by the roadside when he was a yout selling ackee or mango, leaving him either covered in dust or water depending on the weather.

'I had to abandon it in a field three miles outside Negril. It gave up the ghost. It's probably still there now, rusting away.'

'They pull it from the field and get it back up running,' Bangaz said. 'Man sell it to one woman in Kingston mi hear.'

'What? Well she's welcome to it. The parts were beyond me. Well, you couldn't get them. But I was sorry to walk away from her,' Willy smiled to himself, caught in memories. Neither talked. Silences, long silences, were a social norm in Campbell Cove. Often nothing needed to be said. That made sense when you heard what often was said. Willy's breathing slowed and grew shallow until suddenly he needed a deep breath.

'They've all gone,' he said. 'They've all gone. I miss them. You know, Bangaz, sometimes I feel a long way from home, and a little bit lonely.' He nodded ruefully. 'It's comforting to have somebody to talk to,' he said.

Bangaz looked up from his phone. 'Wha' you say?' he said.

'Nothing,' said Willy. 'I was just explaining I don't really have any friends anymore.' Willy's social circle had contracted in three years from about a hundred people to two: Bangaz and Bunna. And he hadn't seen Bunna for weeks, since he came round to borrow the machete and hadn't brought it back. He needed it to help search the verge of the highway. The son of a top businessman had leant out the window to vomit while being driven home, and his head struck an electricity pole and was torn off. An enthusiastic Campbell Cove search party had looked for over an hour until they found it.

'You ever have woman now?' Bangaz said.

'Me? God no.'

'You need to kick the ball, Willy. Every man have to have a spurt. Dribble up the flank, you know?'

'I think I'm a bit old for that.'

'A lie. You need a woman to get you back in motion. Not too young though, maybe take a twenty-one year old. I can find you one, wid ease.'

'It's okay,' Willy said, 'thank you very much.' He stared under the low eave of the porch at the thunderclouds far away across the flat sea. Distant lighting flashed silently.

'We had adventures in that car, Bangaz, touring Jamaica, before the all-inclusives, before.... before it all changed. Before everything went so bland and dull. When men were like you, Bangaz: pirates, buccaneers, dangerous, gutsy. I'd like to try and explain that in the book, the joy and spirit of Jamaican life.'

'You don't forget this is my book, yes? Ready?' asked Bangaz.

Willy nodded.

'Very good,' said Bangaz.

36

Clad in his mesh merino, diamond socks and Clarkes, lying on an expensive towel on a lounger by the pool, rum and chasers beside cell phones and lead lists, Bangaz, with Omar, Toffee and Ample went to work.

When not under a frilly umbrella Bangaz was flying down the highway on his motorbike to Western Union to pick up his cash, which he walked out with, under the pharmacy awning, pleased and proud, no-one asking questions or accusing him of committing a crime.

Sometimes he was so busy nudging clients in America to their bank or their Western Union, he had to send Pauline to pick up the cash. She took a taxi to Lucea with the kids and, holding Jenna by the hand and with little Tanna on her hip, presented her Government ID and came back on the bus to Cove with the money.

It was so common for American citizens to send down money for their relatives for medical bills or construction costs in Jamaica that Bangaz and Pauline didn't attract any trouble or bad attention. Though both of them kept a sharp look out in case Gucci put two and two together and made sixty grand, which was how much they made every couple month.

The first time Bangaz bingo made $10,000 US in one hit he brought the money back, spread it in the bed and stared at. Then he had sex with Pauline on it. Then he bundled it back up into a brick and placed it under his pillow to sleep on, believing it would bring him good luck. He was right. It did.

At night the choppers competed to spend the most money. Bangaz hit a winner with a 85,000J bar bill at Troy's after buying everyone drinks for seven hours, ending up with people arriving from Black River two hours away as the word spread.

Hearing about it, Omar turned up at Troy's shed the next day, ran up a 28,000J bill, and then doused a wad of sixty 1000 J notes in Hennessy and set them on fire in the middle of the floor to win the challenge.

Deliesha stood behind the bar on a beer case smacking the counter shouting, 'DJ! Play your music, Barney,' and the music blasted and thumped, the bass line roll and catch, so dem gyal dash out and whine an go lang bad on each other, and then on the boys, who watched in awe. Bent at their waists wid dem batty cock up in a de air, their hands only supporting their bodies as their heads touched the tiles on the floor. Batty up in the air everything roun a back.

Bangaz slipped out of the bar and wandered across the tarmac onto the sand. The water lay silently in the cove. He was trying to reach his phone to call Pauline but there was so much money in his pockets he couldn't get it out. He looked back at the bar and watched Deliesha on the bar top slapping men who tried to touch her batty. The yout were clothed in the style of Gucci and Gabbana – the people not the designers. Rihanna sang out, as if only to those people in that little bar in Campbell Cove. Like Diamonds in the Sky. Bangaz gazed up into the darkness speckled with stars and felt tears in his eyes. After so long, after hundreds of pain strewn years, he actually felt like smaddy up there finally loved the little people dem of Campbell Cove.

Four years passed which Bangaz and his friends had a glorious time accumulating and spending vast sums of money....

'Ya cya say four year past like that,' said Bangaz.

'Why not?'

'Dem are the glory years, Willy. They are when we are fully happy. Tell them about the birthday parties I keep for Jenna and Tann with 200 friends at mi pool party at fi mi yard.'

'You can't write about every event every year if nothing changes,' Willy said. 'It gets boring.'

'Cho!' admonished Bangaz. 'It would not boring if you is buying ya first Porsche...'

'Okay. I can give the reader a flavour,' said Willy.

'More than a flavour,' said Bangaz. 'Dem tirsty for this, chuss me. Dem mi glory years.'

37

Bangaz and his bredren were not like the drug dealers and the gunmen of the 80s who were mixed up in political violence. They didn't need guns to make their money. They were not thugs. They drank fine champagne and sent their kids to private schools.

Bangaz and Pauline's design for their rapidly growing home was extravagant and expressive, as the Chopping School of Architecture demanded. Barely supported staircases rose to minarets, roman balustrading, Georgian doors, Tuscan tiles, renaissance oriel windows, classical balconies and every other architectural extravagance he and Pauline could find on the internet to pile into the design. And then they painted it magenta red, sunflower yellow, claret and pink.

Pauline bought five acres of extra land and built a swimming pool, garages and a miniature castle and trampoline for Jenna and Tanna. The girls were growing up.

Omar enrolled at college in Montego Bay, where he was conveyed every morning by chauffeur driven Mercedes to study Black History and Politics. The scammer lifestyle of excess felt too empty. On his course, he met other students looking for answers. He and a couple of his new bredren converted to Islam, or turn Muslim, as they put it. He wore long gowns, an embroidered prayer cap and a permanent look of disapproval. During his long, intensely sober hours on the internet he located an architect who he commissioned to build him a circular house with a library and falconry on the hill overlooking Montego Bay. The architect was a bemused Italian who Omar flew over, first class, twice a year to oversee the project.

Back in Campbell Cove, the Chopper Chateaux started popping up all over the place. Ample built his mum a sprawling bungalow where her little board house once stood. Toffee tarmacked four miles of public road to his mum's house, and imported and erected 40 full size street lights 'to cut crime'. Toffee's own house was loosely based on The White House, with twenty-four pillars, a dome, a garage for six cars, a pool hall, boxing ring and private go-go club.

The bars that had sat dark and empty for years were now bursting with light and tump with music. Green Island, which after dark had basically been a dark corridor for the tourist buses to swish through on their way to Negril, was now lit up like Vegas. Droves of yout on motorbikes swarmed from one bar and party to the next, parking their mounts three deep and swaggering into the bar shouting 'Mi bingo!'

'Bartender! Hennessy!'

It was as though the entire community had found an oil well in their own back yard. The waterfall of money was so wide and high, everybody in the community wet up. There was plenty to go round, and when it ran out, more appeared. They were crazy and happy times. These were their glory days.

Bangaz spread the word to all who wanted to know, and people caught on fast. One breezy winter afternoon in 2005, when he went to photocopy the IRS script in the computer centre — a miserable room with plywood cubicles where people toiled over the screen to get some exam surfiticket or other — Bangaz opened the machine to place his document on it and found another, different scamming script on it, this one to do with Life Insurance.

And all day long, the queue at Western Union stretched further than the pharmacy awning. The door swung open every two minutes to release another happy man with a pocket full of money and a head full of dreams into, for him, a new world.

During the working week, Toffee went to live at the Palm Hotel in Lucea because of the time it took to transport the girls up to him in Cove. He lived on the first floor overlooking the car park with the balcony doors open, on take-away food, take-away sex and take-away money.

38

Mr Hawkin's wife, Myrtle, had a batty famous for many miles. It lived lovingly encased in ornate dresses run up by her dressmaker from floral chintz that specially showed off its size and shape. Mr Hawkins himself oversaw the final fitting to check that his wife's booty was fully and boldly displayed. No man walking behind them could keep his envious eyes off it, and Mr Hawkin was inordinately proud of it, opening the passenger door of his car and murmuring 'Delightful lady' as Myrtle squeezed in and settled the famous rump on the lucky car seat.

It was Mr Hawkin's day off from Plantation and he was giving the fabric covered bottom so admired in his community a very special run out. It was an unfortunate fact that the other parts of Mrs Hawkin always had to accompany her bum, but Mr Hawkin made the best of it.

He drove east with the coast on his left through the seaside towns of Lucea, Sandy Bay and Hopewell before reaching the outskirts of Montego Bay where a new mall had sprung up. He pulled up in the car park, mindful of getting a good walk with Myrtle so the traffic on the main got an eyeful of the batty in motion. As he guided his wife across the asphalt, Mr Hawkin allowed himself an indulgent glance over his shoulder to catch the security guards and drivers at the traffic lights admiring his wife's derrière.

'Empress,' murmured Mr Hawkin, as he pulled open the opulent glass door of the brand new Audi dealership in Montego Bay. Here was the kind of place — airconditioned, designer-built with careful attention to detail that only the Germans could achieve — which would attract the calibre of men, and women worthy of a close up walk by of Myrtle's batty. She was built for places like this. So dignified, so unapproachable, but at the same time so lubricious and available. But available, of course, only to Mr Hawkin, who smiled indulgently as he patted the marital buttocks and eased Myrtle forward. She put on her money walk, with an extra slip and slide of the thighs.

'I am looking to replace my present vehicle,' said Mr Hawkin to the gym-fit salesman with a goatee and expensive spectacles. 'I am looking for something with good handling, a strong chassis and attractive curves.' He'd been practising that line for days. Myrtle raised an eyebrow at him. 'As you can observe,' he continued, 'I am habituated to riding something rather special.'

'So I may observe,' said the salesman laughing dutifully as he ran his eye up and down Myrtle in a way that satisfied all three of them, though all for different reasons. Myrtle was pulled magnetically towards a gleaming white Porsche Cayenne with pink leather upholstery and white piping that was parked in the showroom. Mr Hawkin feigned disinterest. He didn't want his wife slavering over something that could never be theirs. The salesman had been quite enough already.

'Madam makes a fine selection.' said the salesman.

Mr Hawkin murmured 'we can't afford it,' and headed to the back of the showroom where the pre-owned vehicles stood close together.

'Don't worry, sir,' the salesman added. 'This vehicle is already sold. Ahh, here comes the new owner now.'

Myrtle thought she'd take a look at him. She turned sideways to the door to give whoever it was a blast of her batty's impressive profile. But she couldn't spot the owner, just some poor country boy dragging a girl behind him. Mr Hawkin recognised the yout: he was the boy he'd fired for a number of infringements including being too black and teaching tourists Patwa. He was about to shout 'Mechanic entrance round back!' when the salesman cut in front of him and scampered to pull the door open.

Bangaz cruised past Myrtle and led Pauline by the hand to the criss Porsche Cayenne. While Pauline opened the doors and boot, Bangaz felt his phone buzz with a message. It was Andy confirming he had sent down another payment for the Fed Ex money: Andy's sixth.

Mr Hawkin watched Bangaz and Pauline get in the car as the salesman drew back the glass window of the showroom. Nobody was looking at Myrtle. Mr Hawkin felt sick to see the young couple skate off inna the new Porsche.

That night, Bangaz took the family down to Troy bar and pulled the cork on a bottle of Hennessy, carefully encircled his Porsche pouring the brandy on the dirt, and then lit the spirit to create a ring of fire around the car. He saw pure enchantment on Marva's face as she stared at the dancing blue flame. Toffee pulled up in a Lexus and bought a bottle of champagne.

'Up top!' called Bangaz.

'When mi flick mi fingers, girl bumflick like ninja,' Toffee informed his friend as he doused the two bikini clad girls who emerged from his car in champagne and gave them a hand up onto his bonnet. He then also emptied a bottle of brandy around the Lexus, and with a flick of his lighter encircled his car in flames, after which he got into the driving to watch the girls press their bodies against his windshield, squirting the washer when they got dry.

On the beach below the bar, a sound crew worked under a plastic gazebo by a throbbing car packed with amps and speakers. Beside a driftwood fire, Troy set up a table of fish and soup and rice, illuminated by spots of light from the street light which Bunna had put a cardboard box over with holes bore in it. Children watched as he delicately balanced the box with a long bamboo pole, inches away from live electricity cables. The ganja smoke caught in thick tongues around the girls' mouths as they ignored the boys who passed close by.

The choppers grouped up against the rail, looking down on their gleaming cars and bikes. They were rich and successful, and they had not done it the whitey way with school and exams and promotions, they had done it the Campbell Cove way: they had demanded it and they had taken it, the way the white man had taken it from them so much times in the past.

Bangaz watched Marva climb into the Porsche. She couldn't drive it but she didn't want to go anywhere. She was finally at her destination, sitting in her son's car, doing her hair in the mirror while Wayne leant against the wing talking to Bunna, though Marva soon warned them sharply from the paintwork.

Standing on the sand, Bangaz watched the people framed in the door and windows. A couple of young choppers turned up and one or two muss bingo because they throw money on the bar for Deliesha to put in her bra and get the girls to dance Puppytail, Kotch and Ramping Shop. The new fun was for the choppers to buy drinks and the girls, dressed only in lingerie, to pour them over their heads and and wet up dem body.

The bar catch a fever, the air so thick with smoke and sweat. Everybody glisten in the red light. Bangaz felt the air coming off the sea like a breath which drifted past him through the shed, cooling everyone's body for a minute as though the ocean took special care of them.

He watched Deliesha under her crown of Hennessy, Johnny Walker Black Label and champagne on the top shelf. The shed tremble with the music. DJ Barney reach for his phone and says 'Hi yeah', and had a conversation ten inches from 10 thousand decibel.

Bangaz walked under a bulb in a almonds tree. He shake him head and smile; took a sip of rum from him cup. Up the lane his ancestors lay dead in the cemetery sprinkled with litter from the last graves-digging. Bangaz wanted to wake them from their sleep to tell them the good news: all of their pain, all of their anger, all of their rage, was avenged right there, in that moment, on the fisherman's beach. At last the little people of Campbell Cove had got some of what was owed. This night was a down-payment.

Wake up! he would shout at the cement gravestones: in this bright future we can forget our past.

Bangaz sat on the side of a ruined canoe, thinking what else he wanted to tell the dead while the water at his feet sipped at the sand. All of the floggings, all of the murders, all of the blood which was shed, all of the rapes, all of the stolen opportunities, all of the firings and the bullshit disciplinary hearings, all of these injustices he wiped clean for them that night.

What else?

All of the hotels that looked like Great Houses with their tall white columns. All of the Plantation diners. All of the places where tourists went to celebrate slavery, not bury it. All of the white gloves they had to wear to serve food to tourists. All of the queues that white people got to the front of. All of the times a police let a white driver pass a roadblock. All of the jobs they'd been denied. All the classes at school with no teacher. All the universities out of reach.

All of it was wiped clean. In that hour. With the patient cove behind him which, over the years, had seen it all.

Now the people whine and sport on the very spot the ancestors had toiled and died. He drained the cup and went to find the family and another flask. As far as Bangaz was concerned, this was just the beginning.

Striding through his community one bleaky morning, when the cloud was low and the sea box against the rocks spoiling for a fight, Bangaz heard some news from America which made whole his happiness. Gucci and Gabbana had finally come to trial, and a jury of the peers had found them guilty.

'God bless 'merica justice!' he called out to Pauline. 'God bless dem white people and dem jury!'

When he was waiting for the fish to come off Troy's grill he felt his phone buzz.

'Marjorie!' he shouted. 'Thank you so ever much for calling back,' he slipped into Mr Patterson from Publishers Clearing House. 'I don't mind telling you we have had to go the extra mile for this account. Yes, yes, I know. Yes there was fraud involved, I am sorry to say. We are very much pursuing the felon. The good news is your winnings are still secure. He did not get his hands on them. You will soon have that swimming pool for your grandkids. Your winnings are finally ready for distribution directly into your bank account. Can you believe how many years it has been! For me to action that today so you have the funds available tomorrow all you need to do is remit a thousand dollars for tax and legal fees...'

39

Gucci and Gabbana were both sentenced in the Federal Court of the Northern District of Indiana to twenty years in prison. They were incarcerated in Terre Haute Federal Prison.

'When was that?' asked Willy, looking up from the keyboard. He picked up his biro and flattened his note book. They were on the porch in the light of a dim bulb. Outside it was an inky, moonless night, the sea kissing and sucking at the rocks out of sight below them. A slow squeaking ceiling fan tried to stir the air in Willy's bedroom, but made no difference.

Bangaz relit his spliff. 'Lang time. That was, er, can be, 2007,' he said.

'Of the twenty years sentence how long are they expected to serve?' Willy asked.

'Bout near, say, fifteen year.'

Willy stared into space and then counted '19, 20, 21 ... but that ... doesn't that mean they get out this year?'

'Gucci already out,' smiled Bangaz. 'So dem say. So me hear.'

'What?' Willy rubbed his forehead and looked at his palm. 'You aren't worried?'

'No man! Wha me a worry for?' Bangaz laughed.

'No, really,' said Willy. 'It's quite serious. You said the man's a killer. No, the man is a killer.'

'Wha you sey?' said Bangaz.

'What if he finds where you live? Or, more importantly, finds where you work. With me? I'm in danger here. Thanks to you.' Willy said. 'That will have a bearing on my fee. It's unavoidable.'

'Yes, Willy. You is now a known associate.'

'I am not madly keen on being murdered,' Willy said.

'Nuh pressure yuh brain Willy. Just worry bout de book. Gucci nuh have nutten to do wid you. Mi will be your saviour dis time.'

'Well I hope you're right. I suppose he could've forgotten. It was all a long time ago. People change. You think he's a reformed man? Many do go straight. Why would he want to go back and make the same mistakes again? You're right, he's probably forgotten all about you.'

'Forget me? No man, dem cya forget me!' Bangaz cried, insulted. 'Gucci tell people inna jail he gonna reach down and murder me. But he put bullet pon me, dem bounce!' Bangaz shouted, throwing his arms wide, puffing out his chest and dancing around. 'I hear Gucci tell every prisoner all the money we choppers make is truly fi him money. That we tief him out!' Bangaz threw his head back and chuckled. 'Ya haffi laugh, man'.

'But he might put bullet pon me,' said Willy. 'And I'm not so confident of them bouncing. And this,' he pointed to the laptop, 'is somewhat incriminating. If he reads this, we are sunk. Plus, I feel it incumbent on me with the prospect of your imminent death, to point out that you have not yet addressed my concerns about payment. My position is not good, Bangaz.'

'Nuh worry yourself bout dat,' Bangaz said with a wave of his hand. 'Me and you a roll, the Kingpin. We fully protected.'

'How are we fully protected?'

'With this ring,' said Bangaz, showing Willy the large cheap signet ring on his finger. 'Nutn can touch me, me have on this. Mi guard ring full a powaz. Nutn.'

Willy sighed.

'Nuh live in fear, white man!' Bangaz shouted. 'You valuable to the posse now. Understand? Okay? Now, stop fret. Start type.'

40

The Member of Parliament for the Parish of St John, The Honourable Herbert Aubyn Harris, Queen's Council and Minister of Justice, piloted his SUV through the gates of his family farm and set off on the road for Kingston, at the other end of the island. He drove on the new smooth highway, paid for by the Europeans, which meant he could avoid going through the little communities of his constituency, where bad things could happen. If there was a land dispute, or another problem with the police, or even just complaints about potholes, the villagers tended to exert their democratic rights by trying to apprehend their MP as he drove through. Using road blocks or honey traps, they brought him to a halt so they could vex with him and give him bad argument while he checked his doors were locked. Herbert, a largely peace-loving man, feared most being dragged from his car, particularly by some of the old women. The most dangerous place had been the fishing hamlet of Campbell Cove where he was once lured to a stop by a man offering fresh snapper and lobster. What followed had not been an enjoyable morning snack between breakfast and lunch, but a mini riot during which the entire community group up on him and drape him up with lyrics. Where was the new housing? Where was the water in the pipe gone? Where was the new school building? Yuh cock up in a big jeep and nah do nutn fi we don't even have a donkey. A dis we vote yuh in?

But on this fine June morning, Herbert tapped his fat fingers on the steering wheel and hummed a happy tune before swerving across the oncoming traffic and taking the turn onto the old road into Campbell Cove. His belly rumbled with hunger as he thought about the fish freshly grilled on the beach by Troy bar. He had not eaten for forty-five minutes and was famished.

He wound down his window. Yes! Going through Campbell Cove with his arm resting on the sill, pickney running out to watch him go by, and women waving from their porches. The election was only a few months away and the people were happy and the people loved him.

He pulled up where the old road faded into the fisherman's beach.

'Boss!' shouted Troy, and fling a lobster pon the grill.

Herbert sneaked a look into the gloom of the bar and waved coyly at Deliesha, whose slimatic body was catching the light in a way that made the Minister twitch. He considered her compact, girlish body and thought it to be exactly the kind of thing which was fair reward for the services to jurisprudence which Herbert had rendered as Minster of State for Justice.

Deliesha, meanwhile, was feasting her eyes on the Minister's steroidal car with its government sticker and attaché case on the passenger seat. Then she came to the door of the bar, put her hands on the lintel, took a long, lingering look at the fat bald head man with glasses and sweating neck, and felt a kick of excitement. Even though she knew no-one could see, she squinch up her pum-pum in anticipation. At last, she told herself, I buck up pon the kind of man I need in my life who cya put a end to mi worries.

Herbert climbed down from the cab, without a body guard and without a licensed firearm in his chubby hand. How things had changed. Sitting on the creaking bamboo bench he watched Troy plate up a snack of lobster, rice and roast plantain.

'Everyting good, mi boss?' Troy said to Herbert.

'Indubitably,' said the MP, eyeing Deliesha as she descended the concrete steps of which every riser and every tread was of a different length and none were parallel. She held out a cup to the Minister.

'You want try my special juice,' she said. 'Taste sweet, and give all the strength a big man need.'

Word reached Bangaz that the Minister was in the hood, and soon the Porsche drew up alongside Troy bar and its driver was bursting out, shouting and laughing and bumping fists and palms. Bangaz was the man who had bought peace and harmony to the Minister's life. Herbert was not certain exactly what business Bangaz was in, but he did know it was profitable, and as far as he could tell nobody was killed, which was often a feature of the other profitable enterprises in the parish.

After a pleasant stop, the Minister punched fists with Bangaz, took one last lingering look at the curve of Deliesha's bumpa, climbed into his vehicle and resumed his journey to the capital. He was particularly looking forward to a meeting with no less than the Ambassador of the United States, probably the most important person on the island, that very afternoon. He allowed himself to daydream about why he was being summoned to the US embassy. Did the man require legal advice on a personal matter? Maybe he wanted some help with a land investment in the country. Rich people had always liked to buy a bit of coastline.

Herbert drove down through the steep hills that surrounded Kingston and across the dusty plane, past old factories and rusted warehouses, into the residential streets that led up the hill towards New Kingston with its tower blocks, gated communities and orderly streets.

The Ambassador was a fine Republican from Kentucky called Brett Mactaggart. Six foot six, blond hair, he was an ex-footballer and property developer from a long line of Kentucky Republicans. He had only recently taken up the appointment of Ambassador after losing his congressional seat, and had frankly hoped for a better posting. But there was some decent golf on the North Coast, and a few of his old buddies came down to weekend with him at one of the beach hotels from time to time. Politically there was little to do but make sure the Jamaicans didn't turn communist, and that looked highly unlikely. Shirley, his wife, and their two kids had stayed for the time being in Kentucky because, well, frankly the schools didn't look so appropriate in Kingston. It could have been worse: he could be in some Arab country or African place where he would have been hated and in constant danger. In Jamaica he was a celebrity. Everybody loved him.

The Minister of Justice was shown into Brett's office looking suitably impressed and, yes, cowed by the magnificence of the building, the marines who guarded it and the majesty of Stars and Stripes that stood to attention behind his desk.

'What may I do for you, your excellency?' Herbert asked.

He shouldn't have used that title, but saw that Brett took it.

'I thought I'd have a quiet chat with you, off the record, to flag up a concern we have about some activities that have come to our attention,' Brett began.

'Of course,' said Herbert. 'What kind of activities are these?' He wondered if it was going to be about the volume of the music the people played at night. A lot of visitors had a problem with that.

'Confidence tricksters, also known as scammers.'

'I'm afraid I don't know what you mean,' said Herbert.

'It has come to the attention of law enforcement agencies in the US that your citizens are using the telephone to engage in illegal financial transactions with US citizens. They are stealing money.'

'Stealing money,' asked Herbert. 'How?'

'It's called scamming.'

Herbert shook his head. 'I'm afraid that doesn't mean anything to me,' he said. He was not telling the truth. He had heard about scamming. From Bangaz, in Campbell Cove. It sounded like some kind of Ponzi scheme he was running in America. Herbert wasn't entirely certain what it involved but he could tell it was an excellent enterprise. Jamaicans were not the ones losing out, and that is what mattered to him. After all the many business failures, something lucrative and peaceful had taken root in his constituency. Yes it might run a bit close to the law, but not in Jamaica, and the laws of another country were not Herbert's affair.

'My own mother-in-law, an elderly lady called Marjorie, has been sending money to someone in Jamaica because she thought she was going to receive a prize.'

Herbert tried not to smile. 'That is reprehensible, your excellency. I am so sorry. But tell me, how did she know these people were from Jamaica?'

'That's what I'm coming to.'

Herbert looked concerned, and tilted his head to one side.

'She sent the money, many hundreds of US dollars, to a Western Union office in a town called Lucea, in the parish of St John. I believe it is in your constituency. Western Union is currently refusing to open up its books to the FBI because of issues of jurisdiction.'

'That is unfortunate,' said Herbert.

'It's in your jurisdiction,' said the Ambassador coldly.

'Of course.'

'We believe that many of the victims in the States are not reporting the crime. They're ashamed. They feel stupid. But from early indications the Bureau has made an estimate that, in 2007, fifty million dollars was stolen from unsuspecting Americans. I believe this year it will be considerably more.'

That explained why things were so happy and peaceful in Campbell Cove.

'It's just a few wildcards, sir; hotheads with cell phones.'

'I want you to understand the severity of the situation.' The Ambassador paused as he picked a file and opened it. 'My mother-in-law, my own mother-in-law, sent eight payments amounting to 2400 US dollars in all to a person named Clive Thompson.'

Herbert cocked his head.

'Clive Thompson?'

'Yes. Do you know him?'

'No. But with a formal application from the FBI we can look into that,' Herbert said.

'There's not going to be a formal process, okay? I'm not dragging my mother-in-law into this. The point is, it must stop. You get it? We're not tolerating your people taking advantage of US citizens. Is that clear? Find these people. Root them out, arrest them, charge them, and sentence them heavily. Do what you need to do. It is your jurisdiction. Take a note of that name.' He looked back at the file. 'Clive Thompson.' He pointed at a little pad on the desk.

'I will do so this very minute,' said Herbert, leaning forward, writing on the pad and tearing the page off which he then folded and held up to the Ambassador. 'This is where the fight against the scammers starts.' He placed it in his pocket.

The Ambassador nodded approvingly. Herbert stood up, shook the Ambassador's hand and thanked him for the meeting. 'Please be assured, your eminence, that everything will be done to root out these miscreants and felons. No stone will go unturned. Consider the problem solved.'

Out in the car park Herbert felt for the note paper. He opened it up and read what he had written: Go suck your madda pussy hole. He screwed it up into a ball and tossed it into the dirt, then got in his car and drove home.

41

The following week, Herbert circle back to Cove. Deliesha skipped to the car and tugged his door open making a play of its weight.

'Minister.'

'Deliesha, always good to see a hard-working young constituent.'

'You know you can get my vote anytime.'

'I know exactly why I am in politics when I see a bright citizen like you.'

She led him into Troy's bar where she was restocking the top shelf with Hennessy, Krug, Grey Goose and Tanqueray. When she reached up high her crop top ride up her body. This she knew. Then she tek up the broom and sweep the confetti of phone credit across the mosaic and into a garbage bin already white with them. That done she entertained the Minister by bending to take up a few bottles and drop them in a case. Quite a few countries laid on fact finding missions for Ministers of State. There was something called Cop 21 coming up in Paris. His forensic brain examined the proposition: Herbert and Deliesha walking arm in arm down the Champs-Élysées on their way back to the Jamaican Government funded hotel bedroom for an afternoon ramp. Definitely a brilliant precedent to establish.

He finished his lobster, dash away the shell in the flames and went to the standpipe to wash his hands. He was thinking of a way to cautiously test the ground by asking Deliesha something like have you ever heard of a place called Paris? when his name was called.

'Mista Herbert! Big man! Up top!' He had asked to meet Bangaz in a quiet spot and recognised the croaky voice. And here the man was, bouncing on the balls of his feet, presenting a fist. 'Minister! Greetings and guidance. Oh my lord it is a blessing to have you among us. The safety of the community is assure. Every pockhole will full!'

'You chat like a politician,' said the Minster, allowing his gaze to linger on Deliesha's bubble butt before turning.

'Mi neva turn politician. Mi hard working business man.'

'Mek we talk in my car,' Herbert said.

They got in, Bangaz rather more easily than the well-padded Minister, and closed the doors.

Herbert said 'I know I can count on your support with the election coming up, but I want to give you some funds to make sure your bredren all go out to vote and put their tick in the right box. For their expenses, only.' Herbert clicked open his attaché case and took out a small wad of Jamaican currency.

'Cho!' admonished Bangaz, waving the money away. It was a paltry sum, and he had more important things to talk to his MP about. 'You know the loyalty of all of my thugs and all of my people is right behind you. I don't need no cash to secure it.' With those words he took the money and put it in his back pocket.

'Good, good, good,' said Herbert. 'Also, I was wondering, do you know if young Deliesha is married, or has a steady boyfriend?'

'Nobody control Deliesha,' Bangaz said. 'Now. I have something to give you.' He withdrew from his pocket a thicker wad of US currency. It was a $1000. Pauline had counted it out before handing it to him.

'What's this for?' Herbert blushed, popping it into the case and shutting the clasps before Bangaz changed his mind. 'I mean what can I do for you? Is it legal advice you need?'

'No. Mi nuh want no legal advice.'

'What is it?'

'You ever hear of consultancy fee?'

Herbert smiled. 'What am I consulting about? I cannot join or condone unlawful behaviour.'

'Cho! Just cool man. Dat nuh go happen.'

'You are a valuable local business, Bangaz, bringing much needed investment into the economy of this parish,' Herbert said. 'And I have always been very pro-business. It is on my record. So how can I help?'

'I need to know what the police plan for us.'

Herbert paused. 'Am I correct in thinking you have something to do with lottery fraud?'

'Can be a possibility.'

'While there remain no Jamaican victims and no violence in Jamaica you will enjoy the support of most people. But I can tell you last week the American Ambassador called me in to complain about scammers. That's what you call yourselves?'

'Some say scammers some say choppers.'

'And I sense the Americans are going to take some action against you.'

'This how you earn your consultancy fee, seen? You know we never use guns or never rob a Jamaican. Make sure the big people in town know that.'

'I will. And I believe the police and government think there are higher priorities for the law enforcement agencies to be pursuing than lottery fraud.'

'Yes. Very good. That just a down payment on any information received.'

Herbert watched a fishing boat approach over the water. He said, 'The FBI are setting up an office in Kingston.'

'To deal with scamming?'

'Yes. A woman called Lieutenant Tilson is going to run it.'

'Dat sound like restraint of trade,' Bangaz said.

Herbert smiled.

Bangaz opened the door. 'Keep me in the loop,' he said. 'I don't want that office to open.'

'It does sound like a bad idea, I agree,' said Herbert. 'Based on what is optimum for the economy.'

'See what you can do, you is the Minister, and come back and I will give you a help towards expenses and sundry costs.'

He jumped down.

Herbert sat in the car, but didn't turn the key in the ignition. He wanted one last glimpse of Deliesha, who was in the shed filling and knotting 50J bags of weed. He was no gallis, Herbert; he was a shy and bookish man. His life had been a lot of hard work in the library, which had propelled him from rural Jamaica to a seat at the top table, via a Rhodes scholarship to Oxford University and a successful legal practice. He had felt called by his country to create order and respect for the rule of law, and he wanted to leave his mark on the nation. He wanted to leave it a better place than he had found it. As a young man he had ambitions to create a Jamaica with an international reputation for being law-abiding, peaceful, hard-working, incorrupt and maybe, as a bonus, quiet. In his college rooms at Oxford he envisaged Jamaica as the Switzerland of the Caribbean, respected all over the world, with a solid currency, a culture of hard work, and an admired, decent society.

Thirty years later he could not exactly shout Mission Accomplished! Deliesha came to the door of Troy bar, pretended to be surprised he was still there, smiled and waved at him. He wondered if maybe there were other aspects of Jamaica he needed to turn his brilliant legal mind to. Deliesha now walked towards him, burning hot and trailing a wake of mischief. As he stared at her supple back, cute botty and toned legs, a plan formed in his brilliant legal mind. Herbert was thinking: foreign trip. Ideally two nights. Revise that: three nights. This was a clear opportunity. He wasn't getting any younger. He had to seize the day. But it wasn't carpe diem, it was carpe Deliesha.

Herbert opened his window and tried to summon some words. He had planned to say does the issue of global warming worry you?'

But Deliesha spoke first. 'Minister,' she said, 'You ever tink of carry a gal like me inna foreign?'

Over the next few weeks, the Minister traded delightful and dangerous texts with Deliesha. She wanted a shoes and a dress for Paris. She needed a coat. She suggested lingerie. Paris: it was an insane idea.

To create cover for their meetings, Herbert dug around for information that could be useful to Bangaz. He would have passed it over for free just to have an excuse to see Deliesha, but that would be odd, so he charged Bangaz for the intelligence. The cash came in useful for the mounting expenses of the Paris trip. When Herbert ran out of secrets, his laser intellect came up with what he called Operation Top-Up. He had started by passing to Bangaz details of all road blocks planned for the parishes of St James and St John. As he grew more horny and Deliesha's demands increased, he had to pay the police to put up road-blocks, the whereabouts of which he then sold at a profit to Bangaz.

Bangaz realised that the flow of solid intelligence depended on the irresistible curve of Deliesha's bumpa and the promise of her smile. He never spoke to Deliesha about it. They were from Campbell Cove. They knew without chat. But he made certain that the bartender and the Minister of State for Justice were not disturbed.

42

The opening of the Federal Bureau of Investigation's satellite office in Kingston was blighted by a number of unfortunate delays. The signage and furniture freighted from the States were lost at the wharf. They finally turned up in Port-Au-Prince. A second consignment was dispatched a month later which did make it through, and the sign was finally fixed above the door of the FBI office in New Kingston, but was stolen two nights later.

At the press launch for the enterprise, Herbert shook hands withSenior Officer Rachel Tilson, a lady with thin lips and red hair pulled back into a tight bunch, while the Gleaner photographed them. As Herbert stood there holding a queasy smile he thought this gonna mash up my majority. His only hope was that Bangaz would explain what really was going on.

The FBI had a tough first few months: Officer Tilson's car was stolen four times and her son, on a short visit, was busted for ganja. She also had to deal with a sex scandal involving two of her officers and some women from Negril. In addition, the electricity to the FBI office was accidentally cut off three times and the water twice, but Officer Tilson was a G woman: tough and determined.

In her spare time, at her home in a gated community, Officer Tilson designed a poster which said:

WANTED:
SCAMMERS
DEAD or ALIVE
For theft of US$ 90,000,000
From US citizens

She fixed the poster to the wall of her office behind her desk, and liked to draw guests' attention to it.

Officer Tilson was aware of the obstacles being put in her way. It was clear the legal and political systems were in no hurry to run these scammers to ground. She was going to have to do it on her own.

The problem boiled down to this: she could find citizens who were scammed in the States, and they could arrest scammers in Jamaica, but until they connected the two, she didn't have a case. She had to get hold of a phone or laptop or PC which had the details of a US citizen who had been defrauded of money.

When arrests were made the police either failed to find any phones, or only seized phones which were broken. If working phones were impounded, the courts always returned them to their owners before Tilson could get her hands on them. It was like everybody was protecting the scammers. On one occasion, Officer Tilson was told the police had seized a couple of phones but, while an officer was driving them over to her at the FBI office, the car hit a bump and both phones flew off the dash board, out of the window and into a river.

'We sent in police diver dem,' the officer told Tilson, shaking his head sadly, 'but we nuh find dem.'

Officer Tilson gave up with the police and instead scheduled an interview with the head of security at Digiflow, the mobile phone network. Had Officer Tilson spent time in Campbell Cove, she would have seen the two mobile phone masts on the hills at each end of the community and walked over the confetti on the floors of the bars where phone credit was sold, and have noticed that most male citizens possessed a minimum of four phones. She would have drawn the conclusion that the phone companies were, like

most other institutions, connected to the scamming industry and were doing very well out of it.

'To root out this criminality,' Tilson explained to the phone executive,
'I need to have access to the mobile phone records of all callers in the Parish of St John. For starters.'

'I see,' said Melvin Cuttler, the head of Security, a gentle bearded man
with a round head and big hands. 'Ultimately I think this would be a matter for the Ministry of Justice to consult on in terms of the Telecoms Act
and The Interception of Communication Act, and to first come to a judgement about the legality of this ...'

'I have already spoken to The Minister, what's he called ... Herbert
Harris.'

'Did you receive the relevant support?'

'No,' Tilson snapped. 'I don't know what's wrong with that man. He
just makes notes and then absolutely nothing happens. Except roadblocks.
The number of roadblocks that man puts up. Total waste of time. He said
he wanted to put it to judicial review which, if he fast tracked, would take
eighteen months to get an initial hearing.'

'I am sorry.'

'I'm not saying we look at everyone's records, right?' said Tilson
through gritted teeth. 'Just the ones we are pretty sure are scammers.'

'We don't ...' started Melvin, then paused and said, 'I would say nobody comes through the door and says, to use your terms, I am a scammer.'

'I am aware of that. Look...' she started again.

'I apologise for interrupting, but our recommendation is you route this
through your consulate or whatever. That way we will see if we cya help.'

To Tilson, it was one of the most maddening features of the Jamaican
language that can't and can sounded exactly the same. Had the man said we
will see if we can't help you it would not have surprised her. She thought
fondly of the day in her training when she had been taught to kill a man
with her bare hands. 'It would be a lot quicker and serve justice better if
you worked directly with us,' she said.

'I agree,' said Melvin. 'Wouldn't it? But unfortunately, it doesn't work that way. Most regrettably. But on the topic of scamming, may I add an observation?'

'What?'

'I know you Americans will look at it differently, but some things point to the gullibility of some of these people getting these calls. You have not entered something, and you have magically won,' he spread his hands in surprise. 'I'm sorry, a free lunch is just not being given away. Maybe your energy could be better spent. Look, this is an "educate the public" situation, do you not agree? In your own country. That's where the trouble start. But then everyone wants a free lunch, so here we are. Aren't we?'

Tilson and her inner circle of officers devised a plan that didn't involve taking Jamaican police into their confidence. When the suspects were arrested and their machines seized, she, with her IT specialist, would surreptitiously load a software reader inside them which could then send information back to the bureau after the computers were returned to the scammer, which they inevitably were.

She combed through the list of suspects and picked a dozen names.

'Come on team, we're going west. We are making arrests and we are making extraditions.'

43

The passport came through and Herbert hurried to Campbell Cove to place it into Deliesha's eager hands.

She stared at the book, examining the photo, while Herbert said, 'This means you can be my plus one for Paris.'

Deliesha closed the passport, looked into Herbert's wise and foolish eyes and said, 'How mi ever gonna pay you back?'

He managed to wangle a temporary diplomatic accreditation out of his colleague in the Diplomatic Department (it was a standard request) so went ahead and purchased Deliesha's ticket, putting her in economy on his flight to London. He daydreamed about leaving first class, walking past her seat and seeing her pretty smile. All would be secret till they touched down in Charles De Gaulle. But even economy cost Herbert over 1200US, leaving him short. He called the Commissioner of the Police and organised two roadblocks and two house searches, netting the Minister sufficient for a set of lingerie and a baby-doll negligee.

One soft romantic evening when the moon flooded the cove with its serene glow, Herbert put Deliesha's Cop 21 lanyard, which had arrived by post that day, around her neck, laying a paternal kiss her on the top of her head, while out of sight she crossed her eyes.

'Are you as excited as I am?' he whispered.

'Mi moss. But mi want one overhead locker bag and neck pillow.'

'I will get you one,' he murmured. 'Whatever you need, you shall have,' adding, 'not literally.'

Herbert would give her his undivided attention in Paris. He wouldn't bother with the conference beyond a quick walk through. He believed anti-global warming policies were a thinly disguised attempt by rich countries to deny Jamaica the fruits of its hard work. It was not an opinion he aired in public. Through back breaking drudgery, smart thinking and determination Jamaicans had earnt cars, international air travel, and a whole heap of electrical contraption. But now they were being told they weren't allowed to use them. At stake? Climate catastrophe. It wasn't a prospect a Jamaican, who lived through regular hurricanes, floods and landslides, thought more catastrophic than losing their car and AC unit. The people of the parish of St John had already been through a two hundred year man-made disaster and were still fighting for survival scores of years later. The Jamaicans in his constituency were not worried about the sea rising forty centimetres, they were already living with it at their chins, economically speaking.

Herbert thought about taking one of his wife's overnight bags from the pile of suitcases under the stairs, but instead wandered round the New Kingston shopping mall in a daze of love looking at every suitcase he could find, imagining Deliesha's lingerie nuzzling up inside it. Yes, Herbert was married, and had been married for over twenty years. But this was the first lunch hour he had spent in a swoon of love over another woman.

In Paris, he would dress Deliesha in their room. Once he had her looking right, they would go out not hesitantly but brazenly, side by side, inviting photographs. That was dangerous territory but nothing he couldn't deal with, since his infatuation had skewered his judgment. Deliesha would be in close attendance at the Governmental level cocktail party on the opening night. He would feel President Macron's eyes rake her body. Sex appeal. Appeal? That was for white people. Deliesha had sex demand. It issued a direct order. No man could disobey its call.

44

Pauline made an appointment to see Liar Reynolds in his new office in Freeport, Montego Bay. Freeport was a recent, high-end housing and hotel development with no potholes, no pedestrians, no music, no litter and no poor people. She strap with the brick of cash Bangaz give her. There was a lift up to the sixth floor, where she waited for an hour in a chair, looking at the people through the glass partition working at their desks, thinking how it was like an American TV show.

Finally, a woman with a headset showed her into a room where Brian Reynolds sat behind a wooden desk.

'I come to talk to you about some land,' Pauline said.

'Sit down, please,' said Reynolds. 'Do I know you?'

'Not really know me, sir. But long time my husband Clive Thompson came to your Negril office with Maas Henry Campbell when he sell out his island at Plantation Hotel.'

A smile bloomed on Reynolds' features. 'Ya man, I remember. Long time.'

'Yes.'

'Your husband is well?'

'Very,' said Pauline.

Mr Reynolds suddenly looked serious. 'This not about Maas Henry is it?'

'No man, no man,' said Pauline.

'Good. How may I be of assistance?'

'I come about some land.'

'The island again? It's 500 for title deed transfer, but you can't use my office. There's a couple of guys in Lucea who will help with that.'

'No. I don't want to sell no land. I want to buy land. I find a nice little piece near our yard. I have money.'

'You have the money?' Reynolds said.

'Yes.'

'How much is it?'

'The man aks for twenty-five grand but we agree twenty-one.'

Pauline looked into her white Vuitton, pulled out the brick and placed it on the desk.

Reynolds stared at it, looked at Pauline, and said 'You can put that away until later. Right. Name of vendor and address?'

Reynolds took her through the formalities, stopping when it came to the buyer's name.

'Clive Thompson,' Pauline said.

'Source of funds?' The lawyer asked.

'What do that mean?' said Pauline.

Reynolds looked up at her. 'Where did the money come from? A gift, a sale, a legacy?'

'It private source of funds.'

He put down his pen. He stood up, went to the door and locked it.

'This conversation is covered by client attorney privilege.'

Pauline stared at him.

'This a secret. Nobody ever gonna hear what we say now. I am inferring that your husband came by these funds in an informal capacity. They are not, for instance, inside the tax system? Or coming with a receipt of payment from their source?'

Pauline slowly nodded.

'Okay. Don't worry. I can look after you. Source of funds is required, but it is mainly by the Americans, and there are certain technical ways we can satisfy them without revealing unnecessary details. You understand?'

'I understand.'

'It will cost 4% of funds.'

'Mi undastan. Mi cool wid dat.'

'Good to do business with you,' Reynolds said.

'And you Mr Reynolds.'

'Please, call me Brian.'

45

Herbert's wife was called Emmeline; she was a tall and handsome woman, with high cheekbones, carved shoulders and a long straight nose which slightly overshot her nostrils. She taught sculpture at the Edna Manley College of Visual and Performing Arts in Kingston and had exhibited her work, without disinterest, in private and public galleries. She now sat beside her husband in the back of his Ministerial car on the way to a cocktail party at the Chinese Embassy. As they cruised the wide streets of New Kingston they made use of the time aligning their diaries.

'The second week of June we go to Miami,' she said.

'Mm. You'll have to do that one without me, I'm afraid. I have some boring government overseas commitment. It's a four-dayer more's the pity. I'll be sorry to miss Thalia and Jake.'

'What is it?'

'What?' asked Herbert feigning vagueness.

'The overseas thing.'

'Er, let me look. A thing called, er, Cop. Very dull. A talking shop about carbon emissions or some such nonsense.'

'That's the global climate crisis conference.'

'Yes. Climate change has many legal implications which the Boss wants me to consider.'

'That's fascinating. My students are all so motivated about it. But hey, isn't it in Paris?'

'Paris? Er, I think so, yes. I didn't really take it in.'

'Oh, but I must come too. June, in Paris? Ooh la la. When you are at the speeches I can wander round the Louvre and the Jeu de Paumes. And at night I will drag you away from the boring old conference and we can have a romantic dinner. Boring? Paris is the city for lovers,' she laughed. 'I'm not going to Miami, I'm coming with you.'

After that conversation Herbert screw face and nuh deal with everybody for two days. He detoured to the fishermen's beach at the first opportunity. Deliesha's carefree skip to his car gave him a stabbing pain in his belly.

He broke the news. 'I'm afraid wifey hear about my trip, and is coming with me. Three would be a crowd.'

Everything she had hoped for slip through her hands: fly on airplane, see another country, brandish new clothes, see shops, see new city, meet new people and most of all: leave Campbell Cove, the backwater where her life was draining away. She feel like her throat cut open. It was the most disappointing and painful moment of her life, but Deliesha looked at him impassively. She would not show him a tear.

'I am so sorry, dear Deliesha. I promise you it is unavoidable.'

In a small, imploring voice, she said 'I can be quiet.'

Herbert felt his phone ring.

'Listen to me, please,' Deliesha said.

He glanced at the screen. 'I have to take this.' He turned away from her. 'Prime Minister.'

'Herbert, I am under some considerable pressure from our American friends to make sure some of the suspects in these scamming cases are charged and extradited. To that end I want you to give me an assurance that no Government agency or private citizen will interfere in the FBI actions over the next few days.'

'The FBI do not have right of arrest in Jamaica, Prime Minister. We cannot set that precedent.'

'Go, then. Go to Paris with your wife,' Deliesha said, turning and walking with heavy feet up the steps and out of sight into the bar. Herbert watched her walk away, the Prime Minister carried on.

'They are asking to place reading and tracking software in the suspects' devices while they are held for questioning. When the suspects are released and they use their devices again, the evidence collected in the US will be sufficient to justify extradition. They have a list of suspects who they are confident they can charge and transfer into the US justice system. We will not stand in their way. Brett Kavanagh said they are planning to hand out severe sentences as a deterrent. Ten years. It's a Federal offence. I've just attended a meeting with Brett and am forwarding the list of the suspects who are being targeted by the FBI. I am asking you, as Justice Minister, not to allow any interference with the process. We have to throw them some red meat, Herbert, or they will start to come after us.'

'I understand,' said Herbert.

'I also understand the argument that these crimes do not fall under our jurisdiction,' said the Prime Minister. 'And I know there is a great deal of sympathy for the young men who are doing no more than selling a dream, like many others have before, and fair criticism of the fools who fall for it. But this is for the good of Jamaica. We must retain the trust and friendship of our American friends who, in the totality of the picture, do so much for us as a nation.'

'I understand. Leave it with me, Prime Minister.'

'Thank you, Herbert. Goodbye.'

Herbert and Emmeline would be flying British Airways to London on the afternoon flight on Monday. From there they were taking a connecting flight to Paris. In the taxi on the way to Norman Manley International, Herbert received an email with the list of suspects due to be arrested.

Clive 'Bangaz' Thompson was the third name on it.

His first instinct was to tell the driver to turn round and drive the four hours to Campbell Cove to meet Bangaz on the beach and tell him of the danger. Then find Deliesha and somehow swap her for Emmeline.

But he couldn't tell Bangaz. It was a trap for Herbert. Officer Tilson would report him to the Prime Minister. He had to let Bangaz go. As soon as Bangaz turned on his computer he was on a fast track to a Federal penitentiary for a ten year stretch. Maybe it was for the best. He was, after all, a scammer. And his association with Herbert was tricky.

Outside Departures, Herbert tipped the driver and summoned a porter to load the bags before heading inside. As they swept, in a triumph of privilege, past the snaking queue for economy, his eyes were caught by a wig the colour of a hi-viz tabard on a girl wearing skin-tight white trousers, a crop top and eyelashes the size of awnings. It was Deliesha, in the line for check-in. Herbert had been too blinded by love to notice that the more he had spent on Deliesha's appearance the faster she had transformed from cute beach gamine to fifty dollar hooker.

'Can you stay with the bags,' he said to Emmeline. 'I've just seen someone I know.'

He dashed back round the corner and found Deliesha. 'What are you doing? Ya cya come. Ya cannot get on the plane.'

'Why?'

'Because you won't be able to deal with Paris on your own. You don't even have a coat.'

'Buy me one.'

'I can't. I told you that. You must leave the airport.'

'I can't go back to Cove now. Me nuh have no money.'

Herbert took out his wallet and peeled off some bills.

'There. That'll get you back safe. I'll see you as soon as I get back. I promise. I promise.'

He dashed back to Emmeline who stood at the desk checking-in.

Emmeline reached for the boarding cards and said to Herbert, 'who was that?'

'Oh, a constituent.'

'Where is she from?'

'Campbell Cove. Did you see her?'

'Did you give her money?'

'Yes, a little help for her first trip abroad.'

'Did I notice she had a Cop 21 lanyard?'

'Yes. She… is… a climate activist.'

'A climate activist from Campbell Cove?'

'Yes.'

'There is yet hope for our beautiful planet.'

On the plane, after a meal and brief siesta, Herbert got out of his seat to stretch his legs. He paused to look fondly at Emmeline asleep, then pushed through the curtain to get his money's worth, parading down the cramped chaotic seating of coach, when he spotted the mat of yellow nylon and spidery eyelashes; his stomach lurched.

'Hi!' she called out, waving and smiling from seat 65C.

'Deliesha,' he hissed through his teeth. 'What are you doing here?' He smiled and nodded at the passengers around her.

She said, 'Mi go a foreign, sah.'

Herbert's first fear, and there were many on the list, was, had he blurted out the name of his hotel while boasting to her at the beach? 'But you have nowhere to go,' he said. 'You cannot stay with me. It's not possible.'

'Mi nuh want fi stay with you,' Deliesha said. 'I don't like you. I will make my own way. Leave me alone. Go back a wifey.'

A woman in the row behind Deliesha stifled a laugh. Herbert grappled his way back up the aisle.

46

Pauline made sure she look pretty pretty for her meetings with Liar Reynolds. She wear a white suit tight pon her body. With his help she bought various lots of land up and across the hill behind Campbell Cove. Liar Reynolds twice introduced her to some old people who needed to sell out and preferred to sell it to Pauline than some white businessman from a foreign.

Pauline looked forward to the days that she and Liar Reynolds met for lunch and drove out together to look at parcels of land. On the way to a poor rural community he said , 'As your legal counsel I would like to draw your attention to the proposed Proceeds of Crime Act. As it may affect your husband's position.'

'We nuh married,' Pauline said.

'That could be advantageous,' said Reynolds. 'You see, if in the future an inquiry into his assets revealed they were gained unlawfully, Mr Thompson could stand to have them confiscated. I would suggest as your attorney that the assets were put in someone else's name to prevent that happening. I offer a service to hold them in trust off shore, if you wanted. For safety's sake. Belt and braces.'

Pauline said, 'Mi haffi go check it out and get back to you.'

Reynolds changed down gear to deal with a steep hill, brushing Pauline's sheer stockings.

'Sorry,' he said.

Later that day she found Bangaz sitting at the kitchen island building a spliff. She explained what Reynolds had suggested, and added that the land should be put in a trust for him in Caymans.

'To keep it out of the feds hands,' said Pauline.

Bangaz licked the wizla, put it to his mouth and lit it.

'I don't want no land in no Cayman trust. Dat foolishness.'

'Okay, hun, mi hear yuh, but if yuh get catch and dem charge you we inna problem for keep the land.'

Marva appeared with a mop in her hand. It was strange how often the floor needed a mop when Bangaz and Pauline talked about money.

'Put all the land in fi you name,' Bangaz said to Pauline.

Marva stop mop and stare at Bangaz.

He said, 'You can protect my money if anything go wrong.'

'Okay. You know you can trust me,' Pauline said.

'I know I can trust you,' Bangaz said. The mop bucket clang.

'Reynolds said if we had any more money he can recommend some more land opportunities.'

'I leave it to you, Pauline. You are my baby madda and you are my empress.'

Marva came out of the laundry room and said, 'Lord, Bangaz you lucky to have a woman so close who you cya trust with your money. Mi wish mi have a sum of money to put down on a piece of land for mi old age.'

'He pay your rent,' Pauline said.

'Rent. Mi nuh want to pay rent. Mi a old woman now, mi nuh want to pay rent all the days of mi life. Mi want sump for myself. Mi cya pay rent till mi dead. Why can't I have a decent sum to buy a property? You is my own son. You know some of dem dutty landlord demand sex for the rent?'

'I think you're safe there,' said Pauline.

47

Standing in the queue to check in at the hotel, feeling he had done a bad thing to Deliesha, Herbert noticed that the receptionist either couldn't or wouldn't speak English, but it didn't matter because Emmeline took over in her fluent French. When they had unpacked, Herbert found his notebook and stared out of the window at two pigeons and some empty balconies. Emmeline was in the bathroom preparing for a walk along the Seine she wanted them to do. Herbert's mind wandered in a different direction: to Deliesha. That had been a close one. He was so relieved that Emmeline, with her familiar ways, was sharing the room with him. He now realised how much he needed his wife. To stiffen his resolve and discipline he wrote HERBERT: DO THE RIGHT THING a little bit too hard in biro at the top of the page.

'What's that?' Emmeline said standing behind him clipping on her ear-rings. She looked cosmopolitan and sophisticated with that dash of that self-belief bordering on defiance that Jamaicans possessed in such abundance.

'My speech. Just going over it.'

Her finger pointed at the paper. 'Herbert. Do the right thing? I never thought you cared about climate change. Do you want to try it on me?'

This was something they sometimes did.

'Okay,' said Herbert, turning in his seat and glancing at the words. 'The Santiago Network was established by the United Nations Framework on Climate Change last year with the aim of providing technical support to help developing countries deal with loss and damage from climate change...'

Emmeline smiled at the opening sentence. It was not oratory to move hearts. She was not married to Nelson Mandela or Dr King. But her little thorough Herbert had inched his way to the top of politics with facts and figures, and legal and technical know-how, which left the opposition flattened behind him. Often, it must said, with boredom.

'....For small island countries like Jamaica, global warming and rising sea levels represent an existential challenge which will cause tremendous damage and lead to massive displacement of people especially from low lying parts of the island. Page 3 of 5 Concrete action accompanied by adequate and predictable funding is, therefore, absolutely essential....'

He droned on for ten minutes ending without a flourish.

When it was over, Emmeline clapped her hands. 'Perfect,' she said. 'You always do the right thing my love. Now come on, let's go out and enjoy this beautiful world before it goes up in flames.'

The next day Emmeline, map in hand, headed to the Pompidou Centre, and Herbert descended into the Metro to ride to the climate conference at Le Bourget. The carriage was filled with young, prosperous, literate and educated Europeans of every hue, hunched over their tablets and phones or engaged in earnest debate. Looking at these delegates, Herbert thought of Deliesha, Bangaz and the yout of Campbell Cove sitting on the bamboo bench. For brains and balls he'd back Deliesha and Bangaz over this lot any day. But Bangaz and Deliesha were forced to take drastic action to carve out a life for themselves. That thought reminded him: where was Deliesha?

Inside the conference hall, he took a sweep through the booths and side rooms looking out for her brass hair. Nothing. He tried to look as though he was on his way to an important meeting with a German Minister, but ran out of steam and ended up standing by a pillar, lost in his thoughts about Deliesha. A horrible truth sliced through him. She disliked her life in Jamaica so much she was prepared to have sex with Herbert to escape it. Herbert – married, 54 and 187 lbs.

There was a break in the session in the main hall, and suddenly the corridors foamed with men and women in loud conversation about the horrors of climate change. A river of people flowed past him, in which Herbert saw someone he recognised: a man he'd been to university with, years before, called Tom Popham.

'Hello! Hello. Do you remember me? Herbert Aubyn.'

He was taller than Herbert with a bald head and big chin. He looked at Herbert and said, 'I do apologise, forgive me. I can't seem to remember. When did we meet?'

'We were in college together,' said Herbert.

'You mean at university? At Oxford?'

'Yes, I was at Oriel with you.'

'What year?'

'Your year! In first year my room was three doors down from you.'

'Was it?' Tom peered at Herbert's name badge.

'Herbert! Of course! Herbert. How the hell are you?'

'I'm very well, thank you.'

'A Cabinet minister!' he read off the badge. 'Well I'll be damned. Congratulations. I'm so pleased for you. Family?'

'My wife is here in Paris and we have two children who currently live in the States. Jason is an attorney.'

'I'm an MP too,' said Tom. 'In fact, I'm chairman of the Foreign Affairs select committee. Are you very involved with, er, this...' he waved his arm around.

'We are a member of the AOSIS, that's the Alliance of Small Island States. I'm giving a brief speech at their fringe meeting this afternoon. 4 o'clock.'

'That sounds a bit like too much excitement for me, but if I'm free I'll put my head around the door.'

Herbert smiled. 'Tell me, Tom, do you have any input into UK foreign investment policy?'

The question irked Tom.

'We always need investment in Jamaica,' Herbert continued. 'And we are a country with a very big future.'

'It is in the committee's remit,' said Tom, and then paused. He put his finger on his chin. 'You know what my best advice is? Get your house in order first. You know what I mean?'

'No, I don't,' said Herbert. 'What do you mean?'

Tom masked his thoughts with a thin smile. He quietly said 'Reparations.'

'Yes?' said Herbert.

'We don't need this subject being brought up in the UK. It's really not helpful to your cause. It's counter-productive, you know, calling for them.'

Herbert was not a man of extreme emotion, but felt himself boil with anger. He had never himself asked for reparations; to him it felt undignified, like begging, but to be silenced by this man with his fine suit and slender arms was too much. Why is it, Herbert asked himself, that Jamaica never got the spoils? Why did they always go to Tom Popham and his kind?

'Look,' said Tom, resting a hand on Herbert's arm. 'Come and see me in The House when you're next in London and we can talk it through...' They exchanged pleasantries and parted company. Herbert wandered aimlessly down the corridors with all the things he wanted to say to Tom but hadn't, ringing in his head. He needed to focus on his speech.

Through the circular window of a double door he saw the podium in a small half-filled lecture hall. Herbert wandered into the chamber and looked up at its raked seats. The moderator introduced himself to Herbert and led him to the stage. As he approached the lectern, he reached for his speech, but felt his hand leave the paper in his pocket as different words bubbled up in his mind. They were urgent words, and angry.

'Bonjour et good afternoon,' Herbert started into the microphone. 'I come from western Jamaica.' He took a deep breath. 'I do not deny the importance of climate change, but I want to talk about the last man made disaster caused by the northern hemisphere that ruined the lives of my people. Which I believe is even more urgent. My constituents were impoverished by slavers and colonisers, whose descendants sit at this conference.'

Almost all of the audience nodded in agreement. With what it was hard to tell.

'But nothing at all has been done to help my constituents,' Herbert said, going a little hoarse. 'We have never had a conference such as this to address our concerns. Nothing has been done to help our plight. Why, for instance, do we not have a university in West Jamaica? And by that I don't mean a few rooms upstairs at a shopping mall where people learn to make a spread sheet and get a certificate. I mean a campus with halls of residence, classrooms, lecture rooms, canteens, student bars, studios, labs, teaching spaces, full faculties, theatres, all laid out attractively, properly funded with secure and safe green spaces. The kind of place that everyone from Europe has access to. And where are our art schools? Or our film schools? Where are our film studios?'

Some people started looking at their phones to see what had happened with the schedule, but others sat passively half listening to Herbert.

'Where are the Spanish and Chinese language courses? And the engineering courses? Where can my constituents be taught to be a mechanic, an engineer, a nurse or doctor? I will tell you: nowhere. You left a wasteland when you went, and you never came back to help us rebuild. And now you ask us to help you with another mess you made for all of us. You know, the only vocational courses available to my constituents are to train our young people – people like you – to be waiters, to bring you cocktails at sunset. Well prepare yourselves. Because now they're bringing you your bill.'

That night, as he settled with his wife into the table for two in the cute restaurant Emmeline had found on the hill in Montmartre, with the winding cobbled street outside, and the glow of candles inside, Emmeline said 'So how did it go today?'

Herbert had expected to be fired for his outburst, but nobody had reported it, and nobody even commented on it on the media, so there were advantages to being entirely ignored by the world's press.

'Today was a good day,' Herbert said. ' I saw a lot and I learnt a lot. So much that I think I am driven to taking some direct action. Today, I did the right thing.'

48

While Emmeline and Herbert sat drinking fine Burgundy and eating garlic snails in Paris, four police took bolt cutters to Bangaz's ornate gates, rushed the yard and hammered on his front door.

Bangaz looked down from his Tuscan balcony. Three cop cars and an unmarked vehicle blocked the lane. The unmarked car was Officer Tilson's, recently back on the road after getting two punctures in one day.

The officers wore balaclavas but Bangaz recognised them. The one who cuffed his hands and pushed him into the squad car was Patrick, pretending not to know him. Bangaz saw Tilson, the white woman with the red hair standing with her arms crossed in the grey light. As he was driven away he saw eight police going into his house.

In the back of the police car Bangaz strong himself fi face it. He had seen the American lady and he prepared himself from that moment for extradition. He was ready to deal with it.

At the lock-up they pulled a grill and pushed Bangaz into a group cell.

A prisoner shouted, 'take off your shoes! You think this a your yard?'

Across the cell the prisoners already had Toffee, and were making him climb the bars of the grill for fun, hitting his fingers with water bottles full of water cork tight. Toffee wore a torn satin shirt and stained white jeans.

'Go pick some ackee!' they shouted at him, forcing him up the bars again again.

Being little, Bangaz grew scared. He was dragged by the collar and presented to two prisoners who'd been in the lock-up on remand for two years. One was called the judge, and the other the liar. The judge was a big bald man with a belly spilling out under his T-shirt. The liar was an old fellow with white hair and missing teeth. Bangaz was made to stand in front of the two of them and present his case, while the judge and the liar listen carefully to every detail while dem blaze dem weed.

Bangaz explained what had happened.

The old man said 'The case dash out. The only problem you have is if the Americans get to see a computer and phone. The Jamaicans don't business wid dat stuff.'

The judge said 'You don't got nutn to worry about: six weeks for ganja possession and you will be free.' He then said 'Now you have to pay liar and court fee.' He handed Bangaz a phone, which had credit and charge, and said 'Get us a food.'

Bangaz rang Pauline.

'Dem take the computer and bangers?' he asked.

'Dem tek everyting outa the house,' she said.

'None o dem sound American? Yuh see nuh FBI?'

'Ongle pure Jamaican only I see. Patrick de deh.'

'Mi see him. Look, mi want you to bring me some food, plenty, for couple a da yout here in the cell block to the lock up in Lucea. Can you do that? And call Liar Reynolds, tell him mi dung here.'

'Him here right now, he reach round after the raid. He's been looking after me and the girl dem.'

Two hours later the guard come to the cell with ten box meal in a white poly, fish, rice, chicken, mutton, goat, yam, plantain, and even in the sauce pot JB white rum. Pauline even sent credit to the judge's phone. Thus Bangaz made friends in the cell and held many good reasoning and meditations with the other prisoners.

On the second day, he heard his name being called.

'Clive Thompson, tek up your tings,' the guard said pulling back the grill.

'Ah,' said a familiar deep voice. 'My client. Guard. Remove those hand cuffs immediately. This is an innocent man.'

'Yes, Mr Reynolds.'

'They treat you good?' Reynolds asked Bangaz as they walked out of the police station.

'Ya man,' nodded Bangaz.

'I have served an order of habeas corpus for your release, and another order for the quick and safe return of any items of yours which were removed illegally from your home. I am just here to clarify and clear up. The computer, laptops and phones were about to be sent to the new IT police lab in town, but they had no evidence to connect them with you as they searched your house without a dated warrant and so seized them illegally.'

'Respect and manners, every time sir.'

'My pleasure. I will be billing you.'

'No problem.'

When Bangaz pushed open his yard gate, Tanna ran towards him for a hug leaving Jenna standing with her arms crossed by the front door. She turned inside before he reached her. She just wanted to get on with her A level biology project which his criminality jeopardised by getting the computer confiscated.

Bangaz drew Pauline into him and said, 'Thank you for the food. It got me through a lot more than just being hungry.' Over her shoulder he saw a police car draw up at the gates and a man get out, fly the hood and reach in for boxes.

'Yes officer,' shouted Bangaz, 'carry them inside. ....' He let the police through his gate, across the yard and into the house, directing him to the new mahogany veneer table. 'Here please.' The boxes were wrapped in a tape that said DO NOT DISTURB CRIME SCENE EVIDENCE.

Jenna said 'Finally,' picked up the computer and placed it on the desk in the corner. She delved in the box and pulled out some leads.

'Bangaz! Bangaz! My son! Come ya,' said Marva rushing in the house and pushing Pauline out of the way to get to him. 'Tank God you is all right mi pickney. Lard Maasa mi come soon as me get the news. You is safe dear god. Mi come as soon as I can. Suppose dem extradite you to 'merica? And what if Pauline haffi go up to help your defence? Nuh worry, mi would look after Jenna and Tanna. But how woulds mi pay for food? Mi nuh know the combination lock of the safe. You never tell me! You never trust me even though I am loyal at your side. You must tell it to me combination jus in case anything…'

Jenna was leaning over the desk plugging leads into the back of the screen and the box. A car approached, bumping and splashing through the potholes of the lane. Bangaz looked through the grill to see the vehicle draw up under the silhouettes of the palm fronds in the dusk sky. Recognising it as Herbert's car, Bangaz went outside to greet him.

'Mi general,' he said. 'Everyting good?'

'I can't stop long,' said Herbert from the car, fidgeting and glancing around. 'You get arrested?' He put the window up so only his eyes could be seen.

'Dem free me up.'

'They seize your computer?'

'Yes. And my liar get it back.'

'Do not turn it on. The FBI tamper with it. Do not turn it on. It is a serious mistake to use it. I can't say any more. I must go now, I may be being watched.'

Bangaz rushed inside to see Jenna settling down in front of the screen, her finger moving towards the power button.

'Nuh turn on it!' he called, reaching behind the desk and pulling the plug out the socket.

'Dad! Chill out. It's for school. Please!' said Jenna.

'Sorry. This computer cya use.'

Bangaz tapped his phone. 'Travis? Come around a check out sump.'

Travis turned up, immaculately groomed in a Liverpool strip, picked up the computer box and placed it on the breakfast counter, tipping it on its side. He took the only high quality screwdriver in Campbell Cove out of his ironed top pocket and pulled out the screws. With the cover off, he bent his head close to the circuit boards.

Pauline and Bangaz leaned in to watch him.

'I cannot see anything out of the usual,' said Travis.

'Check good.'

After a decent search with his phone light, Travis said 'It looks okay to me.'

'Can be they tamper with the software?'

'Sure,' said Travis.

'How yah go know?'

'Maybe, if we turn on it.'

'We cya do that. Tank you Travis.'

Bangaz tipped Travis a few grand and went back to Pauline who was staring at the box.

'Inna my knowledge,' he said. 'Mi just feel sey dem can be recording back everyting me a do right there and then,' he said to Pauline.

'Yes,' she said. 'They enfree you too easy, and send this back too quick.'

'That computer can be just recording everyting back.'

'Mi swear me see the American woman Herbert tell me about. The FBI one.' Bangaz stared across the room. 'What I want to know is, was Liar Reynolds in on this?'

'Brian?' said Pauline. 'Mi doubt it. A him help me.'

'But he ask for the computer dem and get them back fast. I'm not sure. You have to careful, all I am saying.' Bangaz put the computer in a cardboard box, closed the flaps and took it out to the car, placing it in the boot.

49

November time, and Willy hadn't seen Bangaz for a few weeks. The hot and humid summer with its sodden sweaty air had shifted off. The emotional stuff with the sleepless nights and broiling afternoons was done. Cooler, easier weather had blown in: a light breeze played over the sea and the pale sun shone tenderly through the trees. Willy no longer sat and sweated beside the rings of moisture on his desk. He dug out an old linen jacket, bought in Jermyn Street in 1968, gave it a sniff, brushed it with the back of his hand and put it on to keep off the cool morning air.

The leathery leaves of the sea grape tree tapped on the zinc roof. They fell and scratched as the breeze shifted them. Willy wanted to see Bangaz but, after hearing about the FBI tapping phones, did not want to call him. So he missed him.

Bunna was in the yard wearing a flexible hoover hose round his neck like a scarf. One of Bunna's skills was to use tools long after anyone else would have asked their employer for a new one, in the hope that Willy would think he was useful and pay him. He was moving the leaves using a rake with two tines towards a bucket with no handle.

'Bunna stop that, it's futile,' Willy called. 'And I haven't got any money, I'm sorry, I just don't.'

'Nuh worry bout that, Willy. Mi happy to help an old bredren.'

'I'm not that happy about you working for nothing. It really doesn't seem right. Stop, please.'

'The yard want cut,' said Bunna.

'I can give you a drink. You want rum?'

'Tell you the truth mi tirsty, Willy,' said Bunna tapping his chest to add a medical dimension to his thirst.

When Willy found the half Q of Appleton, Bunna came and sat down. Close up, Willy could see how worn and tired he looked. His mouth virtually toothless, his skin dull and eyes lost.

He took a sip and said 'Guard your laptop good, Willy. Tief bad. Dem have a spray they spray into your house while you are asleep that make you can't wake up. Then they come in and take your laptop.'

'That doesn't sound good,' said Willy.

'The only guard against the gassing,' Bunna explained, 'is to sleep with a bucket of water by the bed.'

'Who tell you that? Man who sell bucket?' Willy said.

'If you want mi to stand guard at night, mi happy to do it. You is always kind to me even though you don't got no money same as me said way.'

'Up Top!' they heard. 'Wha gwaan, mi general?'

'Bangaz! There you are! Dear fellow. Good to see you. Everyting cool?'

'So far,' said Bangaz, leaping onto the porch and sitting at the table. 'You good?'

'So far,' said Willy, and they bumped fists.

'Every time,' said Bangaz. Bunna pushed off to finish his rum and sleep in the shade, a productive morning behind him.

'I'm glad to see you. I've got something to tell you,' Willy said. 'Look, at this ...' he turned the laptop to Bangaz. 'I think I mentioned months ago I sent a letter to a publisher mentioning what we were working on.'

'Good, very good,' said Bangaz wafting his lighter over a palm of grabba.

'Well, the woman came back. Yes, she actually answered my email. Not quite but almost a first. And said she was interested in your story, and more importantly, my angle, my telling of it.'

Bangaz scowled and muttered 'My story. Not our story and not your story. My story. Mine. Fi mi. Memba good.'

'All right, calm down. She asked for some pages, so I sent her the first few chapters, and today, after a couple of weeks, I got this:

Dear Willy,

Thank you for your email and the sample chapters. I think this project has potential. I shared it with one of our editors, Shana Sara-Winna, and she responded particularly positively to the way you are setting scamming in the context of the contemporary and historical crimes committed against the scammers themselves. None of us can think of a book which explains and defends scammers in the way you plan to do. The story of his rise from rags to blingdom sounds like a page turner too.

Tell me, have you spoken to anyone about broadcast rights? I have a friend at Netflix who I would like to show this to on an informal basis.

I look forward to hearing from you and reading more.

Zuri Bennet-Henriques

'Bingo,' said Bangaz.

'No, not bingo. But a step in the right direction,' said Willy.

'We muss charge her to read more,' Bangaz said, with a lick of his wizla. 'Handling fee, 200 bucks. Reading fee, 300. Western Union. Mi will give you the name.'

'Zuri Bennet-Henriques is a serious publisher,' said Willy. 'She works for Penguin Random House. You can't scam her. It's a ridiculous notion. She deals with literature and the truth, neither concept with which you are entirely...'

'You can scam anybady,' interrupted Bangaz. 'Chuss me.'

'Well you are not scamming Zuru Bennet-Henriques,' said Willy. 'Where is my notebook?'

'Pon de floor,' said Bangaz.

With a groan, and a creak of the chair, Willy picked it off the red boards.

Bangaz suck teeth. 'Gucci reach down last week,' he said. 'A links atell me he try fi buy a gun.'

'What?' said Willy.

'He reach dung a Mo-Bay. So mi hear,' Bangaz smiled and shrugged.

'This may be a laughing matter for you,' Willy said. 'But I have a sixth sense when it comes to survival, and it's telling me you're a maniac.'

Bangaz unscrewed the lid of his flask, and pointed at the laptop.

'Mek we work.'

'I'm sorry, but I'm not in the mood.'

'Gucci don't scare me,' said Bangaz. 'Bigger dog after my blood than that botty bouy.'

'Don't say that. You're scaring me. It's not nice, either.'

'Not you dem after, Willy.'

'Have you never heard of crossfire? Or stray bullet?' Willy looked over his shoulder.

'Nuh worry yourself, Willy. Nobody know mi here, and mi move undercover.'

'That's bullshit. You can't go anywhere without everybody knowing about it.' He scratched at his thigh, suddenly becoming hot. 'I really don't know why I'm putting myself in danger.'

'I know why,' said Bangaz.

'It's not for the money, unless you're gonna put your hand in your pocket, are you?'

'You are doing it because you is a artist. And you are making one wicked book.'

'No,' Willy shook his head. 'I think it's getting too dangerous now.'

Bangaz came round beside Willy.

'Willy, ongle you can tell my story, and we are going so well, you know? That lady, Zuri, she love it.'

In a moment of desperate insecurity, Willy heard himself ask, 'Do you like what I have done so far?'

'Very much, it very good. Very good,' said Bangaz.

Willy smiled, and swallowed. 'Really?'

'Yes! It top of the line, Willy.'

'It is?'

'For sure, Boss.'

Willy shook his head and reached for his notebook. 'Okay. Maybe let's push on.' Willy turned a few pages, then looked up. 'But I would be happier if we don't meet here anymore. Everybody can see your car parked by my yard. How about I find a hotel up the coast, and we meet there where nobody knows us?'

'Good. Very good. Where?'

'I don't know. Ochi?'

'Ochi. Okay. Give me a shout and I will come.'

'Thanks,' said Willy. He looked back at his note book. 'So ... Right. What happened with the FBI? Were there extraditions?'

'Yes,' said Bangaz. 'Fourteen yout was arrested at that time and ten go up: Catman, Mental, Madhead, Tyson, TJ, Gilroy, Longman, Weedie, Brownman. And one other juvenile from Likkle London.'

'Did you know them all?'

'Not good friend, but mi know dem.'

Silence fell as Willy made some notes. 'I take it they all want to kill you too,' Willy said.

'Cho Willy! Ya bad! You a real sample, man.'

Willy held out his palms.

'Some do want to kill me,' Bangaz admitted, not without pride Willy thought. 'Not all. Most do. Cos dem tink mi sell out dem to the feds to save my sweet ass, because ongle me and mi Campbell Cove bredren get lock up that time and never get extradite.'

'Who?'

'The original gang. Me, Toffee, Ample and Omar. We excape.'

'How?'

'We never turn back on our computer dem when the police return them, like Herbert tell mi.'

'So you told your bredren?'

'Mi haffi. Toffee a mi true gee from lang time. And mi haffi give supportance to Ample and Omar. But first mi haffi locate them, cas the phone too dangerous. Toffee wash him scamming money, yuh know. He now have two go-go bar, a ramping shop motel, and a top of the line bordello in Redlands call Toffee's Pussy Palace. I go from one to the other but mi cya find him so dem tell me to go to a office building in Mo Bay Freeport which he buy for him new moggle agency he start and porn channel. I find him there and we gather up his device dem and go find Ample and Omar. Omar in him house wid it dome. We say Omar, tek up your laptop and computer. He say him son Patrick clever so he must aks him. We tell Omar Patrick six year old. He a pickney. Omar say he six year old true, but him have mental age of a twenty-eight year old. And he gonna take over the business when him eight and let Omar free to do him praying and incanting. In the door come Patrick in him little cap and gown holding a book and a white lady who Omar tell us is him tutor from Harvard. The kid too smart for Jamaica school, Omar say. He have to train his mind with the best. The tutor oversee him education and tests on-line. And Patrick pass all him exams.

'And the boy not call Patrick no more. Him have a new name: Brains. We tell Omar we don't got time for fockry, the feds are closing in. So we leave Brains, throw Omar devices inna the car, pick up Ample, and drive out inna the hills. When we find a gully, Omar, Toffee, Ample and me use rock stone and mash up fi we laptop, pc and phone dem and fling down the pieces inna the river. But, mi tell mi bredren, we is buccaneers, we is privateers. And when one ship sink, we build another.'

'Freebooters,' said Toffee.

'Pirates of the high seas,' said Ample.

Omar said, 'No. We are the Reparation Kings. Come to redeem our people. Yes. Our royal house will stand forever. They ain't gonna see us fall.'

'And we leave that gully all of us inna mi car and leave our mash up devices in the river.'

'Was it a big loss?' Willy asked.

'Everyting was on that computer, Willy. Every ting. All the numbers all the script dem, all the leads and all the clients I was working with. I have to start all over. I still have my money, I still have all the lands Pauline buy, but I don't got no business.' While Willy tapped on the keyboard, Bangaz said, 'Come on, mi tirsty. Mek we go for a drink. See if Troy has a food. Every worker need a rest.'

'Is it, is it actually safe walking around with you? I mean now I have to worry about all the guys who got extradited?'

'We is just two old friend who go a bar. No problem.'

Willy found his slippers and they walked through the broken gate and out onto the quiet old road. A knot of well-dressed Seventh Day Adventists holding their bibles walked by on their way back from a day at church.

Bangaz said, 'Don't be scared.'

'Gucci's in Mo Bay for Christ sake,' Willy said. 'Jesus! What happens when the book comes out, Bangaz? If it does. We don't even know if it will. It might be a relief if it doesn't. That would be a first. That'll be what happens: the one book I don't want anyone to read will be a hit. No, there will be two hits: one in the best seller charts, and one on me by a hitman. Somebody might easily read the book and tell Gucci what I said about him.'

'What do you say in the book about Gucci?'

'I say—no, you say, he virtually invented scamming and he also murdered people.'

'Mi nuh tell lie 'pon him.'

'I think I need to round him out as a character a bit more,' Willy said. 'Make him more sympathetic. Improve his looks, even make him handsome, make him dress well and make him taller. Definitely disguise him so he doesn't recognise himself. Did he keep pets? Maybe I'll give him a nice dog. Warm him up a bit.'

Bangaz brought a flask and two cups out of the bar, poured rum into them and lay the flask sideways on the curves on the bamboo bench.

'How about, this is just an idea,' Willy said, 'but have you considered making peace with Gucci? It was a long time ago. Maybe you can bury the hatchet and shake hands.'

Bangaz smiled at the thought. He was looking at one of his phones.

'Gucci could well have forgotten about you,' Willy said. 'How come he hasn't sent someone to kill you if he was that set on doing it?'

'A dat me aks the woman.'

'Oh?'

'And she say Gucci said he never send down nobody. He don't want anyone else to kill me. He want to do it himself. He said killing me will be better than sex. So he ago do it himself.'

'Christ,' said Willy.

'You know how he said he gonna kill me?'

'Do I want to know?' asked Willy.

'He said he want to kill me "beautifully".'

'Why did you tell me that?' said Willy.

'If he comes with a gun either him or mi ago dead.'

'It better not be me. We are definitely moving location. Definitely.'

The moon came up over the hill, burning through the branches of the trees, shining as brightly as Toffee's personal street lights, and laying a spectral glow over the puffy white clouds out to sea.

When Willy wobbled home that night, he was fumbling for the key to his bedroom and noticed, on the floor by the door, a bucket of water that Bunna had left for his protection.

50

Bangaz had most of the scripts memorised, but the lists were something different. He estimated he had lost 5,000 names and numbers, many of them prime beef. He started to put together some new lists, getting a bredren to supply him with the details of the tourists at an all-inclusive hotel in Negril, but for one reason or another when he called them his strike rate was low.

'Too much couples,' Bangaz explained. 'It better if they live alone and are lonely. Also too much Jamericans, and they can't scam easy. Probably half of them have brother or uncle doing it.'

'Try internet dating customers. They live alone. Mainly,' said Pauline.

But there wasn't a dating site employing staff in Jamaica, and so Bangaz couldn't get his hands on the client lists.

'People with big debts are soft,' said Bangaz.

'You want soft people,' said Marva. 'Idiot who give to charity.'

'Maybe we can get a link in a 'merican bank,' Pauline said.

'I will ask everybody to see who they know,' Bangaz said.

He put out feelers, asking if any bredren knew of relatives or friends who were bank employees in the States, but when Bangaz found someone—a guy called Eden in Chase Bank, Atlanta—he wasn't prepared to sell

Bangaz information. Since the advent of scamming that kind of data was more heavily protected.

It was Maas Henry who made the breakthrough. Like too many Campbell Cove men, Maas Henry had longed to get up to America, and finally he was living there. He had bribed his way onto the Farm Workers' Program, and been flown up to Georgia with a bunch of other Jamaicans to pick blueberries, pecans and spring onions. But Maas Henry always considered himself more management than labour, so ran off the farm and into the nearest city and was now enjoying life as an illegal alien.

He went to Atlanta, which like any self-respecting city had a small Jamaican community which was not difficult to find, much to the annoyance of some Atlanta citizens. These kind people helped Maas Henry get a job cleaning and stacking beer crates at a blues bar called Blind Willie's. The clientele was mainly bank workers winding down after a tough day. When most of them lost their jobs in the banking crisis, the bar shut down and Maas Henry drifted west to Las Vegas.

He ended up sweeping the car park at The Sahara, and sleeping in a shared room in the basement with some Mexicans.

One searing hot and cloudless morning, Maas Henry found a bunch of keys in the sidewalk gutter with a plastic fob on it saying NA Welcome Back which he took through the hotel to Reception. He was made to wait while the receptionist dealt with a departing guest. The man was a tall pale guy with sandy blond hair and a bleeding nose, which he was holding a paper handkerchief to. When he had signed his bill he turned to Maas Henry and said, 'Tell me last night didn't happen. Please!'

Then he grabbed his bag and made off towards the exit.

'Found these keys,' Maas Henry said. 'What happened to him?'

'Dropped forty grand on poker last night,' the receptionist said. 'Might have some explaining to do when he gets home. Thanks.'

Some antennae twitched. Later that day Maas Henry called his old bredren Bangaz and told him what he had seen.

'That man was ready for me to tell him anything, Bangaz. Even that yesterday never happen,' said Maas Henry. 'He was in very torment and in very desperation. And he don't make good decision around money. He look to me like a big fish ready for catch.'

51

In room 1376 of The Sahara Hotel in Las Vegas, Bill Macintyre slept with his shirt on and his trousers wrapped around one ankle. Bright sunshine pushed at the edge of the blackout curtain. An air conditioner fanned cool air from the ceiling. Bill's snoring switched with a grunt to a rasping and then a gurgling.

The bedside phone rang. He woke, and picked up the receiver.

'Reception here, this is a courtesy call to remind your that check-out time is in ten minutes. May we send up a porter to help with your bags?'

Reply was impossible. His mouth and lips were non-operational and his left nostril bunged up with what felt like builders' plaster. Staggering to the bathroom he bent over the sink and directed water from the tap into and around his cracked lips and crusty nose.

It started coming back to him. The whole sprawling disaster of his night. In tortuous detail. The guys in his party had tried to persuade Bill to go with them to a strip club. Oh, why had he not gone with them? Bill had said he wanted to turn in early as they were leaving in the morning. But on his way to the lift he had veered onto the plush carpet, into the casino and over to the cashier.

He bought a $100 of chips and headed to the rattle of the ball in the roulette wheel; he deserved a bit of fun before bed. He picked his son's birthday, height and age to be his lucky numbers. The little ball tickled and settled on different numbers, none of them Bill's. In four spins, he lost all his chips. He went to the toilet telling himself he was on the way to the elevator, but got a bag of coke out of his pocket and gave it a good dig with his car key. A sharp sniff, a brief check in the mirror and he was on his way out of the rest room. He turned not towards the elevator and bedroom, but the cashier and catastrophe. The gloves were off. This time he meant business. He bought $1000 of chips.

He lost them too. He had another sharpener in the toilet, and was back to the cashiers. He had emptied his current account, so looked for his savings account card, which he found, and passed over to the cashier.

'Give me five grand,' Bill said. He had eighteen grand in the account.

When she pushed the card machine back at him and requested his pin number he stared down at the buttons and realised he didn't know it. It was on a slip of paper in his desk. And he could hardly ring his wife and ask her for it.

He stepped aside to let the person behind him get to the cashier, and put the card away. When he looked in his wallet he noticed he had the card for his son Ted's college fund. And the pin number was written on it backwards.

His wife Essie's college friend, Samuel, who played guitar in a successful indie band and who was Ted's godfather, had opened an account and paid $5000 US into it yearly on Ted's birthday since Ted was one. Ted was now eleven. Essie and Bill occasionally paid for school books or exam fees out of the account, which is why Bill had the card and pin number on him.

He got back in the queue.

Placing the card on the counter he said 'Give me twenty thousand please.'

Things were made worse when, thirty minutes later, Bill found himself seventy grand up. Once he had put the twenty back in Ted's College Fund and accounted for the first hour of losses he was still nearly fifty grand to the good. To the very good. He told the croupier to guard his chips and went back to the toilet, emerging a few minutes later flattening down his hair, feeling like a General entering a conquered city.

Riding the wave of a few big wins, looking round and grinning at the other players, he started commenting quite loudly on his plays.

'They said it couldn't be done. They said it was impossible! But I am here my friends to tell you they are wrong! And a neat one hundred on 16 and five hundred on 22 and three hundred on red and two grand on even and come on my little bouncing dancing ball of destiny. Come to me baby. Let it roll!'

Two hours later he cleaned out Ted's college fund, losing every last cent in a lurching, sickening descent. He hoovered the last of the coke off his credit card, that useless bit of plastic, and stared at himself in the restroom mirror whispering What have you done, man? What kind of asshole are we? Is this really where we are? He dragged himself up to his room and crashed out across the bed with his trousers round one ankle.

While he was in the bathroom dry heaving into the toilet the next morning, he heard his phone ring. That would be his wife. He just knew. Essie was a mid-ranking executive in a recruitment company. She'd be at the office. Bill had lost his job at a building supply company and was now working in an old folks' home, doing admin and staff rotas. The ring tone seemed like the trumpeter of the apocalypse but this was considerably worse than the end of the world, because Bill was going to have to live through it. That was the answer: suicide. It was the only way out of the path of shame that he was about to be shoved down. He thought about facing Ted with Essie, telling him that his dad had gambled away his college fund.

He looked at the phone. It wasn't Essie. It was an unknown number.

It was actually Bangaz, from the minaret, tipping back his chair and resting his feet on his desk, the coastline laid out majestically before him. While Bill had slept, Maas Henry and Bangaz had been busy. Maas Henry had had a word with a waitress who born and raised in Green Island, only five miles from Campbell Cove, who worked in the casino. She had told him she had seen a man lose heavily at roulette, had read the name off the bar tabs and, in return for twenty bucks, had given it to Maas Henry. Holding a pair of car keys in his hand, Maas Henry went to reception at a dead time of night, posing as a valet, and found a listless junior manager.

'These are Mr Macintyre's keys. Room 1376,' he put them on the hook. 'He ask me to message him his parking lot number. Can I check his phone number?'

'Go ahead.' The woman leant forward and swiped the machine with her lanyard.

Maas Henry had watched the receptionists work the system, so clicked on the room number and saw the information on the screen. He wrote down the phone number and the address, and for good measure Mr Macintyre's middle name.

Bill looked at his cell phone. If it wasn't Essie it was probably one of the guys in the party telling him about where they were getting the cab for the airport. The plane that would speed him back into the arrivals hall of hell. But it wasn't.

'Hello, is that William Pensley Mocintyre of 6537 Railton Highway, Little Rock Arkansas?'

'Yes, who is that?'

'I am calling from The International Publishing Clearance House in Columbus, Ohio. I am informing you that your ticket is one of our lottery winners. Can you confirm your name, address and that you did purchase a lottery ticket?'

Bangaz spark up him spliff, poured a likkle JB from flask to cup and survey him kingdom.

'Yes, my name is William Macintyre. I can confirm I do enter the lottery...' Bill sat on the side of the bed.

'Are you in possession of Ticket 548769X56?' Bangaz asked.

'I may be. I am not certain I have kept a copy. Is that a problem?'

'Not necessarily. Please confirm your address.'

'I live at 6537 Railton Highway, Little Rock, Arkansas. 68901.'

'Very good. That is a match.'

'Did you say I had a win? How much?'

'Hold the line Mister Mocintyre. I am just imputing the data into our system. Here we are. Yes. You have won 865,873 dollars and 46 cents. Do you wish to tick the box for publicity? We recommend this, so we can tell your friends on social media of your good fortune.'

'No. No, definitely no publicity.'

'Are you certain?'

'Yes.'

'I will tick the no publicity option.' Said Bangaz.

'Is this ... are you, I mean are you real? Did I really win? How much again?'

'Yes sir. You are a winner. I will repeat the figure: 865,873 dollars and 46 cents. Can we proceed with processing as I have seven more winners to processise before the payment window closes.'

'Let's proceed, sure, yeah.'

'Hold the line I am just imputing that upload into our database. That is now correctly tabulated on our database.'

'So, what happens now? Do I just get the money?' Bill asked.

'I will give you all those relevant details. Hold the line.'

Bill sat on the bed. The blinding sunlight peeping at the edge of the blackout which was such a threat earlier now seemed full of hope and promise. Oh sweet life! Eight hundred and sixty grand.

'Hullo. Mr Mocintyre,' said Bangaz.

'Yes,' said Bill.

'I am confirming you wish us not to inform your spouse of this win?'

'No, no no. I mean, yes. Do not inform her.'

'Hold on. I will input that updated status information. Okay. Next question. Do you wish to pay US State and Federal Tax?'

There was a pause.

'Well, what are my options here?' Bill laughed. Oh, he felt so good, so bright, so light, so fine.

'State and Federal taxes accrue at a sum total of 231,789. Which gives you a win of 634,086 and 34 cents.'

'That's a chunk, eh?'

'It can be avoided by going the route of the off-shore winner under the Gaming and Lottery Act of 2015. That way your taxation burden would be $US 36,765.'

'I see,' said Bill. He knew Essie would have said Bill, just pay the full amount with the tax, but this was his money. Not hers.

'Well, I don't mind paying that. We gotta pay tax right for schools and defence? That seems a fair figure. How does the off shore route work?'

'It is all totally legal and above board, I assure you. The Company send the funds off shore to an accredited legal attorney, who we work with on a regular basis, and it is then taxed in that jurisdiction and sent to you at an account of your choosing.'

To an account of your choosing. What sweeter words were there in the English language?

'Please give me account numbers of all your accounts and designate which one you require the payment to be submitted into.'

'Okay, hold on,' Bill reached for his wallet and tipped out his cards.

When he had read out the numbers of his accounts, Bangaz said, 'First I must do some background checks now we have found you. I will call you tomorrow and please have your bank details to hand. My name is Mr Stephens. Good day.'

Bill slipped forward onto the carpet, got on his knees and raised his arms upwards.

'Thank you, Lord! Oh, Thank you Lord my God,' tears spurted from his eyes. 'For this and all thine many, many blessings I thank thee Lord for taking pity on a sinner. I will never forget this. Ever. And I swear I will never gamble again. Or take money from Ted's college fund account. I swear. I will spend some of the winnings on going to rehab and sorting out my problem. I love Essie. I love Ted. I love my home. I have a problem. But this will help me face it and sort out the issue. Ye have taught me with thy lesson of this win. I repent,' he sniffed. 'Oh sweet world,' he sobbed with relief and joy.

This changed everything. While he was shaving and showering, having decided not to kill himself, Bill remembered when he bought the lottery ticket. It was on a rainy day, Essie was on a never-ending sequence of Zoom meetings meaning he couldn't use the lounge because that was her background, so he had gone out for a walk. It must have been before he went into a bar that he got it at a kiosk. He had thrown away all the receipts and betting slips in his coat pocket in a hurry when Essie rang to say he was late for picking Ted up. That's when he must have lost it.

After the flight back to Arkansas, which he spent in a state of quivering excitement, he opened his front door to the smell of Essie's Neapolitan spaghetti sauce.

'Hi honey,' Essie called from the kitchen. 'Have a good time in Vegas?'

'I had a great time, my darling wife, but am I glad to be back home!'

'You look well.'

'I am.'

52

Bangaz spoke to Bill Mocintyre, as he called him in an attempt not to sound Jamaican, from Willy's swimming pool, straight after landing another fish from Maas Henry: a woman who had lost eighty-five grand at craps. She too, didn't want to pay tax.

'I've paid enough tax,' she yelled at Bangaz.

'Also you is a senior citizen.'

'Dead right. Fuck 'em. So how do I get my money?'

'The process is not difficult, I will take you through the honoration procedure step by step ...'

Bill answered before the first ring was over. He was sitting on the bed sweating and breathing heavily, but when he heard Mr Stephens' voice his anxiety was swept aside and in its place came the wonderful, muted excitement of the tremendous, life changing news.

Essie was in a Zoom meeting. Ted was at school. Mr Stephens said, 'Before we make out the full payment we need to take tax and legal fees from the principal sum. They must be paid in advance.'

That didn't sound right to Bill. Was this some kind of con? 'What do you mean in advance?' he asked.

'The fees and tax are paid first, then you receive the full payment.'

His stomach sank. A pair of big double doors opened in his imagination and he was ushered back into the hell of his pre-win life, with the lies and the debts and the empty college fund. 'Why can't you just take it out of my winnings?' he croaked. 'I'm not comfortable with this, you rang me to say I had a big win.'

'Yes Mr Mocintyre. Of course we will pay the tax out of your winnings. You don't have to pay anything.'

Bill found himself laughing. 'Of course, sorry,' he said. 'I'm not having to pay anything, right?'

'You are a winner,' said Mr Stephens. 'We are paying you.'

Bill made a kind of involuntary yelp of joy.

'We at International Publishing Clearing House are making a special numbered personal account which we have put your prize money in and you are going to take it out and pay it to the lawyer off-shore. It is all from your winnings, nothing else.'

'Okay. How do we do this?'

'Please have a pen and paper by your side. Hold the line. I am just waiting for the account allocation to be upload on my screen. Right. You are on the database. That means you have been cleared for payment. Take down this number.'

Mr Stephens dictated the winner's account number to Bill, which Bill carefully wrote down, double checking the digits.

Mr Macintyre did not recognise that the account number was his own savings account, which had $18,000 in it. He wrote the numbers with such care and such excitement, it blinded him to the truth.

'That is the special payment account,' Mr Stephens explained. 'From this account you will pay the lawyer and the tax. Please now go to your car and drive to your Chase bank. Please leave your phone connected at all time. That is procedure.'

Bill did as he was told, and drove through the sleet onto the overpass. 'I'm here,' he said.

'You are at the car park. Park in the second line of cars from the bank.'

'Uh huh.'

'Leave the car. Take your ID and the account number and go to the teller on the very left or the very right.'

Bangaz liked to keep them on a tight leash. It was good sport.

Mr Macintyre pushed through the glass door and went to the teller on the left. This was the moment he was going to find out if this whole thing was for real. He pushed across his ID and said, as he had been told to, 'I would like to withdraw six thousand dollars in cash from this account. Large bills.' Bangaz had told him to stipulate that.

The teller glanced at her screen, checked his ID, smiled at Bill and said, 'Of course, sir.'

Bill watched her counting six thousand in cash with rising excitement, not knowing that it was money from his own savings account. How fast her fingers moved. Each bill was a 100. Sixty of them. His breathing almost ceased, and he felt so light, so elated, like he was going to lift off the floor and leave behind all the troubles of his old, gravity-run life.

Bill almost skipped to the car, picked up the phone and said, 'Hello. I got it! And I godda say I'm feeling much less anxious.' He now let the guy at the lottery company take charge. Mr Stephens was going to make everything work out fine. Everything was legit. Here was the proof: six grand in cash. The remaining 800 grand was just round the corner.

'Okay. Very good. Did they give you all the cash in one envelope or did they give it to you in separate envelopes?'

'I got it in one envelope.'

'Very good, that information is correct,' said Bangaz, showboating to himself. He had not known there was 6000 in the savings account, so he too was happy at the outcome. 'Now we see that everything is on track,' he said. 'You will now drive to Walmart.'

There was another pause of ten minutes as Mr Macintyre drove his brown Cherokee across a suburb to the Walmart car park, where Bangaz made him park to the left of the main entrance.

'I am here,' Bill said. Sleet fell softly and silently on his windscreen.

'Okay get a bit of paper and pen. Make sure there's no mistake made, no mistake whatsoever so please make sure you are listen correctly and write everything down. The first name you are going to write down is Gerald Binks.' Bangaz took him through the spelling. 'You will go into Walmart and say "I would like to make a deposit to a family friend." That the word you use.'

'Er, Mr Stephens, but why am I sending money to Gerald Binks, and saying that he's a family friend? I don't know any Gerald Binks.'

'Why?' huffed an indignant Bangaz. 'You are keeping it private and confidential with the offshore lawyers. You are not hiding the money, just doing it properly. When the offshore company receive the cash then they release the winning to your account.'

'I just present this Western Union receipt to the bank and they give me the winnings?'

'Mr Mocintyre, as I explained to you from before there is nothing for you to be uncomfortable about because that is the reason the payment has been issued and for the declarance to be made because this receipt you are going to be getting is just like a certified cheque. When you hold that receipt you hold your wins of 800 thousand. Tell us when you are finished and you are back to the parking lot.'

In Walmart, Bill Macintyre passed the money with the name to the teller, a young pale man with a narrow head and big eyes.

Bangaz put the phone to his ear. He heard the Western Union cashier say, 'Here is your receipt. May I do anything else for you?'

'No thanks,' said Mr Macintyre. 'Thank you very much.'

Then Mr Macintyre said, hoarse of breath, coasting on adrenalin, ready to receive his 800 grand. 'Okay, I am back in the car.' He was staring at the receipt. The tax and fees were all paid. This bit of paper in his hand was worth 800 grand.

'Okay very good. At 3 o'clock p.m,' Bangaz said, 'the settlement is transferred. That is when you must be at the bank to receive it.'

'That's the 860 grand, right?'

'No. Eight hundred in a bank cheque, sixty grand kiash. That receipt you have, that is just like a certified cheque. Everything is in because now the quantification is timed. You have nothing to worry about. Everything is all in your favour.'

'I have the payment receipt right here,' said Mr Macintyre. 'I guess it's this one, right. PC 7693569. Is that all I need to receive the payment?'

'Correct. Now I must go as I have another winner to take through the procedure.'

Bangaz switched off the call and shouted. 'Bunna, get me a cold Red Stripe.' He waved to Troy who was coming back into harbour.

53

Bangaz rang Gerald in New Orleans. He was a links of Maas Henry. Gerald confirmed he'd received Macintyre's six grand payment. Bangaz directed him to send the cash by Western Union to Jamaica in Marva's name, who was the only person in Bangaz's circle who had not been blocked from receiving cash at Western Union. She had capitalised on this by charging Bangaz 4% to pick up the money. She had taken to the work well. She used a variety of Western Unions across West Jamaica, spinning a rich mix of colourful stories about the payments to anyone who asked.

'They call me a saint, but me no saint! Cho! Mi just see the tourist baby drop inna the river and me jump after him and scoop him up and return him to her madda and fadda. Dem too scare of the current, cos it run fast. They leave back up a foreign with them baby and send down a little help to me for save the pickney life. It could be any grampickney. Lord knows I did not do it fi no money.'

She enjoyed dressing up and travelling by bus to Montego Bay, Grange Hill, Savannah La Mar, and even as far as Santa Cruz and Black River, looking up old friends and inventing stories to tell them that reflected well on her. She was on the road almost every day, earning a good sum. She glowed with the cash. Bangaz once saw Marva work out 4% of $3750 faster than he could do it on his phone.

While Marva was taking route taxis up and down the line, Pauline was investing the cash in land and building projects with Liar Reynolds. They used to drive out together in Pauline's SUV or Reynold's Merc to park up and stare at hillsides, or blank pieces of flat bush, unfolding maps on their laps. He had a reassuring calm manner, a pleasant contrast to Bangaz's frenetic presence. There was a problem with the doorhandle on Reynolds' passenger door, and sometimes he had to lean right across Pauline to open her door. When his arm brushed her body she didn't flinch. If they left the car to look at a plot, Liar Reynolds offered his reliable arm to steady her on rough terrain.

Brian Reynolds thought Pauline was wasted on Bangaz, and desired her for himself. Her determined eyes, her pressing body and her urgent ambition, all encased in her tight white suits, beguiled him. The rich click of her Manolos. The promise of her neck. Her well-manicured but tough hands. She was a woman to contend with, a woman of consequence.

Bangaz was in his minaret or at Willy's villa working his cell phone, landing more catch from Las Vegas. Maas Henry link up with a receptionist at the MGM Grand, which turned out to be a rich new fishing ground. Every day, Bangaz received contact details of more big losers to phone and cheer up with great news.

54

Marva came by the swimming pool office and waited for Bangaz to finish his call.

'Mi nuh get troo,' she said.

'Wha' dem say?'

'Money never send dung.'

'Which branch of Western Union?'

'Lucea.'

'Which cashier?'

'Sidi.'

'The one with cast eye?'

'She. You owe me tree hundred for taxi fare. And a hundred for patty.' She put out her hand. Bangaz wriggled around to find a bill, and put 500 in it.

'Just little bitty payments I get here and there,' Marva said to no-one. 'Boy, mi want a certain portion of cash, to set up mi life.'

'They say they have no record of transfer?' Bangaz said.

'Ya man.'

'And when you show them the Money Transfer Number what dem say?'

'It not a real number. Or maybe it have mistake in it, but dem nuh have nutn on fi dem system for me. So me lef out and reach dung to tell you.'

'Show me the paper with the number on it.'

Marva opened her purse and handed Bangaz the bit of paper he had given to her the day before.

Bangaz compared it with the text from Gerald. 'One moment,' he said to Marva. He dialled Gerald. 'The Western Union transfer you sent yesterday.'

'Five grand eight.'

'Yes. It don't reach dung. Call them and check it out.'

'Sure, no problem.'

Bangaz looked out to sea and suck teeth.

Marva said, 'Can be Gerald tief it.'

The phone rang. Gerald said: 'Dem say it already pick up.'

Bangaz waved Marva away and turned out towards the ocean. 'Who pick it up?'

'In the name of Marva Thompson.'

Bangaz looked at Marva, who twitched impatiently in the shade.

As usual, he spoke to Pauline about it. He always wanted to know what she thought.

'Marva jinall you?' Pauline said. 'She tief ya money?'

'Mi nuh know. Mi nuh sure. Mi cya believe it. She nuh so stupid.'

'Wha you say?' said Pauline. 'But serious, I don't think it's Marva who is taking the cash. Have you seen how unhappy she is? She would glow if she had her hands on some funds.'

A day later Bangaz went to visit Omar, who greeted him softly at his door wearing a long white cloak and a little hat. He said, 'Come this way, let me show you my library,' and led Bangaz into a circular room with a view of the sparkling bay and the seething city of Montego Bay far beyond. A silent woman and a boy in robes brought in a brass circular tray of bush tea.

'Bangaz, this is my son.'

Bangaz looked at the chubby boy. 'Mi remember Mario. You good?'

'We call him Brains,' said Omar.

'You top of the class at school?' Bangaz said.

'He don't go to school. Him too intelligent for school. He have him private tutor at home.'

When the boy had left, Bangaz said. 'Tell me bout Western Union. I heard you had trouble, Ample tell me.'

'I don't use that place now. I sent down money and it disappeared.'

'What did they say?'

'They said we collected it, but my own sister went and I know she didn't,' Omar said, looking into the tea pot and replacing the lid.

'Same thing happen to me, said way,' Bangaz said.

'And I don't want no investigation in case the police and the Feds get involved,' said Omar lifting the teapot.

'Uh, huh,' said Bangaz. 'Which branch your sister go to?'

'Lucea.'

'Any teller?'

'We always use a girl with one bad eye cos she used to deal with us quick and smartly.'

'Sidi?'

'I think that is her name. He offered Bangaz a plate of biscuits. Bangaz was busting for a spliff but Omar had asked him not to burn weed in the house as it was a "spiritually pure environment."

'I figured,' Omar continued, 'that one of the tellers had seen the pattern of my transfers with Western Union. They knew it was choppings and they knew who I was sending to pick up the cash. So the teller just marked the transfer as been picked up and took the cash themself, knowing that if I started inquiries Western Union would call the sender, which would be a problem. The Feds would not be far behind. So I never made a complaint.'

'Same with me, said way,' said Bangaz, adding 'Bumboclaat,' making Omar wince.

'Please,' said Omar, 'remember Allah is always listening.'

'Sure,' said Bangaz.

'We start to use a different Western Union branch, in Negril,' Omar said, 'and the same thing happen. Smaddy in Western Union must be recognising scams and teif fi wi money. And we cya do nutn bout it.'

'Sidi is this same girl who said fi mi money already pick up.'

'We don't know it is her. But I am never using that place again,' Omar said.

'What do you do?' ask Bangaz.

'I get smaddy to carry dung the kiash direct from 'merica on a flight. I don't trust the Feds. They're watching all our data, you know?'

'I do.'

'I want to show you something special, my friend,' said Omar, reaching for a leather book tooled in gold. 'This a gift for you.'

'Me?' said Bangaz.

'Do you ever think about your soul, Bangaz? Is it thirsty? Does it ever call for a drink?'

'Whole heap o time Omar. So me carry me JB.' He handed the book back to his friend and took his flask out of his pocket.

Bangaz drove back down the coast straight into the setting sun, seeing it sinking through the flaming palms into the fiery sea. His radio was tuned loud to Irie FM, and the car was brimful to bursting point with Vybz Kartel singing dance hall lyrics, praising the scammers to the skies.

On a bend outside Lucea, police were pulling drivers over to make it look like they were after choppers. To Bangaz, roadblocks were no different from a toll booth. He slowed down, lowered his glass, gave the officer some cash and accelerated off.

In the town, he parked over a puddle in the old mall next to Western Union, turned off the engine and waited. Half an hour later, Sidi appeared under the pharmacy's canopy. She waddled towards a car wearing a knapsack. It looked new. So did her shoes. She stopped and reached in her knapsack for a pair of sunglasses. They, too, were new.

Bangaz started the engine.

55

Bangaz walked around the swimming pool with two limes in his hand, squeezing Mr Macintyre to control him fully. He made Macintyre withdraw extra cash for Gambling Tax, Local Tax, Federal Tax, Transaction Tax, Winning Tax and Transfer Duty, slowly draining Bill's savings account. Bill didn't mind, because he believed it was all an advance out of his prize money. The more he withdrew from what he thought was his prize account, the more confident he felt that this thing was for real. When Bangaz told him about a new payment, Bill just sighed and said, 'More red tape, huh?'

Finally, one day, Bill went to the bank and the teller said, 'I am afraid there are insufficient funds for that request, sir.'

Bill took that as good news. That account was designated to pay the costs associated with his win. If it had run dry it must mean the principal sum was ready to be transferred. The world was such a beautiful place. He bounced into his kitchen at breakfast, ruffled Ted's hair and beamed at Essie.

'You look happy this morning,' Essie said.

He hadn't told his wife or son because he had decided to break the news with a new car in the drive. A Lexus. Something to make it tangible. It may even happen the next day things were moving so fast.

Up in America, and inevitably always on the hustle, Maas Henry had asked his bank worker acquaintances in Atlanta if they had any smart ideas a scammer might use. A tall slim man of Maas Henry's acquaintance called Eden Parks had told Maas Henry that the biggest way to make money in banking was scamming, but he had at the last moment declined to steal data for Bangaz. Four years later, burnt by the banking crash, redundant and in debt, Eden remembered Maas Henry and called him.

Maas Henry of course remembered the bank worker. 'Eden! Wha gwaan? You good? Everyting cool?'

Eden was in arrears on his rent and his car payments. He didn't want to send the Merc back, but getting a job at his old pay was impossible. So he told Maas Henry he had a bit information that would be useful to scammers, and was looking for some cash for it.

Bangaz told Eden that if it was useful and worked, every time he used it he would send Eden 10% of whatever he could make. The information concerned automatic overdrafts given to senior citizens who had been loyal customers of Chase Bank. It was a policy born in the heady days before the banking crash, when to have a big loan was considered a human right. Some customers, particularly elderly ones, refused to take out loans. They didn't want them and they didn't need them. It was Eden's job to weaken the criteria on which loans were given, so basically everyone ended up with one. It was decided that whatever these old folks spent up to 20K would be honoured, and given to them as an overdraft even if they didn't have any money in their accounts. The banks didn't care if they couldn't pay them off. They'd get their cash when the customers died. They were certainly first in line. And in the meantime, they could charge a tidy rate of interest. Bonuses all round.

The computer code worked but had a glitch, which Eden was tasked with debugging just before he was let go from Chase Bank. You could go into your bank and pay your credit card debt off with one of these accounts simply by knowing their routing number, name and address. You didn't need their signature or pin number, or any form of consent from the payer. And, here was what made it interesting, the money would be available on your card immediately. It was all because the bank was trying to create debt. The other account would be debited even if it was at zero. An overdraft would instantly be created. But the money could only be used to pay off a credit card.

Bangaz had established that poor old Bill Macintyre had three credit cards, and each of them had a couple of grand debt on them. Now all he needed was to locate a Chase Bank customer over seventy, which would have been easy had he not lost his lists in the FBI raid. Then he remembered his first notebooks, which for some sentimental reason he had never thrown away; they were under some sedimentary layers of clothing in a cupboard at his yard. He went to dig for them, took them up to the minaret and started leafing his way through the pages of scribbled names and numbers.

After a long and leisurely spliff he found the word Chase Bank and, beside it, the name Marjorie Bell. Marjorie! He remembered her. But she was years ago, and if she wasn't dead she'd probably have closed her bank accounts, especially as he had scammed her.

But Bangaz knew that banking was an art, not a science, and that strange unpredictable behaviour was the way of people. Who would have thought that Bill Macintyre would not check his own savings account for months? Maybe it was because somewhere, dark in a mine sunk deep in his soul, he feared he was being conned and couldn't face finding out. Or maybe he thought if he looked at the money in his account he might start gambling again.

Bill was confident. After all, the lottery company had paid out around sixteen grand already, and no scammer or con man would do that. It was only taking time because he was going the tax-free route and saving himself over 200 grand. It was all good. All good.

Mr Stephens explained to him that he needed to make sure he had no debt on his credit cards because the financial institutions all talked to each other and credit card debt in combination with a big cash deposit might trigger an investigation by the IRS. 'We cannot have any tamperification,

Mr Mocintyre.' But Bill didn't have to worry because Mr Stephens was going to get the credit card debt paid off by the company. It was just going to take a little time. But if it saved 200K in tax, heck it was worth it.

'You have to receive two payments. One on top of each other. From the special winners account allocation we have in your name. Take down this routing number.'

Bangaz gave him Marjorie's account number. It didn't matter if there was no money in her account; because of Eden's glitch, the credit card would be paid up to a limit of twenty grand.

'If it is expedited we may make the October payment window,' Bangaz explained.

It was a kind of gobbledeegook but Bill trusted Mr Stephens and went along with it. After all, it wasn't his money.

Bangaz had learnt some more lingo watching a movie set in a bank that afternoon. He used it to keep himself sound official. He particularly liked tamperification, although he coined that word himself.

'Hold on,' he said to Macintyre, 'I have to call you back after a meeting with my supervisor who is questioning your payment. I will call you back.'

Bangaz stood up and went down the spiral staircase to look for a lighter which worked. At all times he knew he could lose Mr Macintyre, and he didn't want the fish to break the line. He had to be very careful. He had often pulled a fish right to the boat and watched it jump off the hook. Not a good feeling.

'Mr Mocintyre. This information that is going to be putting through at the regions has to be given to you as they have to give you documents that prove that everything will be going through. Now please hold the line, Mrs Williams gonna speak to you just a minute. Hold the line, I have her right here...'

Bangaz morphed into a Mrs Williams, a friendly southern matron. He placed his hand on his hip and hitched his voice up a register or two, throwing in a southern twang that oozed kindness.

'Hello? Pleasant good morning, Mr Macintyre. Soo good to talk with you. How're you doing? Wunnerful! Now what we want to just explain to you is all the information they will be declaring this morning. That is why they made sure that all your credit cards have been paid off.'

It turned out Mrs Williams also talked gibberish, but Mr Macintyre was soothed by a woman's voice. He was sitting in his icy car warming his hand on the heating vent.

'I just wanted to be certain I was doing the right thing,' he said.

'If this is not cleared immediately by the bank, why, they gonna be closing the payment down!' Mrs Williams exclaimed. 'Sure thing! So this is why this has to be cleared, so all we are requesting you to do is for the otheration for the Regions' bank. So please hold the line and Mister Stephens here gonna take you through the process. Hold the line. I'll pass you back to Mr Stephens. You just follow procedure now, Mr Macintyre, okay?'

Bangaz shook off happy Mrs Williams and reverted to serious Mr Stephens: 'We are near the completion of the payment protocol. So there can be data in the information to lead into you so nothing can be left over because this has to be cleared...'

Thus he led poor Mr Macintyre round in some more tight circles.

Bill gave the account number which he believed was the lottery's but which was actually Marjorie's and paid off his credit cards.

The teller tapped in some numbers and said, 'Mr Macintyre, your balance is now zero.'

He had had thousands of debt on his card, and it had been wiped off. This is what winning felt like.

Bangaz held out the limes and gave them a squeeze.

'You go to the teller and say you need 8000 cash advance from your card. They are going to ask you how you need the cash. You say large bills.'

'Can you explain why I am asking for an advance? That bit I don't quite get,' Mr Macintyre's common sense said.

'The Publishing Clearing House has paid off your cards as part of your prize. You are now going to pay the final instalment of the offshore fees and accrued expenses so you will be clear to receive the full $860,000. Is that clear?'

'But why am I doing it in cash?'

'Because this is right at your fingertips,' replied Bangaz. 'You go into the teller, you give your ID and the curds and you say "Good morning. I'd like eight thousand cash advance on each card. Sixteen in total."'

'I'm not, you know, really sure about this,' Mr Macintyre said, turning off the engine. 'Like, how do I know this is above board, real?' His common sense was having one last plea before having a pillow pressed over its face by his hopes and dreams.

'How could someone pay your bills off if they were trying to fraud you? Would we just pay your bills off? This is legit, we give you legit information, legit money for everything to be done.'

When he had the $16,000 back at the house, Bangaz suggested he take a thousand for himself and take his wife out to dinner, or go and buy a shirt. Bill said he'd like two new tyres for his truck.

'Go ahead,' said Bangaz. 'For a sum this size the company will organise a personal courier,' he told Bill, 'to expedite it straight to the offshore lawyer and they will trigger the full and final payment into your account. This should happen by close of business tomorrow.'

Bangaz told Mr Macintyre to put the cash in an envelope and be ready to hand it over when the courier came to the door.

56

DJ Barney stood in the corner of Troy bar on him decks. He worked in a service industry to the scammer trade, and was used to being dragged out of his yard at every hour of the day and night to play dancehall music for a bingo. Other service industries had popped up around the choppers: pastors and obeah men sold incantations and oils which improved performance on the cell phone, and an enterprising business man imported a container full of bright and boasty rings which he said could ward off any danger including the FBI, and soften the defences of American clients.

It was the fourth bingo in a row in two days, and Troy tyad bad. At 3 am there were still twelve motorbikes tethered out front, and the bar was a madhouse of yout, gal dem, smoke and music so loud it bend the boards. In the glow of the bulb under the counter two bartenders pop beers, spoon shards of ice into cups, and pass out single cigarettes. With the music audible four miles up the line, DJ Barney felt in his pocket, answered his phone 'Yuh?' and had a conversation ten inches from the speakers about another booking.

The choppers provided a solid economic base for the community. Pretty well everybody felt the benefit. The fishermen got a good price per pound, the bars were full, the shop busy and the builders had work for months. But even the people like Bunna, who was slow, or Gutta who stutter bad and could not scam, were looked after, bought drinks, and given a help when they need it.

Later, the motorbikes buzzed off with a skid of gravel and a crackle of backfires in twos and threes to go to club and look women. The bartenders closed the shutters, got their pay and took their taxis back to them yard. Troy walked out onto the beach, settled in his hammock, and lost himself in the folds for a short nap. He woke an hour later, in a moonless night, the sea inky and the road quiet. He realised that Toffee's street light was dark. Current gone. Maybe the JPS were fixing it down the line. Or maybe it lock off for a smuggling operation. Some of the big people did that. It made it easier for the boat at sea to find the flashlight on the fisherman beach if there was a major power cut.

Troy knew the sounds of the smugglers. Trawlers came out of the dark ocean, motoring in close with no lights on, the huge diesel engines throbbing, and waited for one of the Cove boats to go out to them. They couldn't send a tender in because only people from Cove knew the lanes through the coral, and when strangers tried to cross it they buck up on the coral and mash up dem boat and can be sink it. There was a long slender boat from Cayman which had been coming to Cove for so long the captain could navigate the coral in the dark. He used to sweep in before sunset, hide his boat in the mangroves, loaded it with ganja, and then party at Troy's bar till late with bartenders before heading back to Cayman, a day's sail to the west.

Troy recognised a different engine. It had a high pitch and was coming straight over the coral, which in places was only a foot deep. A black, inflatable, flat-bottomed boat unlike anything in the Campbell Cove fishing fleet swished right up onto the beach. These were the Haitians. Dem crazy.

Since the earthquake and uprising and revolution and fire and brimstone on Haiti, the army and police lose control of the island and whole heap o guns fall into the hands of the little people. They had no money, and nobody wanted their currency, so they traded guns for what they needed. And they need everyting.

At first they came for ganja and coke and paid in hand guns. But they get hungry and mad, and started turning up with rifle and machine gun which they exchange for frozen meat. There was a report of them taking a live donkey on a boat to sell fresh meat at home.

Some people splashed out of the boat speaking a language Troy had never heard. He lay still in the hammock while they loaded the boat. It could have been ganja. From the men's breathing, it sounded heavy. Then he heard a new sound. The sound of clinking metal followed by the lowered tones of awed conversation. He lifted his head to see five men, one shining a flashlight into a duffer which they were pulling guns from. Troy slowly lowered his head. The group split, some went back to the highway, some into the boat.

Then Troy heard a man stutter 'Wey-wey-wey-wey-wey!'

Gutta. The eighteen-year-old yout from the next community. Troy looked up to check. It was Gutta in the company of Bookal, Maas Henry's grandson, another yout who could not scam. They had spent the night holding beers watching them bredren celebrate a 10,000 J bingo. All they got was four Red Stripe.

Gutta try and learn mechanics but they run him off when he stood and observed the men working on the vehicles – which was the established apprenticeship. He try and get in tourism but he don't spell too good or speak English fast enough with his stutter. Gutta got his nick name from when an English teacher in school asked him to spell guitar and then laughed at him for writing gutta.

Bookal took some cash from his pocket. There were sharp words, then murmurs. Then silence. The two yout leave the boat and walk right past the hammock. So Gutta get him gun. Gutta was in a hurry to make his mark amongst his bredren, so he had to use it.

The Haitians started the engine and pushed off over the coral.

57

'Leroy! Leroy!' a man called progressively louder in Pang's direction, 'Leroy!' Pang remembered that Leroy was his name on this job and he turned his head. Pang had registered as Leroy Hibbert because he didn't want any IRS or Social Security or even Immigration hassles using his own name. At the time he'd been listening to Leroy Stibbles on his headphones, the old Jamaican reggae singer, and Leroy was the first name that came up.

'Yeah, sorry,' he said.

'You deaf? We're moving.' It was Rico, the boss, calling them out of the café back to the truck.

Pang sat on a pile of bags of cement enjoying the sun on his face until they pulled over in a suburban street and had to get to work. He was down in Vegas for the college holiday making as much cash as he could, paving and tarmacking driveways and patios.

Maas Henry, cap on his head, his knobbly legs sticking out of wide shorts, stood on his driveway watching the workers arrive. Maas Henry had moved up in the world, quit the shared basement room with the Mexican dem, and was now renting a two bed bungalow with a two car garage and a yard out back. For months, Maas Henry had been supplying fish from Vegas so fat and slow that Bangaz's problem was not getting the money out of them, but getting the money into to Campbell Cove.

Blocked, and now stolen, by Western Union and Moneygram, Bangaz decided to follow Ample and arrange for the money to be brought down in cash on a commercial flight. But for this, Maas Henry had to find people for Bangaz who could travel to Jamaica. Many of the men in the Jamaican diaspora who could be relied on to do a fairly simple thing for a few hundred bucks had an immigration status which didn't allow them to fly to Jamaica. While an application for US citizenship was in process, the applicant had to remain in the US. Almost all other people in the diaspora who Maas Henry asked turned out to be illegals, so they couldn't leave because they would never get back in.

Pang was sitting looking at his phone when Maas Henry approached him.

'Whuppen?'

'I'm good,' said Pang. Pang had a Vietnamese mother and Jamaican dad, but had never met either because he was adopted by a white family in Boston.

'You a Yardie?' Maas Henry had heard them calling him Leroy.

'I'm American, but have Jamaican heritage.'

That was enough for Maas Henry.

'You got a valid passport?' he asked.

'Yeah, why?'

'You want to earn a bit of extra money?' Maas Henry asked, crouching down near Pang.

'I don't want to break the law.'

'No, nothing like that. This is easy and simple. You go to a man's house. You pick up a envelope. You go to the airport and fly to Jamaica and give it to a man and fly back.'

'What is in the envelope?'

'Cash.'

'How much?'

'Between five and thirty grand.'

'Okay. How much for me?'

'One grand. Plus fares. It won't take more than two day.'

'Is this drugs money?'

'No.'

'Is it—'

'—No more questions. You interested?'

'Yeh, yeh. I'm interested.'

'Okay Leroy, give me your number. Tell nobody. Nobody. We'll call you.'

Four days later, Pang caught a taxi at Little Rock airport and read off a bit of paper to the driver: '6537 Railton Highway'. He sat back to be taken through tree lined avenues, pulling up in front of a neat clapboard house with a pick-up truck out front.

'Wait here, please,' said Pang to the driver.

He walked the path to the porch and rang the doorbell, telling himself he had not done anything wrong. Ringing a door bell was not a crime, but he looked up to see if there was a camera anyway, and there wasn't. The door opened and a middle-aged man with thinning hair and a face raked by anxiety answered the door.

'I am here to collect a package from Mister William Macintrye,' Pang said.

'Yes, yes. I have it right here.' Bill picked a thick envelope off the table behind him and gave it to Pang, who put in the inside pocket of his coat.

'I await to hear from the lawyers about the, er, outcome,' he said. 'I mean the date of final transfer of funds to my account.'

Pang had been instructed to say nothing so he smiled, turned and walked back to the car. Within two hours he was on a plane to O'Hare international, Chicago, from where he had been told to go to another address and pick up a second package, before returning to the airport and boarding a flight to Montego Bay.

The second pick up was for Ample, whose client lived in a trailer. Curtis Miller was a tall, slow-moving man with a bald head, beard and sad eyes. He had not lived in a trailer when he had first spoken to Ample. He'd lived in a house with his wife, his grown-up daughter and her toddler. Over the course of a year he had spent all his savings and sold the house to access his big win. His wife, at her wits end, had left him after an escalating series of fights.

Curtis had told his daughter, Ellie, to prepare to receive the big money because he was handing over the final payment. She had rushed round to his trailer stop him. So when Pang knocked on the caravan door he heard a shrill woman shout. 'No, Dad! No! You don't do that!'

The door opened and Curtis said 'Excuse her.'

'Courier. I'm here to pick up a package,' Pang said.

Ellie grabbed her dad from behind and tried to get hold of the envelope. 'No, Dad. No. For god's sake. Get away from him!' she screamed at Pang.

'Take it,' said Curtis. 'Go.'

In the back of the taxi to O'Hare, Pang opened the envelope and glanced into it. In departures, he counted out five hundred bucks and, instead of boarding his flight to Jamaica, bought a flight to New York.

58

Pang and his girlfriend, Topik, were in the bedroom of their rented home in New Jersey with the door locked, even though the house was empty. Topik was a short, chubby young woman with a pretty face and straightened hair. Pang was counting cash on the bed while Topik was counting the contents of another envelope on the dressing table.

'It's fifteen,' she said.

'And twenty in this one.'

Pang and Topik stared at the money.

'They think you're on the plane right now?' Topik said.

'If we're not going to do it, I have to call him right away with an excuse so I can get down there tomorrow.'

'What would you say?'

'I dunno. I had a medical emergency? Car accident?'

'Yuh,' said Topik. 'You never said your real name to the guys on the building crew?'

'No. Hardly anybody spoke to me and I never said Pang or Richard, and I definitely never used Heaton.'

'Did you ever talk about friends, or me?'

Pang thought for a moment. 'I don't think so.'

'Some boyfriend you are.'

'Could turn out to be a good thing, baby,' said Pang. 'The crew were, like, Spanish speaking and kept themselves to themselves.'

Topik said, 'Shit.'

'Yeah,' said Pang.

'Thirty-five grand. That's our deposit right there. That's our house. What address did you give for Leroy Hibbert?'

'I gave some bullshit address.'

'Which one?'

'I gave an address I lived at in college, like six years ago. It's a student house. 1067 Fairland Boulevard, San Diego 21170. Hundreds of kids went through that house.'

They both sat in silence going back and forward over it in their heads.

Pang said, 'It's safe. It is.'

'But these are Jamaicans, baby, and as we say dem nuh easy.' Topik was born and raised in Jamaica but moved to the USA in her late teens and was now a citizen.

'They can't find me,' Pang said. 'No way can they find me.'

Topik thought hard for a while, and then said, 'Oh my god, honey, you got us a home! You got us a home!'

59

When Bill Macintyre stopped hearing from Mr Stephens he presumed he'd misunderstood his instruction about accessing his prize. He took the transfer receipt to his bank and presented it over the counter and said he was informed it would trigger a payment of the $800,000. But there was some kind of problem, because the bank were not aware of the payment. Bill called Mr Stephens but couldn't get through. Bill knew he was now acting strangely because Essie kept saying, 'What the hell's gotten into you? You're so antsy.'

As the days went by, Bill constructed reasons for the delay. Mr Stephens had been ill, busy, transferred to another branch or promoted to head office. He would get back to Bill as soon as he could. One positive thing was that he definitely heard no bad news, so that was good.

Finally he heard from Mr Stephens.

'It is so good to hear your voice,' said Bill, flushed with joy and relief. 'When I am to receive the money?'

'We are doing triple security checks here at head office,' Mr Stephens said. 'May I ask a couple of questions?'

'Sure.'

'Date of birth, mother's maiden name and brief description of the courier who picked the cash up. 'I didn't get much of a look but I think he was kind of Asian. Everything okay? We ready for the transfer of funds?'

'I will revert back to you, Mr Macintyre. Good day.'

Ample called his client.

'Can you describe the courier?'

'He was Asian, about thirty,' said Curtis Miller. 'Has he complained? I apologise for that. That was my daughter. She cannot ... she refuses to see the big picture. Everything still on track?'

Bangaz sent Maas Henry to talk to the contractor who paved his drive, to ask about Leroy Hibbert. The contractor gave Maas Henry an address and his phone number – that was all he had on the guy. He had only been on the crew for a month. Maas Henry sent a contact round to check out the house in San Francisco. It was a student hall of residence, and nobody had heard of Leroy Hibbert.

Bangaz vex bad that he lose Mr Macintyre's fifteen grand. And Ample angry about his twenty.

'Ya too soft,' Marva said. 'Dat why dem rob you. A good business man strike first. Pre-emptive.'

''Tap ya noise Marva. I'm thinking.'

'Thinking of how much money you lose? Oh – what I would do with that money. A likkle house, car and put some aside for mi retirement.'

'I'm a white collar criminal, Marva. Like Teacher say. I don't use no violence.'

'You want to be popular, sure. Be popular, while your poor old mumma don't have hardly no money to eat. But dat don't matter cos her son is popular.'

But while one fish get away, another bite the bait and, lying around Willy's pool, he pulled them in.

'Boy, have you saved my bacon,' the old man on the phone laughed. He was called Terence.

'May I please take you through the data input procedure to expedite the payment of your winnings, sir?'

A week later Bangaz had Terence, with an envelope containing $23,000 at his apartment, but no runner to pick it up. After losing Mr Macintyre's bingo, Bangaz wasn't too impressed with Maas Henry's choice of courier.

'Boy am I excited about telling my son about this win,' Terence had babbled to Bangaz.

'You haven't told him?' Bangaz asked.

'No. I godda look at his face when I tell him.'

Bangaz was experienced enough to recognise danger. Informing adult children about a big win: it never went well.

'When are you seeing him?'

'He's coming over this afternoon. Within the hour. He is gonna be over the moon. I'm sharing the prize with him. 50/50. Did I tell you?'

Bangaz had an hour. The man lived in Naples, Florida. His geography of America was a little hazy but he remembered that name from the past. It was the town where the man who he scammed in his FedEx script came from. He opened the drawer of the desk: wizla, lighter, broken scissor, advil and the school exercise book.

He leafed through the pages, and found the name amongst the scribblings, numbers and words: Andy. And beside it a landline number. He picked up his phone and called.

'Dick's hotdogs. You love hot dogs, you'll love dicks,' said Andy.

'May I speak with Andy.'

'Sure, what is it in connection with? I will see if he is available.'

'I've been recommended I speak to Andy by an associate. I need some help.'

'With what?'

'I need someone to do a service for me, which is urgent.'

'I don't do escort work anymore,' Andy said.

'It's some courier work.'

'Courier? I could do that. If you pay me.'

'I am paying. It is very simple. I want you to go to an address in Naples and pick up an envelope and fly down to Montego Bay and give it to me.'

'Cool. I dig Mexico.'

'It's Jamaica.'

'It's Jamaica? Cooler! What's in the envelope?'

'Cash is in the envelope, Andy. Nothing else. And it is my cash and I need it in Jamaica.'

'How much?'

'23,000 dollars.'

'Is this drugs business?'

'No.'

'I want to know what it is. I am not doing it unless you tell me where the money came from. I'm the one taking the risk here.'

'It is a private matter.'

'So how much are you offering?'

'2,000 dollars plus air fare.'

'Okay. Well I'm interested. How about if you give me two grand and a hotel for two nights in Jamaica. And two tickets, not one.'

'Okay.'

'Cool. When do I do it?'

'That is the thing, Andy, it is urgent you go and make the pick-up from my client in the next half hour.'

'What's the address?'

'7603 Ocean West Building, 93rd North Road.'

'I know it. It's close.'

'Very good. Very good.'

'What if this guy doesn't hand the money over?'

'He will.'

'I'm not getting into any kind of argument or fight am I?'

'No, he is purchasing a service. A legal service. But you must get round there right away because if you don't, the deal will fall through. That's why I am asking a stranger.'

'If he doesn't want to give me the money I'm just leaving, okay?'

'Nothing gonna go wrong, Andy, chuss me. Call me when you get back home.'

Andy put down the phone, took his car keys out of the basket and made for the door. He was definitely going to go over to the address. He was 99% sure there wasn't going to be an envelope with twenty-three grand in it, but what if there was? He got a trip to sunny Jamaica with a girlfriend and two grand spending money.

Andy knew the apartment block. He had been there many times because a couple of his motorisation units were faulty and the owners wouldn't stop pestering him to fix them. He parked the car under a palm tree that sprinkled a little shade and headed for the main door. He pressed bell 39, said 'Courier!' and was admitted without any questions. In the elevator going to the third floor he thought that was positive. Along the corridor the doors were well spaced; it was a high-end apartment block. He found number 39, and rang the bell. It immediately opened, and standing on front of him was Mr Leakey, an old gay dude who was a real ball-ache when it came to making his blinds motorise.

Andy said 'Courier.'

Terence handed him an envelope and said, 'Don't I know you?'

'No sir,' said Andy 'I don't believe we've met.'

'Aren't you the motorisation man?'

'No sir, I'm in the courier business.'

Andy got away as fast as possible. As soon as he had the car door shut he tore open the envelope and saw the cash. He didn't count it all then, but it could easily be twenty-three grand. He put the car in drive and went home.

After talking to Bangaz and agreeing to fly down the next day, Andy thought about who to take as his love interest. It needed to be someone who wouldn't get all naggy about only having one room. Andy did not have time or the inclination for a tiring romantic seduction. That only really left one person: the woman he had officially broken up with four times, the last time being six months ago: He rang her up.

'I don't know if I should,' she said. 'After all the things you said to me.'

'I know. I'm sorry, honey. I'm a work in progress. No, I'm fucked up. That's the technical psychological term for it.'

Danielle laughed. She so wished she hadn't. She just could not resist the idiot.

'I thought a weekend in the Caribbean would be a way to make it up to you. Jamaica's in the Caribbean, isn't it?'

'Really?'

'Yeah. You don't even need to get time off. We leave tomorrow, return Sunday evening.'

'I was going to work some overtime.'

'Oh, come with me.'

Danielle said, 'Am I going to have to pay for this?'

'No no no, it's fully funded. All expenses paid. This one is on me.'

Danielle said nothing.

'Really,' said Andy. 'Look I know what you're thinking, but I have the cash, I will buy the tickets and pay for the hotel. I swear.'

'Okay,' said Danielle. ' Okay. Ahh, it'll be fun. Jamaica, right?'

'Jamaica,' said Andy. 'Like they say, No problem.'

60

With Archie (or rather Willy) abroad on an extended European trip, Bangaz had completely taken over his house. Bunna tried to defend the place against the worst of Bangaz's outrages but it was useless. The pool was dotted with sodden bank notes, a reminder of a party the night before when the scammers threw cash into the water to make the girls jump in and wet up for it. There were still a handful of party girls lying on the sun loungers under the tree, with another couple asleep in Willy's bed. Bunna was walking around clearing up bokkle and plastic cup.

At midday, Bangaz climbed into his car and headed to Mo Bay airport. He left the Audi to bake in the car park and walked over to the glass doors outside arrivals which breathed out gusts of cold air when they drew back, as if the temperate north started just the other side of them. You weren't allowed in, so Bangaz stood by a pillar monitoring the arriving passengers.

An exhausted man with baby buggy and guitar, his dream dying. Fat Americans dressed as huge toddlers. Then a few tall lean preppy wasps glided by, usually the woman in front, sometimes vaguely themed. Khaki and pale blue.

Andy emerged in front of Danielle in a straw hat, cargo shorts, flip flops and a T-shirt that said GOD IS DOPE. Danielle was in pale blue jeans and white T-shirt. Andy took off his hat and waved it around, and by the time it was back on his head Bangaz was saying 'Good afternoon, sir, welcome to Jamaica. May I kindly take your bag?'

Andy had not wanted Danielle to know about the money. She always accused him of being too shady, and it would just complicate matters if she knew. Bangaz understood, and suggested he pretend to be a taxi driver and that when he dropped them off at Plantation, where Bangaz had arranged a cash deal with Mr Hawkin, Andy would leave the money in a bag of litter in the footwell of the car.

Bangaz was picking up Danielle's overhead bag when he suddenly noticed, coming through the glass doors, the unmistaken crumpled old school Englishman that was Willy Loxley-Gordon, with a leather suitcase, in a dirty linen suit, sweating profusely, looking flat broke and on a major come-down. He may not have known him well – at that point – but Bangaz had seen Willy around the village all his life and recognised him anywhere.

Willy was returning to Jamaica after a few months in Britain. Originally, he had been going to stay with his brother in Fulham for a fortnight to celebrate his nephew's wedding. But he met up with some old chums at the reception including Patrick Lichfield and the Count, who both invited Willy to the country, so he delayed his return date four times in total while he enjoyed a stately, six week bender.

Willy finally had to board a plane to Jamaica because he had a long-standing arrangement with his ex to have Holly to stay in Campbell Cove for a week in the Easter holiday. It would be her first overnight visit alone, but Willy had suggested that now Holly was thirteen it was the right thing to do. It had actually been Holly's idea, so Kayenne, her mum, had reluctantly agreed to it. All Willy had to do was make sure he was there at the house when they turned up. Unfortunately, his plane had been delayed and he was now running twenty-four-hours late. He had emerged blinking into the Montego Bay sunlight at 11am and was due to welcome Holly at 11.30am at Campbell Cove, an hour's drive away. There was nothing else he could do but hurry back as fast as possible and hope that they didn't mind waiting quietly in the yard for him.

As Bangaz walked to the car, he fumbled for his phone and dialled Ample.

Ample answered and said, 'You find Leroy?'

'No, no sign of that. Him gone, mi a tell you. Can you get over to Willy villa and tell them Willy at the airport and gonna reach soon.'

'Okay, okay. Mi will tell them.'

'Make sure the girl dem lef.'

Bangaz piled the luggage into the Audi, hurried Andy and Danielle into the back, barged the long queue to leave the car park, pushing in front of some tourist in a rental. He then sped back down the coast road, scattering pupils crossing the road in Sandy Bay with a blast of his horn.

'Wow,' said Danielle. 'It's the Monaco Grand Prix but with crowds of children and oncoming traffic.'

At Campbell Cove, Bangaz swerved off the highway and shot down the lane, pulling up outside Willy's villa and telling his passengers to wait in the car.

'Soon come,' he said and trotted into the yard where it was mayhem. Bunna was in a flat panic, holding a mop with two strands on it, and dragging furniture from the pool towards the house. Indoors there were bottles and ashtrays and cups on the beds, chairs, tables and floor. A girl was braiding a woman's hair on the porch.

'Leave,' said Bangaz, 'you haffi lef now. Tek up your stuff and go. Party done.'

He shook a sleeping girl and removed a red wig from Willy's bedpost.

'Move yourself gal. Spread up back the bed now.'

He left the house to find a pretty teenage girl, holding a suitcase, standing next to a woman who vex bad. Bangaz approached the woman and said 'You look for Toffee? You can meet him at him go-go in Negril. Take her there.'

He got back in the car and left Bunna standing at the gate looking overwhelmed as he watched a taxi with Willy in it pull up. Willy paid the taxi driver, left his suitcase inside the gate and went to look for Holly and Kayenne.

'What the hell is going on here? Wha gwaan?' he shouted to two girls as they looked for their slippers on his porch. 'Bunna. Who are these people?' he called.

A small voice said, 'Hello, Daddy.'

Kayenne emerged from the shade, Holly in tow, and said, 'You really are pathetic. You can't stop even on the day you know your daughter's coming. Well done Willy. Holly, take my hand. We're going. I'm not leaving you here in this Soddom and Gomorrah.'

The small voice said, 'Bye bye Daddy.'

61

'Go and buy me a flask,' Willy said. 'Christ, Bangaz.'

'Wha' you say?'

'And get me four, no five Craven A.'

'What's wrong?'

Willy shifted in his chair and scratched his head. 'You've just brought it all back to me with that story. That was the first time I had seen Holly in four years. My relationship with her was very fragile, almost non-existent. And you totally fucked it up. You know?'

'Let me get you that drink,' Bangaz loped off towards Troy bar.

When he returned, Willy poured a good portion of the flask into his cup. 'Holly didn't get over it, even though I said it was nutn to do with me.'

'Boss, I never know it was so serious. I am sorry, Willy. I never understand. Hush.'

'She was never allowed to stay after that. She comes to see me now but still she never stays. Years later.'

Bangaz seemed to shrink. 'Mi sorry man. Serious. Serious ting.' He had never seen Willy's face look so ... tired, beaten and miserable. 'Mi sorry Willy.'

'Mmm,' said Willy. 'It was a fucking disaster. A crawsis situation if I ever saw one. I did ask to see her. I wanted to keep in touch. But Kayenne, she was so bloody obstructive. I suppose I could have given more money, but I didn't have any. A meeting would be arranged. Not here. Holly was banned from here. Some depressing tourist café. Holly would sit opposite me with Kayenne at another table, staring at me like I was about to attack the girl or poison her. One time, it was in Mo-Bay down by the public beach, Holly sat for an hour with me and didn't say a single word. Not one. I did my best asking her about school and hobbies and plans for the future but she just stared at me and didn't say a word. Never answered a question.'

'Dat disrespectful. Enuh?'

'No no no,' Willy shook his head. 'She was upset and young and confused. I don't blame her. I couldn't meet her eyes. I was feeling so guilty.'

'Wha' you say?' said Bangaz.

Willy waved him away. 'No. It was my fault, the whole mess, it was.'

Bangaz sat down and for once appeared to be listening quietly.

'And when I plucked up my courage and looked into Holly's eyes I saw that she was crying. Without any movement or sound. I hadn't noticed. Tears were coming down her face. It was horrible.'

Willy shook his head. Bangaz stared at him.

Willy said, 'It was not what you would've wanted as a father.'

They fell silent.

'That bad,' said Bangaz. 'But she your daughter, she haffi love you. She muss. Take her out widout her madder. Take her gambling along the hip strip Montego bay, on the machines, and then Burger King. Kids dem love it.'

Willy ignored that.

'How old you say she was then?' Bangaz asked.

'About thirteen.'

'Too young for strip club,' Bangaz said.

'Yes,' said Willy.

'Dat sixteen.'

'You take Jenna to strip club?' Willy asked.

'No, mi try, but she get rude pon me. Thirteen girls like to go gamble.'

'You took your daughters gambling at thirteen?'

'Tanna love it. I take her and her friend dem to Hip Strip in Montego Bay, fi gamble and go a Burger King. Try that with Holly.'

'She's s bit old for that now.' He reached for his phone, wiped the screen on his thigh, tapped a few keys and showed Bangaz a photo of Holly. 'She's 23 now. Pretty, isn't she? And very bright too.' Bangaz looked at the picture, nodded, and had the sense not to say what was on his mind. 'That day she came here and I was late and the place was a ramping shop,' Willy said, 'I think it broke her heart.'

'That is not good Willy,' said Bangaz.

'No, you can say that again.'

'Mi apologise,' said Bangaz. 'One day mi can be meet her and explain wha gwaan that day.'

Willy grunted.

62

The barrier at Plantation rose as Bangaz drove towards it and Mr Hawkin himself rushed out of reception to welcome the guests and grab his cash from Bangaz.

Andy got out the passenger seat, leaving the duty-free bag in the foot-well containing a couple of cardboard coffee cups, a half-eaten sandwich and $21,000. As Danielle headed inside she glanced into the car and said, 'Andy, take your trash. You're such an animal.'

'It's okay. I am happy to dispose of it,' Bangaz said.

Danielle opened the door, and grabbed the bag, saying, 'that's very kind of you but we can take care of our garbage. Andy.'

Bangaz and Andy watched her go inside with the bag.

Bangaz said, giving Andy a warning look, 'I will contact you later.'

Andy nodded and went after Danielle who was looking for a garbage bin when she saw something better: an actual cleaner, a thin woman with a kind, leathery face, shining the floor beyond a yellow plastic sign, pulling a little garbage trolley behind her. She handed the bag to her and said, 'May I give you this? Thank you.'

Andy, a few steps behind made started making some strange choking noises.

'Are you all right?' Dannielle said.

'I just remembered it's not all garbage,' Andy said, and snatched the bag from the cleaner.

'What are you doing?' Danielle said.

'There's something in it I need, I just remembered.'

'What?'

'A biro,' Andy said, striding towards reception, sweat breaking out from nearly every pore on his body.

'Well find your biro,' Danielle said. 'You're not walking around a nice hotel with a trash bag. What's wrong with you?'

'It's fine. I just don't want to throw it away. I'll look for it in the room.'

Danielle rolled her eyes and approached the woman in the high heels behind the desk. There was some delay with the wrist bands so they got their key and were told the bands would be sent up to them.

Their room was on the first floor with a view through the palm fronds of the garden, then on to the beach.

'This is dope!' Danielle said. 'I mean awesome. My god it's so beautiful.'

Andy was only thinking about keeping the bag out of Danielle's hands. He was blind to everything else. He badly needed her to leave the room so he could retrieve the cash. When Danielle slid back the glass door and stepped onto the balcony, he stuffed the bag in the dustbin to keep it out of her hands.

His phone pinged and there was a message from Bangaz saying to meet in the water sports office at six. That gave Andy an hour.

There was a knock on the door, and Danielle went to open it to reveal a man in a white tunic holding a clip board. 'A very pleasant good afternoon, milady,' he said. 'I have your wrist bands.'

'Oh great,' she said putting out her wrist.

When both their bands were clipped on, the man said, 'Please sign here to say you are in receipt.'

'Sure,' said Danielle, taking the pen which was attached to the clip board on a kinked brass chain. She scribbled her name but no ink came out. 'I think your biro's finished.'

The man started feeling in his pockets, and said, 'I will go and carry another one from reception,' and turned to leave.

'Don't,' said Danielle, 'we have one. A very important one, according to my boyfriend.' She laughed and rolled her eyes.

Andy watched her walk from the door to the dustbin, pick out the plastic bag, untie the handles and look inside. He scrambled off the bed and tried to pull it out of her hands.

'I'll look,' he shouted.

'Why?' Danielle asked.

'I ... I know it better,' Andy said. He knew as he said the wprds, it was a desperate and probably fatal line.

'You know the litter bag better than me?' Danielle said. 'Are you on drugs already?'

'No, it's just that I remember where I threw the biro.' With Danielle staring at him with her arms folded, Andy looked into the bag, rummaged around a bit and said, 'Oh it's not there. I must have left it on the plane.'

Danielle said to the waiter: 'Excuse my boyfriend, he's an imbecile.'

When the waiter promised to return with a serviceable pen, Danielle closed the door, turned sharply and said, with narrowed eyes, 'What the fuck is in that bag, Andy?'

Andy fished out the envelope and said 'Okay, okay, okay. This.' He passed her a thick brown envelope.

Danielle looked inside.

'Woah,' she said.

'Twenty-one grand,' said Andy.

'Where did you get that from?'

'Long story.'

'No, Andy, short story. Where did you get it from?'

Andy sank back down on the bed, rubbing his temples. 'A guy rang me and asked if I would do a courier job. That's what I had to bring down to Jamaica.'

'Who're you giving it to?'

'The taxi driver. Well that was the plan.'

'Oh right. Yeah. Of course. And, you know, who is he?'

'He's called Bangaz.'

'Yeah, yeah, sounds legit.' Her sarcasm was perfectly pitched. 'What's the money from?'

'He didn't tell me. But it felt cool to me. I think I've got a pretty good feel for these things.'

'Do you, Andy?'

'It was all going great till you picked the bag up out of the car.'

'Why didn't you tell me?'

'Because it's like a finely tuned operation that I could not allow you to jeopardise. It was on a need to know only basis.'

Danielle walked round the room, thinking. 'How, and why did he get in touch with you?'

'He rang the apartment. He said he was recommended me by an associate.'

'Who?'

'I don't know. I am quite well known.'

'What as, an idiot?'

'No! I'm an ex-porn star. I'm quite famous.'

Danielle tutted. 'What have you got yourself involved in?'

'Easy, Danielle. I got us two grand, plus a little holiday. So I'm not that much of an idiot. I was gonna give you a grand.'

'That's why you didn't tell me,' Danielle said. 'You're so cheap, Andy.'

'What, honey?'

'You didn't want me to know you were being paid. You were not going to give me a grand.' She folded her arms and shifted her weight onto one hip.

'I was! I wanted it to be a surprise.'

'And you don't know where the money came from? Drugs I guess.'

'No, not drugs. I asked him. So I could judge the risk. I'm not stupid!' Danielle tried not to smile.

'What did he say it was?'

'He wouldn't tell me.'

'But you took the job.'

'I assessed the risk, Danielle.'

'What are you going to do with the money now?'

'I'm meeting him in the water sports hut at 6pm. Which gives us time to go and get a drink at the bar.' He stood up now, feeling like the interrogation might be over. 'Come on, beautiful, come and have a cocktail with your big bad gangsta boyfriend.'

They left the room, crossed the reception area with the busy restaurant beyond, walked out onto the deck and spotted a thatch bar right down on the beach, strung with pepper lights.

'That looks cute,' said Danielle, and they walked onto the warm soft and soothing sand of Negril beach.

While they were having a drink Danielle said, 'You know what I'm thinking?'

'How hot I am in bed?'

'I can't believe it, Andy, but for once I am not. Hey, come here, thanks for this beautiful beach and that amazing sunset.'

Andy leaned in for a little kiss under the warm light of the multi-coloured festoon. Danielle let him, but then pulled away with a serious expression on her face.

'No, I'm thinking this courier thing might be something to do with the guy who scammed you. Remember? Pablo who apparently worked for FedEx who was going to transfer ten million bucks to you? I remember there was a Jamaican connection in that scam. Something Jamaican.'

'No, this guy is legit. I mean, I've already got my money.'

At 6 o'clock, Danielle insisted on chaperoning Andy to the water sports hut; a wooden weatherboard shed near a landing jetty. One wall was full of fins, masks, regulators and all the other paraphernalia of scuba diving. A few guys in shorts and Life Guard T-shirts melted away when Andy asked if Bangaz was around. A small door opened at the back of the shop and Bangaz came in.

'Hello. Andy. Respect. You have my envelope.' It wasn't a question.

Andy handed over the envelope which Bangaz took, extracted the money and counted it out in a way that made Danielle think he had done many times before.

'Okay. We're good. We're done,' said Bangaz. 'The hotel will sort out your taxi to the airport on Sunday.'

As they trooped out of the shed, Mr Hawkin, wandering the hotel grounds, spotted them and changed course, heading in their direction.

'Aha! I see my alumni is taking you on a perambulation of the facility and amenities!' he said. 'You did not know that your friend Clive here used to be in the employ of this establishment. Mr Clive Thompson,' Mr Hawkin put his arm around Bangaz's shoulders, 'was a treasured member of staff. We were so sad the day you left. We clapped him out in a guard of honour.'

'That must have been incredible,' said Danielle. 'Did you say Clive Thompson?'

'Yes,' said Mr Hawkin. 'I knew he would make a success of himself. And now he honours us with a return visit as a top business man, and pillar of the community.'

'You people please enjoy your pleasant evening,' said Bangaz. 'I must unfortunately be detained by a prior engagement,' he explained, remembering his Hawkin tourist English.

'Oh come on, come and have a drink with us,' said Danielle, grabbing Bangaz's hand and leading him back to the thatched beach bar.

It was not an environment in which disagreement with a tourist was easy, and the grip she had on his wrist was not to be slipped out of without her consent.

'Sure, no problem,' said Bangaz. 'Give me a shot of JB and a Boom chaser.'

'I have no idea what that is, but I'll give it a go,' said Andy. 'Irie vibes.'

Bangaz went and sat at a table on the sand, smiling at the tourists and stretching out his legs.

Under the thatch of the bar, Danielle and Andy waited for the drinks.

Danielle turned and nodded to Andy. 'He's Pablo from FedEx,' she said, resolutely.

'Are you crazy? Pablo's in a wheelchair.'

Danielle sighed.

'And he was young. Twenty-one,' said Andy. 'Plus he came from The Caymans, not Jamaica.' Also,' he thought for a bit, 'he really let me down, Pablo. And this guy Bangaz seems pretty cool. I mean, he's come through for us.'

'Just give me a minute with him, stay here and wait for the drinks.' Danielle said.

Danielle took a seat on the bench opposite Bangaz and said, coolly, 'What I want to know is, where you got Andy's name and phone number to ask him to do this job?'

'It was supplied by an associate who recommended Andy as reliable and above board.'

'That sounds likely,' Danielle said. She looked him squarely in the face. 'You're Pablo, aren't you? From FedEx? You scammed Andy, didn't you? Don't get up. I have those two transfers I made to you somewhere, a thousand each if I remember. And I should remember as I ended paying for them. From what I read in the newspapers and see on the TV, the FBI should take an interest in you. Plus I know your real name: Clive Thompson. It just so happens to be the name of an uncle of mine, so I remembered when the manager said it.'

'This is one very big misunderstanding,' Bangaz said.

'No it's not,' Danielle carefully raised her voice. 'You stole money from us and I want it back.' Some tourists at the bar – not Andy – and a young couple sitting at another table, stopped talking and looked at her.

Bangaz smiled and laughed. 'No problem, Danielle, no problem.'

'Follow me back to the hut,' she snapped, standing up. She had been nervous confronting Bangaz but was now, after remembering the two-thousand bucks he stole, beginning to enjoy herself. The door on the weather-beaten shed was still open. She flicked on the light.

'You are going to give me the two-thousand you took from Andy. I know you have cash on you, so come on.'

Bangaz reached into his shorts for the envelope, took it out and counted the bills onto the table between the sea-glass and fins.

Danielle picked it up, checked it, folded it in half and did something she had often wanted to do but had never been put in the position; slipped it into her bra. In all, she was very pleased with her performance.

'Goodbye,' she said.

Her hand was on the doorhandle when Bangaz said, 'Hol' on.'

'What?' She swallowed nervously.

'Let me put something to you,' he said. 'Are you interested in a business opportunity?'

'Probably not,' she said. 'What is it?'

'Would you do another run for me?' asked Bangaz.

Danielle paused, her hand still on the handle.

'I admit we have had our difficulties but we overcome them, and I now I want to start afresh and am asking if you want to work for me.'

'Why me?'

'Because you're white and you won't be questioned at customs and immigration if you reach down for a couple of days each month. You just a regular tourist.'

'How many trips are we talking about?' Danielle turned and walked back towards Bangaz.

'At the moment, to tell you the honest truth, I am looking to carry down maybe six bingo a week. Total about 120 grand. One trip a month.'

'That's a big chunk,' said Danielle.

'The Feds have started searching Jamaicans coming back for quick trips with kiash, but they never search no white tourists coming to Jamaica.'

'What's our cut?'

'This is between you and me, Danielle. Not Andy.'

'Okay. So what's my cut?'

'Two grand a pick up, plus expenses including hotel for two nights, cos it must look like a holiday.'

'So.... about forty-eight grand a month, plus a holiday in Jamaica.'

'You cya turn that down,' chuckled Bangaz.

'I can. I'm not an idiot.' Danielle was enjoying playing the hard boiled gangster woman. 'I take it this is cash you scammed out of people like you scammed Andy. And I presume you're gonna ask me to collect it from their door. The people you scam are gonna report me to the police and it won't take long before they're looking for me. It's a very big risk.'

'No. That is not the case, Danielle. Let me explain. Terence, when he gave Andy that twenty-three grand, it was not his money. It was money I sent to his credit card from a third party. So when that third party find the money gone from their account, which they will, they gonna discover that Terence rob it. They are gonna report it to the police, and the cops will go and see Terence, and what is Terence gonna say? A man came to my house and I gave him all the cash. I don't know who he was. He's gone. Nobody gonna believe Terence. They will arrest Terence, not look for Andy. Or you, if you do this.'

Danielle let that sink in and said, 'That is an incredible scam. It's almost beautiful.' She asked a couple of questions about the bank protocols, on which Bangaz satisfied her. 'How did you think of that?' she said. 'It's brilliant.'

'Tank you, Danielle.'

'Did you make up the FedEx scam?'

Bangaz smiled. 'You liked it?'

'You asshole,' she smiled. 'Pablo, Ange?'

'All made up,' said Bangaz.

'You should be in a legit business.'

'I should be Danielle. But mi cya be. Mi cya travel and nobady will give me a chance here. You people nuh give we nutn fi put down, as the song goes.'

'What does that mean?'

Bangaz had a think and said 'You never re-invested any of the money you took from slavery days. It basically say that.'

'Oh,' said Danielle, shocked.

'You know the hotel manager? The bludclaat fired my ass, him don't sorry to see me go. That is bullshit. Mi work hard for him, and he fired me for nothing. And when mi left I couldn't get no job to feed my family. There was nothing except for scamming.'

The conversation continued, until Bangaz brought it back to business. 'One thing you must know Danielle: these payments are not always for me. Sometimes we pick up for other business men, and if any money goes missing I don't response for what might happen. Dem heavy, you know? So no funny business.'

'Sure,' she said. 'Have faith.'

They shook hands and left the shed. Danielle went to look for Andy, who was by the beach bar dancing with two female guests, giving them plenty of pelvis. When he saw Danielle he shouted, 'There you are! I've been looking everywhere! Meet these two gorgeous ladies. I don't have any idea of names, but I think mine is Andy. And this is Danielle, the love of my life.'

Danielle said hello while Andy staggered across the sand to order more drinks. He came back with a tray.

One of the women said 'We love Andy!'

When Andy returned he said quietly to Danielle, 'I think they recognise me.'

She said, 'Not with your clothes on, Andy.'

'You look happy,' he said. 'Give me a kiss.'

'I am,' Danielle said, 'tonight I've decided to finally quit selling real estate.'

63

For weeks, Topik had been trawling through newspapers, scrolling realtor websites, scanning realtor windows and dragging Pang around the far end of New Jersey hunting a place to buy. She located a one-bedroom apartment in a half decent block, near the station. She could get to the care home and Pang could get to college with only a ten minute walk to the train. They went over to the realtor to confirm their offer on a gloomy night after work, and on the way home, tired and excited, they treated themselves to a steak.

As she took off her coat and settled herself into the booth, Topik glanced at her phone, opened a message from her mum and said 'Oh, oh no, no, no ...'

'Whats up, hun?'

'They murdered two aunty.'

'What?' said Pang looking up from the menu.

'Miss Myra and Miss Hannah,' she stared at the screen, her mouth open. 'Dem wicked.'

'Was it, like, a robbery?'

'They don't know. They shot them and set the house on fire.'

'That's brutal,' said Pang. 'They must have some idea why?'

'Nobody know, mumma say. Sometimes I wonder why I emigrated but then I remember things like this.'

'Did you know them well?'

'I remember them. They were like kind old aunties when I was little. They let me get the eggs from the fowl coop.'

'Is this common in Jamaica? I mean, wow.'

'Just so senseless,' Topik said.

They sat in respectful silence, then Pang said, 'The view from the bedroom window in that apartment will be awesome in the summer with the trees all in leaf.'

64

Ample had heard Gutta was a gun for hire, and spoke to him one night in Lucea town in a bar. It was tucked away down a dark and noxious waterfront alley where street girls met their men and rats scurried over the garbage.

Ample had told Gutta, 'You go to the yard. You kill one woman and tell the other, "This because you disrespect the scammer and steal we money." Repeat that to me.'

'Th-th-th- this because you dis-dis-dis- respect the scammer and st-st-st- steal we money.'

'Practise it, okay?' said Ample. They agreed the $400 US fee and Ample put down $300, the remaining balance to be handed over after the job was done.

Gutta drove through Negril and took the Sav road, passing the big police station, on his way to Little London. He found the board house set back off a quiet street. He drove off into the bush and waited for the community to drop asleep before kickstarting the bike and driving quietly back to the house with no lights on. A half-moon showed him his way.

He left the bike under a tree and walked around the back of the house, a pack of dogs barking in the distance, crickets ratchetting closer by. There was a dull glow in one window. He found the back door and took the gun out of the back of his waist band. With a kick of his boot the rotten door sprang open. In the gloom he saw the face of an alarmed old lady. He felt his belly churn and turn, but he raised the gun, aimed, shut his eyes and squeezed the trigger. When he opened his eyes there were two old ladies, one on the floor, one by her side looking down at her.

'Th-th-th- this because you dis-dis-dis-dis....' Gutta stuttered.

'Why you do this?' screamed the woman. 'Wha you wan'?'

'Be-be-be-be-'

'Wha you wan'?' said the old lady cupping hear ear. 'Mi nuh anner-stan. Please, sir, please ...' the old lady implored. His stutter had stopped him getting into tourism, stopped him chopping and now mash up him gunman life.

'Re-re-re- respect the ...' And then he accidentally said stammer instead of scammer, adding, 'Nuh tief we money.'

The old lady said, 'But mi neva disrespect your stammer.'

Gutta snapped. He knew he wasn't up to repeating it. He didn't have the time, for a start, as people must have heard the gun shots. In a spasm of anger he raised the pistol and shot the second lady, who fell backwards onto a table knocking over an oil lamp which sent licks of flame across the wooden floor. Gutta turned and fled.

Ample was not happy that Gutta had shot both women and failed to get the message over, but Gutta insisted he was owed the final $100 and Ample paid it. Ample was going to need a better messenger so he paid a yout from Negril to go and kill Dalton Hibbert, a young man in the same family, and make sure this time they knew why he was murdered.

65

It was Topik and Pang's first home, and when, a couple of weeks after their steak dinner, the realtor left them alone in the house with their own front door key for the first time it felt like one of life's romantic set pieces. As they kissed, Topik's phone pinged. She looked at it and tutted.

'Wha?' she said 'they kill Dalton.'

'Who is Dalton?'

'My little cousin.'

'They murdered him?'

'At him yard.'

'Why?'

She was reading. 'It's in the Gleaner. A gunman approached his yard in Oakley Drive, Little London, Westmorland and opened fire. The victim was rushed to hospital but succumbed to his wounds.'

'Was he mixed up in something?'

'No! He was a top performer at Savanah La Mar High School.'

Topik called her madda to ask about it. She said, 'people say it sump to do wid scamming. The shooter say that nuhbadi should tief scammer money. But she nuh know no scammer.'

Topik turned off the phone and told Pang.

Neither of them said anything, until Pang said, 'Wow. Bad times.' Then he looked over at Topik, who was glaring at him, eyes wide, waiting for his brain to register something, 'What? Why you looking at me like that?'

'It's us, Pang.'

There was a horrible sinking feeling in Pang's bowels, but he said, 'It's not us. I gave them a false name and there is no way they can trace it back to me.'

'The false name you gave was Leroy Hibbert.'

'Yeah?'

'And Hibbert is my name. All these people they murder all called Hibbert. They track down my family. Jamaica is not that big, Pang.'

'Dalton, he was a Hibbert?'

'Yes, and Miss Myra and Hannah. Both Hibberts.'

'But none of them knew a Leroy Hibbert.'

'They don't know the name is fake,' She said through gritted teeth.

'Jesus.' Topik put her hand to her heart. It was galloping. 'You got to give the money back,' she said.

'Who to? I don't know whose it is. I don't know who I was meeting. Plus we've spent it.'

'They're gonna go on killing,' Topik said. 'I know Jamaica.'

'I can't stop them now. How can I stop them?'

'Why didn't I think of this?' Topik said.

'It might be random,' said Pang, feeling himself falling into a churning vat of fear and guilt, 'it might be nothing to do with us. You're always saying how bad the violence is there.'

The atmosphere in their new home, which had been so joyful, turned deadly. But they pressed on and painted the lounge and bedroom together, and while Pang retiled the bathroom, Topic sewed and hung the curtains. They were looking at a rug they had bought for the hall in a thrift store when Pang said 'Okay. Okay. I can't have any more on my conscience. I'm going to ring the guy in Vegas who set it up, Henry, and say we want to give back as much as we can.'

'You have his number?'

'It's on the old phone.'

Pang went to the drawer and picked up the Samsung he had turned off the night he left Chicago with the money. He considered it.

'Can they track it if you turn it on?' Topik said.

'The FBI can, but not a private citizen,' said Pang. 'And it's sure not the FBI after us.' He paused, adding, 'it's worse than that.'

He plugged in the charger and they went into the kitchen to anxiety snack on nachos.

'Get the phone,' Topik said, emptying the dust down her throat.

Pang came back, the phone came to life. 'Forty-two voicemails. Twenty three messages.'

'Play the voicemails,' Topik said.

The first one was calm:

Hi, I am waiting outside arrivals for you but don't see you. Wave your cap above your head please.

'I guess that's the guy,' Pang said.

'Unless he sent somebody else to meet you.'

Can you ring me to confirm you have landed?

I can't find you. Please pick up.

Call me as soon as you hear this.

This is serious, Leroy, you have my money. So call me.

But another voice could be heard in the background of this one, saying 'Bangaz! Uptop! Big man! Bangaz Thompson. Jah-jah. Good to see you.'

Then a new voice on a new message:

Leroy this is Henry here in Vegas. Has there been a problem? Call me.

You better call straight way, man.

What the fuck is going on man? You better not rob that money. That would be a big mistake. Believe me.

Leroy. Just call me.

They got to the end and Topik said, 'play that one again with the man hailing up the caller.'

Pang found it, they listened to it and Topik said, 'Bangaz Thompson.'

'You heard of him?' Pang asked.

'No,' said Topik.

'Good,' said Pang. 'At least he's not a famous gangsta. So I'm gonna get in touch, tell him I'll return his money, and we'll sell the house. What a fuck up.'

'There is another option,' Topik said, opening a fresh packet and digging salsa with a corn chip. ' Pang, I don't want to give up this place. Do you? How are we ever gonna be able to afford a place like this again? I don't want my relatives murdered, so, it's simple: We kill this Bangaz guy. I mean, he started it. We stop it.'

Pang looked aghast. 'You planning on sending me down to Jamaica to assassinate a gangster? I'm not sure that's in my skill set.'

'No. We pay a gunman to do it.'

'You gonna google one?'

'You probably can. That's Jamaica. Loads of them have gun and will do it for money.'

'Isn't that like making it worse? I am not feeling good about this,' he felt his stomach churn. He was close to vomiting.

'Let me make a call.' She said.

Pang tried get his mind off the nightmare, and found something to do in the bathroom: the grouting behind the shower control needed touching up, so he went to get the sponge and grout. As he passed the kitchen he heard Topik say, 'Yuh. Mi have a job for someone who really serious bout dem work.'

66

The gory details of the double death of the two old ladies were picked over by the people dem up and down the line. As they sat on porches, threw dice onto dudi tables, slapped down dominoes outside sheds, waited for buses on the roadside or chat pon dem phone, they revelled in the details: the empty shell casings scattered on the porch; the charred bodies, the faithful dog staring at the blackened ruins. Everybody agree the gun man wicked and heartless.

To improve his standing with the dogs and the girls, Gutta let it be known that he was the gunman. He swaggered around with his pants and belt half way between his knees and his waist, his gun in him back pocket visible to any who looked. He adopted a dark and dangerous expression and told people he only ever smiled after a killing.

After the shaky start, Gutta's business began to grow. The number of customers who were prepared to pay around 400 bucks to have someone killed was encouragingly high. The only challenge to his business model was the police, and luckily for Gutta they took little interest in his activities. If forced to by an irate population, the police could be relied on to arrest and charge the wrong person. As the golden era of scamming passed, so the golden era of gunmen began. The jobs came in thick and fast. You could say Gutta was just in the right place at the right time. He purchased more guns and ammunition, and got himself a high grade girl: Tanna

Thompson, the slimatic teenage daughter of Bangaz Thompson, the original famous scammer.

There were setbacks: unfortunately he killed another old woman accidentally in cross fire, and people joked that he only killed old ladies. But that apart, Gutta's world was complete. He lived up in a yard in the bush with his bredren, enjoying the rebel life of motorbikes, guns, ganja and other people's choppings.

As his reputation grew so he began to get requests to kill more prominent people. For this he could charge whole heap of money.

When he was offered 2,000 US dollars for a hit, Gutta knew he had made it into the big time. Then he heard who it was: Bangaz Thompson.

Gutta was speaking to his client in America. He said 'Bangaz Thompson? Dis no pram push ting. A big man ting. Dis a gonna cost yuh major dollars.'

'How much?'

'Three grand. US.'

'Okay. That's okay. The lady says three grand is okay.'

'One now and two when the job is complete,' said Gutta.

It was true that Gutta liked Bangaz and was in a relationship with his daughter, but those things did not count. He was a gunman. He killed people for money. He couldn't let his feelings get in the way of business. And anyway, he didn't have any feelings left.

67

The last dab of gold paint had been applied to the tip of the minaret and the spikes on the gate of Bangaz's palace. Marva drew up in a cab and shooed the gardener out of the way as she approached the Georgian front door.

Pauline, glowing with prosperity and power, sat at the breakfast counter with Bangaz. She was going over some new land opportunities and telling Bangaz about a shopping mall in Mandeville he was now a partner in.

Marva stamped in and said, 'Why you let that gardener sit in the shade?'

'Cos him tired after work from early,' Bangaz said.

'If he take a break make him sit in the sun or he start enjoy it too much and don't do work properly. You have more cash for me to pick up?'

'We don't pick up no more,' said Pauline. 'Western Union a too much problem for we right now.'

'That just Sidi. Sidi a small fry. You can solve dat problem with ease,' Marva snapped her fingers. 'Eliminate it. Then we can move forward with Western Union.'

'We have another way to get the cash down now.'

Marva dropped her bag heavily onto the counter. 'So wha about me?'

'We nuh need you right now,' said Pauline.

Marva said to Bangaz: 'Dem nuh fraid of you at Western Union you know. You let them tief your money and you nuh defend it. Ya too quiet so dem take you for a fool. That's how you reach this fockry.'

Pauline said, 'Leave dat alone Marva. Dat nuh concern you.'

'It haffi concern me. What about my percent? Mi nuh count as nutn? What about my likkle dividends? Mi want help out mi son, but now him just brush mi aside like dirty cloth.'

'You cya gwaan do sump elkse, I will look,' said Bangaz.

'Do the shopping,' said Pauline, 'and stop chat at mi head. A land we a deal with, things that are important.'

Pauline turned away from Marva to explain to Bangaz the structure of a deal she and Liar Reynolds had put together with some Chinese investors. Marva stared at her with screw face.

While she was talking, Pauline pushed a pad of paper and pen at Marva.

'Write a list,' she said to Marva. 'We want irish, yam, chicken part.'

'My son don't eat chicken part,' said Marva. 'Him want leg and thigh. He your husband and mi haffi tell you that.'

'Lasco,' said Pauline, pointing at the list.

Marva wrote down the words:

Tin Milk

Rice

Peas

Kill Sidi

Foil

Okra

Oranges

'Ya get everyting?' Pauline said, dipping in her Vuitton. She gave Marva some money but Marva remained staring at the cash in her hand until Pauline added some more to it, when Marva put it in her pocket and left to go a market and find Gutta.

With the house quiet but for the little squeak of the ceiling fan, Bangaz looked closely at Pauline's face and tilted his head.

'You start bleach?' He asked softly.

Pauline put a hand to her face and shrugged her shoulders. She had been using a skin-lightening lotion for the past few weeks but hoped he wouldn't notice.

'How long you bleach?' Bangaz said, and kiss his teeth.

She did it because Liar Reynolds liked it. But she couldn't tell Bangaz that. She gave a fast shake of her head and looked back at the planning maps.

'You know we don't bleach in this family,' Bangaz said. 'We nuh bleach and we nuh pick up gun. You know that.'

But Pauline bleached.

68

Bigz Hibbert was fast in his bus, but slow on foot. A big man with shoulders sloped from years of resignation, he spent the day behind the wheel of his black people carrier driving dozing hotel workers to and from their shifts in Negril. He liked a quiet life, always avoiding pock-hole and trouble, and at the end of each day returning safe to his yard and his wife, to eat a food, and watch TV till him drop asleep. His survival mechanism was to swerve conflict at all costs. It was easy to nuh deal wid other drivers, and Bigz humble with a long fuse.

When Auntie Hanna and Myra were murdered, Bigz called it mistaken identity. When Bigz's son, Dalton, lay in the morgue different rumours travelled as fast as any taxi up and down the line. Three people had heard the gunman shout that it was because Dalton tief scammer money.

Dalton had a college friend called Romario, who people said was a known scammer. Romario arrived at school on a new bike with a new knapsack and new girl every week. He had funds. Furthermore, Romario had been Dalton's best friend, and it was an established fact in west Jamaica that your best friend was also your enemy and your enemy your best friend. Everybody agreed: Romario and Dalton must have got into some scamming business and something had gone wrong, as it tended to with chopping.

Bigz had never lived with his son and had not been close to him, it was true, but it burn him bad when he had to go to Dalton's nine-night, wake, graves-digging and funeral. Everybody up and down the line in all the little communities he passed through; Little London, Wakefield, Ferris Cross, Cave, all of them want to know wha gwaan. Bigz shrugged and said, 'bwoy mi ne'evn know miself, because him nevva trouble people, Dalton was a good boy, so man dem jus wicked. E'en police dem not even a do them work so we cyah know nothing.'

Bigz couldn't see the point of looking for perpetrators. What good would it do to find out who kill Dalton? It would just kick up more trouble. Dalton was dead. But Dalton's madda Stacey came to find Bigz and race him up.

'Yuh son dead and yuh nuh do nutn bout it! Ya coward! Everybadi a seh a Romario kill him'.

Bigz was gingerly stepping down from the Voxy after a long shift. His foot and foot bottom swell up with bad circulation and dem painful to use. He wearily raised a hand to his wife, who was standing on his porch watching.

'Two aunty dead, Dalton dead,' said Bigz to Dalton's mumma, 'I don't want no more, so just forget 'bout it and don't make more trouble.'

Stacey, a tall woman with a scooped nose and strong body went to lick Bigz, but stopped herself at the last moment. 'Yah wasteman,' she shout at him instead. 'Yuh nuh serve nuh purpose. Yuh neva help when him a pickney, all now him dead yuh still nah help.'

Romario was murdered four days later. His bullet ridden remains were left half in the gutter at the front of a local beauty supply store where he had gone to purchase bleaching lotion.

He had a lavish and emotional schoolkid's funeral, with the girls looking glamorous and bawling to the cameras. The police were there to keep an eye on a swarm of chopper dem on motorbikes which turned up and buzzed through the gathering, but when the police charged them they turned their bikes and drove at the police sending them running for cover.

GOOD SCAMMER

Savannah La Mar College got an enviable reputation for creating rich and successful scammers. Tales were told of Romario's bingos and, of course, his fatal feud with Dalton. On the porches, under the almond and mango trees, in the sheds and in the bars, the people listened carefully and took sides. Some say Romario at fault, others Dalton, but all revelled in the notoriety it brought the school and community. The well attended and televised funerals proved it. It hot inna de air with stories of Dalton, Romario and the police rout. From porch to bar to minibus to taxi, word spread east. And it soon reach down to the corporate area, St Andrew, and Kingston town itself. And the yout, some of them good, some of them bad, roused themselves and made plans to travel out to the west end of the island to join the gold rush.

69

Willy for once rose eagerly and early to get on his way to meet Bangaz in their secret location in Ocho Rios. He was feeling enthusiastic about the project and wanted to make sure he squeezed the last bit of story out of Bangaz before he was killed — 'he' referring to both of them in that sentence.

In the dawn light the sea was pan flat and utterly silent, its surface one transparent flexing plane over the coral reef. When the sun hit the hills, the rising heat would draw air from the ocean and obscure the underwater garden with ripples. Bangaz went to his battered Toyota, revved it up and drove east. For the first ten miles he was on familiar tarmac and knew each of the potholes personally. The most famous pothole was the one at the hospital turn in Lucea, where the right of way was given for anyone with someone ill in their car. Many drivers meet in accident there. The pothole was a yard wide and so deep it destroyed any wheel that dropped into it. Everybody understood that cars swerved across the centre line to avoid it and made allowances by giving them space. The pothole only became a problem if someone drove the road who didn't know about it.

Willy decided to meet at a place he found called the Sea Breeze Hotel, in Ocho Rios, about a three hour drive away. It had started life as The Colonial Hotel in the 40s. Constructed in a time before sunbathing, it had no beach, just a concrete path by the shallow water. This was the cause of its slow and demeaning demise. It served an era when everyone made every effort to be as white as possible. In every meaning of the word. Hotel design had since changed from colonial outpost to tropical paradise.now, a hotel without a beach had become a restaurant without a kitchen. As he drove down the coast he passed many new all-inclusives with modernist buildings lurking behind generous greenery.

Willy parked in the empty car park by a derelict building with a lop sided sign saying Ocho Rios Arts Gallery & Café. The façade of the old hotel was now seedy and in full decay. The heat was hanging around, and his clothes began to stick to him.

He passed between the battered pillars and entered the cavernous reception area which echoed with a TV watched by a caretaker lying on a fake leather couch. Only six inches of the receptionist was visible because she stood behind a desk five feet high. A sign behind her said Cash Only. She slid the tiny key over a counter so wide that impulsive grabs for money or her throat were impossible.

The caretaker roused himself to show Willy to his room without offering to take his bag. They walked along an open gallery with pipes weeping liquid down the concrete and wist falling from the mossy roof. The swimming pool was taped off, and the pool house had a bow in the roof and gaps in the shingles like missing teeth in a drunken smile.

Expectations were low as Willy entered the gloomy room, and they were fully met. The French windows were so dirty he only realised he had a sea view when he opened them to let out some stale air. Outside he discovered a concrete balcony with the charm of a World War II bunker, but with a view of a fairy tale bay.

He heard a knock on the hotel door.

'Yes mi bredda,' Bangaz said as he touched knuckles, loped past Willy and dug into his shoulder bag for his weed and wizla.

'You good?' asked Willy. 'Y pree?'

'Everyting smooth and cool. You good?'

'Yes. Now here are the rules, Bangaz, and I expect you to keep to them for the safety of us both: we only meet here in the room, we are not seen together anywhere, okay? Not even entering the hotel or around it. I am not taking any chances. Are you staying in Ochi?'

'Mi turn wid mi bredren pon the hill.'

'Well keep your head down. Be discrete. Be aware that bad people dem look for you to kill you. Don't tell nobody you work with me. Don't tell nobody we are here.'

'.... Dem nah get chance fi kill me Willy. Dat naah go happen.'

'Well just be careful.'

Bangaz suck him teeth and reach in him bag for lighter.

'What you want to hear bout?' he said.

Willy held out his palms. 'Over to you.'

'Let me tell you bout Sidi, the girl at Western Union. One day after I see Omar I was driving out to get a chicken at Barry. I like to go there and sit and hol' a reasoning wid Barry and couple of fi we bredren, watch the car dem drive past and buy chicken to carry home. As I drive back through Green Island I see whole heap o' people all over the road and higgler selling beer and soft drink from the back of the car so I slow down to ask wha gwaan? A bredda say it a wake. I say who dead? And he answer Sidi. Dem murder her in Lucea.'

'Christ,' said Willy. 'Who killed her?'

'Some likkle gunman, but who pay him nobody know. Mi wan' a drink. You want a beer?'

'May as well,' Willy said.

Bangaz left the hotel room. Willy opened the laptop, fired it up and found a pen in his bag. He started making notes. When Bangaz came back he took him through the crazy sequence of events leading up to Sidi's death and the aftermath.

Bangaz thought about who knew Sidi was a tief. He did, Pauline did, Marva did, Omar did and probably Omar's sister did. He called Omar. He asked Omar if it was he who put out a contract on Sidi. Omar said 'she never dead?' Omar assured him he was nutn to do with it, and Bangaz believe him. Sidi could well have been robbing other choppers but some hunch made him think Marva was involved.

He tracked her down in his own kitchen, where she spent most days either sitting on his couch or standing at his fridge. Jenna was at the desk on the computer looking at pictures of coral reefs for her biology A level coursework.

'Where is Tanna?' Bangaz asked.

'Mi nuh know,' shrugged Marva.

'She gon a road,' said Jenna without looking away from the screen.

'Who with?'

'Mi nuh know,' Marva said. 'Mi baby-sitter? How can I know where she go?'

'She gone with Bookal and Gutta.'

Bangaz suck teeth. 'Marva, come with me. Mi want fi talk.'

Marva made a great play of the inconvenience of having to get off the couch and move. They went into a bare concrete room with the washing machine in one corner and two plastic washing tubs in the other.

Bangaz closed the door and said 'Did you pay smaddy fi kill Sidi?'

Marva twitched, but then crossed her arms defiantly at her chest.'Yes. Because you fraid to do it. People will see her dead and respect you.'

Bangaz said 'Bludclaat,' and moved to leave the room before he lost his temper, but then turned around and confronted her. 'Who give you the money?' he said.

Marva sighed, as if his questions was an inconvenience. 'I take it from the housekeeping and shopping money,' she said.

Bangaz shook his head slowly, rubbing his eyes with a thumb and forefinger.

'Don't worry about it,' Marva said, adding 'Look, nobady nah suspect me of killing nobody.'

Bangaz rolled his head back. 'I did,' he said quietly, to the ceiling.

70

Willy held up his hand to stop Bangaz talking, to catch up with his notes. Bangaz went out onto the balcony, and then spun round, put his finger to his lips and beckoned Willy.

On the balcony, Bangaz could hear a man talking in the next room. Bangaz tilted his head, listened, and stifled laughter. Willy tried to hear what was being said.

'......according to the rules and regulations, when there are overseas transactions under your name, you need to pay the full portion of the transaction fees to the IRS Department, which you never did.....'

'Chopper!' Bangaz mouthed.

The man droned on: 'they have investigated each and everything, and they have filed a lawsuit complaint against your name...'

Willy could tell what was about to come. They went back in the room. Bangaz was delighted with his discovery. 'Some time half a hotel full up with scammer. Like a office block,' he giggled. 'Ya cya believe it, de honest truth.'

'So, let me guess. Sidi's people vex bad and want revenge,' Willy said.

'A dat, mi general,' Bangaz said filling his plastic cup from the flask. 'Dem decide to kill me and find some dog from Sav to do the work. It easy to find gunman. But the man don't know me, so Sidi dem show him a photo of my Audi with the big foglamp.' Bangaz puff on him spliff, then said 'what they don't know is I like to buy new car all the time, and I had just buy another, a BMW X, black. And my old car get sold to a old man called Harold Firbank, worked on the trains in England for thirty years before retiring to Jamaica, where him born. How mi know? Cos dem publish it in the Sunday Gleaner. The killer full up the Audi and Harold with bullet out at Bogue, Montego Bay way. A dat the paper say.'

'Christ,' said Willy. 'What a mess.'

'A dat, mi general,' said Bangaz.

Willy looked up the murder of the returnee in the Gleaner. Page 5. A washed out photo of the bullet holes in the Audi. A quote from his daughter about senseless violence and wicked people. A statement from the local pastor calling for better protection of returnees who were being targeted by local gangsters.

'So this was when the guns really arrived,' sighed Willy, patting the newspaper on the bed for his cellophane with four Craven A in it.

'This was when the guns come, Willy,' said Bangaz. The sun had set, the night moved in and they were sitting in the room as it got darker. 'And it change everyting. Everyting mash up bad. Dem Haitian bwoy bad, and nutten normal. They treat the fisherman beach like one Walmart. The whole a the north coast in fact. Like a supermarket whey you pay for everyting in gun and ammunition.'

'Desperate people I expect,' said Willy.

'You could trade anything with them for a tool. Even diet Pepsi. Even hair cream. Even bleaching lotion.....'

'Who was buying the guns?'

'Some local yout, but whole heap o' bwoy draw west by lure of riches, dem mumma send them to come to get a big house, spike heel shoe and false hair.'

They sat in silence. The man next door either lose the fish off the hook or bingo, because he wasn't making any noise.

'When scamming meet guns it like gasoline and lighter,' Bangaz said, sparking him spliff and shaking his head. 'It get mad. Everybody run, who can. But nobody can excape.'

71

On a still afternoon at the fisherman beach, nothing stirred; Troy was sitting in the shade with his feet up when he recognised an engine coming down the old road. It was Herbert. The Minister pulled over onto the sand and got out to look around.

'Afternoon, sir,' call Troy. 'Lobster done. You want drink?'

'No, no, I'm all right thank you.' He wandered over the litter strewn beach towards Troy. There had been a bingo the night before.

'All good?' Troy asked him.

'Indubitably,' smiled Herbert. 'Can you call Bangaz?'

'Yes boss.' Troy took out his phone and said a few words into it.

They settled into a comfortable Campbell Cove silence, watching the sea lapping onto the sand and gulping at the rocks.

Herbert took a deep breath and said, 'You don't hear from Deliesha?'.

'Deliesha gone up.'

'You don't know where?'

'Inna foreign me hear,' said Troy.

Herbert said, 'I guess you miss her at the bar.'

'Everybody miss Deliesha, dem haffi.' Troy said.

'Yes. She lit the place up,' said Herbert.

'A dat. The glory days,' said Troy.

'When it came to having fun, she truly raised the bar high,' said Herbert.

'She raise the whole bar truly high,' said Troy.

Bangaz drove his black BMW down to the beach side. There he saw the Minister's car.

Herbert was standing holding his keys talking to Troy.

'You want a drink?' Bangaz called.

'I will take a beer,' said Herbert.

'Hot or cold,' asked Troy.

'Give me a hot Red Stripe.'

Troy bought the beers with the caps half on and turned on his heels to disappear in the bar. He knew big man ting when he saw it. Bangaz poured a sip of beer onto the sand.

Herbert looked around and then said quietly 'Wha a gwaan?'

'Wha?' asked Bangaz.

'Serious, man, serious ting, what has happened to this community?'

Bangaz suck teeth.

'What have you done?' said Herbert. 'It's a war zone.'

'That is not me,' said Bangaz. 'You know that is not me. If they don't listen to me the first time, I talk softer. That is my style. I don't pick up no gun.'

'Well I can't protect you anymore,' Herbert said. 'Do you know how many gun murders there are in this constituency? Thirty-four in the last four months. Campbell Cove and the villages on this side have a higher murder rate than Pittsburgh. A higher number of victims than Australia, New Zealand and the United Kingdom combined! In this one constituency where 100,000 people live.'

'It just foolishness,' said Bangaz. 'It soon sekkle.'

'I'm out. I can't help you anymore, even if I wanted to. I'm no longer the Minister of Justice. The boss has moved me. The Americans told him to. I'm on roads and infrastructure. You also need to know the Americans want to bring the army in. You know they're after you?'

Bangaz thought, if they were going to bring Bangaz down, Herbert nuh wanna get sink himself.

'You muss worry mi ago talk if dem arrest me,' Bangaz said.

Herbert shrugged.

'Mi would nevva sell you out Herbert. You cool.'

'Well, I appreciate that...'

'If you want to help me and stop them pressure me for information, you can do one thing for me.'

'Sure. What's that?'

Bangaz kicked at the sand. He was cornered. He said: 'You can get me out of the country.'

'What do you need?'

'Clean my Police recard. And get a invitation letter from some big person, one of your links dem in the states.'

'I cannot help with the police record. I regret that the FBI are too involved now. That is too much for me to do.'

Bangaz nodded slowly, the sharp point of panic beginning to creep into his blood. 'How can I get out?' Bangaz said.

'I don't know,' said Herbert. 'I don't think there's a legal way, to be honest. You are on every watch list. FBI. Homeland Security, Interpol...'

A shooterman waded ashore dragging his canoe behind him on a string. Bangaz saw there were three lobster, four fish and an innertube-powered harpoon gun in the boat.

'I have to go,' said Herbert. 'We can't meet again. I'm sorry I can't help.'

'No problem,' said Bangaz, thinking the opposite.

Bangaz watched the Minister get in his car and hurry onto the highway and get away and thought, now another man want mi dead.

72

Danielle was buzzing. Spliff in one hand, Red Stripe in the other, dancehall music exploding around her. She'd hit the ground running at Donald Sangster International, been met at arrivals by Bangaz and Ample, handed them 135 grand, received $28,000 US in cash, and was now standing outside Troy bar in the tropical warmth of the evening, mingling with the good people dem.

'One of mi bredren bingo,' Bangaz shouted at her.

As the saying went: there is nothing with more promise than the Jamaican night.

It was her eighth run into Montego Bay, nothing had gone wrong and she had become good friends with the guys, and better friends with Jamaica. It had turned from a suspicious acquaintanceship into a fiery love affair. Ample kept smiling at her from where he stood chatting and laughing with bredren. He could make her feel gorgeous with those melting eyes and goofy grin.

She tapped her foot in time to the rhythm. The music felt so good with Bangaz and Ample. She felt invisibly protected by them. Mercifully her Patwa wasn't good enough to understand the lyrics. 'Treat my nuts like cashew,' the artist implored. 'Leg in the air like chandelier. She smell better than a barbeque.'

Sometimes Andy did the trip with her, but honestly it was easier without him, and it was good to get home and find him waiting so patiently and attentively, particularly as she usually walked back into the apartment with twenty-five grand. Andy wasn't cut out for the world of work. Danielle was.

She had had a uniform made for her. It was her idea and her design: a green short sleeved shirt with the words Legal Courier and a logo of a piece of A4 with wings on her chest. She wore a cap of the same green with a peak piped in yellow. They were matched with green McJob elasticated slacks and a pair of minimum wage sneakers. In addition she had a green shoulder bag also with the logo and the words Fast & Legal emblazoned on it. She looked convincing.

'Official,' said Bangaz.

'Official,' agreed Ample.

The bar start hot up with DJ Barney on the decks. The place pack. Danielle was forced back against the wall watching the crowd dancing, smoking and drinking. The women danced Leggo the Bird, Stir fry, Dirt and Bounce. A yout shouted through the music at the bartender for a 50 bag of weed and chopped it on the block on the bar. When he put the spliff to his lips he was palmed a lighter by a friend without asking or looking. Danielle watched Bangaz stand with his back against the wall telling a woman a story, and she felt Ample beside her. The place was growing hot and skin glistened with sweat. The bartender dipped into the freezer for a bottle of frozen water, took a knife to the plastic, peeled it back and hacked the tube of ice into shards. Outside from the dark, the air stirred and a caring breath of ocean breeze wafted through the bar and over the people.

Wearing a striped hoody and with his belt barely above his knees, Gutta sat on the Armco barrier and watched Danielle leave the bar with Ample and get into the Audi. They were going back to Plantation to have fun.

With the woman tourist out of the way it was safe for Gutta to move in and kill Bangaz. It had been on his to-do list for months but he chill with a gang of scammers in Redland, Negril. Gutta's instinct was to walk straight into the bar and kill Bangaz in front of everybody, to advertise his business and spread his fame, but even Gutta could see that with Bangaz's popularity that plan could back-fire. So he sneaked up the side of Troy bar, had a quick glance inside, spotted Bangaz on the far wall, swung his gun through the window and, without looking, squeezed the trigger.

The pistol leapt in his hand and flame spiked from its muzzle. Something lick the air and sent people flying. He kept pulling the trigger. The cracks sounded like god smack the shed. Some shout, some bawl, all fled fighting to get outside. Gutta was already fifty yards up the highway, holding his buckle, sprinting to the tree where he left his bike. He dash into the bush and wait for the people to simmer down, but the pack ran after him, thinking they were running from trouble. He took out his gun and shot over them, turning them terrified like fowl, so they all sprinted back down the highway away from him, screaming into the darkness.

Bangaz had taken cover under the shed bottom in the area behind a bamboo fence where they cooked on an open fire. The hand coming through the window waving the pistol was seared on his brain. He heard the crowd shouting far away and went back into the bar where the pepper lights illuminated the chaos: the decks and amps had spilled over and cables were tangled in fallen furniture, and there along the bottom of the bar, one arm behind his back, nose and face against a pool of blood, lay a dead man: Bunna.

73

Everybody start fi chat when the first Jamaica Defence Force unit pass through. The army now run ting. They appeared in a column of dark green, open sided jeeps each loaded with soldiers in camouflage. Campbell Cove had never seen the army before, except parading pon TV at official ceremonies. They looked foreign to Bangaz: unlike the police their equipment was in good condition. Their uniforms were new, their boots strong. They were silent. They were disciplined. They were not friendly. How could they even be Jamaican?

General Gordon, a polished officer with a tight uniform and bristly moustache, came on to TV with the Prime Minister to reassure the people.

'Quiet,' said Bangaz from the couch, waving at Marva. She was enjoying a conversation with Tanna she returned to whenever Bangaz was in earshot. It was about what she would do if she won the Lotto.

'Mi woulda buy miself a nice likkle house wid good yard space, cuz mi cya afford fi a worry bout security at my age. Mi wuda buy a likkle car. Lawd, it must feel so nice to have a car.' She gazed into space basking in the thoughts of owning her own motor vehicle, and then stared pointedly at Bangaz. 'Mi body too old to cramp up and bungle up in a taxi or bus. Lord God, I hope I get likkle good luck 'cuz from when I was born mi have bad luck, like mi neva christen. Mi life is not sweet like yours you know young gal. I wish it could be easy like yours. But you have a daddy who look after you, who will buy you big house uptown and car and let fly go a Miami first class.'

'Shh, woman!' Bangaz hissed. He was listening to the rules of the State of Emergency: detention without charge for thirty-five days. Searches without warrants. Any equipment deemed to be connected with telephone fraud, criminal. Withholding password: criminal offence. No appeals. Bangaz scanned the group of men on the screen squeezed together to give themselves confidence. He knew none of them. The police had been demoted. Even removed.

The next day, Bangaz drove through a road block outside Lances Bay. Patrick flagged him down so Bangaz slowed to hail him up, chat and give him a little help, in the traditional manner. But then he saw, in the deep shade behind Patrick, four heavily armed camouflaged soldiers. They didn't smile, they didn't even nod at Bangaz when he acknowledged them. They weren't flabby and relaxed and pale on the fat of corruption, like Patrick. They were fit and black skinned, from working hard in the sunshine. The metal on their M16s showed wear. This was not Gutta or some Negril dog with a Haitian pistol and ten bullets. This was a killing machine.

Patrick asked Bangaz to step out the car. The police looked serious and anxious, so Bangaz played along. Two police searched his car. A soldier stood behind and said 'Trunk'.

Bangaz opened the boot, and let the police search around spare tyre. To most Jamaican men the car was considered a more intimate space than the body, and they did not like it interfered with, but Bangaz remained relaxed. 'Glove box,' said the soldier.

Bangaz was clean, and they let him through. But many other choppers were pulled over, busted and sent to the lock up in Montego Bay. The scammers smashed the phones with their fists as they approached the blocks. If the authorities got into a scammer's phone it was a problem situation. No liar could get you out of that, because under the State Of Emergency no attorneys were allowed for suspected scammers. It could even mean extradition and a ten year sentence in America. The Army didn't need evidence.

They just dragged the yout from the car, sometimes through the window, and trow them in the lock up. The arms of the scammers waved out of the slit windows at the crowd of mummas and aunties on the roadside calling for justice for their yout dem.

The judiciary and some NGOs made calls to respect human rights, but they were ignored. Even the many big people who benefit from the chopping industry begin to think twice. The murders were a factor. When the big people travel to the States they had to listen to the reputation of Jamaica being dragged through not just the mud but the do-do. But no real Jamaican cared about that. A real Jamaican was secretly proud to be from the badderest country on earth. What did vex the big people dem was how difficult the scammers made any kind of business transaction. Want to make a bank transfer to your daughter in college in the States? Forget it. Just as the Americans pressure Western Union and Moneygram so they get tough on the banks. The moment the big people used their credit cards in Jamaica they were blocked. Buying real estate, buying boats, buying new cars became tiresome and invasive. Everybody had to ask questions because the Americans demanded it. You couldn't even get a phone without proving your ID.

Bangaz felt the mood change. Too much people supported the crackdown. Too much people knew somebody who had been killed. And too much people hated the police, and were happy to see them humiliated by the army. Things came to a head in Negril when the army were hunting down a friend of Gutta who had paid the police to protect him. The army opened fire on the police and wounded three of them, much to the delight of the people of Campbell Cove.

Marva started talking again. 'You have your daddy,' Marva was telling Tanna. 'Lord, I never get a rich daddy. I muss live with that sin. I cannot complain to share a room in a house with three other old people as I get old. I will be fine. As long as you your sister Jenna and my favourites, come and check me and bright up my day with a visit ...'

'Hush up now, Marva,' said Bangaz. 'Let me listen.'

The US Ambassador was being interviewed after the press conference. 'We consider it reprehensible that two of Jamaica's leading rap artists released a song with lyrics saying that the scammers are stars and the money they steal is reparations. We are encouraged that new government in Jamaica has finally passed some new laws targeting the scammers, but I am deeply troubled that it has taken Jamaica so long — years — before getting serious about this problem. For far too long, Jamaican authorities turned a blind eye to this fraud, which was illegally bringing an estimated $300 million annually to their economy ...'

Bangaz stood up, shaking his head, found his car keys and drove to Bunna nine-night.

74

When Bangaz turned up at the fisherman beach he only saw six cangle lit for Bunna. He found a yout, gave him some cash and told him to go to Sharon fi three dozen cangle and paper bag. When the bike returned Bangaz told the yout to fill the bags with sand and line the path to the shed with them. Bangaz then planted the candles into the sand and bent down and lit each one so the bags glowed in the dusk.

The people were still shaken from the shooting at Troy bar, and were nervous about going back in the shed, though all had briefly to approach in hushed reverence the spot where Bunna's blood stained the boards at the base of the bar.

Large gatherings, including nine-nights, graves-digging, wake and funeral were banned under The State of Emergency. A few days later Bangaz attended a much reduced graves digging for Bunna. At dawn he arrived at the cemetery with two bottles of JB white rum, the traditional diggers' drink. He had paid for the cement and marl which Bunna's friends were already mixing as the daylight approached. Six men worked all day to dig the hole, line it in blocks and cast the top. Buckets passed from hand to hand in a human chain. When one man lay the shovel down another would step up and start scraping and mixing. By the end the job was done and them stagger away drunk, stiff with rum.

Bangaz choose Bunna's casket and pay for the funeral; him get a bands fi com play a the wake because Bunna people dem a Christian so him insist on live gospel. The band performed from a pick-up truck which made a stately progress through the village drawing people behind it to the cemetery. Bunna's madda, a tiny bent woman in a long skirt and dreads, came down from the hills to walk behind the casket alongside a couple of her sistren.

The choppers and the dogs stayed away, scared of the police and nervous of the people. They hid behind zinc fences in the ghetto or deep in the bush, feeling the pressure. Nobody could buy a good lead list or a script that wasn't now widely known in America. It became increasingly difficult to hook and land a fish. They spent most of the day calling a number and being told to go to hell. Which was strange because that was where they were, hunted by the army, penniless and hated by the community.

Up in the States, The Prize Patrol from the genuine Publishers' Clearing House, whose job it was to inform real lottery winners by turning up at their house with a cheque the size of a lilo, were beaten up in San Diego by a mob who had took them for scammers.

The young choppers put their trust in bizarre superstitions and outlandish rituals. Smoking formaldehyde and drinking the blood from a severed goat's head were believed to improve the chances of a bingo. Worthless guard rings changed hands for thousands of dollars because they brought protection from the army and police.

It was a dark, blood-stained time lived against a blistering soundtrack of devil music. The original scammer dancehall tunes spoke of peace, prosperity, and justice, but these ones ranted about war and greed. Jenna skip school and climb up pan Gutta bike gone a Redhill in a Negril where all dem do is pop Molly and grind and talk her daddy business. When the army came near she put back on her uniform and smuggled the gang's phones through the roadblocks.

Bangaz was awake and fidgeting at 4 am when he noticed the phone signal drop out. He hadn't been expecting any messages but could not stop checking his phone.

The army lock off the phone masts and arrived in force at the eastern end of Campbell Cove. General Gordon sent a column of jeeps to the far end of the community to stop anybody escaping, put more men on the hill, and a platoon down by the fisherman beach to keep an eye on the boats. The army had the place encircled, and then it went from door to door. Everybody out. Everybody. Each house was searched room by room for laptops, phones, lists, CDs, USB cables. The people cuss and use bad words but the army silent. They don't even swagger. They just do them duty.

Bangaz heard the shouting on the lane as people were bundled out of houses, and went to find who was in charge. He needed to speak to Patrick. Right at his gates he met General Gordon.

'The very man,' said the General. 'Open these gates.'

'Please come in,' said Bangaz.

'Search the place, and hold this man,' said the General.

Tanna woke up at the commotion. She stole silently across her room to a chest of drawers. She put her slender arm into the clothes and felt around, listening to soldiers stamping around the kitchen. She pulled out an iPhone, removed its sim card and swallowed it. Then she held the phone in her hand and punched its face with her fist until it cracked the glass, biting back the pain. She placed it back in the drawer and took out a Samsung Galaxy, removed its SIM card and punched its glass until it cracked, blinking back the tears. She was swallowing a third sim card and punching the phone when the doorhandle rattled.

'Mi a com,' she called, ramming the phone back under her dresses. She opened the door and was grabbed by a soldier and led outside to where Bangaz and Pauline stood beside Jenna, who wore an expression of fury, as if to say this is not my mess.

Bangaz watched them carry his laptop, desktop and cell phones past him, knowing they weren't going to find anything beyond a huge list of dancehall videos on YouTube and a bit of light porn.

'Come with me please,' the General said to Bangaz. 'And you,' he nodded at Tanna.

They were led into Tanna's room. A soldier in camo, mask, and helmet with a machine gun over his shoulder was holding a drawer of girl's dresses, while another was holding three phones.

'You find a dress that fits?' Tanna said.

'What are these?' The General asked.

'Phones,' said Tanna.

'Whose?' asked the General.

'Mi nuh know.'

'What are they doing in your room?'

Bangaz looked at his daughter.

'If I see broken phones I pick them up,' she said, 'because I hope to fix them one day and sell them to make money because my father doesn't give me enough money. I find them on the roadside near roadblocks.'

The General looked at the phone and looked into Jenna's innocent eyes. She felt a drop of blood oozing out of the wound on her knuckles. It dropped onto the tiled floor.

'You know if you carry phones for scammers we will charge you and try you and sentence you to go to prison?'

'I would never do that, sah.'

'Good.'

Twenty minutes later the General moved down the lane to another house where men were pulled out of the undergrowth at the edge of the yard and led in handcuffs to a van.

Bangaz ushered the women back into the house, closed the door and took a deep breath.

'Why you do that, Tanna?' he snapped at his daughter. 'You a walk and tek up bruk phone? You a get mad? Them can arrest you and charge you likkle girl.'

Tann turned to go to her room.

Jenna said 'She a liard. She never find di phone dem pon the roadside.' She grabbed Tanna's wrist and turned her hand palm down. Her knuckles were torn and bleeding. Jenna shook her hand free.

'Lef me alone. Why you do that?'

'Cos me care about you,' Jenna said. 'And you catch up in dangerous things.'

Tanna kiss teeth and walked off.

'Why you vex? She her daddy daughter,' said Jenna staring defiantly at Bangaz.

75

Bangaz drove out to Mo Bay to cruise the smooth tarmac of Freeport and park before the gleaming building where Liar Reynolds now practised law. He took the elevator to the 6th floor and waited briefly on his feet before the woman with a headset showed him into a room, where Brian Reynolds sat behind the same wooden desk Bangaz recognised from Negril.

If Reynolds looked sick it would not have been a surprise. Ever since Bangaz had said he had something important to talk about he had thought Pauline must have let something slip, and Bangaz was coming to kill him.

'Bangaz,' said Reynolds, putting out his hand. 'A honour that you grace us with your presence.'

'Wha gwaan?' Bangaz said.

'All good. Can I get you a coffee or glass of mineral water?'

'Get me a flask of JB, Red Bull chaser.'

Reynolds sent a secretary off somewhere to secure that; he had no idea where.

'Office look good,' Bangaz said.

'You remember my place in Negril?'

'Of course! Mi haffi. I come there as a boy with Maas Henry.'

'We've both come a long way since then. Sit, please.'

'A dat.'

'What can I do for you? I assume Pauline has been keeping you up to date with the property portfolio?' He said, moving some papers to avoid direct eye contact.

'Ya man. Mi cool with that. I come for another reason.'

Reynolds leant back, lightly reassured. 'Oh? What can I help you with?'

'I need to get a visa,' Bangaz said.

'For what country?'

'I need to get to the States or to England. I have to get the family out. Things too crazy.'

'Right.' He blinked. 'Well, you could probably get to South America. Brazil, Columbia ... Mexico?'

'Pauline don't want to go those places. Dem nuh chat English and dem nuh proper place. Pauline nah gonna like dem place deh.'

The secretary came in with a flask, can and glass on a tray. Bangaz popped the can and filled the glass.

'You can't get to the States,' Reynolds said, folding his hands on the desk and leaning forwards.

'I just need a invitation letter,' Bangaz said.

'No, that's not good enough for a man in your situation. Look, you are on every single watch list there is, we can be certain . They are all going to block you, and if they didn't I would be very suspicious that it would be a trap to arrest you the moment you set foot on American soil.'

'Wey you say?'

'I'm sorry, Bangaz, I'm only telling you the truth.'

'Bludclaat.'

'We could look into other countries. Nigeria, possibly....'

'Bumboclaat. Mi nuh come this far fi a go back a Africa,' Bangaz said.

'Sure,' said Reynolds.

Bangaz then said quietly, eyes cast down, 'Mi cya let Pauline and the girls stay a yard. It too dangerous. And Pauline well want to go up. You haffi find a way for me go with her.'

'It's difficult, Bangaz.'

'Tell me the loop hole,' he said, his voice raising, 'mi know how dem ting run. There is always a loop hole dem leave for high colour white people.'

Reynolds took a breath, put his forefinger and thumb to his temple, telling himself he better make this look good.

'There is one thing.'

'What?'

'Extraordinary ability.'

'What that?'

'If in your field of activity you are pre-eminent.' Reynolds loved to throw in some erudite English to impress the cheap seats.

'What that mean?' said Bangaz, not impressed.

'If you are, like, a top footballer, or top artist, or top actor, then you can get a visa for the States under a category called extraordinary ability.'

Bangaz spread his arm and stood up. 'Me that. Serious. It me,' he said.

'They don't have a section for scammers,' Reynolds said, 'but if they did it would be a—'

'—cake walk,' finished Bangaz. ' A cake walk! Extraordinary ability. Dat me a have! For sure.' He poured out his flask and drank it off. 'Bumboclaat,' he said.

'It's tricky,' said Reynolds pressing his fingertips together to make Bangaz think he was looking for a solution.

'What if a big person, really big man in America invite me?'

'Like who? The President?'

'Mi nuh know.'

'A politically influential sponsor could help, but unless you make firm friends with the chairman of Google or Netflix I would not put too much hope in it.'

'Bludclaat.' Bangaz lay his fist firmly, but quietly, on the desk. 'Mi try and lef this place from me a yout. It only true mi grandaddy dead mi lose mi paper dem,' Bangaz suck teeth.

'What are you going to do?'

'Mi ago buy a boat and sail off this jamrock. Sail up to British Virgin Island or Nassau and reach up to Florida that way. Mi run through the border if a dat me haffi do.'

76

Despite it being winter, when the island was desiccated and windblown, it was the tourist season because it was still much colder in America and Europe. That meant the tourist coaches hammered up the highway often appearing two abreast around a corner, kneeling on one front wheel. Willy added them to the list of dangers on his inner map of potholes on the road to Ochi.

Bangaz had been living in hiding in a community above the town called Exchange. Willy nosed through its narrow lanes between zinc and bare block walls. The hard blue line of the sea's horizon sometimes appeared between the treetops and the unfinished concrete houses. When he passed a bar he heard shouts for him to stop.

'Yo! White man! Willy!' a man shouted.

Willy stopped and wound down the window.

'How you know my name?' he smiled.

'The boss tell me. Him gone a barber gone trim. He soon come.'

'Thanks,' said Willy.

He turned off the car, opened the window and felt the Christmas breeze, a cool wind that blew from the wintry north.

Bangaz appeared in the rear view mirror and got in the car.

'Up top mi general,' he said.

'How come they know our names? You're supposed to be under cover.'

'A mi bredren dem. Dem cool.' He pointed down the hill.

They drove to the Sea Breeze and parked on the waste land by three sleeping dogs. Willy paid for the room and took the key, trying to shoo Bangaz away when he stood too close.

Safely in the room Bangaz reached for his weed and wizla while Willy set up his laptop and opened the doors onto the balcony and the fairy tale bay.

A huge plastic catamaran with a tiny jib, overflowing with tourists drinking and dancing, chugged across the sea. To the left, an opulent motor yacht with blacked out windows and no markings or flags rested at anchor.

'Scammer,' said Bangaz. 'After car and villa now dem want yacht.'

'How do you know that's a scammer's? It's a bit big. Do you know how much they cost?'

Bangaz lifted his phone to his ear. 'Run up mi flag,' he said and turned off the phone.

A man appeared on the deck of the yacht and sent a flag up the pole which caught the breeze and stretched out rippling. It was the Jamaican flag: green for the land, gold for the sun and black for the people.

'That's your boat?' said Willy.

Bangaz stared at the craft. Nodded.

'Really? Really? In that case, can't we do these interviews on board? Nobody would see us. Does it have a well-stocked cocktail cabinet? It looks like it should. And a shady deck to take the breeze?'

'Tek it dung,' said Bangaz into his phone.

The flag rapidly came down the pole.

'Dat a fi mi boat,' said Bangaz. He suck teeth. 'To look at. But me cya use it.'

'You should get a pirate flag,' Willy said.

'Dis a pirate flag. It the flag of Jamaica.'

'I know what you mean,' said Willy.

'We learnt from the biggest pirates of them all,' Bangaz said. 'You British. We are your child. But you abandon us. You run we away.'

'Only some. I keep the faith,' Willy said. 'I care about you.'

Bangaz kiss teeth.

'You certainly have our exceptionalism,' Willy said. 'You believe you are special. You are,' said Willy. 'Look, are you certain we can't go on board?'

'The Feds are watching. So mi cya risk it. If they catch me out at sea there is no witness. Dem will shoot me for sure.'

Bangaz went back inside to budge a sideboard away from the socket so he could plug in a phone and a battery, then looked out of the window, 'See weh mi a tell you?' he pointed.

A police boat cruised round the point where the Jamaica Inn Hotel started, and headed across the bay towards the boat. Two police were on deck, one with his hands on his hips, scanning the land.

'Dem see mi signal and look for me,' Bangaz said, backing into the room. Willy went down on his haunches behind the parapet. 'Ow,' he said.

After five minutes Bangaz came to the door. 'Dem gone,' he said.

'Not sure I'm going to be able to stand up.' When Willy crept back through the doors he stared at his screen for a couple of minutes and said, 'We've got some good news.'

He turned the screen of his laptop to Bangaz, but Bangaz said 'Read it.'

'It's from the woman at the movie company,' said Willy. 'Dear William. My friend and ex-colleague Ala passed your intriguing manuscript to me. I see the working title is THE GOOD SCAMMER. I'm not certain about that but I am certain about the content: fast, funny and authentic. A bright new voice crying out for justice. This is the kind of story we are looking for here at Netflix. Would you be interested in allowing us to develop it into a ten part series for streaming?'

Willy stood up 'Boom!' he said. 'Boom! Shake mi hand brudder. I love you, Bangaz! No, give me a fucking big hug. No, you don't do that.' He blew out a huge lungful of air. 'I tell you, if I am honest, I never thought we'd get this far. This is very, very good news indeed...' tears were actually forming in his eyes. Tears of joy, tears of gratitude, and, as he looked through them at the little man with the gleaming smile jiggling about in front of him, tears of love.

'Very good,' said Bangaz. 'Very good Willy.'

'This calls for a drink.' As Willy unscrewed the top of the flask he looked back at the screen.

'Hold on, there's more,' he touched the pad. 'Er.... On no.... Oh no....'

'What is the problem?'

'I think she thinks ... no, she definitely thinks I'm black.'

'And she change her mind? Dem racist people deh wicked, Willy. Explain you is white; we can still work with her. We have to just deal with that stuff.'

'No. If she thinks I am white she will not want to do the project. Look.'

He spun the laptop on the glass top of the frilly cane table and pointed to the paragraph.

Bangaz said, 'Read it.'

'I am flying down to Jamaica on a short vacation next month and I have to meet you. We can discuss how you see the end, talk about casting maybe, and of course enjoy a Red Stripe or Rum back a yard. Ya mon! We only have one rule in my division of Netflix: No white directors and no white writers! It's the perfect creative home for you. (My ancestry is part Jamaican I am proud to say.) Yours with warmest wishes, Ala Alagidi. Responds to pronouns she/her.' Willy placed his cup on the table top and said 'Bumboclaat.'

'What responds to pronouns she or her mean?' Bangaz asked.

'Some people out there have vagina but want to be called he.'

'Like Patwa?'

'No, because some people have penis and want to be called she.'

'A lie,' said Bangaz and kissteet.

'People are allowed to do something called self-identify and make people call them what they personally wish.'

'Why dem let them do that?'

Willy sighed. 'Can we talk about that some other time? Right now we have a more pressing problem. What am I going to do when she turns up? She wants to check me out, talk about the story. Say I'm ill? How long can I keep that up for? Of course we have to meet. Some time.' He held his head in his hands. 'Shit.'

'When she a com?'

'Willy glanced at the screen. 'She don't say.'

'Answer her and tell her you look forward to chill wid her when she reach dung a Jamaica.'

'And then say I sick out, when she gets here? The problem is, my dear friend, that this is just going to arise again. At some point I'm going to have to meet her and the chances are she'll notice that I'm white. It's like a fucked up situation and there is no way out.'

'There is always a way out. You never learn nothing from kingpin?''

'You don't understand, the book, the film, it'll just fall apart when she finds out I'm actually white. And, you know, I'm old, too ...'

'I will meet her, mi will represent we,' Bangaz said, slapping his chest. 'No problem. Wid ease. Mi go a her hotel, chat bout book, anything she want fi hear and tell her sey a me name William.'

Willy leant forward and stared at the worn beige tiles on the floor. He had a long think and said 'You're suggesting you go and pretend to be me?'

'Wid ease. No problem.'

'Can you do that?' Willy asked.

Bangaz raised both his eyebrows. 'Nutn can wrong. Never forget mi a coot.'

'Of course you can,' said Willy quietly. 'You've been training for it all your life.'

'This my story,' said Bangaz walking around, 'not your story, not his story. I know it more fully than even you, Willy. It gonna be a cake walk. Chuss me. A cake walk. Very good. Now write a email back to her. Aks which hotel, which time, and sign it from me and say me prefer pronoun Kingpin or The Boss and me don't got no vagina.'

77

It had always been the way that a pool of yout in Campbell Cove was available to dip into if Bangaz needed some labourers to do something in his yard. If he sent word out in the afternoon, the next day a couple of men would be at his gate ready to do what he wanted. But the pile of topsoil he needed to spread into a lawn was beginning to grass over. Since the yout all turn scammer, he couldn't interest anyone in the work. In an environment in which some sixteen-year-olds were making $500 US a day it was hard to get people to turn up for $20.

Bangaz turned away from the window. He was feeling anxious. He had heard gunshots in the lane in the middle of the night. They could have been anything but he felt it was smaddy intimidating him. He had gone to check on the girls: Jenna, to see if she was scared, Tanna, to see if she was there.

Jenna was sitting up in bed reading a book.

'Yuh hear dat?' she said.

'Yes. Nuh worry yourself, ano nutn. Just some foolish yout.'

'Yes.'

'What are you reading?'

'A book written by a man in the community. A white man.' She held it up. Bangaz recognised it.

'It can gwaan?'

'It's good. He's funny.'

'You get some sleep. It late.'

Tanna was fast asleep sprawled carelessly over her bed, without a worry in her head.

The next morning Bangaz woke early. Pauline said she was getting home around breakfast, which sounded wrong. If she was so close how come she had spent the night away? When she drew up he saw that Liar Reynolds was in a car behind her. Bangaz thought there must be a money problem. Maybe they had lost some cash on a deal.

They both came in the house, Pauline looking flustered.

'Wha gwaan?' Bangaz said.

Reynolds stood behind her as she said 'I have something important to tell you.'

'Wha'? You lose money?'

'No, not that.'

'What? Tell me.'

Bangaz checked to see where Marva was, but she was outside moving a couple of goats she had bought to try to show Bangaz how poor she was. The girls were upstairs getting ready for school.

'Talk,' said Bangaz.

She caught her breath. 'Bangaz, mi sorry. There is no other way to say this: I am leaving you. Mi a leff,' she said, 'mi haffi. And me carry the pickney dem with me, to 'merica. They cya be here no longer. It nuh safe fi dem nuh longer.'

'Wha?' He pointed at Reynolds. 'Wha you a do here?'

'Brian helped me,' Pauline said. 'With visa dem, and travel plan', she turned and smiled at Liar Reynolds. 'Him a 'merican citizen. Him born ova der.'

Bangaz said to Reynolds, 'Com outa mi house. Mi wan' talk wid my wife.'

'No,' said Pauline. 'He is with me now.' She reached out and held onto Reynolds' arm. 'We're getting married.'

'Weh you say?' croaked Bangaz. 'You do what?'

'Pauline has agreed to be my wife,' said Reynolds.

'Bumboclaat,' Bangaz said quietly.

'We haffi marry to get green card,' Pauline said.

'What! Jesus Christ. A muss joke dis.' He started pacing round the kitchen, staring dangerously at Reynolds.

'Mi wife and mi liar turn scammer!' Bangaz shouted.

Pauline placed her bag on the counter. 'I'm going to tell the girls.'

Liar Reynolds shifted his weight on his feet. Bangaz suck teeth.

'You apply fi visa fi dem?'

'Yes.'

'And you get through?'

'Yes,' said Reynolds, adding, 'it is for the best.'

Bangaz suck teeth again.

'No,' said Reynolds. 'I know how dangerous the situation is. And I know your daughters. And I think they respect me.'

'.....Jesus....' said Bangaz.

'I can give them what they need. A secure life and a good education in America. Jenna is very bright. Do you want them to grow up lawyers, or grow up scammers?'

'Same ting,' Bangaz spat.

Reynolds straightened his tie. Bangaz reached for his weed.

'Tanna is already getting mixed up in chopping,' said Reynolds. 'You know that? You must let her go up, for her sake, before she dash away her life.'

The girls came down the stairs, looking sullen and confused, each carrying a small suitcase.

'Go and get in the car,' Pauline said.

'Can we say goodbye?' Tanna said.

'Say goodbye.'

'Com ya,' said Bangaz, pulling her to him. He wondered if it was the last time he would look down into her pretty slender face so held her gaze trying not to shed a tear. He pulled away and busied himself unfastening the slenderest of the four gold chains round his neck. 'This will keep you safe till next time we meet.' He fastened it round Tanna's neck and kissed her on her head. He then took a ring off his right hand and passed it to Jenna. She seemed ambivalent about taking it, so he put it in her pocket.

'Go careful, yuh hear?' he said to her.

'You too, Daddy,' she replied.

'When will we see you?' Tanna asked.

'I can't be sure for now.' Bangaz had a stab of the pain he felt when he thought about his mother, dying in the hospital before she could know or love him.

'Go to the car,' Pauline said.

When the girls were out of the room Pauline took a brick out of her bag.

'Here is a hundred grand,' she said.

Bangaz looked at it. He thought for a few seconds and said, 'Now I understand. All the land is in fi you name.'

'Yes,' said Pauline.

'I don't got none?'

'You have fourteen acres I put in your name uppa Blenheim side.'

'How many do you have?'

'In my name, seven hundred and fifty.'

'Bludclaat,' said Bangaz.

'It's for the girls,' said Pauline. 'Not me. Put that in the safe,' she pointed at the money. 'Memba the combination? The girls' birthdays and fi you birthday.'

Bangaz stared at Pauline, his hand on the money, his mouth open, the room spinning around him.

'Pauline, wait ... How you can do this to me?'

'It is for Tanna and Jenna,' she said quietly.

'Raas,' Bangaz said. 'Mi raaasclaat!'

'Come on,' she said to Reynolds.

'Yes,' he said, looking at his watch.

Bangaz put his hands on the bars at the window as he watched his family walk to the cars, get in and drive off. Then he moved the fridge, picked the cash of the table and placed it in the wall safe. When he pushed the fridge back Marva appeared from the laundry holding a bucket and mop.

'Wha you want?' Bangaz said.

She put down the bucket and said: 'Mi never like to say, but mi told you so.'

Bangaz suck teeth.

'Son,' said Marva. 'You know you can trust me.'

Bangaz grunted.

'Mi a ya madda. A mi a yuh madda.'

'Yah man, and you is one bad madda. You never love me, you never send me a school or buy me a uniform or a shoes. You run me and Pauline outa de yard when she get belly. You ungle come to find me cos mi turn big man. You is a bad bad madda. Forget it.'

78

Bangaz burn him spliff until night fall and moths clustered around the light bulb. He had been scammed. By who he trusted and loved. The remembrance made his body flex and stiffen and his knuckles crack.

The moth was believed in Cove to be the returning soul of the recently dead. He looked at a large brown and white one, the size of a pickney hand, and wondered if it was Bunna coming back to comfort him. Bangaz could almost smell the breath of death on his neck: spoiled and rotten. He took out his cloth, wiped the sweat and walked the stairs to the minaret. The police wanted him dead. The army wanted him dead. Gucci wanted him dead. Herbert, no doubt, would not mind if he turned up as a corpse in a culvert. And now he could be pretty certain Liar Reynolds wanted him dead. Maybe even Pauline. And there was the gunman who killed Bunna. Was he still after Bangaz? If he wanted his pay he had to be.

Between the fronds of coconut and the arcs of the palms, Bangaz watched the headlights pass on the highway as people made their way home or drove out to find a food or party. Happy people, without cares, who had taken a different path. From this high point, he could also see if anyone was approaching the compound. For the moment the streets were empty except for the usual idlers sparking up spliffs while children played around the rusty Lada under the street light. The pickney dem in the street at least were no threat. Rat-bats sped from their caves, swooping and swerving through the trees, and the crickets and tree frogs began their chirruping, croaking and ratchetting, officially starting the night service.

Over the tree tops, on the water of the cove, he could just pick out in the last light the silver lines of the wake of a fishing boat going out onto the dark sea, and beside it the eery glow on the water of a shooterman with an underwater torch looking for fish on the reef. Suddenly they seemed such easeful things to be doing. The people of the fisherman's beach had taken a different turn to him, and it was too late to turn back and sit with them and watch the people go by.

Music pulsed through the darkness from boxes on bar tops, programmed by bored bartenders scrolling their phones in an empty shop.

Bangaz sat at the desk and closed his eyes, but the stress hold him. His head was too full of numbers, names, sums of money, aliases, strategems and tricks. He reached for his weed, placed it on his chopping board and build a spliff. A few lungfuls turned the volume down on the chatter and chaos. Instinctively he picked up his phone, reached into an empty drawer and peeled a bit of paper adhered to its underside. But what use was another brick of cash if he was going to be dead? He put down the cell phone.

He went downstairs to check the grills were locked, and stood in a doorway staring at the old top-loader washing-machine with its rusting dial. It had once been his pride and joy. The floor the washing-machine stood on he had cast and tiled with his own hands. And he and Pauline and the pickney had once lived in this utility room on one bed.

A jet twinkled in the darkness. The planes banked and turned above Cove to make their approach into Donald Sangster International Airport. American Airlines. British Airways. Jet Blue. By day you could read fi dem name. Virgin. Montego Bay was an international Airport for everyone but Jamaicans. They said sweet sweet Jamaica, and it was, if you nuh live there. Jamaica was Bangaz's prison. It was only 120 miles from end to end and there was nowhere to hide.

He was thinking about going to get something to eat when his phone buzzed. He read the text. It was Pauline.

Meet me car park Progressive Foods.

His frustration and anger boiled up, but did not hiss on the cooker. He seethed with her betrayal, and showed nothing to the outside world. But now he suddenly needed two things: a char-grilled fillet steak, and a gun. In Campbell Cove one was a lot easier to get than the other, so he ended up driving to Mo-Bay with a portion of chicken on the passenger seat. Every minute that passed intensified his pain. Whatever happened he could not go on living with things as they stood. He twisted in his seat. He shouted out NO! NO! NO! And he developed a plan, which was simple: shoot Pauline, yes, that was how angry and out of control he was, take back the girls, kill Liar Reynolds. Bribe the police. Live happy ever after.

In the shopping mall car park he pulled up under the half-lit sign, parked, and finished his chicken. He looked at the Glock, and the Glock looked at him. The green light from the 'gressive sign glint on the barrel, and light his finger on the trigger and his thumb the safety. The metal heavy and warm. This the first time he was going to use a gun, and it was on his own wife. He pictured blood spreading across her white jacket as he pulled her body from the car and pushed it down a gully. He would drive away, clean the car and report her missing. Just another unsolved murder. He looked at his phone. Bad to think too much about a killing before you do it. He'd heard gunman say that. He placed the loaded gun in the side pocket.

His thoughts were interrupted by Pauline getting into the car.

'I haven't got long,' she said.

Maybe two minutes, Bangaz thought, feeling the gun he kept out of sight by his side. He would turn that suit red with blood. 'You have to hurry back to Mr Lover-Lover?' he said.

'I'm not interested in him,' Pauline said. 'Reynolds? Mi nuh business wid dat. That's what I come to explain.'

'Ya nuh business wid dat?' Bangaz said.

'You think I love him? Mi nuh love him. Mi nuh like him. I'm doing this for the girls. I'm using Reynolds to get them and me out of here and into America. And to keep all your land out of the hands of the Feds. I'm not staying here in this fockry, and dead. And we are not forgetting you, understand?'

'You take Tanna and Jenna.'

'To keep them safe.'

'Why you with Reynolds?'

'He file for we. Smaddy must do the paperwork.'

'You friend wid him?'

'Mi friend wid him.'

Bangaz suck teeth.

'Mi haffi. Jesus. But mi nuh love him. Mi nuh want him.'

'Wha' you say?'

She took his hand and looked into his eyes. He looked angry, but under that, she could see he was frightened. She smiled softly and squeezed his hand tenderly, bringing it to her lips. 'It's you I love,' she said. 'You. You taught me it a hustler world, Bangaz, and I always thought ongle one thing in this world was not a scam. Ongle one thing in this wide world: your love for me and the girls. Is that still true?'

Bangaz stared at her, studying her eyes. Nobody ever looked at him with the kindness and care she possessed.

'Of course it a true,' he said. 'So you nuh leave me?'

'Never. Me and the girls just go somewhere safe and wait for you.'

'Oh,' said Bangaz, trying to put the gun back in the pocket without making any noise.

'What is that?'

'Wha'?'

'There, what is that down there?' Pauline said.

'This?' he raised the gun.

'Why you carry that?'

'I was about to kill you,' he said.

'A lie,' she laughed. 'I am your wife and your woman,' she said.

'You love me?' Bangaz said.

'Always. Every time,' she said. 'You are my G. Till the end of time. Come ya.'

She gave him a kiss so tender it was a protection against all the harshness of his childhood, and the dangers of the world he found himself in.

'Bludclaat,' she chuckled. 'You ago kill me?'

Bangaz skin teeth.

'That good,' she said.

'Why?' he asked.

'Dat show you really love me.' Pauline smiled.

Bangaz grunted. 'Yuh nuh easy, gal,' he said. 'You know I do love you, and only you.'

'Nutn has changed,' she said, and jumped out the car. 'See you in 'merica.'

79

Bangaz drove home, his heart tumbling in his chest like it boomflick. He lay back on the couch and picked up the remote, racing across the channels. He ended up watching a documentary about Mario Puzo, the man who wrote The Godfather. Something stopped him flicking over. He never usually watched anything for more than two minutes, but he saw this film through to Puzo's death of heart failure in New York. The documentary made lavish use of Coppola's movies, which Bangaz had never seen but which his senses revelled in now. Marlon Brando, Al Pacino, James Caan. Bangaz was all of them.

The next morning was a hot and humid July day, and Bangaz went to Willy's yard. He stood on the invisible border and called 'Willy yo! Y pree?'

'Hello,' said Willy, coming to the rail on his porch. His slippers didn't match and his hair was wild. He recognised the man standing in front of him, but didn't know him well. 'I know you, but forgive me, I've forgotten your name...'

'Mi name Bangaz.'

'Of course. I remember you. From long time. You used to sell ackee and mango on the roadside by the bridge when you were a little boy.'

'Ya man,' said Bangaz, 'and you used to drive past and wet up me with puddle splash.'

'I do apologise,' said Willy.

'Mi born and raise in Orange Hill and mi live yasso from long time.'

'You good?' asked Willy.

'Top of the line. Can I talk wid you?'

'Yes, yes,... come up here, have a seat. You haven't got a cigarette on you have you? I don't really smoke.'

Bangaz gave Willy a Craven A, sat down briefly, then stood up moving from foot to foot.

'Everyting cool?' Willy asked.

'Wha?' said Bangaz. 'Of course! Give tanks and praises for the guidance and supportance. Look. Willy, mi want fi you a write a book bout me.' Bangaz's bulbous eyes blazed with certainty, and his small wiry body buzzed with crackling energy. Sweat glistened on his skin.

'Say that again,' said the old man.

'You a writer, yes? I need you to write one book bout me.'

'Are you in trouble?' Willy asked.

'Wha? Of course not. Dem never touch me. Mi just want mi story write down.'

'I'm afraid I write my own books, not other people's.'

'Yes, Willy, good. Good. But you will write mine.'

'Well ... why me?'

'Mi pickney read one of your book dem and she say it can gwaan.'

'But I write comedy,' Willy said.

'Jenna tell me dat,' he gleamed. 'And dat good, because mi want you fi sweet up my life story wid joke.'

'Oh, are you planning to pay me?'

'Cho! No! Mi cyaa pay you. Me a scammer Willy. You lucky me nuh charge you. No. You will write it and you will sell it to the big people dem that publish book, and get ole eap o money from dem.'

'I very much doubt that. I'm afraid I am not a name any more my friend.'

'When dem read it dem will love it. Truss me. Cho. And you are the ongle writer I know. You haffi do this. Plus white people more easy to get books published.'

'I would not be so sure of that.' Willy sighed and said quietly, 'those were the days ...'

Bangaz twitched. 'Willy. You muss do this for me, you know? I cannot spell good and mi cya write. Ya haffi help mi.'

80

If you want to go back in time to the order and deference of the colonial era, The Jamaica Inn is your place. It's the only place in Jamaica where music is played at volume 2.

Bangaz walked through the colonnaded reception area holding a spliff and a plastic cup of JB rum. He was greeted by a reassuring tableaux of order: the closely mown lawn and clipped flower beds of the hotel garden, beyond which was a half-moon of pale sandy beach. It said private. It said expensive. It said Are you sure you belong here?

But Bangaz ignored that question. As a successful movie writer he wandered coolly onto the terrace where waiters in white gloves were serving tables of guests. A lady in her thirties with an African head dress, hooped earrings, leather sandals and silver wrist watch, waved at him. She was sitting next to a guy with a baseball cap with a long peak, suede sneakers and a book.

'William Loxley-Gordon,' she said, shaking Bangaz's limp hand. 'This is an honour. I am Ala Alagidi. This is my husband Eliot.'

Eliot was a quiet, friendly guy with an easy smile and diplomatic manner.

'I used to be called Sandra Facey.' Ala said. 'My grand-father was Jamaican. But that was a slave name. I changed it to Ala Alagidi. Means Maker of Dreams. Quite appropriate for a film producer, wouldn't you say?'

'You can choose any name you wan'?' Bangaz inquired.

'Of course. That's what emancipation should have meant. Not more incarceration. My slave name is my dead name. I live a new life with my new name. Sit, please.'

The waiter came and peered down at the plastic slippers on Bangaz's tiny legs sticking out of the voluminous sateen shorts.

'A very pleasant good evening.'

'What will you drink?' asked Ala.

'Gimme shot of JB, double, and a Boom.'

'And we will have two Red Stripe light,' said Ala. She sat back and looked at Bangaz slouching in his chair. 'So tell me,' she said, 'where did you learn to write?'

'I didn't hardly get to school. Dem nuh teach me nutn. Streetside college mi learn. You nuh like it?'

'Not at all. I love it. I just wondered if you ever did a course ...'

'Mi graduate from the university of marketing and persuasion.'

Eliot laughed at that.

'You like my story?' Bangaz asked.

'Very much,' said Eliot. 'Very much.'

'I can see where we need a few nip and tucks,' said Ala, 'but the story is basically there.'

'Good. Very good,' said Bangaz. He had her on the hook but resisted saying are you in the age group 50 to 55, 55 to 60, etc.

'I envisage taking what you have given to me to utilise as a foundation. Tell me, do you object to other writers working on your material?'

Bangaz frowned.

'All of African heritage, of course,' she said.

'If they cya spell good, that is cool with me,' he said.

Ala smiled, enjoying the little joke. 'Great. I will find some writers, I already have a few in mind. They can take it forwards to its next iteration.'

'Next iteration. No problem.' Bangaz liked the word, it sounded Jamaican.

'You realise they may alter your narrative in some way, to fit the form of a TV series? I want you to understand that.'

'Mi understand dat. Mi overstand it.'

The waiter placed down the drinks. Bangaz slopped a sip of his rum onto the flowers' bed.'

'I know what that's for,' smiled Ala. 'You always remember the fallen.'

'Good friends we have, good friends we lost,' said Bangaz, 'along the way. So, you gonna buy mi story?' he asked.

'You are very straightforward,' Ala laughed. 'But the answer is, I may well want to buy it.'

'How about money? How much you ago pay me?'

'That is a whole discussion,' Ala said.

'You must make payment before the data window close on my accounts in six days from now.'

'I see you know the value of your material.'

'As soon as I have my new account I will give it to you for the transfer. I do not accept Western Union.'

'I bet!' laughed Ala, 'another drink?'

'If you want, sure,' like he was doing her a favour.

'Of course. Waiter, please?'

'Get me two flask white rum,' Bangaz said with his customary sense of entitlement., 'two chaser Red Bull and two pack Craven A.'

'William Loxley-Gordon,' said Ala, 'A name that is soon to be known all around the world.

Bangaz frowned, then said: 'Mi nah go under no slave name William Loxley-Gordon. Mi adorn mi self like a real African chief.' He tump him chest with his fist. 'I will get a new name.'

'What name will you choose?' asked Ala.

'Mi haffi think 'bout that. If you need to talk to me you wattsap me, annerstan? Here is my number. Don't email. The Feds are looking at my email. And I will pick a new name,' he said as he sent his number to Ala. 'And let you know. For the contract.'

Ala smiled indulgently at her protégée. Then she raised her right arm and waved at someone across the terrace. An elegant woman with long dreads and a long print skirt approached them. There was something familiar about her. Then he recognised who she was: the woman on Willy's phone. His daughter, Holly.

'Hello darling!'

'Hiya Ala! Eliot! What's poppin?'

'Holly!' said Eliot, standing up. They all kissed each other, alarming Bangaz, who would never kiss anybody in public, but he held his ground.

'Holly, let me introduce me to a new writer I am trying — no going — to work with.'

Bangaz realised that he was about to be introduced as William Loxley-Gordon to Willy's daughter.

'Nuh say mi old name,' he said to Ala. 'That name dead. I don't go by my slave name, from this moment.'

'Wow,' said Ala, 'I'm impressed.'

Holly nodded. 'We have to bury our past,' she said.

'Call me General,' Bangaz said. 'Till me chose mi Africa name.' He crossed his arms defensively and nodded, as was his habit when he met someone for the first time.

'I will have to let you read some of his work, Holly. You'll adore his fresh take on your turbulent and vivid culture.'

'I look forward to it,' smiled Holly. 'Wha gwaan?'

'Mi good,' said Bangaz.

'I will talk to the team and let you know what we decide,' Ala said to Bangaz, sounding an alarm bell.

Bangaz walked away and said, 'Ala, mek we talk.'

She left Holly and Eliot gossiping.

'You don't got time to talk to no team,' Bangaz said shaking his head. 'Serious ting. You need to hurry or my Feb window will be closing for offer inputs, and it will not be open till June. Mi want twenty-five grand, that's twenty five thousand US dollars or I will have to offer this to a next person who is serious. Is you serious?'

'I am serious, of course I am,' Ala said. 'That's why I invited you here.'

'Ok, good. Very good. Do not let yourself down. Because this is at your fingertips. You must transfer it directly. Directly. Or I can accept kiash. That is a option.'

'But ... but... but,' said Ala.

'Ya cya "but" now. Ya haffi move forward or drop out.'

'There will be paperwork, a contract, was all I was going to say,' Ala said.

'Good. Very good,' said Bangaz. 'Plus one more thing I must have. You have a pen and paper? '

'I'll remember it,' she said.

'Good. Memba this carefully. You must get me a visa to go up to America.'

'Okay,' said Ala. 'I guess I can ask the lawyers to look at it.'

'You is Netflix, right?'

Ala nodded.

'You can do it. Outstanding ability. Dat me have. Tell dem. If you want my story you haffi file for me and get me up there. Don't forget. Very good.'

Ala said, 'I understand, we'll see what we can do.'

'Mi touch road,' Bangaz said. 'You let me know what is happening. And pure black writers. No white man on this.'

'Of course. Just the authentic voice.'

'A dat.'

Bangaz said good bye to Eliot and Holly, and breezed through reception stuffing the cigarettes and flasks of rum he had ordered in his pockets.

Ala said to Eliot, 'Isn't he great?' She picked up her light beer and sighed. 'That's what I call lived experience.'

81

Willy sat in the Sea Breeze hotel restaurant at a table level with his chest, staring at the laminated menu and worrying about how it was going over at the Jamaica Inn with Bangaz and Ala.

'What have you got?' he asked the waitress, trying to break through her boredom.

She shrugged. 'You want frozen fish of the day?'

'No. Give me a burger, please.'

The waitress suck teeth and wandered off, not in the direction of the kitchen but towards the large section of the restaurant designated for staff to lounge and eat.

Twenty minutes later a man appeared. 'You order burger?'

'Yes.'

'Excellent choice, captain.'

'Is it coming soon?'

'No problem.'

In a dining room of fifty covers there were, including Willy, five guests so it was hard to understand why it took forty minutes to produce a burger, but it did. The food eventually appeared through a sinister hatch as though it was created somewhere so unspeakable it had to be hidden behind a wall and passed through a hole.

Willy ate some of his food with plastic cutlery, paid the bill and returned to the room. He sat on the balcony watching the raucous booze
cruise pass in front of the lavender and gold sunset.

The door opened and Bangaz advanced into the room, looking
pensive.

Willy said 'What's wrong? What happened?'

'Be honest, Willy, fish seem like it gonna drop off that line.' He closed
the door behind him.

'What? What happened?'

'The woman, Ala, she not sure, to tell you the truth.'

'What happened?'

'Well,' he sighed. 'She don't like it, Willy. She don't want it.'

'What? What did she say?'

'She say it too ...' here Bangaz paused.

'What?' said Willy. 'It was too what?'

Bangaz hadn't thought through what he was going to tell Willy, and
being rude about the book wasn't in his nature.

'She said it too good.'

'What? Dat a fockry,' said Willy. 'It bullshit.'

'That what she say,' said Bangaz.

'Mi nuh idiot. You're just being kind to me aren't you? Don't worry,'
he turned away and searched in his bag for something. 'I can imagine what
she said. And thank you Bangaz for your kindness. But she said she didn't
think it was any good, didn't she? Don't worry, I know. And I can take it.
What did she really say?'

'She said it too high class.'

'Right. Well that wasn't what she actually thought, I assure you. They
are not good people, Bangaz. Movie people. You can't trust them. None
of them say what they really think when they're rejecting a manuscript. I
should know. It's what you would call my area of expertise.'

'Honest Willy. She said it was too good for her. She say dem mainly do
like trashy ting, and this too quality.'

'Did she work out you aren't the writer? She smell a rat?' Willy said. 'If that's what happened I should go and see her and explain...'

'No, she never doubt me. She just don't like it,' said Bangaz.

Willy's body sagged, and tiny tears of disappointment pricked his eyes which he quickly wiped away with his cuff.

'I am sorry,' said Bangaz. 'She don't really tell me fully why.'

Willy sighed, shook his head, put his face in his hand and let out an anguished moan. 'Ugggh. Fuck it. Fuck it.' He looked up at Bangaz. Bangaz was taking it well, and even managed a smile. In the face of such a diabolical set back. How magnificent were the Jamaicans, Willy thought. Titanium people. Nothing can break them. Nothing. 'Why oh why do I believe in myself when I am obviously totally shit?' He shuddered. Then he looked up at Bangaz, and said. 'We tried man, we fucking tried.' He was crestfallen, punctured, with hope whistling out of him. 'Why do I get my hopes up? After all this time, after all these failures you'd think I'd learn my lesson. But I'm so fucking stupid and naive. Did Ala suggest any alterations that might make her change her mind? No notes, no hints...?'

Bangaz shook his head. He suck teeth. 'Bludclaat woman,' he said.

Willy held out a plastic cup.

'Life go on,' said Bangaz.

'You are right. Tank you. Right. Back to work.' He pulled his laptop out of his old briefcase.

'But book done, Willy,' said Bangaz. 'Dis over.'

'We have to finish the book,' Willy said

'Mi done with that,' Bangaz said.

Willy said 'We can't give up. I know tings tough, but always remember, my friend, the darkest hour is right before the dawn. We must stay positive.' He looked at Bangaz urgently. 'This is not over. We've got to believe.'

'No, it is,' said Bangaz.

'What?' said Willy.

'Mi haffi touch road.' Bangaz emptied the last drop of rum from his flask, and made for the door with a spring in his step. Willy followed him out onto the gallery and stood with him on the stained concrete under a dripping AC unit. Bangaz bounced off, humming a tune.

'That's it. Keep your spirits up,' said Willy. 'Chin up. Set backs just prepare us for the final triumph. See you soon,' he called. 'This not over.'

'For sure,' said Bangaz. But it had to be over for Bangaz, because he certainly couldn't face Willy again after this. The thought didn't make him happy, but business was business.

'Stay positive,' Willy called as Bangaz trotted down the stairs.

Willy returned to his room. As the door clicked shut he felt the full weight of failure press down on him, flattening his soul. He lay on the bed, turned off the light and came to the realisation things could not be any worse: the project on which he had pinned his artistic, social and financial hopes had collapsed, leaving him in the darkness with nothing. Nothing. Then he heard a mosquito, and his misery was complete. When it circled his right ear he slapped his hand against his head so hard he saw starbursts in the dark. He waited to see if he had got it. Silence, but for the shuddering AC and the barks of some far away dogs. Sometimes Willy wondered if partial hearing loss meant he wasn't able to detect mosquitos. But no, they were one of the few things he could hear with absolute clarity.

His thoughts again turned to the abyss he was falling into. He had lied when he told Bangaz he didn't think there was any prospect of making money out of the book. He had been banking on it himself, and was now calamitously in debt with no way of bailing himself out. He had borrowed money from Holly. It shamed him to think of it. Then he heard the mosquito again. He felt for the thin towel and held the end of it in his hand while he waited for the insect to circle. It returned like a stuka in his left ear, and he lashed it with the towel that whipped his face. 'You fucking little thing,' he shouted in the dark. He lay there in pain, and then heard the mosquito circling again, so he lashed out, hardly even bothering to aim.

He just wanted to punish himself for everything going wrong. He ended up kneeling on the bed lashing the towel around his head and onto the pillow and bed. He remembered that a single mosquito bite released a chemical message which could be read by other mosquitoes as far as a mile away.

82

The Jamaican sunrise was the salve to all wounds. When Willy was feeling beaten and depressed the weather could be relied on to revive him with a series of blisteringly beautiful tropical mornings: blue sky, warm breeze, bright sunshine and placid sea. However bad things had looked, the overwhelming beauty and optimism of the morning sunshine gave everybody hope. Even Willy.

But Willy woke to discover a sea storm had skulked in overnight under a thick layer of churning cloud. His lonely and sad feelings were intensified. A look in the mirror revealed both welts and mosquito bites.

At reception he slid the little key back across the wide expanse of desk and left. The ocean had mislaid its Xanax and Valium and was in a right state, soaking the road where it crashed over the barriers. The waves rolled in with an alarming pulse, thrashing the north shore.

When Willy got to the hospital pothole the traffic was backed up for a mile. The hole was so deep you'd have to change gear to get out of it. Some might have to be towed. There were probably fish in it. People had sentimental attachment to the hole as they'd known it since it was an inch deep and the width of a plate. Now it was virtually a local beauty spot. Everybody knew traffic had to detour into the oncoming traffic to get round it.

From Willy's porch the pulse on the ocean was deeper and stronger, sending waves exploding into the rocks. The wind whipped the salt onto the house, making everything sticky. The trees and flowers took a thrashing. Over the next week their beaten leaves would drop from the branches, creating an instant winter.

By dusk the waves came in relentlessly, booming in the darkness and hissing with white foam. Willy's desk, furniture and cushions wet up so he sat in his bedroom thinking bleak and doom laden thoughts, like being washed away by a tsunami.

He realised that during the time he had been listening to Bangaz's story and inhabiting Bangaz's world he had been getting progressively more optimistic and excited about the project. He had actually thought it was good. And he now resolutely refused to believe that, after Ala had turned it down, Zuri Bennet-Henriques at Random House would go near it. It was a failure. He was washed up. Due to a lack of talent and judgement, the experiment had failed.

He hit the bottle. He drank rum hard. For two days the angry and sad sea beat against the land. For two days and nights Willy drank and shouted into the storm.

'You heard about what's his name? Loxley Gordon?' he said into the wind. 'Poor man. Lost it totally I heard. Too long in the tropics. Completely deluded. Perfectly nice chap, just stark raving mad. Embarrassing that he ever thought he should go on writing. Pathetic really.'

At dawn on the third day the sea was settling back, upset and tired. Broken trees and foliage washed down the river and clogged the cove. Bunna once said to him, 'Nature have its course, Willy, sometimes angry sometimes sad,' but Bunna dead.

At dawn on the fourth day, Willy woke to feel the storm receding. The ocean settle down, the booming weaken. The pulse had diminished in power and frequency. The water was soupy with churned up sand and seaweed. It looked bruised as though after a fight. It gave a last few sobs before going to sleep, and the sun came through the cloud for the first time in days.

Willy looked around for his shoes, found his laptop, and opened it. There was an email from Ala.

Dear Baban Zamba

Oh glory, how great it was to meet you! Give thanks and praises to highest. And so awesome to talk about Good Scammer, which I believe can be mega if you get it out to the world it in the right way – and by that I mean with Zuri at Penguin Random House and with the TV rights coming to me and the team at NETFLIX.

Even though we both agree there is still work to do on the manuscript, there is sufficient here for me to proceed. I will assemble a team of top writers. All of them I assure you will be of African heritage, as you demanded.

I am happy you are prepared to sign a two year option for $25,000. I have spoken to the accountant and he says that it can be transferred to any account you nominate, so we await your instruction. I asked about your request to have it paid in cash but I am afraid it is against NETFLIX policy.

It's all good news! It a happen! It haffi happen!

I will return to the States to get the ball rolling, the paperwork in place, and if the lawyers can sort out your visa, I look forward to seeing you in Los Angeles before the year is out.

Irie vibes every time.
Ala

83

Bangaz was in Exchange, leaning with his back against a bar and his arms outstretched either side of him. Five bredren and a couple of sistren were listening to him chat, for he was as usual telling a story. This one was about Omar's son, the one who had been home-schooled by a tutor from Harvard because he was too clever for school. The reading, writing and maths tests the child did online showed he was at genius level they all called him Brains. But when Brains had to take a public examination to get into high school, he failed it. It turned out Brains couldn't read or write or add up. For two years, the home-school tutor from Harvard had been doing all of Brains' assignments for him.

Willy walked into the bar, just as everyone was laughing, and seeing his screw face, the place fell quiet.

'I see you are holding forth,' Willy said.

'Mi holding forth, mi holding fifth and mi holding sixth, Willy,' Bangaz said. 'You want drink?'

'No. I want a word, in private. Pay your bill, mek we go.'

Willy stood at the open door watching Bangaz pay and leave. The car was up the lane under a tree by a tethered goat.

When they were in the car Willy said 'Who the fuck is Baban Zamba?'

'Dat?' said Bangaz, 'Dat, dat a mi Africa name.'

'What?'

'It mean Writer of Wisdom!' Bangaz beamed.

'Raas,' said Willy.

'Ala love it.'

'Does she?' said Willy.

They drove on in silence.

'Where we ago?' Bangaz asked.

'How the fuck can you try and scam me, Bangaz?' Willy said dropping gear and heading down the hill.

Bangaz said 'Don't use mi dead name. Mi name Baban.'

'We are meant to be friends,' Willy said. 'Bredren. We are involved in a creative project. Doesn't that mean anything to you? Jesus, is there nobody you won't scam?'

'Where are we going?' Bangaz said.

'To the hotel. To talk.'

'No problem boss,' said Bangaz. 'No problem.'

They got the old hotel room, the one with the mosquito. Willy looked at the bed wondering if he recognised the sheets. He pushed open the door onto the balcony.

'I got an email from Ala which was meant for you,' Willy said.

'Very good,' said Bangaz.

'You try to tief my work from me. How can you do that?'

'I am a scammer, Willy, you know that.'

'You can't scam me, I'm your bredren.'

Bangaz waved his arm. 'You know nutn. You neva grow in Jamaica. You just come here to live. You is rich. You don't understand nutn.'

'I understand loyalty.'

Bangaz suck teeth. 'You should thank me, Willy,' he said. 'I am the man who save this project. You are right, if she think a white man write it, it a problem situation. I hear the way she talk about she ongle work with black artists. Like me.'

'You are not an artist, you are not a writer,' said Willy.

'You ever hear of lived experience?' countered Bangaz.

Willy said nothing.

'Dat what me have.'

'She wants some changes,' Willy said. 'How're you gonna do them?'

'With mi team of writer dem. Dem ago do it. Fi mi writer dem with Africa heritage.'

'What about the twenty-five grand?'

'That is mine,' said Bangaz, 'I negotiate that.'

'I am going to write to Ala today and tell her exactly what you've done. I will explain it is a multi-racial project. A co-operation between black and white. She will restore me as the writer.'

'She don't want multiracial, Willy. That time done. She want lived experience, seen? Pure black man ting. You will mash up the whole deal, Willy. Chuss me. She never give you twenty-five grand, Willy. Never. She nuh ago work with you. She want me, not you. Serious ting.'

Willy twitched his neck in frustration.

'Let me deal with this,' Bangaz said. 'And in mi new name: Baban Zamba.'

'You should have told me,' said Willy.

'How could I tell you? You would mash up it if I told you she like it.'

'So she like it?' Willy said.

'Ya man. She love it.'

Willy stared at Bangaz.

'And she never suspect I am not the writer. Mi craft her mind good! Mi have outstanding ability!' Bangaz said.

Willy drifted off into his own world, glowing with happiness. 'Really,' he croaked. 'She said she love it?'

'She say it real and rude.'

Willy chuckled. He was under a waterfall of joy.

'That is gratifying to hear,' he said.

'Don't fuck it up now, Willy.'

'So you are suggesting you continue to front it?' Willy said.

'Dat haffi happen, Willy.'

Willy nodded. 'I guess if my name isn't on it, I won't get killed, at least, for being a snitch.'

'Good. Very good. Very good. That is a advantage. You live to tell the tale.'

'I live to tell the tale indeed,' said Willy.

'Good. Very good Willy. You turn scammer at last.'

'There is the matter of my invoice to settle. I trust you will pay outstanding accounts...'

'Wha you say? Cho! I muss look after you. You mi bredren. Muss. And you know Willy, you is my good friend, you know dat?'

'I hope so. You see I have run up a lot of expenses on this job...' Willy was angling for five hundred dollars. That would be enough to cover his bill at Troy and give him a few hundred to see him through till the next miracle.

'Ala give me twenty-five grand for a two year option,' Bangaz said.

'Yes, I was hoping...' said Willy.

'.... and 250 for full purchase price.'

Willy swallowed. 'Two hundred and fifty thousand dollars? US?' He checked.

'Outstanding ability,' Bangaz said.

'If they buy it,' said Willy.

'Dem ago buy it, Willy. Wid ease. And we still have the publishing rights. Seen? With a Netflix option dem easy fi sell.'

'How do you know about them?'

'Cos me listen smartly. We can aks twenty grand for worldwide rights.'

'I'll be impressed if you pull that off,' Willy said.

'To be honest wid you Willy, after me scam five tousan clients over ten year, dealing with Netflix a cake walk. Me give you ten grand US expenses now, and more when she buy it.'

'US? That would be ... that would be very helpful,' Willy said, annoyed that he was so transparently grateful.

'Right now mi want you to write back to Ala, Willy, to accept her offer and say there is one more thing she must do. Get me that visa,' Bangaz said. 'That must be clear to her.'

'Okay.'

Bangaz pointed at the laptop. 'We do that now. It important. It a deal breaker. You must tell her. I have outstanding ability. That is what dem want.'

'Surely not a deal breaker?' Willy said.

'Yes. I must go up,' said Bangaz. 'Muss.'

With the email sent, Bangaz built another spliff, lit it, sat back and blew a cone of blue grey smoke into the room. 'So the people ago read mi book. Mi happy! Mi tell mi story, and people will read a lot and find sense and knowledgable. It fulfilling, heart breaking. It will touch people around the globe.'

'Spoken like a first time published writer,' Willy said. 'Prepare for disappointment.'

'As I tell my story to you, I always thought someone might read this book and think I will really help this person. And that person will get a breakthrough.'

84

While Bangaz lay on the bed daydreaming of his success, Willy fancied a drink – he owed himself a little celebration – and went downstairs. He wandered out onto the cracked terrace to get a cold beer. Weeds sprouted between the paving and paint peeled off the plumbing pipe used as a guard-rail. It was here in December 1957 that Evelyn Waugh, Noel Coward and Ian Fleming met for lunch before a rafting trip on the Rio Grande. The three greats of 20th century English literature. All English, all white, all male, all middle aged. Fleming was working on Diamonds Are Forever, Waugh had just sent Officers & Gentlemen to his New York publisher, and Noel Coward had just completed a sold out run of cabaret in Las Vegas. Evelyn wore blue silk pyjamas and a Panama hat with a pink ribbon. Lunch was served by a huge number of waiters all wearing white gloves and all doing something tiny, like placing the spoon down by the bowl after another waiter had brought the soup, and a third had laid the napkin across a lap. Waugh had the hotel fill biscuit tins with ice to keep his wine cold on the outing. Talking in clipped, upper class English accents, smoking cigarettes from Bakelite holders, they were the pinnacle and the absolute end of an era.

Willy placed his large bum in a plastic seat at a plastic table and waited for the waitress, who he could see at a table inside eating. He was quietly gruntled: the opposite of disgruntled. His work was being acknowledged, albeit anonymously. Ten thousand United States Federal Reserve Dollars were flying in his direction.

Willy still meant something. He added up to something. After a ten-minute wait for the waitress he ambled over to the bar. He didn't hold with things like bucket lists, but for a moment he indulged in the thought of one. What would be on it? No skydiving, or white river rafting. Before he died, Willy wanted to do two things which had long been in his old hardened heart: to be known and respected for his work. Not famous or rich, just acknowledged as a little better than average. As someone a bit special in the writing department. The other wish was to be able to sit with Holly without rancour. To see her happy to be with him.

There were four stools at the bar, one occupied. Willy took one of them and looked for a bartender. Another customer in a colourful shirt sat down beside him. Willy got a Red Stripe and took a sip. He was feeling buoyant, particularly when he remembered the depth he had sunk to during the storm. What was the stand out event? Easy: when Bangaz told him that Ala had liked the story, had engaged with it. What joy that brought him. Willy took a sip on the cold beer and stared at the classic design of the bottle, watching the condensation run down its curves.

He had worried in the hotel room that Bangaz was humiliating him, and stealing his glory, but there was another way of looking at it. He was not Bangaz's bitch, he was Bangaz's puppeteer. Bangaz thought he was the boss, but he would find out when they asked him to write something new that he was merely a conduit for Willy's talent. Willy now had a face acceptable to the new world of arts and culture. If all went well, Bangaz could front book after book and TV series after series for Willy. It was a perfect arrangement.

The man beside him walked out in front of this happy thought-taxi.

'You on vacation?' he asked.

Apart from the patterned short-sleeved shirt, he sported leather trousers, a neckerchief, and sunglasses.

'No, I've been based here,' Willy said, 'well down the coast in the parish of St John, for nearly thirty-five years, for my sins. Are you on holiday?'

'I guess you must know lots of, like, local people,' the man said. There was something familiar about him, but Willy couldn't put his finger on it.

'Of course,' Willy said. 'Well the Jamaicans are lovely and lively people. I count many as friends.'

'I'd sure like to meet some. I've been staying in Sandals.'

'Hard to meet people apart from tourists in the all-inclusives,' Willy said. 'Still you've managed to get out. You've just got to be friendly and open.'

'I thought I recognised you earlier with an old friend of mine.'

'Oh yes?'

'A man called Bangaz Thompson.'

The penny dropped. Gucci. It was Gucci. It was Gucci. Willy recognised him from photos in the Gleaner.

'Who?'

'Bangaz Thompson.' Gucci said. 'He a friend of yours?'

'Is his name Thompson? I just know him as good old Bangaz. Not well, not at all well.' Willy finished his beer, smiled and started getting off the stool.

'You walk away,' Gucci said quietly, 'I'll kill you. Shall I tell you how I will kill you? I will knock you semi-unconscious with two swipes, I will then introduce you to my friend Bud. Bud is my oyster shucker. A blunt knife but strong. I will find the gap between your fourth and fifth vertebrae and work into your spinal column. It will be painful. Then I will put my boot on your face and will press it until I hear your teeth breaking. That's how I will start.'

'I wasn't going anywhere,' said Willy getting back on the stool.

'Where is your friend?' Gucci asked.

'Who?' said Willy.

'Bangaz Thompson.'

'He's not really my friend,' said Willy.

Gucci said, 'I have been rotting in jail for sixteen years waiting for this day to dawn. This is my day of judgement. On this day will the wrong be righted. After dreaming about it in that hell-hole, I'm finally gonna get me some justice.'

'I have no idea about what happened between the two of you in the past,' Willy said, 'but after sixteen years, I hope you don't mind me saying, isn't it time maybe to forgive and forget? Wouldn't that be a better thing all round? Nobody wins with revenge...'

'He stole my fucking life. And I heard he's very rich. That hurts, you know? That grinds my guts. So now I am going to hurt him. Get off the stool and lead me to him. Go on. Or I will drag you to my room and kill you. Which do you want?'

'Put like that...'

Frightened and confused, Willy led Gucci through reception, up the steps and onto the galley. Just as he had established Bangaz as a convincing person to front his work and usher him into a few last years of success, this bastard had turned up to take it all away. And possibly kill Willy, though right then that seemed less annoying.

Outside the bedroom door Gucci slipped his beringed hand into a small bag and took out a gun. He indicated for Willy to use his key go in. Willy turned the key in the spongy handle, opened the door and saw that Bangaz was still on the bed.

'There he is,' Willy said, standing back to let Gucci in.

Gucci prodded Willy in the side with the gun and made him enter the room.

'Sit down,' Gucci said to Willy, pointing to the plastic chair. 'Don't move.'

Bangaz slept peacefully, an empty cup held in both hands on his chest. Gucci pointed a gun down over his face.

'Bangaz,' he said.

Bangaz opened his eyes, saw the gun, and then Gucci, and smiled.

'You good?' he said.

'Very,' said Gucci. 'Because this is the last time you'll ever wake up.'

'You don't need to shoot me,' Willy said. 'I'm very much just a writer. Like a piano player. Totally unnecessary to shoot. We are trained not to tell.'

'You just said you're a fucking writer. Put your hands behind your head.' While Gucci searched Bangaz he pressed the barrel of his gun into Bangaz's crotch. 'Who's he?' he asked.

'Bredren.'

'I'm not really a bredren, as such,' said Willy, 'you make me sound like an accomplice. I am a lowly writer, of no importance.'

'What is he writing?' Gucci asked.

'A book about my life,' smiled Bangaz. 'Because mi a big man.'

Willy thought, why can't you be humble and compliant just once in your life? He also thought, there is now a hole in my bucket list because I am about to die.

'He told you about Call-Sure?' Gucci asked Willy.

'What's Call-Sure?' Willy said. 'We've been focussing very much on Bangaz's humanitarian and philanthropic activities. Not so much the business stuff—'

'Give me your phone,' Willy passed it over. 'Give me the laptop.'

Gucci slid the laptop and Willy and Bangaz's phones into the side of his holdall. Then he cable-tied Willy to a plastic chair by his wrists and ankles. Willy worked out there was only way of moving, and that was to tip forward onto his face still attached to the chair, so he stayed still. From the main compartment of the holdall, Gucci removed duct tape, cable ties, wires, battery and what looked to Willy, horribly, like a pack of TNT about the size of a pack of cigarettes.

'You gonna kill me?' Bangaz said.

'Yes. Want to know how?' Gucci asked, taking a bottle of lube from the bag.

'Beautifully,' said Gucci. 'You will record it,' he said to Willy.

Gucci spun Bangaz onto his front bringing his hands behind his back and cable tying them. He then tied his ankles and pulled his shorts and drawers down, leaving his batty naked.

'I'm not looking,' Willy said.

'Shut the fuck up,' said Gucci. He held the explosive and said 'When you confine an organism in a tight space you know what results?'

Willy smiled helplessly in a futile attempt to be liked.

'They get twisted.'

Willy nodded, he hoped sympathetically. Was Gucci likely to be softened by him? No.

'We get twisted,' Gucci said, examining the explosive. 'Right? Like a corkscrew. Our minds. You ever seen a man take a shit out of his mouth?'

'Me?' said Willy. 'No, I think I'd remember that.'

'Bangaz,' he cuffed him across the back of his head. 'I'm taking this explosive and shoving it up your ass. Like a long way. Deep.'

'Dat nuh nice,' said Bangaz. 'Nuh suh.' He started to rock on the bed until Gucci struck him on the back of the skull with his gun.

'Because that's what you did to me when you stole my lists. You fucked me in the ass. Okay? So now I'm gonna attach this to this phone,' he held up a banger phone. 'When it ring it's gonna blow your tripe through your belly hole, and your shit out your mouth.'

Gucci lovingly connected the wires to the packet of explosive with a careful twist of his fingers. It looked to Willy like it was going to be painful enough going in, forget coming out. 'After I insert the device, I am going to leave the room,' Gucci said, 'cos I don't want to dirty my shirt. I will post on Facebook anyone wants some free money can ring this number. The first person who rings will detonate the explosive and kill you. You will stay here,' he said to Willy. 'If you're not killed, you'll write about his death.'

'It's okay, I doubt I will put it in. I definitely don't need to see it.'

'I have a hundred grand, US.' Bangaz said.

Gucci was sitting on the bed squeezing lube over the explosive.

'You do?'

'I can give it to you.'

Gucci said 'Where?'

'At my home. In the safe.'

Gucci looked at the explosive. A dribble of lube dropped onto Bangaz's buttocks. Willy knew exactly how much that would mad Bangaz.

'There's a hundred grand in cash. I can give it to you.' He sounded so calm.

Gucci said nothing. Willy got the feeling Gucci wanted to insert the leading edge into Bangaz's anus more than he wanted a hundred grand, which was a problem.

'What's the code of the safe?' Gucci asked.

'I will tell you when we reach. You can't get in the house without me. It lock. Serious.'

Gucci pressed the sharp corner into Bangaz's ass. 'What is the code?'

'Spin left to 4, right to 9, left to 18 and right to 6. Then 1 and 18.'

'What do you want in return?' Gucci liked asking this as he had no intention of giving Bangaz anything. As soon as he had the cash he was going to kill him.

'Set me free and I will give you another hundred grand in four weeks,' Bangaz said.

Smooth move, Willy thought, though the level of trust between these two was unlikely to support the plan.

'Okay,' said Gucci. 'Tell me the code again.'

'You spin left to 4, right to 9, left to 18 and right to 6,' said Bangaz. 'See I am honest,' he added.

'Or a scammer,' said Gucci. 'Who is at your house?'

'Nobody. My wife and kids are in the States.'

Gucci replaced the cap on the lube, took a rag from the bag and wrapped the explosive before placing it in the holdall.

'Okay,' he said, 'we're going for a drive.'

'Have a good trip,' said Willy.

'You are driving,' said Gucci.

Gucci walked them in front of him through reception and out to the car. He placed Willy in the driving seat, Bangaz cuffed in the passenger seat, and sat behind them with his gun in his hand.

'You fuck around, I kill Bangaz first then I kill you. Get that?'

'Yes,' said Willy. 'I think that's clear.'

'Drive.'

'Can me build a spliff?' Bangaz asked.

'No.'

As they passed the buses drawing into Dunn's River Falls, full of their anxious hunched white people, Gucci kept the two of them up to date with his latest plans.

Willy's hands were damp with sweat on the steering wheel and his mouth dry. His heart flapped like a throttled dove. Gucci was either going to get the cash and shoot Bangaz, or find there was no cash and shoot Bangaz. That much was certain. And because Willy was a witness he too would have to be murdered. The best he could hope for was not to meet Bud first.

And now he realised he was going to spend a significant portion of his last hours alive trying to cross the most frustrating box junction in the world outside KFC in Montego Bay. The rule that you didn't enter the yellow box unless you could see your way out on the other side was not closely observed. If you hesitated before crossing it, three cars cut in ahead of you and gridlocked the traffic as if it were a patriotic duty. Willy smiled lamely at a couple of men who came down the line selling peanuts, steering-wheel covers and donuts. Inching out of the city, he drove free of its stranglehold and hit the highway, heading straight towards a huge, plump, setting sun.

In Lucea, the hospital turn pothole had created a three-mile tailback, and Willy crawled through the sour streets past the pavement vendors in second gear. Nobody in the line of traffic particularly complained. A delay often promised more fun than a destination and most drivers either hailed up old friends or flirted with new ones.

As they climbed the hill past the old merchant houses, with their fancy verandas eaten out by termite and falling into rot and ruin, Willy formulated a plan. He was going to drive as fast as he could straight into the hospital turn pothole. His tyres, like him, were worn and balding. Surely they would blow, and with so many cars crawling by a crowd would soon assemble as people liked to get involved with a breakdown and give unbidden advice, particularly if it was wrong. There was little chance of Gucci using his firearm and getting away.

Up ahead the cars detoured round the puddle forcing the oncoming traffic onto the verge. Willy touched the accelerator and drove straight at the pothole. The right front wheel thumped into it, the car shuddered, Gucci shouted 'What the fuck are you doing, man?' But the vehicle, instead of collapsing with a broken axle, climbed out the other side. The back wheel then dropped into the pool with a hopeful thunk, though again climbed out.

Willy said 'Sorry, didn't see that.'

Gucci said 'You wanna meet Bud? You wanna meet Bud? Pull a stunt like that again I'll shoot you through the seat and butcher you with him. You get that?'

'I get that,' Willy said.

Bangaz laughed, 'Ya bad, Willy!'

That was the last throw of the dice. It was six miles to Bangaz's yard. Which meant he probably had sixty minutes left of his life. He felt like a rum and a Craven A, though they were said to reduce life expectancy even further. It didn't help that Bangaz was smiling and humming a tune as if he was on his way to pick up a bingo.

Closing in on Campbell Cove and Bangaz's yard, Willy thought about driving off the road, but was too cowardly for that. If he did, he would certainly get himself shot in the back, as opposed to being shot in the front at Bangaz's.

As he drove the long bend at Lances Bay, the place where three oncoming vehicles often appeared in a line coming towards you, Willy saw an army road block strung across the road, set to catch scammers. Two soldiers with M16 machine guns stood in front of a barrier, and others lurked in the shade of a tree. Willy knew the drill: you slowed down, lowered all windows, and let the soldiers look into the car. If they saw something they didn't like, you were directed to the roadside to be searched and interrogated, if they didn't spot anything that interested them, they waved you through.

Bangaz knew when the cold-eyed soldier with the face mask and forage cap spotted cable ties on his wrists they would be pulled over. He knew if he hid his hands they would be pulled over, and probably shot forthwith. Willy thought, even though Gucci could hide the gun out of sight, the soldier would probably recognise Bangaz and pull them over. Then they would find Gucci's gun, and the solders would kill all three of them. A sadness pressed upon him. He looked at the steep embankment with tufts of goat nibbled vegetation and sprinkling of litter as he slowed to a halt. It was a pretty nondescript spot, but it was to be the last place he was ever to see. They inched forward in the queue, with three cars ahead of them and a few behind. A u-turn would be literally suicidal. Willy had to get them waved through. He lowered the window and put his arm on the sill, letting the unbuttoned cuff on his old striped Gieves and Hawkes shirt fall down his pink forearm.

Gucci held the gun low and out of sight. As soon as the soldier looked in the car he would shoot the squaddie in the face. Straight afterwards he would kill Bangaz and, if he had time before he died, the old white man.

The soldier enjoyed his work. He couldn't get a bribe out of the scammers to let them pass, like the police used to, but he could have the fun of killing them in cold blood, for which he got rewards for his unit like weekends at an all-inclusive.

The soldier scanned the approaching cars. He spotted a couple of anxious yout twitching in the front seats of a mark X Toyota, the signature ride of a chopper. His finger moved off the guard and onto the trigger in case they tried to shoot first. But in front of them there was a car with a white man driving. He needed to get him through. The soldiers didn't want a white man around when the killing started.

Willy, Bangaz and Gucci saw the soldier stare at them and lose interest, moving his eyes onto the car behind them and waving them through.

'Bludclaat racist,' Bangaz said.

''Top ya noise,' said Gucci. 'Drive.'

85

In his yard deep in the hills Gutta come out of the house, pull up him belt and blink at the sun. He felt in his pockets for money, pushing his jeans back down towards his knees, leaving a good expanse of tartan boxer. He could hear a couple of bredren working their phones in the gloom of the house. The candles which give them power over the clients had burnt out, and nobody bingo for days. Even though they smoked formaldehyde spliff and drank goats' blood, both of which they paid top dollar for because the man tell them they will craft the client mind, still nobody bingo for days.

Gutta was hungry, he want a breakfast but don't got no kiash, and his car nearly burn outa gas. He sat on a concrete block and considered his options, which were robbing a house or a shop. He stood up. He had forgotten he could still collect two thousand bucks if he killed Bangaz. Since his failed attempt at Troy bar he had gone off the project. But now Tanna gone a foreign it made it all easier.

Gutta looked around for his old balaclava, took up his gun and bullet dem from under the kitchen sink and go look for a jug of gas. Before he left he could not resist going back inside and dipping a spliff in the form-aldehyde, which he lit as he stood in the doorway, spinning into a muffled cloudy dream which he walked through on his way to his car.

86

Marva was staring at the safe and try fi memba the date of Bangaz's birth. His earthstrong. She thought the month was February so, after entering Tanna and Jenna's birthdays, spun the dial to 2 and then back to every number from 1 to 31. She was at the 14 when she heard a car draw up and the clank of the gate being opened. She pushed the fridge back in front of the safe and picked up a broom, but when she heard a strange voice, which did not sound friendly, peered through the grill. A short thick set man was walking Bangaz and the white man who lived by the fisherman beach at gunpoint towards the house. The short man look tough and, from the way him walk stiff, him vex bad, so she move quietly across the kitchen and was about to go up the stairs when the handle turned so she disappeared into the broom cupboard bringing the door to.

Gucci dragged two of the Chinese made Georgian dining chairs across the floor and cable-tied Bangaz and Willy by their ankles and wrists to them, double checking they were secure by kicking Bangaz in the back so he tipped over and landed on his face, then picking him up and leaving him upright with a bleeding nose.

'Right. Where's the safe?'

'Behind the fridge,' Bangaz said.

Gucci went to the double doored fridge and dragged it out of its space. He swung it across the tiles until the safe was visible. Gucci stared at it.

'What is the combination?' he said, then took a breath. 'No. Before you tell me that, I want to show you something.' He put the Glock into the back of his belt and went over to his holdall. He removed a short stubby knife. 'Meet Bud,' he said. 'Bud likes pain. I want you to remember that when you tell me the combination. Might jog the memory.'

'Tell Bud fi chill out and relax. Nutn can wrong. You is gonna open that safe, get your money and then you and Bud can lef me,' Bangaz said.

'And me,' said Willy.

'Sure,' said Gucci. 'Now, the safe please.'

'Spin left to 4, right to 9.'

Gucci breathed hard as he stood at the safe, the dial clicking as it turned. His left hand was by his side holding the Glock. 'Next,' he said.

'Go lef' to 18 and right to 6.'

In the cupboard, Marva recognised the kids' birthdays: Jenna 4th September, Tanna's 18th June.'

Gucci turned the dial again.

'Now 2 and 18,' Bangaz said.

The 18th of February. That was his birthday. She had been so close. She listened as the safe click open.

The money lastic up in brick dem. Gucci take it, and place it pon table by his duffer. He started to try and count it. 'It 'ondred grand,' Bangaz said. 'US.'

Marva realised what was going on. Bangaz had lied to her about the safe being empty. No surprise there. A strange man, one of her son's many enemies, tief the hundred grand from under her nose. White hot fury heated on the coals of years of injustice, fanned by many, many resentments, bubbled up inside her. That money was fi her. No man was going to get between Marva and that cash. Not Bangaz, not this other man, no man. Her body flexed and twitched with anger at the thought of losing it, and her elbow touched a broom handle which knocked against the wall. She heard the silence. The shuffling feet stopped. They had heard it.

Gucci picked up the gun and advanced silently towards the door of the broom cupboard. Marva could see his shadow on the tiles through the gap. She decided to let him get closer before bursting out. But Gucci stood back, raised his gun and shot through the door. Marva had anticipated this and had drawn herself up against the side, but a bullet grazed her forearm. She looked at it, saw the blood dripping from the stinging gash, and made absolutely no noise. She was that tough, Marva, when there was a hundred grand at stake.

Hearing no sound, Gucci relaxed and approached the cupboard to look inside. As he reached for the door it flew open in his face and knocked him backwards. As he recovered his balance, he looked up to see Marva charging him down, her blood-flecked arms pumping, her fists flying. The wound had detonated her. She tump Gucci to the floor, she took his hand and bit a lump out of it like a beef patty and sent his gun spinning across the tiles. With her knee on his chest she punch him like she a contender. She handle him like a man. As she attack him she shout, 'You feel it some batty boy gunman you a deal with? A real bad gangsta woman dis you a deal wid. Real Jamaican girl dis. Yuh undestan?'

Marva grab Gucci's hair and smash his skull again and again on the white floor till his limbs dropped limp and blood dripped from the corner of his mouth.

She stood up, turned to Bangaz and said. 'Ow you say you nuh have no money inna ya safe?'

With her trapped audience she took the money and stuffed it in her bag. When Gucci groaned she went over and kick his head again till him hush up.

'Cut we loose, Marva,' Bangaz said.

'If it's not too much trouble,' said Willy.

She picked up Gucci's firearm and weighed it in her hand. Then she stood in front of Bangaz.

'Tank you,' Bangaz said.

She said 'Tell me what kind of madda mi de.'

'What?' said Bangaz.

'Mi a good madda or a bad madda?'

Bangaz suck teeth.

Marva raised the gun to his forehead. 'Mi good or mi bad?'

'Raas. Untie mi hand, Marva, and 'tap ya fockry.'

'Mi good madda or mi bad madda?'

'Marva mi don't got time for dis.'

'Mi nevva raise you good? Ami nuh love you and tek care a you?' Willy said. 'He often said what a big part of his life you were.'

''Top ya noise white man,' Marva said raising her arm to Willy.

'Mi love you very much,' said Bangaz.

'Yes,' said Marva.

'And mi want you to have the kiash deh.'

'Good. What else?'

'Wha?' Bangaz said, blinking.

'A place to live.'

'Yes. You must have a plot of land. I will give it to you.'

'Good,' said Marva. 'Why?'

'Cos me love you.'

'And?'

'You raise me good.'

'A dat. Okay.'

She went to a kitchen drawer, put the gun on the counter, picked up a knife and came back to cut Bangaz and Willy loose. While she was down on one knee, the door behind her swung slowly open and a slim man with a black hood over his face with a Glock pistol in his gloved hand stood in the threshold.

Gutta took in the scene, which was confounding enough without the formaldehyde fog filter. His first concern was not to kill the woman. He didn't want to cement his reputation as a gunman who killed old women.

'Clear outa the way,' Gutta said to Marva. 'Mi nuh come for you.'

Marva half stood up, bowing submissively to Gutta, keeping her eyes on the floor.

'Mi sorry sah,' she said.

He was just trying to make sense of the scene in front of him when Marva, who was shuffling meekly away, swung out her arm and stabbed the blade deep into his bicep.

Gutta gasped and clutched the wound. She pulled the knife out and lick him across the face with her other fist. He groaned and fell forwards onto the tiles, his gun slipping from his hand. Marva picked up the gun.

Bangaz shouted, 'Official! You one good madda!'

Marva pulled off Gutta's mask.

'Gutta! Ya a idiot,' she said, and box him round him head with her fists till he whimper and bawl.

When Marva had cut Bangaz loose he said 'Gutta, you is a friend of mi daughter and mi know you just a yout, so me gwaan let you go.'

'Tank you, Bangaz, tank you.'

'But you haffi take this gentleman with you.'

They dragged Gucci groaning to Gutta's car and bundled him onto the back seat. Without Gutta seeing, Bangaz took both the guns off Marva and put them in the footwell below Gucci's body.

'You must go now,' Bangaz said, guiding Gutta into the driving seat. 'You deal with him, you understand?'

'Yes, boss,' said Gutta.

'Do not drive to Negril, there's a army roadblock on the road. Drive to Lucea.'

'Sure boss.'

'Go,' said Bangaz.

'Nuh let him go,' Marva said. 'Him try fi kill you Bangaz. He must die.'

'He just a yout, Marva. Nu worry yaself.'

'Ya too soft,' she said.

'Go,' said Bangaz to Gutta.

'Tank you.'

Bangaz, Marva and Willy watched the car go down the lane, stop under Toffee's streetlight and turn right at the highway towards Lucea.

'Why you let him go?' Marva said. 'He will come back to kill you.'

'I don't let him go,' said Bangaz. 'Der a army roadblock two mile down the road. Dem will kill them both, for sure. Dem ago dead. The army cya deal wid dem bodies. It more easy.'

They stood there for a moment considering this.

Willy said 'Have you got a drink? I think I need one.'

87

Three years later, on a sultry summer afternoon just after rain fall and the sun sparkle the wet leaves, Willy sat on his porch gazing into the distance. The sea was pan calm, back on its tranquilisers, and mud from the river was dissolving over the reef.

Willy heard a car draw up and smiled when he recognised Holly's white SUV. He cast about for empty bottles and hid them, along with an ashtray, in his bedroom cupboard.

'I carry some pear for you,' she said, placing two huge glossy avocadoes on the table. Willy knew them to be buttery at that time of year. Their thin skin made them unexportable. Like most of the best things from Jamaica, you had to be in Jamaica to enjoy them.

'Thank you, Holly, that is so kind.'

'Wha gwaan?' Holly said, smiling as she sat down. 'You look well.'

'Mi healty and hearty,' Willy said.

'Hey! You got the pool up and running.'

'You must come for a swim.'

'Next time,' she said. 'You got some money?'

'Some royalties arrived in the nick of time,' Willy said.

'Good.' Holly said. 'That's great.'

'I bought myself a television,' Willy said.

'Great. Do you have Netflix?' she asked.

'No, I wish I did,' he said.

'There's some good stuff on it,' she said. 'I can give you my password.'

'Really?'

'It's allowed. I'll do it now.' She took out her phone.

Willy said 'Do you want a cup of tea?'

'Yes please.'

He tottered off to the kitchen in the middle of the yard where he filled the kettle and watched it come to the boil. It was funny she should mention Netflix. With Ala's help, and a visa application filed by the legal department of Netflix in Los Angeles, Bangaz reach up to America. The book, now Baban Zamba's book, had been made into an eight part series by the streaming service. Bangaz had kept his word and, over the course of two years, sent Willy many thousands of dollars, couriered in cash by Danielle.

Willy returned to the porch with the mugs of tea.

'I've done it. Just enter the password I've sent you. You must watch my friend Ala's series about scammers,' Holly said. 'It's called King of Scam. It's dope.'

'Oh,' said Willy.

'It misses a lot out,' Holly said. 'But it was pretty good. I actually met the writer once with Ala. At The Jamaica Inn. Baban Zamba. Great name. It means Truth Teller.'

Bangaz had told Willy Baban Zamba meant Writer of Wisdom, but he let it go.

'Baban lives in the States now,' Holly continued. 'He's, like, really famous Ala said, doing all kinds of things like chat shows and adverts. Over four million Insta followers. And he came from round here, would you believe it?' Holly took a sip, said 'Mmm,' and then, 'I'm glad you left it to a Jamaican.'

'What?'

'Weren't you going to write about choppers once?'

Willy drank his tea, which he had topped up with rum. He said 'Actually, I...' and stopped.

'What?' said Holly.

'Nothing,' said Willy.

They spent an hour together. They were getting to know each other, and it felt right. It definitely no longer felt painful.

After Holly left, a thought struck Willy: what did Baban Zamba actually mean? He unearthed his laptop, fired it up and googled African languages. He then went to Translate and typed in Baban Zamba, trying to see which one of them it was. After trying Ebo and Yoruba, he got the correct one: Hausa, from northern Nigeria. Baban Zamba. Its English translation was not Truth Teller or Writer of Wisdom. It was King of Scam.

Other books by the author

One People
Sunbathing Naked
Bird Brain
Time To Go
The Accidental Collector
Foot Notes